A Strange Boy

A Strange Boy

JOHN L. JEWELL

authorHOUSE®

AuthorHouse™ UK
1663 Liberty Drive
Bloomington, IN 47403 USA
www.authorhouse.co.uk
Phone: 0800.197.4150

Published by AuthorHouse 03/08/2016

ISBN: 978-1-5049-9338-8 (sc)
ISBN: 978-1-5049-9336-4 (hc)
ISBN: 978-1-5049-9337-1 (e)

Print information available on the last page.

This book is printed on acid-free paper.

Contents

Prologue

The boy sat pensively at the window, his elbows resting on the sill with his chin cradled in his hands. He looked out onto the streets and the far-off fields. Night was closing in over the town as one by one the streetlights sputtered into life, casting golden halos into the ever-darkening gloom of a February evening. The boy, deep in thought, had barely noticed his father enter the unlit bedroom.

The narrow shaft of light from the landing widened with the opening door, framing the dark silhouette of his father's outline, which alerted the boy to his presence. The man seemed to glide as he crossed the bedroom in the yellow glow from the light. He laid his hand gently upon the boy's head. 'How are you, son?' he asked with some trepidation. 'Are you worried about tomorrow? It'll be fine. I'm sure of it!'

The boy turned from the window and looked penetratingly into his father's eyes. The man's voice had been calm, but his eyes betrayed his deep concern, a feeling that all was not well with his son. What dangers lay ahead for him? The man decided he would leave his son to reveal his version of events when he felt ready to confide in him. If he tried to push, to force the issue, he may learn nothing; he may even destroy the fragile relationship existing between them. He would do all in his power to prevent that.

The man wished his son a good night and left him as quietly as he had entered, the shaft of light shrinking back into darkness as the door closed behind him.

The boy returned his gaze to the scene outside the window, and for a brief moment, the moon cast an eerie silver light across the sad grey slate rooftops opposite and then was gone. The gathering clouds swallowed the silver orb as they swept hurriedly across the darkening sky. The melodic song of a blackbird roosting in a tree close to a street light was returned by another somewhere nearby.

His thoughts drifted between the events that had led up to this moment and his meeting tomorrow with 'Someone from the Authorities'. Later in the week he was to talk to a 'Senior Police Investigator'. His mind was in turmoil. What should he say to them, to his father? Could he confide in anyone? His inner caution told him *no*! Who would believe the word of a sixteen-year-old boy, a 'problem child', a 'strange boy'. How he had grown to detest that title.

His adversary would be a man with infinite resources – a man of impeccable reputation in the eyes of the world, a person respected for his numerous charitable deeds and his positions of trust on committees and school boards of governors. His reputation within the church and his influences in the realms of commerce were legendary. The man could call upon the great and the good to attest to his character, benevolence, and sound principled judgement in all things. What support could the boy rely upon?

He had the word of another boy, Thomas, but Thomas had disappeared into thin air. He had the word of a friend, Perry – a man who had instinctively sensed the aura of a boy with unique abilities. But he could not call upon Perry. The man himself had been subject to ridicule and mistrust. Poor, dear Perry was dead now, so he must do this alone.

The boy felt himself a fraud, an upstart, a boy with secrets he was not about to reveal to all and sundry. He had to expose the wrongdoings but contain his own secrets. Could he achieve this? If not, then how would he fare in the aftermath? They may brand him forever as 'a strange boy'. They may lock him away in one of those places they put 'strange people'. Should he take a chance and risk all or keep his secrets hidden, locked in the cabinet behind the impenetrable door, in a house none could find? His fortress – his secret haven from a sea of deceit, jealousy, betrayal, and ridicule – needed no armies or weapons to defend it.

He had learned from an early age that people who were different, who had very special skills or gifts, were to be shunned and ridiculed. They were not to be trusted. Above all, they were people to fear.

The night sky seemed to grow gloomier the longer the boy sat looking through the window. Was it the weather or his mood?

Illuminated by the pale amber glow of the street lights, flurries of snow had begun to fall. They danced in swirls around the golden lamps as they swiftly gathered pace. The wind strengthened by the second, sending the flurries scattering in all directions. The snow fell thicker and faster and then, sounds from downstairs distracted him from his thoughts. He could hear his father raking the embers in the fireplace with the poker. He could make out the harsh grating sound of the coal as it slid from the old scuttle into the welcoming grate. A few further clunks and rattles sounded as his father evened out the coals, and then came the chink of the poker being returned to its place on the firedog, nestling up against its companions on the hearth.

Outside, the snow had spread into an enveloping cloak, taking captive everything in sight, a gleaming shroud of white that obliterated boundaries, kerbs, pathways, and roads. The different roof tiles and slates that distinguished one house from another were now uniformly white, as though one roof only served the row of terraced cottages opposite.

From the bedroom next to his, the boy could hear the muffled drone of a man's voice announcing the nightly news on the radio; it was his sister's room. She would often hum or sing along to whatever song was the fashionable fancy among teenage girls at that moment. He knew she would be scanning the local newspapers for stories that had mystery about them. She was two years his senior. She had dark hair, black like many of her moods, whilst his was fair. She had dark green eyes; his were a radiant blue. In fact, the siblings were as dissimilar in appearance as they were in temperament and tastes. She outwardly conformed, but she was a skilled manipulator, letting people see her in a favourable light. She was capable of wearing a false demeanour like a veil, of masking her true self. Worst of all, she could be very bossy, demanding, and commanding. Her character changed as the mood took her. He loved her deeply for her defence and support of him; he would not be here today without her!

Nothing moved in the silent street below. All sounds were deadened by the blanketing mantle of snow. The clock on the mantelpiece in the front room below sounded the hour. His father's footsteps on the stairs signalled it was time for bed. Nine…ten…eleven. The last chime lingered as his father switched off the lights on the landing and stairs. The click of the cord pull indicated he had entered the bathroom at the end of the landing. A few minutes passed, and he heard again the clicks of the cord pull. 'Goodnight, all. Sleep tight.'

'Goodnight, Dad,' his children replied in unison.

The boy had decided a good sleep would clear his mind and would enable him to arrange his thoughts more clearly in the morning. He had just one more thing to do before retiring.

He entered a house in a kingdom to which no other person had right of access, a realm in which he alone was the occupant, guardian, and keeper of 'the Secrets'. An upstairs room was accessible only by way of a thick steel door with no visible gaps or spaces between the door and the frame; it was seamless. The door had no lock, no hinges, and no handle, no apparent way to open it. The boy had the only key – a key that could not be lost or found, copied or forged. The key was in his mind, and only he could enter. Three words – he only had to bring those three words to mind when standing in front of the door.

Facing the door as he had done on many occasions, he uttered the three words.

Silently the door vanished. Beyond the open doorway lay a room that contained no lights but was nonetheless brightly lit. A desk stood in front of the window with views out over a lake with a launch moored at a jetty, ready to take him wherever he fancied. On the courtyard below awaited a black limousine, in the kitchen, a hearty meal or simple snack; the choice was his.

There were shelves stacked full of books, which he had read and committed to memory. Every book he would ever read would place itself in its rightful place, among the many and varied titles already established. The books were classified according to content – fiction, sciences, languages, history, geography, and so on. These were his trusted confidants, his true, abiding loyal friends. These books found their way into his realm with no assistance from him; they had their own passport into his kingdom, and books needed no key; they belonged automatically.

From a drawer of the desk, he took a sheet of paper and wrote his thoughts regarding recent events and points of interest. He opened a drawer of a filing cabinet and removed a folder, placed the sheet of paper inside, and returned the folder to the cabinet drawer. He left the room, looking back to make sure the door closed securely, the room could not be opened without him!

In an instant, he was in bed, tired but comfortable. And how soft the pillow felt, how safe he felt with the blankets pulled up tightly around his neck. He could no longer hear the radio. All he could hear was the sound of the howling and whistling wind outside his window.

Chapter 1

Howard house

It was early September 1957. The car that had conveyed them from Felixstowe early that morning turned off from the road into a double gateway ahead of a long tarmac avenue. A plaque on the right-hand pillar of the entrance proudly announced 'The Sir Giles Woodford Village for Children'. Just inside the gateway, they passed the 'Lodge' on the left. The car swept gracefully along the tree-lined avenue, eventually giving way to a shingle forecourt. The golden pebbles crunched beneath the tyres as the car came to a halt in front of a large imposing mansion.

Jackson, in his black livery and cap emblazoned with the Woodford coat of arms, got out of the car and went around to the rear passenger side. He looked up towards the entrance of the mansion before opening the door, indicating to the occupants they should alight. From the front door of the building, a neatly dressed maid quickly descended the steps to the parked car. Her uniform was also black but with white trim on the collar and cuffs. She wore a full white starched apron tied in at the waist, which rustled as she moved; black stockings; and shiny black patent leather shoes. Some wisps of blonde hair struggled to escape from beneath a white mobcap. She must have been in her early twenties, her pale complexion a testament to long hours spent working indoors.

'My name is Susan; you are to come with me and the dean will see you shortly'. Susan turned to the chauffer, 'Jackson, the master wishes you to remain with the car for now.'

'Very well, Miss Susan,' he replied, turning to search in the boot of the car for the cloth to clean the windscreen.

Susan took the boy and girl in each hand and nimbly guided them up the steps to the front door that stood slightly ajar. A polished brass plaque beside the doorway read 'Howard House'.

Once inside, Susan urged the children to wipe their shoes on the thick coir mat just inside the door. She helped them to remove their light summer jackets and hung them on a dark oak hallstand and then ushered them across the hall towards a pair of large oak doors with ornate panelling and brass doorknobs. Leslie surmised that someone must spend a lot of time polishing.

Beyond the oak doors, they entered a very large room with a high ceiling. Directly in front of them, two large windows faced onto a courtyard. To the right, two more windows looked out onto the front drive, through which Jackson could be seen buffing the rear bumper of the black Wolseley. To the left of the room was a single oak door, a large fireplace that cut across the corner angle of the room. It had a white marble surround and mantelpiece, above which was a coat of arms. *The same one that Jackson has on his cap*, thought Leslie. A dark grey slate hearth held a coal scuttle, a large wicker basket full of logs, and a brass firedog with well-used accoutrements; there was also a folding fireguard and a brass hearth surround.

All the wall spaces were lined with shelves from floor to ceiling that contained books, many thousands of them. *A reader's paradise*, Leslie thought. *Every subject written of would be encompassed in this myriad of books.* He had never seen so many in his short life.

Set between the two windows facing them stood a large, polished oak writing desk. Neatly arranged on top were a large leather desk pad, double inkwells containing black and red inks, a pen stand, a mahogany and brass curved blotter, a telephone, and a neat stack of papers. Behind the desk was a large, oak and green leather, button-backed swivel chair with brass studs around the edges of the leather. And facing the desk stood two hard wooden chairs with unpadded seats.

In front of each of the windows to the right stood oak tables, one with four chairs and one with only two. In each corner of the room were pairs of sumptuous armchairs, places to indulge oneself in the pleasures of reading and absorbing knowledge and, perhaps, to discuss.

Susan led the children across the expanse of parquet floor towards the two unwelcoming chairs in front of the desk. 'You are to sit here and wait. When the master enters, you are to stand and not to sit until told.'

She raised her right index finger to her lips. 'You are not to speak unless invited to do so. Do you understand?'

Both children nodded their compliance.

They sat in silence for what seemed eternity. The girl bit her nails (as was her habit) and fidgeted uncomfortably on the hard wooden chair. The boy sat with his hands tucked under his thighs, his head bowed, watching his legs kicking slowly back and forth in opposite directions. The girl gave him a sharp slap on the knee that made him wince. 'Don't do that. You're making me nervous,' she said, inspecting her fingers, as if to decide which one needed chewing next.

Leslie's face was sullen as he contemplated the red weal developing on his left knee. He was about to say, 'That hurt!' when they heard a man's voice. It came from beyond the single door as it opened.

'I shall be discussing that with him later!' the man said to someone in the adjoining room. The children heard the sound of another door opening and a woman's reply, 'As you wish, sir.' The door closed.

The man entering the room was tall and perhaps in his late forties or early fifties. Imposing and well-dressed, with short neatly trimmed black hair greying at the temples, he was clean shaven, and a faint scent of cologne followed him across the room. His stature was athletic without being muscular, and he bore a presence that brooked no nonsense. To the boy, the figure before him appeared be a man of confidence in all things, a commander of men, and a man to obey.

He had no need to be adored; such things mattered little to him. Reputation, education, wisdom, finesse, and the pursuit of perfection – these were the essential ingredients required to make a success of one's life and one's work – not self-exaltation. He shunned the limelight and the press. He considered the press as imposing, intruding, assuming, and no, he had no time for them.

His mission in life, he purported, was to impart his qualities to others. And who better than children to shape and nurture for good? He rejoiced in his ability to sculpt and shape young minds and took great satisfaction in the culmination of his years of hard work – the masterpieces he had created from so little, and all to his advantage! This was his true reward.

His heels clicked as he strode across the floor to the chair behind the desk. The children had sprang to their feet the instant the door had opened. They looked neither right nor left. The girl with her head slightly bowed fixed her gaze on a leg of the desk; the boy just stared at his shoes.

The man lowered himself into the ample chair and began to flick through the stack of papers. He separated them into two neat piles, removed two manila folders from a drawer of the desk, and wrote a few words on the cover of each one. He screwed the top onto the pen and replaced it on the stand.

'You may sit,' he said in a soft but firm tone. 'Do you know how you come to be here in our village?' he asked, looking in the direction of the girl.

'Well…um…er…um, no, sir,' she replied nervously, twisting her fingers whilst maintaining her gaze on the desk leg.

'Firstly, I should introduce myself. I am Sir Alastair Woodford, dean and patron of this village. My grandfather Sir Giles Woodford founded this institution in 1850. My father, Sir Howard, succeeded him in 1898. And I, in the family tradition, assumed the role upon the death of my father in 1936. My father had this house built to replace the original, which burnt to the ground in 1916.

'This library,' he said, indicating round the room with an expansive wave of his arm, 'was built by my father to bring together the family's vast book collections, to which I have contributed many more recent publications.' A proud smile lit his face as he continued, 'It is accessible to all children within our care who may wish to improve his or her knowledge and depth of understanding. We have a librarian with whom you may make arrangements should you wish to avail yourself of this facility.'

He glanced down at the desk and opened one of the folders. 'Now to business,' he said, looking directly at the girl. 'I need to check that the information I have about you is correct.'

He flicked the pages back and forth again, and looking straight at the girl, he said, 'I see that you are Mary Johns, born 5 October 1948. Your brother here is Leslie Johns, born 26 October 1950. You're both of the Isle of Sheppey. Your father, Will Johns, born 6 June 1926 is currently serving in the armed forces and posted abroad. Your mother, Nerys, was born 12 May 1928. Her current whereabouts are unknown. In April 1953, your parents divorced and your father was awarded custody of you both. Due to his military duties, he was unable to fulfil his parental responsibilities. Therefore, in November of that year, he placed you in the care of the St Vincent's children's home, to which he paid a regular financial contribution. You remained there until June of this year. You have been in foster care with the Morton family in Felixstowe until this morning. Am I correct?'

Mary, still looking at the desk leg, replied, 'Yes sir,' a glum expression on her face.

All the while, Leslie did not look up and said nothing, but he had taken in every spoken word.

He had not known his mother's name because no one ever talked of her. He had noticed earlier that he had tied one of his shoelaces unevenly and wondered if he should get down from the chair and retie it. He had decided not to, but it concerned him, for punishments awaited those not meticulous in their habits.

Sir Alastair looked again in the folder and, after a brief pause, said to Mary, 'Tell me something of your education and about you.'

The girl looked decidedly uncomfortable and continued to fidget as she looked up at him, 'Well sir, we…um…we was at the town school in St Vincent's but not in the same class, sir. I didn't like it there. The teachers were horrible, an' the other kids used to bully us because we was from the home. They called us names an' that an' wouldn't let us play with them.' She babbled on about the 'nasty kids', barely pausing for breath, until Sir Alastair held up a hand. 'Enough!' he said.

'Tell me what you are good at. What do you enjoy doing out of school?'

The girl fidgeted as she spoke 'Well sir, I like skipping an' hula hoops an' colouring books an' making quilts an' stuff…'

Sir Alastair looked bemused. 'Your recent stay with the Morton family in Felixstowe, how did you find that?'

'Well we had a lot of good times, sir. We was next to a farm with pigs an' cows an' big fields of corn as tall as me an' Leslie, an' we played in the woods an' the stream. An' Mrs Morton was nice an' good at cooking and stuff—'

Sir Alastair stopped her again with the raised hand; he thought she might expire from lack of breath! 'On the subject of Mrs Morton, I believe you have a letter for me.'

'Yes, sir. It's in my jacket pocket in the hall.'

'Very well. You may give it to me later.' His eyes narrowed slightly as he looked at Mary. 'We will need to do some work on your diction and vocabulary.

'Sir?' the girl looked at him quizzically.

'Did you share your schooling with goats? You referred several times to "kids". One could suppose that your education took place in that farmyard in Felixstowe!'

The girl's face reddened. The glum expression became a look of defiance.

'I see also that you have the disgusting habit of biting your nails, and that, we can deal with promptly.'

She swiftly hid her hands behind her back.

'Now to you, master Leslie. Tell me something of your earliest memories to enlighten me, for you have said nothing all this while.'

For the first time since the dean entered, Leslie raised his head. He looked Sir Alastair full in the face. An icy cold finger ran down his spine. He tightly gripped the edges of the hard chair with both hands. This man had the darkest, blackest eyes the boy had ever seen – sharp, piercing eyes. They seemed to glint menacingly in the light from the windows.

He controlled his fear and spoke. 'I remember the flood in Sheerness, sir. That is the earliest I can remember,' he said, quietly waiting for the man's response.

'That would have been about 1953?'

The boy noticed how Sir Alastair had turned a statement into a question.

'You would have been very young at that time'

On 31 January 1953, I was two years, three months, and five days of age. The boy did not reply, he did not see the remark as a question

'Do you have any pastimes? What do you enjoy doing?'

The boy sat silently for a moment, gathering his thoughts before speaking. 'I like reading, sir, drawing, looking at the stars in the night, and puzzles.'

'Do you know what groups of stars are called?'

'Yes, sir. They are called constillations.'

The man's impassive face broke into a smile. 'Constellations, my boy. Con–*stell*–ations.'

The boy looked slightly abashed. Of course, he knew—

'Can you name any constellations?'

The boy thought for a moment. 'The Plough, Orion the Hunter, and Gemini,' he said with some affected pride. *Ursa Major, Orion, Cygnus, Taurus, Pegasus, Draco, Polaris.* He could identify them and many more, and draw them in their positions and proximities to each other.

'That is good for one so young, who taught you?'

'I learned them from a book,' he replied. A sudden realisation hit him; *I may have given too much away.*

The man stroked his chin pensively, rose from his chair, and reached towards a bookshelf.

Searching the book spines, he selected a tome, opened it (apparently at random) and placed the volume on the desk in front of the young boy. 'Read a passage for me from this page,' he said.

The boy placed a hand on the open page. With the other, he flipped the cover over. It was a heavy hardback volume from a collection of similar books.

The old book, bound in brown leather hide and tooled with gold lettering fascinated the boy. He turned back to the open page and glanced at the writing the dean had indicated.

Another icy finger shivered down his back. With some dismay, he silently read the title of the verse to himself – There is a place. Had the dean opened at this page intentionally? Or was it just chance? How could he know of the secret?

'Well?' the dean said. 'May we hear you read?'

Leslie began in a faltering stutter and then composed himself:

There is a place where I conceal
Those things I wish not to reveal.
There is a place where I retreat
When troubles clamour at my feet.
There is a place that comfort gives
Where peaceful thinking always lives.
There is a place so free and calm
That keeps my soul from hurt and harm.
There is a place where I rejoice,
Ignore the malice in the voice.
There is a place that calls to me
Not of this land or sky or sea.
There is a place as oft I've said
Residing here within in my head.

'You may stop there, Master Leslie. Do you understand the meaning of the verse?'

Leslie thought for a moment. 'Not really, sir,' was his reply. He understood perfectly the meaning of the verse and felt it pertinent to him and to his secret place.

'Perhaps when you are a little older you may be able to understand and appreciate it. However, you read it well.'

Leslie felt somewhat pleased, having managed to impress this man of importance without exposing his secret. But, that shoelace still worried him...

'You may retrieve your jacket from the hall, young lady,' the dean said to Mary, rising up from behind the desk. 'Oh, and the letter please.' He ushered the girl towards the double doors the children had entered through and opened the one on the left.

Leslie remained seated, reciting the poem in its entirety in his head. And such beautiful verse he felt; he must read more from this poet. He made a mental note of the volume and the page.

Meanwhile, Mary returned to the room, jacket clutched in one hand, the letter offered with the other. 'For you, sir.'

'Thank you,' he replied, taking the white envelope from her grasp.

As he unsealed the envelope, the dean walked back toward the desk. He stood facing the window, absorbing the contents of the letter. It seemed like hours later when he turned towards Leslie; a frown furrowed his otherwise smooth features.

'I am sorely disappointed' said the dean, glaring at the boy, 'it seems that you are considered a boy not to be trusted or believed.'

A look of horror spread across the boy's face, and a wave of heat flushed his pale cheeks.

'Tell me of this business with the coins,' the dean demanded sternly.

Leslie sunk deeper onto his chair, his shoulders drooping and involuntarily swinging his legs back and forth.

'Do not slouch, boy,' the dean commanded. 'Sit up straight. I wish to hear what you have to say for yourself.'

'He said he had swallowed three, one-penny coins,' piped up Mary. 'Mrs Morton said he was a liar because them coins is too big to swallow an'...'

'I was talking to your brother, and I wish to hear it from him, thank you.'

Two pairs of eyes focussed on the poor wretched boy.

'Well?' The voice had taken on a menacing tone that made Leslie fear that he was about to be punished. Would it be the switch, a belt, or the crippling ridge?

'It is true,' he blurted out. 'I did swallow the coins, and it hurt my throat and tummy so much. And no one helped me, no one ever believes me, and it is not true that I put the coins in the toilet.' There was a hint of defiance in the boy's voice.

'How many coins were in the toilet?' asked the dean.

'I did not see them, but Mrs Morton said there were three. She said I must have put them there to make her believe I swallowed them. I couldn't understand why she would say that. I liked her, but she upset me saying that I lied.' The defiance now gone, tears welled up in the boy's eyes.

Mary placed a hand on her brother's knee as a tear rolled down his cheek and onto his lap. 'Is he in trouble, sir?' Mary asked in a timid manner.

Sir Alastair looked again at the letter, sat in his chair, and looked at the boy and his sister. Directing a question at the boy, he asked, 'What do you know about the human digestive system?'

The children looked at each other with puzzled expressions.

Leslie turned back to the dean. 'Nothing, sir. I have not seen any books about that, and they do not teach us that at school.'

'Very well. We shall make it part of your education plan.

'Now, I will arrange for you both to undergo an assessment to establish your educational requirements. Mary I allocate to Miss Weston in Epping House, pending the assessment results. Leslie, you will be in Roding House with Mr and Mrs Atkins.

'We shall treat you fairly with care and respect; we expect the same from you towards all the staff and the other children. Our aim is to provide the best care and education within our power.'

Mary fidgeted anxiously, constantly shifting her bottom on the hard seat of the chair.

'What is the matter, child?' the dean snapped, breaking his train of thought. 'Do you need the bathroom?'

'Er...no, sir. It's just that Daddy said we would be kept together an' I was to look after Leslie—'

The hand raised again. 'I am afraid that is not possible here. We do not have mixed houses. You may see each other in recreation time; your houses are opposite each other.'

'But Daddy—'

The hand! 'You repeat yourself, young lady. Your brother will be well cared for.'

The dean flicked through the folder on which he had written 'Leslie Johns' and removed a slip of paper. 'I trust you have been informed of your father's situation.' Without waiting for confirmation, he continued, 'This is the telegram from his commanding officer: Reported missing in action, he was involved in a skirmish that resulted in deaths and severe casualties. He was not among the injured; therefore, he is presumed dead or captured.'

The news struck the children like a thunderbolt. Mary's face blanched; Leslie sat rigid with tears falling freely down his cheeks in rivulets. His bottom lip quivered, but he uttered no sound. Mary raised one hand to her stomach and the other to her mouth.

The dean already had the telephone receiver in his hand. 'Send in Susan please and ask Dr Hendricks to meet me in the west library. Oh, and tell Susan to bring Joan with her. Thank you.' There was an audible click as the recipient of the call replaced the handset. Immediately, a bell sounded down the hall, and a few moments later, the sound of muffled voices approached the double doors.

Leslie was now sobbing and shaking, a darkening wet patch spreading across his short grey trousers. Sir Alastair observed with dismay the results of his announcement, and then a light knock came at the door. 'Come in, come in please.' For once, the dean felt out of his depth. He did not deal with emotions well, he had people who could do that far more successfully than he could, and this was his first time he was faced with this situation. He was like a fish out of water. How could he have been so unfeeling when dealing with small children, susceptible creatures?

Emotions had been systematically removed from him. He had himself been placed in a school, an institution similar to this – a boarding school, where such displays of emotion were frowned upon, stiff upper lip and all that. Then later had come the training academy, where leaders of men could not, in any way, display such self-indulgent emotions. Tears were for women, children, and babies.

Susan and Joan entered the room. Susan looked towards the dean. The merest signal on the dean's face indicated the actions required. She took both children by the hand and led them away towards the hall. Joan glanced at the boy's shorts; lifted the chair on which Leslie had sat; and, in turn, headed towards the open door. Susan stopped and turned. 'If I may, sir?'

The dean nodded.

'They must be frightful hungry after such a long journey.'

'Yes, Susan, how remiss of me. Have them cleaned and fed and return them to me when you are ready. And, Susan, thank you.'

The slight hint of softness in his voice was not something Susan had heard before. Surely, the lord and master had a soft spot and perhaps a very slight chink in the family armour? He best take care; if this got out, goodness knows what would happen. However, it would not come from her lips; she was the very soul of discretion.

Susan led the children hurriedly down the hall to a room off to the left in the corridor. She took Leslie into a washroom through one of the doors at the far end of the room. She gestured towards the basin and soap and gave him a large towel from a rail fixed to the wall. She left the room, quietly closing the door behind her.

Mary had sat alone with her thoughts when a door opened. A stout red-faced woman, dressed in white, peered around the room. She saw the girl sitting alone. 'Oh, I beg your pardon!' she said and disappeared in an instant.

A few moments passed before Susan returned. She asked Mary if she was feeling better, and Mary replied that she was, a little.

'I must attend your brother. Joan will be here directly to attend you.' She collected some clothes from a cupboard and left, accompanied by the rustling of the starched apron.

Leslie stood wrapped in the large comforting towel he had wrapped around himself as tightly as he could. He exuded the aroma of carbolic soap – pungent, heady, clean, and powerful. His urine-soaked clothes, neatly folded, he placed on the seat of the white painted chair with a deep fear of punishment to follow.

Susan entered the washroom, a bundle of clean clothes under one arm, a clean towel and a white laundry bag under the other. She handed the clean clothes to the boy and told him to dress. She turned and placed the clean towel on the brass rail and then, with a deft sweep of her hand, she scooped up the wet clothes from the chair and stuffed them into the waiting laundry bag. She cleaned up the washroom and wiped the chair with a solution of disinfectant. Leslie had put on the clean underpants and navy blue shorts. Susan helped him with the oversized short-sleeved shirt and the vest. She sat him upon the chair and placed his socks and shoes on his feet. She deposited the laundry bag outside the door as she made to return to Mary with the boy in tow.

They entered the room where Susan had left Mary, but it was empty. Susan placed two chairs at a small table against one of the walls. From a drawer beneath the table, she removed a crisp white tablecloth and two white napkins, and with a single flourish, the cloth covered the table evenly, perfectly. From a sideboard, she removed some cutlery and two white china plates. She arranged the items into two place settings and conducted it swiftly, rhythmically, and efficiently. Leslie was in awe of her! Never had he seen such dexterity, such grace of movements. Nothing, it seemed, came between her and the task. *It must require a lot of dedication to achieve such perfection*, he thought.

A door opened, and Joan entered with Mary. Susan bade the children sit at the table, whilst Joan exited for a few moments. The children surveyed the table before them. What were the folded squares of cloth for? they wondered. Joan returned pushing a trolley that contained two glasses of milk, a plate of sandwiches neatly cut into triangles with the crusts removed, and two fresh pears ahead of her. Susan placed the items on the table, 'You may eat now,' she said softly.

The boy realised that he was hungry; it had been a long time since breakfast. The bacon, egg, and the toast with home-made preserve had done well to set them up for the day ahead. Susan's soft gentle hands lightly brushed his skin as she tucked the napkin under his chin; it felt like a caress to his unaccustomed skin.

The meal finished, Susan indicated they should dab their mouths with the napkins. She mimicked the action, and they copied. She held out her hands to take the children back to the library. Leslie felt overcome by an urge to cling to Susan like a limpet. *She should have been my mother.* Quietly, they walked the length of the hall. Susan was no stranger to the whims and fancies of children. She knew how to deflate their bubbles if they misbehaved. This boy was different she felt, and she had a soft spot for the waif that had been without a mother's love.

All Leslie had of his mother was a vague memory of water. It was a memory he could not store, a memory best left unvisited.

Susan led the children to the library. She smoothed the wrinkles from her apron before knocking on the oak doors.

'You may enter,' came the calm voice of the dean.

Susan entered and glided across the floor, her two charges in tow. A nod from the dean indicated that it was permissible for the children to sit.

'Will that be all, sir?'

'It will for now. Thank you, Susan.'

She made her exit in her quiet manner.

The dean had been writing. He gathered two sheets of paper and placed them in one folder, one in the other. He sat pensively for a moment with that now familiar mannerism of stroking his chin. 'I trust you are refreshed?' he said, looking from one to the other.

They both nodded.

He was about to admonish them (a question requires an answer) but let it go unsaid, the children had had an eventful day.

Leslie was aware of the slightly pungent aroma of disinfectant; Joan had washed the chair before replacing it.

The dean began to outline the facilities of the village. 'We have our own chapel and school and a small cottage hospital with an on-call doctor, an optician, and a dentist. There are six houses of residence, each staffed by a master or mistress and two maids, and there are usually six children in each house. The house staff members all live in; they have their own quarters. Your food, clothing, and education we provide within the village. You will, however, be expected to perform minor tasks within your respective residences. These tasks will be allocated to you by the housemaster, who will take account of your age and ability.'

The telephone interrupted the dean. He lifted the receiver to his ear. 'Yes?' He listened to the voice for a few moments. 'Thank you, Ernest. I will be with you directly.' Then he clicked the button on the top of the telephone and dialled a single number. 'Would you send in Susan, please? Thank you.' He replaced the handset. The bell sounded down the hall, and moments later, the sound of a knock came at the door. 'Come in, Susan,' the dean responded.

'Mary is to stay at Epping House. Accompany her. And then leave the boy's luggage at Roding House. Here is a list of some things I require. Please obtain them for me on my account. And thank you.'

'As you wish, sir.' Susan took the list in one hand and the girl by the other. They both disappeared into the hall, the door closing quietly behind them.

The room was silent. The dean sat in contemplation, looking at the small boy in front of him. Leslie looked up at the man, and their eyes met – the boy was almost transfixed by those piercing black orbs. He felt they could see into his very soul; no thought in his head could hide from the scrutiny. He felt a slight tremor; was it fear? But what did he need to fear from this man?

The dean pushed the book of verse in front of the boy. 'I have a small matter to deal with.' He consulted a gold hunter from a waistcoat pocket and then snapped it shut with a click. 'You may read if you wish.' He headed towards the single door by which he had entered.

On entering the next room, he had left the door very slightly ajar. Leslie could hear the voices of two men. One was the dean's; the other was also a man, a softer higher tone and slightly muffled. Leslie surmised that this unknown man probably had his back towards the door or was some distance from it.

The boy opened the book, searching the index for another poem by the same author. Before he had found the page, he could make out some of the conversation next door:

'Letter ... the Mortons-'
'History...lying...St Vincent's-'
'A strange boy—'

Leslie froze – that description of him; the one they had used at St Vincent's; the one he dreaded, hated, and feared with every fibre of his being. Please, no... They cannot use that here. The words rang loudly in his ears – *A strange boy.*

He could still hear the voices:

'Benefit of the doubt, but if it is true—'

'Punish—' The other voice was indistinct, and Leslie could not discern what the unknown man said. There were a few more muffled words: 'Fool that I am, I am afraid I handled the situation badly...assumed too much... they knew about—'

'They should have been told at St Vincent's.'

'With hindsight, I should have left that for you to deal with, and you are the expert doctor—'

The dean's voice grew louder and more distinct. He was returning. 'Come. You should meet him.' The door opened.

The dean's heels clicked across the floor towards the desk. He was closely followed by a shorter rotund man who bore a striking resemblance to a picture the boy had seen of Mr Pickwick from a book called 'The Pickwick Papers' by Charles Dickens. The boy stood up, closing the book on the desk and remained silent. 'Mr Pickwick' smiled at the small fair-haired boy in borrowed clothes. The man extended a hand towards him.

'This is doctor Hendricks' the dean said.

'Leslie Johns, sir,' the boy replied, lightly grasping the open hand.

'You and I will spend some little time together shortly. We will be the good friends, I am sure, will we not?'

Although the boy was just short of seven years, he analysed the man. He noted the slightly clipped speech and unusual turn of phrase. The man was foreign, possibly of Germanic origin, a jovial type. Perhaps they could be friends. 'Yes, sir,' the boy replied.

'Today is Thursday, is it not? So perhaps we can have some little talk on Saturday. Tomorrow you will like to find your feet no?'

Such an odd manner of speech the boy found amusing. He controlled the urge to giggle, sensing that it would be inappropriate. 'As you wish, sir.'

Doctor Hendricks and the boy briefly discussed St Vincent's, Felixstowe, and how the boy felt about being at the village. Leslie had not been at the village long enough to form an opinion, but showed some enthusiasm regarding his future there. (Especially as he had not received any punishments for his laces and wetting his shorts.)

The sun now shone directly into Leslie's eyes, and he shielded them with his hand. The dean raised himself from his chair and beckoned Leslie and the doctor over to the other side of the room, away from the glare. The doctor asked Leslie what he had read, the kind of books he enjoyed reading, and what sort of pictures he liked to draw. It was almost three hours since Susan and Mary had left; the dean consulted his Hunter again for the second time.

The sound of the car crunching the loose shingle signalled the return of Susan and Jackson. Hurried footsteps sounded in the hall and then came a light knock at the door. 'Enter, Susan.' The dean made a few notes and slipped the paper into the folder with the boy's name on it.

Susan stood behind the boy's chair. 'Sir?'

'Did you manage to get those items for me?'

'Yes, sir, eventually.'

'Good. You may escort the boy to Roding House. Ask Jackson to garage the Wolseley on his return and make ready the Bentley. I am expected elsewhere. I should return around seven.'

'Will you require tea before you leave, sir?'

'I fear I will not have the time Susan. Please ask Cook to have something prepared for eight o'clock. I must now freshen up before I leave. Thank you, Susan. You may go now.'

'Sir.' Susan glanced at the boy and took his hand, leading him into the hall.

'Come, Ernest, you may fill me in on your thoughts…' The dean's voice faded as Susan closed the door.

Susan and Leslie walked swiftly down the hall, collected the boy's jacket, and then went out to the waiting car. Jackson held open the rear passenger door as Susan gently ushered the boy inside. She climbed in beside him. The car glided smoothly over the shingle forecourt. Leslie gazed at Susan, still clutching her hand. The crunching of the shingle ceased as they turned onto a tarmac avenue. 'Is doctor Hendricks foreign?' the boy asked.

Susan remained silent. She gave the boy's hand a very light squeeze; it was enough to tell him that one did not ask such questions. The journey took only a matter of minutes before they arrived at the large double-fronted house. A brass plaque announced, 'Roding House.'

Chapter 2

Of Epping, Roding, and Settling In

Earlier during her car journey to Epping House, Mary had contemplated the leaden cloud above the tree-lined avenue. It was as if such a cloud had crashed down on her, destroying the very fabric of her world – her mother was gone; her father was gone; her little brother torn from her, no longer hers to control; everything had now been taken from her. The dark empty hollow she saw looming before her would be her life from now on. The gloomy thoughts pressed down upon her, crushing, squeezing, dissolving every semblance of all she had had and could never regain. Devoid of all hope, encompassed by despair that tugged and wrenched at her, she felt feeble, useless, and powerless. These were sensations that had previously been unknown to her – new, unwanted, and uninvited. *How could God let this happen? He's a wicked God, a God with no feeling for a child.*

They arrived at Epping House, and as Susan and the girl approached the front door, Jackson removed two small suitcases from the boot of the car. He carried the one bearing a brown label, tied with coarse string to the handle, Mary Johns printed in black capitals. Susan took the suitcase from him and thanked him and rang the doorbell. From inside, the girl could hear *ding-dong*. They waited a few moments. The door opened, and a stout woman, wearing a green tweed two-piece, stepped out onto the large polished, red painted step under the entrance porch. 'Miss Weston, this is Mary Johns for your care.'

'Thank you, Susan. Welcome, child. I expect you'll be hungry and tired.'

Jackson had delivered the other suitcase to the house opposite and was holding open the car door for Susan. As he closed the door, he tipped the peak of his cap in the direction of Miss Weston. She, in return, gave a slight nod. Mary was certainly feeling tired but had no interest in eating. She felt sick, despondent, and deposed, a lost waif in this unknown place. She hated the dean for stealing her authority, her responsibility, and her reason for living.

***

'Good afternoon Master Leslie, I am Miss Lola, come this way please.' The short olive-skinned woman led him through the entrance into a large hallway dominated by a wide flight of stairs that curved around three walls leading to the top floor. As the maid helped him with his jacket, Leslie looked around. On the right, just past the bottom of the stairs, was a white painted door with a nameplate, 'Private'. Straight ahead, an open door revealed a kitchen, the smell of toast and melting cheese wafted through the hallway. Next to the doorway, a brass gong suspended from a wooden frame, and on the wall to the left, a large portrait hung from a wooden picture rail, a portrait of Sir Alastair… But no! The nameplate at the bottom announced, 'Sir Giles Woodford. Founder and Benefactor, 1802–1898.' The resemblance was remarkable. The tall, elegant, well-dressed man looking down at him had those same black piercing eyes.

'I am Mr Atkins.' The voice from behind him startled Leslie. He had not heard or noticed the man arrive and turned to face him. 'Miss Lola will take care of your needs for now,' he said, looking at the maid. 'I am the housemaster, and you may address me as master.'

Leslie looked from one face to the other. 'You will have something to eat with the rest of the boys. Then Miss Lola may show you around.' He turned and disappeared into the private room. Miss Lola hung the boy's jacket on an empty peg at the end of a row of jackets. She took hold of his suitcase, which Jackson had left just inside the entrance hall. On lifting it, she remarked, 'Dios mio, que tienes dentro, hijo?

'Oh, sorry,' she said, realising she had reverted to her native tongue. 'Is heavy. What do you have inside?'

She led him across the hall and turned into a corridor on the left. A short way along she opened a door and told the boy to wash his hands. Inside was a toilet and washbasin and a white painted chair, just like the one at Howard House. Against one wall stood a white painted cabinet with glass-panelled doors. He could see clean, folded towels inside. He washed and dried his face and hands. He re-joined Miss Lola and held her hand, and they continued to an open door at the end of the corridor.

Arranged inside the large room, tables and chairs indicated that this was the dining room.

A large fireplace dominated the far end of the room with the usual accessories, a brass fireguard in the front and an ornate clock on the mantelpiece. To the right of the room were two tables, each of them next to a window. They each had four chairs but only three place settings. On the left, there were also two tables; one had two chairs and place settings, and the other had four. The wall behind them had an oak dresser, the shelves lined with white china plates. From a row of hooks under the bottom shelf hung a dozen white china cups.

A boy of about nine attended to the place settings on each table. With most of them completed, the boy moved quietly and efficiently, pausing to check each table. And as he passed, he gave a nod towards the new boy. He removed two water jugs from a wooden trolley and placed them in the centre of each table on the left, ensuring that a large coaster centred under each of them, and left the room.

Miss Lola led Leslie to the nearest table on the right and sat him down. She placed his suitcase on the chair next to him, where there was no place setting. Just then, a gong sounded a single note that echoed through the house. After a few moments, a single file of five boys walked into the room and took their places, each of them standing behind a chair at the tables on the right. The older boy he had seen earlier stood behind the chair directly opposite Leslie. He made a lifting motion with his hand. Leslie quickly jumped up from the chair and stood behind it, earning a slight nod from the older boy.

Mr Atkins entered the room accompanied by a woman with a sallow complexion (Mrs Atkins?), They were followed by Miss Lola, another maid, a woman dressed in white, and a teenage girl. Mr Atkins and the sallow woman stood behind the chairs of the first table on the left, the others at the remaining table. Everyone bowed his or her head, hands clasped and eyes closed. Leslie followed suit.

'We thank you, Lord, for your bounteous gifts. We welcome to our family Leslie Johns and beseech you to watch over him as you watch over us all. By your grace, O Lord.'

'Amen,' they said in unison.

'You may be seated.'

The children waited for the master and his wife to sit before doing likewise. The staff left in the direction of the kitchen, and the children sat in quiet anticipation.

The staff returned with four trolleys, two laden with platters of hot cheese on toast, one with two jugs of cold milk and two bowls of fresh apples, and the other holding a teapot and milk jug and two plates of sliced fruit cake. Miss Lola distributed the platters to each table and served the boys with glasses of milk. The other maid poured tea and served the master and his wife. She wheeled the trolley to the staff table and poured four more cups.

The children tucked into the Welsh rarebit with gusto, accompanied by smiles and licking of lips. *This must be a collective favourite*, thought Leslie. And it was really very tasty! The meal passed with not a word spoken.

When the meal was over, Mr and Mrs Atkins thanked the maids and left the room. The older boy organised the others in clearing the tables and placing the items on the trolleys. It didn't take long to clear and tidy the room. The older boy turned to speak to Leslie, and a smile lit his face. Leslie sat, head on one side, fast asleep.

***

He no longer was a boy of nearly seven but a young man in his early twenties. He stepped from the motor launch, gathering his fishing gear and a basket of fish. He walked slowly along the wooden jetty, pleased with his day's catch. He had not enjoyed a fresh fish supper for some time and looked forward to it in anticipation. It had been a glorious balmy day, the sunlight reflecting off the glittering surface of the water. A light easterly breeze just took the edge off the harshness of the hot summer sun. The gulls screeched, wheeled, and dived for the scraps he had thrown them – the remains of his lunch and the entrails of the gutted fish. He was going to inspect the garden this evening and had some thoughts about the lawn area leading down to the coppiced wood: *A summer house set against the backdrop of the trees and, perhaps, an avenue of poplars, leading from the formal beds to the wilder parts of the garden. Yes, the poplars could follow the line of the small lake, offering shade when the sun was too harsh. Yes, that's it.*

***

Leslie awoke with a start; the older boy was shaking him by the shoulder. 'It is seven thirty. You must get up now!'

Leslie looked around him in confusion. Where was he? He raised himself from the bed and sat on the edge, rubbing the sleep from his eyes.

The older boy looked at him and grinned. 'You fell asleep at the dining table. Miss Lola and I brought you upstairs and put you to bed. You did not even wake up when the other boys came to bed.

Leslie yawned and ran his fingers through his hair, 'I had not realised I was so tired,' he said.

The older boy introduced himself. 'My name is Paul Goodwin. I am the head boy and have been tasked with getting you settled in.'

The boys shook hands.

Leslie looked around the room. There were eight beds, each with a wooden chair and a locker, four on each side of the room. At the far end of the room were two double wardrobes, one each side of a doorway. The nearest wall mirrored the far wall. Above the nearby wardrobe, Leslie noticed his suitcase.

'Oh, I took the liberty of unpacking your things. I hope you do not mind. Your clothes are in here.' Paul indicated the wardrobe. 'And your belongings are in the locker.'

Leslie opened the locker. On a shelf was his book, he removed it and hugged it like a long-lost friend. It was a rather shabby tome, scuffed and scratched; some of the thick board cover was fraying. It was *A Dictionary of the English Language*, and it was large and heavy.

'Come. We must get you washed and dressed. Your wash things are in your locker.'

Leslie collected them from the locker drawer, and Paul led him to the door nearest them. Inside was a large washroom. Paul showed his charge to a basin and handed him the towel from the rail. 'This will be your basin and towel. Clean the basin when you are finished. Dirty laundry you place in there.' He indicated a large basket by the door. 'I will return shortly,' he said, closing the door behind him.

About twenty-five to thirty minutes had passed when Paul entered the dormitory to find Leslie sitting on the chair by his bed, putting on his shoes. He passed by and went into the washroom to check that all was in order. He noticed that Leslie had placed his toothbrush, toothpaste, and comb in the vacant beaker. The basin was clean, the towel folded and replaced, and no water splashes were on the floor. He felt he was going to like this boy because he learned fast.

Returning to Leslie, he checked under the pillow, the pyjamas were there and neatly folded.

'Breakfast,' he said, leading the boy out onto the landing. As they descended the stairs, Paul explained that later, he would show Leslie how to make the bed, and that each boy made his own bed and changed the sheets on Mondays, ready for the wash.

They arrived at the same room of the previous evening, and at the table was a single place setting. Paul related that the other boys were already in school. He told Leslie to sit and eat. And as he ate his bread and jam, Paul told him, 'The two maids are Miss Lola Lopez and Miss Maria Carmen del Amo. Miss Lola's proper name is Dolores, and although shortening a name is not usually acceptable here, it is how she refers to herself. I believe it is a common practice in Spain...'

Paul's talk of Miss Lola made Leslie think of Miss Lola's remark. *Dios mio, que tienes dentro, hijo?* He repeated the words in his mind and avowed to learn this language; it would not be beyond his powers!

Paul's voice recaptured his attention. 'You are taking notice I hope.'

'Yes, sir,' the boy replied.

Paul chuckled. 'No, I am not sir. Sir or master is for adults. Just Paul will do.' Yes, indeed, he was going to like this little waif! 'So, today we are both excused from classes. You will start school on Monday. Would you like me to show you around?'

The boy smiled. 'Yes, please, sir... Oh...sorry, yes, please, Paul.'

They began by clearing the dishes to the kitchen, where they encountered a large woman of about forty, dressed in white who Leslie recalled from the previous evening, her hands covered in flour. 'This is Cook,' said Paul. 'I am sure she has a name, but for the life of me, I do not recall ever hearing it.'

The woman made a mock swipe at Paul, sending a white puff of flour in his direction, 'Cook is just fine. 'Tis what I am and what I do.' A big smile lit her face. 'Off with you now. I've work to do. Now where is that lazy girl?' she said, looking about her.

'That will be Joyce, her daughter.' Paul explained.

The two boys left the kitchen by a door at the back, passing various storerooms on the way. They exited onto a concreted yard at the back of the house. Paul pointed out the brick shed standing next to a wooden fence.

'That is the coal shed. When it is cold, they light the fires in the house, and we have to keep the fires going. You know, fill the coalscuttles. But you are too small for such a task yet.'

Beyond the fence, they could see two men picking fruit in an orchard that stretched right over to the high wall that surrounded the village. The trees were laden with fruits. Some trees had bright red apples, some had green, and others bore apples varying from yellow to brown and orange. In between them were trees full of pears, cherries, damsons, and plums.

They skirted the outside of the building, and then they were out onto the road at the front of the house. The road, bordered on each side by grass verges, had a long line of tall slim trees. *Poplars!* Leslie thought. Paul pointed to the house opposite. 'Epping House, one of the girl's houses.' Leslie knew this but said nothing. They turned to the right and followed the road down the hill, passing two more houses, Forest and Hill. Eventually, they reached large, locked double gates, and Leslie wondered if they were to keep people out or to keep them in.

Turning away from the gates, Leslie saw that the road forked. To the left was the road they had used, and to the right, the road led away into a distant wooded area and arced midway around the hill on which the village stood.

As the boys walked along, they could see the river at the bottom of the hill. 'Ooh. Can we go down there, Paul?' Leslie asked excitedly.

'Of course. Race you down there.'

They careered headlong across the grassed meadow. Paul was older, stronger, and taller, so he had the advantage; he reached the riverbank well ahead of Leslie. The younger boy arrived puffing, his face red from the exertion. They sat on the trunk of a fallen elm tree with Leslie gasping to regain his breath.

The two boys sat for some time, gazing into the clear shallow waters, observing the pebbles, the minnows, and the pond skaters skimming over the surface. The water gurgled and swirled in eddies as it made its way down to a bend, further downstream. On the far bank, a wooded area obscured the high boundary wall. The bank itself was about three feet or so above the level of the water. 'The water is usually a lot higher, but the dry summer is the reason it isn't deep at all.'

'Oh. Can you put a boat on it then, when it's higher I mean?' asked Leslie.

'Yes, there's a boathouse on the other side of the woods,' Paul replied, pointing ahead of them. 'We can go that way.'

Rested, the pair ambled along the track beside the river, enjoying the warmth of the late summer morning and subconsciously building a relationship. Paul ducked under a swarm of midges dancing near the water's edge, and as they entered the wooded area, it became noticeably cooler and darker but more humid.

The sunlight danced as it reflected from the water's surface, sending flickers of light like fiery fingers through the trees and into the canopy above. After a while, the woodland thinned out onto a sloping grassy field dotted with shrubs and wildflowers. Just ahead of them, Leslie could see the wooden boathouse and a small jetty. As the boys approached, they could see that the boathouse was padlocked. Through a window at the side, they saw an upturned rowing boat that someone had been working on. Leslie could make out some shelves with assorted tins and jars with brushes in them. On the floor near the door lay a coil of thick rope and some rags.

'Let's be going now,' said Paul. 'The water's too shallow for a boat trip anyway.'

Leslie followed him to the other side of the boathouse.

They continued along the path, and on the far bank now, saw some large willow trees, the branches trailing down like arms with their fingers trying to grab at the water. Here was the bend in the river they had seen from way upstream. Just at the bend, the bank on the far side jutted out. It was an area covered with reeds, and they extended for some distance downstream. Farther on, a bridge crossed the river where it veered sharply to the right and away from the village. The high boundary wall extended up to the bridge and then continued from the other side.

Paul steered Leslie to the left, the path now leading them up the hill. The heat was becoming more intense. Paul took a handkerchief from his pocket and dabbed his forehead and face as they continued up the hill.

Sometime later, they reached an assortment of buildings. 'The stores,' said Paul, pointing to the right 'have everything we need for the village.'

They walked on for a few minutes more, and at the bend in the path, they could see the chapel and, beside it, a cottage. It had neatly cut lawns and tidy flower beds full of colour. 'The vicar is a keen gardener. He likes to care for his garden.' Sure enough, as they passed, a slim short man with a bald patch on his head waved at them from beyond a low-cut hedge.

A little farther on, they came to the school. It had two entrance doors, boys one side, girls the other. Leslie commented that there was no playground. Paul explained that they did not have playtime and that he would find this school very different from his previous one. On the opposite side of the road stood a row of cottages. 'Accommodations for the teachers, Mr Jackson, and other employees of the estate,' said Paul.

Next to the school stood a tall fir hedge, neatly clipped and trimmed. And beyond that, Leslie recognised Howard House. It was set back from the road with its own driveway and shingle forecourt, and to Leslie, from this different aspect it looked grander today with its tall chimneystacks jutting up above the roofline than it had approaching from the gates. From the angle they were standing, the boy could see the windows of the second room, the West Library.

'We must be going now. It is nearly lunchtime.'

Leslie did not realise they had been away so for long. They turned and headed down the hill along the avenue past two more houses, River and Bridge. All the houses looked the same apart from the gardens and the flower beds. And soon they reached Roding House.

Paul pushed open the door, and they both went in. They washed their hands and then went into the dining room. Miss Maria was laying up the tables. She gave a sharp look to Paul.

'I am so sorry, Miss Maria. We lost track of the time.'

Leslie felt a little guilty. After all, he had taken up Paul's time exploring the village. Paul busied himself finishing the tables, checking each one. He hurried over to the sideboard and retrieved four large coasters. He swept around the room, deftly placing a coaster in the centre of each table. Another swift glance around – yes, he was satisfied all was in order – and he left the room. A few moments later, the gong sounded, Leslie stood behind his chair as the other boys trooped in.

Lunch consisted of very simple fare – cold meats and salad, and there were also assorted pickles and bread and butter, followed by steaming hot, ground rice pudding with strawberry jam.

After lunch, Leslie helped Paul with the clearing away. The other boys hurried off back to school.

Their chores done, Paul led Leslie across the entrance hall to the opposite wing of the house. They passed a door on the right. 'Storeroom,' said Paul, 'a broom cupboard really,' he said, grinning, 'and opposite, another cloakroom. With twelve occupants, a house cannot have too many cloakrooms.'

He opened the door at the end of the corridor. It led to a room the same size as the dining room. A fireplace dominated the far wall, as in the other wing. A large table stood in the centre with chairs around it, and various armchairs dotted the room. There were two bookshelves and two cabinets with panelled doors. Two matching carpets covered most of the floor area.

Paul went to a cabinet and opened it. Inside it was an assortment of board games – Snakes and Ladders, Ludo, draughts, chess, and so on. Paul closed the door. 'We can play with them, but everything has to be returned to its rightful place.'

Leslie went over to look at the books. Most were children's books – Hans Christian Andersen, the Brothers Grimm, a few colouring books, boy's annuals, and adventure stories. But he didn't see a single reference book – *how disappointing!*

Leslie went back to Paul, who led the boy back to the entrance hall.

As they ascended the stairs, Paul said, 'I will show you how to make your bed.' At the top of the stairs, there was a door to the left and one in front of them. They turned to the right and entered the door at the end of the landing. Pausing for a moment, Paul whispered, 'All the other rooms are out of bounds.' He indicated the doors they had passed.

Leslie's bed was made, but Paul removed the blankets and sheets, placing them on the chair. Leslie watched as Paul smoothed the first sheet over the mattress, tucking the four corners with great skill and speed, and giving instructions as he worked. He spread the top sheet over and offered Leslie a try. After the third attempt, Paul seemed satisfied. Leslie then continued with a single grey blanket.

'Perfect,' Paul said. 'You really learn well.'

I must be careful not to be too good! thought the boy.

'Now, do you play draughts?' Paul enquired with a grin.

'No,' was the reply.

'I could teach you. It is not difficult to learn. All the boys here can play.'

Leslie thought, *it can't do any harm to learn if they all play.* 'Yes, please, Paul.'

They went back down the stairs and into the leisure room.

Paul collected the game from the cabinet and took it to the table. They sat facing each other, and Paul opened a black-and-white chequered board and removed the small black-and-white wooden discs from the box. Arranging the discs on the board, he began to outline the objective of the game. He explained all the moves and directions permitted and occasionally rearranged the pieces to emphasize a move or a move not permitted. He explained what happens when reaching the opposing rear rank, where the normal rules changed. Leslie appeared a little confused. 'Let us play a few games, and you will soon learn.'

Paul led with the first move, and the game carried on until Paul had him easily beaten.

Paul then explained that, as with chess, one needs to think ahead of the moves made. Leslie had never played draughts or chess before.

Paul set up his pieces, and Leslie did the same. This time, Leslie moved first. He could see many ways to advance but decided to mimic Paul's moves of the first game. He lost again. Of course, Paul had not copied Leslie's moves.

Paul won the third and fourth games, and Leslie could now see every possible move. *How soon should I beat him?*

They continued playing until the other boys returned from school.

'I have to go now,' Paul said. 'I must supervise the boys for a while.'

Leslie had gone upstairs to study his dictionary and sat on the chair by his bed. Distracted by raised voices from below, he turned to a window overlooking the yard. Outside he could see Cook and Joyce, her teenaged daughter, a girl of about sixteen. Cook looked furious; with both hands on her hips, her chin jutted out, and her head leaned forward. The girl bore a sheepish expression, both hands tucked under her chin, slightly cowering as though about to receive a slap.

'How many times must I tell you? You stupid girl. Now get inside before I forget myself.'

The girl sidled past Cook and entered through the back door, Cook following close on her heels.

Leslie remained at the window and could see beyond the orchard to the wall of the village. He strolled over to the windows on the other side of the room and could see past Epping House and the distant wall beyond the river where they had walked that morning. Looking to the left, he could see the rooftops of the chapel and the stores. From this vantage point, he saw beyond the stores to a large collection of sombre-looking red-bricked buildings, partly obscured by trees and a continuation of the wall. *We did not see that this morning,* he realised. He considered that the building might be the hospital the had dean mentioned but then remembered that Sir Alastair had said it was a small hospital. *Ah, we could not see it because we were at the bottom of the hill.* He now saw that the high wall had prevented their view. Woods and trees had lined most of their walk as they'd come up the hill, and their backs were turned to it. *I will ask Paul,* he told himself.

The other boys returned from school, washed, changed their clothes, and tidied the room. It would be some time yet before tea, and Paul waved a hand at Leslie, beckoning him closer. 'Now listen, boys. We did not have the opportunity for introductions yesterday. Leslie Johns this is Michael Eastwood – he is six. Peter and Ralph Welch, "the twins", are five. And David March is six.' The nine-year-old had a natural flair for organising and motivating.

Leslie sat on his chair as Paul chivvied the others into finishing their tidying and then set off towards the door. 'Are you coming, Leslie? Not time for bed yet, you know.'

The boys all chuckled, and Leslie grinned. 'I shall be down in a minute or two.' He had to catch up on his reading without making a fuss or drawing attention.

'See you directly then,' came Paul's voice as he disappeared, the door closing quietly behind him.

Leslie retrieved his book from the bedside locker and opened it at page 256. He scanned the contents from 'fancy' to 'fastidious' and closed the book. He closed his eyes and saw the words and meanings clearly in his mind. He replaced the book and recalled the reason for this obsession…

He had not been much more than five years old at the time, and in the classroom, the children had a book of verse to learn. He had no problem with the verse. The poem was by an author called 'Anonymous!' He had enquired as to why the person only had one name. The teacher laughed at him derisively but explained that it meant the author was unknown; it was not his name! Confounded by a lack of vocabulary, he had saved up his pocket money and purchased the second-hand dictionary. Ever since he'd become the proud owner, Leslie had avowed to read a page each day. On many occasions, he consulted the dictionary whenever he came across a new word. This book was power to him, and he could learn many things quickly. Most importantly, he could understand the meanings and uses of new words.

On re-joining the other boys in the leisure room, Leslie found that the twins were already engaged in a battle of wits on the draughtboard. David struggled with a jigsaw puzzle, and Michael coloured in one of the books from the shelf. Paul had in front of him a similar chequered board to the one earlier. However, this board had uniquely different pieces. *This must be chess*, Leslie presumed.

'Are you interested in learning this game?' enquired Paul.

'That looks difficult,' said Leslie. 'But you can show me.'

As before, Paul outlined the purpose of the game and the ways the various pieces could move around the board. He emphasised that it was a game of mental skill and planning.

'This is a game very highly rated by many people; some even compete at national and international levels.'

'Wow,' exclaimed Leslie. 'I never would have thought a game could be so important.' He lied; the importance of the game of chess had been explained in his book.

Paul led and controlled the game all the way to its inevitable conclusion.

'One more before teatime?' said the victor.

'Yes, but it is more complicated than draughts.'

Paul smiled at the lad. 'You will pick it up soon enough. You are a fast learner.' A warning bell sounded in Leslie's head!

The games and puzzles neatly stored away, the children went to wash their hands. Paul attended his chores in the dining room, and Leslie sat alone. He retraced all the chess moves in his head and then played an imaginary game. Plotting the moves one by one, he made a note of mistakes and revised the moves—

The gong sounded, and he lined up with the other boys. They entered the dining room, followed by the Atkins and the staff.

During the evening meal, Leslie noticed, through the large window beside the table, a young man of about eighteen or twenty. The man struggled with a wheelbarrow that almost tipped sideways it was so laden with potted plants and bags of bulbs. He rested the barrow, mopped his face and brow with a wipe of his rolled-up sleeve, and searched around him. His expression changed, indicating that he had found whatever he had been looking for. He passed out of view to one side of the window. A moment later, Leslie could hear the sound of digging and raking. A man's voice from nearby, but out of sight, was instructing him to place the hydrangeas at the back of the border so they avoided blocking the smaller plants when they were at full height. 'You can plant those closer together. They look better in blocks. Don't forget to stake and tie them. They'll be down with a strong wind.' There was a lilt to the man's voice, and Leslie surmised that this must be the head gardener, Joseph Breen.

After they'd eaten, Leslie assisted Paul and the others to clear the tables and tidy the room. It was still early, and there was plenty of time left before bedtime. Leslie decided that he would go and look at the flower beds outside the window. Paul was going to play chess with David.

Outside, the early evening air carried the scent of freshly turned earth. The man Leslie had seen through the window sat on an ageing tree stump, rolling a cigarette. The man removed a match and struck it on the side of the box, cupped his hands, and lit the cigarette. Small puffs of smoke escaped from the cupped hands, and Leslie could smell the aromatic fragrance of the tobacco.

Puffing on the skinny cigarette, the man looked at Leslie. 'Who might you be then, young sir?'

'Oh, I'm not a sir. I'm Leslie Johns.

'I'm Robert Lane, you can call me Rob if you like.' He gave a grin that showed a gap where a tooth was missing. Rob noticed the boy staring and said, 'Lost that when I trod on a rake. Come up and smacked me full in the mouth it did.'

'That must have really hurt,' said Leslie with some concern.

'Nah, bin in worse hurt than that; did sting a bit though.'

Leslie cast his eyes across the newly turned flower bed, observing the hydrangeas and wallflowers, the stocks and primroses, and a swathe of brightly coloured nasturtiums. 'Which house are you in?' Leslie said, looking back at Rob.

'Gawd no. I ain't one of you lot. We live in a cottage up near the stores there, across the road from the school.' He waved an arm in the direction of the stores. 'Yeah, there's me, the gaffer, his wife, and two other lads.

'One of the lads used to be here in one of these here houses like you. Talks posh like. Stevie we calls him. He hated it at first, being called Stevie I mean. Came here as a nipper by all accounts. Good worker, but don't say much though. Tell you what, he knows his stuff – a right proper Percy—'

'What is a Percy?' piped up Leslie.

'Lord, I thought you lot was supposed to be educated' he said with some surprise, 'Percy Thrower, the bloke on the radio, knows all there is to know about gardening, and what Percy don't know ain't worth learning, lad.'

Leslie was thinking. Rob seemed quite chatty, and he lived near the stores. 'Is that red building over the back where you live?'

'What, that rambling old place you mean? Nah, we don't live there, lad, and wouldn't to want to neither. That's the asylum, you know, where they put funny people.' His hand made a small circular motion at his temple.

Leslie felt a chill run down his spine. He knew what an asylum was, and it terrified him.

'I like those,' Leslie said, changing the subject and pointing to the nasturtiums. 'They are bright and full of colour.'

'Yeah, the beds should look better with the other stuff in flower next year. Now don't you go eatin' them now.'

Leslie giggled. 'They're flowers. We can't eat them.'

'Course you can. You can eat lots of flowers and plants; you just have to know what to eat and what not to! Take them foxgloves over there by the trees,' he said waving a trowel vaguely in their direction. 'Them's just seed heads now, but they got lovely spikes of flowers early on. Them you don't eat cause they are poisonous.'

Leslie observed the dried spikes of seed heads. 'How do you know what you can eat or not?'

'It's like this, lad. Over lotsa years, people passed their knowledge from one to another. I s'pose the first one that ate them poison ones got ill or maybe died. Other people learned from them. Take mushrooms; some looks much like another, but they ain't, see, and some's really poisonous.

'That tree, the other side there,' he added, again waving his trowel, this time in the direction of the other side of the garden, 'that's a bay tree, a type of laurel. We gives the leaves to the kitchens for cooking with, but you can't use any of the other laurels. Like I said, you got to know your stuff.'

Rob scraped the sandy brown soil from his boots with the trowel. He cleaned the gardening tools and wiped them with an old rag that smelled of oil. Leslie observed his every move, full of interest. He didn't often get the chance to observe a man at work. 'Keeps 'em from rusting,' Rob said. 'A good worker always looks after his tools!' He loaded the tools onto the wheelbarrow. 'I best be getting on now. I'll have the guv'nor on me back, and that won't do, will it, lad?'

'Have you finished now?' Leslie looked a little disappointed.

'Nah, still got these to do,' he said, nodding at the bags of bulbs. 'Got to plant these along the avenue there, daffs and crocuses. Won't be done today, shouldn't think.'

'But what about your tea? Won't Mr Breen be expecting you?'

Rob let out a loud laugh. 'You mean old Paddy? Nah, we don't have teatime like you young 'uns. We has to get the work done see! 'Sides, his wife, Joan, will still be up at the big house.'

Leslie asked with interest, 'Is that the maid who works with Miss Susan?'

'Ah yes, that's her. That Miss Susan now, she's a fine young woman and no mistake! Took a fancy to her meself, but I reckon she's only got eyes for his lordship, according to what Joan says anyway.'

'But isn't the dean married then?'

'Oh, years ago. She died young, givin' birth to their son it's said. Don't see much of 'im though, the boy I mean. Went to Eton I think or somewhere like that. Studyin' now at Oxford, or was it Cambridge? One of them top colleges anyway. Comes home for the odd Christmas now and then. They say he likes to travel. South America he went to last year. Got into some bother over there I heard; cost his dad a pretty penny by all accounts. There were lawyers in an' out of that house for weeks. I reckon his dad's a bit disappointed with him!'

Talking all the while, the new friends stopped occasionally, planting groups of bulbs into the grass on the verge along one side of the avenue. Rob made the holes with a dibber, and Leslie dropped in the bulbs. 'You'll be doing me out of a job, lad,' Rob remarked with a smile.

'I have really enjoyed myself,' remarked the boy.

Just then, a distant voice called, 'Leslie, Leslie!'

The boy turned in the direction of the voice. He could see Mary standing far back along the road, outside Epping House. 'Got to go now,' he said to Rob. 'Will I see you tomorrow?'

'Yep, reckon you will, lad, still plenty to do be done yet, and thanks for the help.'

Leslie ran down the avenue towards his sister.

'What are you doing with that man? Look at your hands! I can see they just let you run around like a stray dog. Daddy was right; you need me to look after you after all!'

Before Leslie had had a chance to explain, Paul appeared. 'There you are. I thought you had gone to bed,' he said with a cheeky grin on his face.

'No, I was—'

Mary cut him off mid-sentence. 'Are you supposed to be looking after my little brother? You are not doing a very good job of it. His hands are dirty, there's mud on his shoes, and I bet he hasn't combed his hair all day,' she said, running her fingers through Leslie's locks.

Paul stood mouth agape, opening and closing without a sound, trying to get a word in but prevented by this 'firebrand in pigtails' – it was the only way he could think of her. Mary gave her brother a push towards Paul. 'An' don't let him go talking to strangers.'

In just a few short seconds, Mary had reprimanded her brother and left a boy, a head boy nonetheless, speechless and shell-shocked. Mary turned on her heels and flounced into Epping House. The two boys stood in the road nonplussed.

'That is my sister, Mary,' said Leslie in a state of embarrassment.

'I am so, so sorry for you,' replied Paul, he related his view of her.

They ran around the side of Roding House and entered through the kitchen backdoor, giggling all the while at the new nickname for Mary.

Passing through the kitchen, they could smell the heavenly aroma of freshly baked bread. Cook peered at them over the top of her spectacles, her hands white with flour, and her cheeks flushed red with the heat from the ovens. She wiped her hands on a towel and grabbed some thick oven-cloths. From the open oven, she withdrew a large tray of deliciously golden sultana scones and placed it on a pair of trivets. 'Where is that girl again?' she said in frustration. 'I swear I'll swing for her one of these days—'

The boys made a quick exit. One irate female was enough for today!

'Where did you go to after tea?' asked Paul.

'I went to look at what Rob had been doing in the garden. He planted some hydrangeas under the window.'

'Oh, you mean the man I saw at teatime?'

'Yes. We planted a lot of daffodils and crocuses along the drive as well. Rob says it will look a picture in the spring.'

'I have seen him around,' said Paul. 'I think Mr Breen keeps them pretty busy.'

'Old Paddy,' said Leslie, grinning.

'That may be how your friend refers to him, but I would not repeat it if I was you. By the way, Mr Atkins says to remind you that you have an appointment with Dr Hendricks in the morning after breakfast. I will show you where to go. I have an errand to do tomorrow, and it is on my way.'

'Thank you Paul. Is it far?' Leslie was thinking that his appointment would be at the cottage hospital up near the stores.

'Not at all,' Paul replied. 'He lives in the lodge next to the gates.'

***

After breakfast and the usual chores, Paul looked Leslie up and down, making sure that he looked presentable. 'Right, let's be off then.' They stopped for a moment at the 'private' door. Paul knocked, and Mr Atkins opened the door about halfway and passed a small envelope to Paul. Through the gap, Leslie could see Mrs Atkins sitting in an upright armchair listening to a radio. The door shut abruptly, and Paul led the way out of the front door.

They walked at a brisk pace up the avenue toward Howard House. Leslie indicated the patches in the verge where he and Rob had planted the bulbs the previous day and talked excitedly about the work still to be completed. Before long, they reached the turning in the road and headed to the left. They had not had the time on their previous outing to explore this area of the village. The open swathe of lawn to their right gave way to neatly clipped box hedging surrounding formal flower beds and, to their right, grassed pathways between the beds and borders. Leslie could see a wall at the left side of Howard House with two terracotta urns each side of a gateway. The urns, filled with a dazzling display of colourful trailing plants, caught the eye.

They continued along the main drive, passing woods of larch trees and silver birch. Blackbirds darted back and forth, squabbling over territory. A robin on a branch overhanging the avenue sang until it seemed the little bird would burst. Ahead, Leslie could see the double gates.

They reached the drive to the lodge, and Paul told Leslie that he was expected and that he should ring the front doorbell. 'I will see you later. Good luck.' Paul waved a hand as he disappeared through the open gates and into the world outside.

Leslie stood at the door, waiting for a response to the jingle jangle of the bell.

A woman probably in her late fifties or early sixties opened the door. She smiled and offered her hand. 'Master Leslie, is it?'

Leslie replied that it was and took her hand. She led him through the house to a conservatory at the rear.

The wall of glass gave a view onto the most exquisite garden the boy had ever seen. Not noticing the man seated at a wicker table in a white trilby and safari suit, he gazed at the steps leading up to a pool with a fountain. The musical sound of the waterspout emptying into the pool fascinated him, as did the gravel paths surrounding the pool and how all the borders were lined with hollyhocks and delphiniums. Carpets of golden thyme spilled onto the pathways, and tall columns were topped with baskets of trailing plants, a myriad of colours dangling from their edges and cascading towards flagstone squares below.

'Good morning, young man.'

The voice snapped Leslie from his reverie. 'Oh, so sorry, sir. Good morning to you also.'

'I thought you might like to be in here. It's comfortable, no?'

That now familiar mannerism made Leslie smile. 'Most pleasurable, sir,' he replied with a slight bow and a flourish of his hand.

'Oh, I can see we shall be the good friends indeed, you agree?'

'Indeed, sir, we shall.' Leslie affected a medieval response.

This behaviour appeared to amuse the doctor immensely. 'Would you like that we have some cold drink and perhaps some biscuits?'

Well, Leslie thought, *can I stay here with you?* 'Ooh, yes, please, sir.'

The doctor tapped a brass bell. 'Perhaps before we begin, you would like to walk the garden no?'

'Yes, please, sir. I have never seen one as beautiful as this.'

'You will come with me this way no?'

The boy followed him through double doors that led onto a flagstone path. Dwarf walls bordered the pathway, over which trailed lobelias and geraniums. In the raised border behind the walls danced blue and red anemones and fuchsia bushes with their dripping flowers of red and white. He took in the mock orange with its pale green leaves, the gay pink Lavatera, and the Buddleias with their long purple spikes. All the while, the tinkling sound of water finding its way down to the pool from the stream somewhere behind the bushes filled the garden with a sense of magic. The doctor and the small boy strolled along the path, past the pool and up two steps to a semi-circular lawn.

A wooden garden bench stood next to a summer house, and beyond that, a curving path led away to a wooded area. The path was bordered with shrubs, and their varied shades of greens, greys, and reds contrasted with each other. A great deal of skill had created this haven. Whoever had designed it had knowledge of the soil and the requirements of such different plants, of the flow of the stream, of how to soften the sharp edges of the flagstones; the gardener had used gravels and flagstones to create different sensations when walking through the garden, had mastered the balance and contrast of the colours, had known the different scents that wafted occasionally through this paradise. *I wish I could stay here forever,* the boy mused.

'Now to the cold drinks and biscuits, no?' said the doctor.

They returned along the gravel path and as they passed the pool, Leslie noticed the fish darting in and out of the reeds and lily pads. Golden yellows, orange, white with speckles of black. Some were as long as his forearm, glimmering as they surfaced and caught the sun's rays. A slight *plop* sounded as they dived back into the depths of the pool.

'The fish they like you and they come to say hello.'

'Hello, fishes. How do you do? I am Leslie.'

'Oh, they know you are Leslie.'

'How do they know, sir?'

'Because I tell them everything. They know as much as I do.'

'Then they must be very clever fish, sir.'

The doctor laughed as he took the boy by the hand. 'You give me too much honour.'

They both laughed, hand in hand.

Arriving back at the conservatory, they found the table laid with a cloth, two glasses of lemonade, and a plate containing a variety of biscuits, many of which Leslie had never seen or tasted. There were two side plates and napkins. They sat, and the doctor invited the boy to tuck in. 'You may call me sir, Ernest, or just Hendricks, after all, we are friends, are we not?'

The boy sat deep in thought. 'Would it be all right if I call you Doctor?'

'But of course dear boy, call me whatever suits you. You told the dean the things you like doing, no. You may tell me if you like what your most favourite thing is, it may be a toy, an idea, a person or something else.'

Leslie saw the hook before it hit the water. The boy had to think carefully for this man was well skilled.

The surroundings were relaxing and comfortable. *Beware!* The voice in his head warned him, he could ignore the warning but he knew it would be a terrible mistake to do so. 'Well, I like the river down the hill and I wish I could go on a boat on it.'

'Can you swim?'

'Oh no, sir! I like to paddle in the shallows but not in deep water.'

'So, if you were in a boat, how deep would you need the water to be?'

'I never thought about how deep, because I have never been on a boat, but not too deep I think.'

'You would surely need enough water to prevent the boat from running aground no? therefore, deep enough to swim in I suspect, would you agree with that?'

'It does make sense when you put it like that, I would have to ensure that I did not fall out of the boat though.'

The doctor smiled and offered the plate of biscuits towards the boy. He eyed them with pleasure and chose a half-coated chocolate biscuit. He took a bite, leaning over the side plate. The biscuit broke, and crumbs cascaded onto the plate.

The doctor smiled and said, 'I never can eat them without the crumbs and the chocolate making the mess.'

Devouring the last of the biscuit, the boy regarded his sticky fingers covered in soft, warm chocolate. The doctor mimicked licking his fingers and said, 'It is allowed the licking of fingers in such circumstances.'

They sat drinking lemonade, and after two more biscuits, the boy sat back in the chair patting his stomach with an air of great satisfaction, and his old friend Thomas came to his mind.

***

Thomas was a boy Leslie knew from his previous orphanage, a good friend to Leslie when they were together at St Vincent's' and Thomas had an enormous influence upon Leslie, especially with regard to keeping his talents secret. Thomas knew Leslie inside out, and though Thomas was only two years older he had many skills, talents that Leslie never knew of, and perhaps why he had told Leslie to hide his talents because he knew from his own experiences the torments his young friend could suffer. So Leslie engaged with the doctor in the games ahead with an air of caution.

***

'So, we now can put these over here,' the doctor said, pulling a small side table towards him.

They cleared the main table, and the doctor produced some pictures from a briefcase beside him. He placed one in front of the boy. 'Tell me what you see here please.'

Leslie looked at an abstract black-and-white design. 'A horse's head.'

The doctor made a note on a sheet of paper, but the boy could not see what he wrote.

'And this one please?'

'A candlestick like they have in church.'

This continued for twenty minutes or so, and each time Leslie gave an answer, the doctor made brief notes.

'Now, I have for you something different.' The doctor produced a jigsaw puzzle, but the pieces had no picture. There was no detail or picture to guide where the pieces may belong. *Beware Leslie.* an inner voice told him.

The boy looked hard at the pieces. He saw the outlines of them and, in his mind, fitted them all together before he had even touched the first piece. He made a display of twisting and turning the pieces, separating the edge pieces first and slowly fitting them into a framework. The central pieces he made a struggle of, trying this piece and then that and moving to one side the ones that would not fit comfortably. Thirty minutes had passed when he completed the last piece. 'That was difficult for you I see.'

'I got it in the end doctor' he said with glee. Mostly his glee was from fooling the doctor. He could not demonstrate his level of intellect or mental acuity. He could have put the pieces together in thirty seconds, not minutes.

'Perhaps now a better game.' The doctor replaced the puzzle in its box and put it in the briefcase. 'You will please to close your eyes for me.'

Leslie could hear the doctor remove the lid from a wooden box and place twelve items on the table in a random fashion. 'You may now open the eyes.'

A cloth covered the items on the table. 'I will take away the cloth, and you have only ten seconds to look and remember as many as you can.'

The boy nodded without looking up. His eyes concentrated on the cloth. The doctor removed the cloth, and click, his mind recorded every object in an instant, *horse, boat, cup, soldier, pencil, pocketknife, teaspoon, glass marble, sugar cube, matchstick, chess piece, toffee.*

With the ten seconds up, the doctor covered the table, and with pen and paper at the ready, the doctor asked him to recall the objects. Leslie had worked out the purpose of this game, a test of sight and memory, he could not expose his mind or his power by giving a perfect result. He began falteringly, 'a, a horse, a toffee, a wrapped wrapped toffee, a marble, oh…a soldier, um…a boat with a sail, er…a…er…a pencil, oh, a piece from a chess game.' The boy bobbed excitedly in pretence on his seat as he recalled each item. 'A spoon…a cup…sugar, a square of sugar,' he said at last, just convincing the doctor that he was good at the games but not special.

Leslie could not reveal his secret, not even to this man he felt comfortable with.

'That is good, very good.' The notes made, the doctor put the items back in the box and replaced them in the briefcase. 'Now perhaps you will like some more lemonade?'

'Yes, please, Doctor.' The boy said with much enthusiasm.

'My housekeeper makes the good lemonade I think.'

'Indeed she does, doctor.'

'You wish to ask me something?'

The boy looked a little perplexed, thinking he had been remiss in some way. 'Sir?'

Noticing the boy's dilemma, the doctor said, 'No. I mean is there anything you wish me to tell you?'

The housekeeper brought a fresh jug of lemonade and set it upon the small table. The doctor poured two glasses and handed one to the boy.

Leslie took a long sip, thinking. What could he ask? 'Do we have any more games, sir?'

'Why? Do you wish to leave?'

'Oh no, sir, I like games especially the ones that test the brain.'

The doctor smiled, 'Yes I think we have another here.' He reached into the magic bag and pulled out a deck of playing cards.

The man separated and removed the Kings, Queens and Knaves cards and shuffled the remainder. He laid them face down on the table. 'You may pick three cards. You must turn each one, look at it, and place it back on the table face down before you turn the next one. You must remember the numbers and add them together in your head. You may let me see the cards, and you will do this quickly please.'

The boy studied the cards. It was not important which cards he chose, and he turned three in quick succession – ace, seven, nine.

'Seventeen, doctor.'

'Good, now three more.'

'Do they have to be different?'

'If you remember and choose the same ones, there is no point in the game, no?'

The boy thought about his actions, he knew where the cards were that he had chosen. He moved the cards around with his eyes shut. He opened them and turned three more – three, nine, six.

'Eighteen.'

He repeated this five more times, leaving a second or two before giving an answer.

'I think you are too good for this game,' said the doctor. 'But it is for small children, no?' He cleared the cards away.

'The items I covered with the cloth earlier, tell me now what you remember.'

Horse, boat, cup, soldier, pencil, pocketknife, teaspoon, glass marble, sugar cube, matchstick, chess piece, toffee.

'A sailboat; a horse; a pencil; a sweet…a toffee, sugar cube, uh, uh, a marble; a boat. No, I said boat. Oh, yes, a spoon, a teaspoon; a cup, yes; a soldier, a pocketknife, yes, a knife with a red handle; a matchstick.'

The doctor said, 'I believe you did well. Now perhaps you will read for me from this book.' He leaned across to a book on a shelf just behind him, opened the book, and indicated a passage to read. It was a bible and the passage, Genesis chapter 41. The boy began to read aloud:

> 'And it came to pass at the end of two full years, that Pharaoh dreamed: and, behold, he stood by the river. And, behold, there came up out of the river seven well favoured kine and fat-fleshed; and they fed in a meadow. And, behold, seven other kine came up after them out of the river, ill-favoured and lean-fleshed; and stood by the other kine upon the brink of the river. And the ill-favoured and lean-fleshed kine did eat up the seven well favoured and fat kine. So Pharaoh awoke.'

The doctor stopped him there. 'You read well but do you understand what you have read?'

The boy thought. 'I know the story of Joseph and the Pharaoh, the seven good years followed by the seven bad ones, sir. We learned it at Sunday school.'

'Good. And you remembered it well. But what do you understand "kine" to be?'

'They are cattle, sir. We were told it is the old English plural for cows.'

'Excellent indeed.'

The doctor replaced the bible upon its shelf and took an old pipe from his pocket. He cleaned it with a small pocketknife and then stuffed it with tobacco from a pouch. He puffed as he lit it, sending small clouds of smoke up to the ceiling. He sat quietly in thought, cradling the bowl of the pipe in his hand and taking the occasional puff.

'You will stay with us for some lunch, no?'

'I think they will be expecting me back at Roding House, doctor,' Leslie replied.

'I can call them on the telephone if you like to stay. I have other puzzles for you yet if I have not tired you…'

'Very well, doctor, thank you' said Leslie.

It was past mid-afternoon when Leslie returned to Roding House and where he met Paul outside the entrance.

'We thought he had eaten you for lunch,' said Paul, grinning from ear to ear.

'I had lunch with the doctor, chicken and leek pie, it was delicious I can tell you.'

Leslie felt slightly downbeat after his visit to the lodge and did not really wish to engage in more conversation, but he did not wish to appear rude to his friend. He wanted some space, some time alone to concentrate his thoughts. The last game had involved a list of twenty words, and he'd had to write down the meanings of the words. He hoped that what he had written was not like reading from a dictionary, which could give the game away! He had hoped that he might meet Rob on the way back, but the man was nowhere in sight.

'Do you fancy a game of chess, Leslie?' said Paul.

The boy felt he had done enough brainwork for one day! 'I think I may just go for a walk, perhaps to the river?'

'See you later then but do not get your shoes dirty, or your sister will be after me.'

Leslie gave a smile and wave without looking back.

***

Walking slowly down the hill, he could not shake off the strange mood that entrapped him. He had enjoyed the games and puzzles, but he felt a kind of darkness bearing down upon him. He sauntered along, watching his feet moving one in front of the other, and to him it was a strange experience.

He decided to cut through the wooded area down to the track instead of going all the way to the gates. He followed a narrow trail made by the regular inhabitants of the woods. From time to time, the trail led into dense thorny undergrowth, making the boy skirt around before finding the trail again. He could smell the musty scent emanating from a fox's den.

He climbed a bank and stumbled down the other side to the road, head down. He walked on toward the river, kicking at the occasional stone or twig. Arriving at the riverbank, he sat on the fallen elm, swishing a stick, and he soon heard voices from the far riverbank.

Three boys made their way along the bank carrying fishing poles and a net. They were about eight or nine years old, and by their attire, Leslie could tell they were not from the village.

Suddenly, a man's voice shouted to them from the wooded area. 'Oi, what's you lot doing here then?'

Leslie recognised Rob's voice. The man was walking along the track towards him from the direction of the boathouse. 'You lots not supposed to be in here.'

Leslie noticed that the boys were wearing Wellington boots. They must have waded under the bridge, upstream where the road first crosses the river. He leaped from the elm trunk and ran towards Rob.

'Hello there, young 'un. Out for a spot of mischief then?'

'Oh, no, sir. I was just taking a rest. I had to see Dr Hendricks today, and I'm feeling a bit weary I suppose.'

'What's up with you then? Got bats in the belfry?'

'Pardon me?'

'Well, he's one of them shrinks, you know, a head doctor. Thought as how you might have something wrong in yer head...'

Leslie had a sickening, sinking feeling in the pit of his stomach. He remembered Thomas, his friend from St Vincent's. Thomas had gone to see a psychologist several times, and then one day he'd just disappeared. The vicar had told Leslie that the boy had gone home, but Thomas had told him he was an orphan and had no family. Someone else said a couple had adopted him. But the two boys had been inseparable. Leslie would have known if someone had visited to adopt his friend. Other boys said Thomas had run away during the night, but only Leslie knew that Thomas was afraid to be alone in the dark. Thomas knew about Leslie's special skills and was the one who told him to keep them secret – told him that, if anyone found out, they would take him away and lock him up! How he missed his friend Thomas. He'd always had his doubts about what had happened to him; Thomas also had special skills.

Despite the hot afternoon sun, the boy felt chilled to the bone.

'Say, you all-right, Master Leslie? You gone awful pale.' His concern showed in his face as he said, 'Here, sit you down here beside me lad. I reckon you been running round too much lad.'

***

Leslie awoke feeling sick and with an immense throbbing in his head. 'There now, you just lay back and rest. You had a nasty fall by all accounts.' It was a woman's voice, a voice unfamiliar to him, and slowly he focused his eyes.

The room was white, all white; the woman talking was dressed in white, and she had a watch in her hand and her fingers holding his wrist. 'I think you'll live young man, mind you, that is quite a bump on your head.'

Leslie could feel the bandages as he moved his hand around his head and felt the bump on the left side. 'Ouch!'

'You just leave it now. It won't get better with you prodding at it.' The nurse walked away towards a glass-panelled door.

At about two in the morning, Leslie lay awake in the hospital bed and recalled the boys on the riverbank and Rob shouting at them. Then he remembered what Rob had told him about the doctor. He shut his eyes and recounted every second of the day's events.

The strangest thing happened! Leslie, through no conscious will, elevated from the bed. He looked down and could see himself. He was there, in the bed with his eyes closed but not sleeping. What was happening? It was a most peculiar sensation. Somehow, he floated above himself… But this was not possible to his mind. He must be dreaming or under the influence of medication. He opened his eyes, and all was exactly as before – a nurse behind the glass door and screen illuminated by a night light, and he, still in the bed. He closed his eyes again.

He slept soundly until the sound of the nurse's trolley woke him at six thirty. 'It is time to take your temperature, young sir. Turn over please!' She took his pulse and checked the bandage. 'You have a slight temperature; I think it is better to keep you here for now young man.' She returned to her desk outside of the room.

After he ate some breakfast, he felt a little better, although the headache still pained him. He shut his eyes to block out the growing daylight that entered through the window.

He was floating again. *But this is not possible; the bang on the head has affected my brain.* He remained looking at his own body for a few seconds.

A thought occurred to him. He could perhaps move around. But what if the nurse saw him? No sooner had he thought of the nurse than he was there standing in front of her. She was talking on the telephone and looking right at him, or so he thought at first, but she was looking through him, right through him! She could not see him, and he could not believe what was happening.

He could hear her say, 'His temperature is a little high, so I am keeping him here to monitor him.'

He found it difficult to believe that he could hear Dr Hendricks' voice on the telephone as though speaking directly to him. 'Well if his condition does not change by midday you will please to call me back.'

'Yes, Doctor. Should I get him some lunch here?'

'Yes, for now it will be the best option, no? I will telephone Mr Atkins and to inform him of the progress.'

Leslie put a hand to his head. 'Ow.' He felt the bump.

He was now awake in the bed, and his thoughts assailed him. How could he hear the nurse and the unmistakeable voice of Dr Hendricks from here? The door between them was closed, and the doctor was at the other end of the telephone! He decided he would wait for the nurse to come back and somehow find out.

He lay pondering this unbelievable idea that he could leave his body when a thought struck him. This was going to be another secret he would have to keep. If he said anything, they would think he was mad. He thought he was going mad, so why shouldn't others?

He wrestled with his thoughts and concluded that it was the bump to the head; it was making him imagine things. Yes, that was it – the bump.

At midday, the nurse arrived with a steaming bowl of tomato soup and two slices of bread and butter. She propped up his pillows and put the tray on his lap.

'How long will I be here for?' he asked.

'That depends, young man, on how soon your temperature drops.'

'But won't they be worried about me at Roding House, for I have not told them—'

'Oh, you need not worry yourself. The doctor has telephoned them this morning to explain everything. Come now and eat your lunch whilst it's hot.'

Leslie realised that what had occurred was not in his imagination after all, but he was still not entirely convinced.

'What happened to me?' he asked, trying to fill the blank space after he'd talked to Rob.

'Well, the gardener, Mr Lane I believe, said the pair of you were talking down by the river on the path leading to the woods. He said you had been running along the riverbank before you reached him. You were chatting, and you just went all white and collapsed. You banged your head quite hard on the path; there must have been a sharp stone or something. You've got a nasty gash on your head, and we had to put four stitches in it.'

That's it, he thought, *that bump and the stitches. Maybe they used something to clean the wound that had some kind of weird effect. Well, it was like a strange dream really and best not to mention it… Head doctor, bats and belfries, Thomas,* and then the boy passed out again.

***

When Leslie arrived back at Roding House two weeks later, he was something of a celebrity with his head swathed in bandages and having had a prolonged stay in hospital. There had been many telephone calls, and the dean himself had come to see Mr Atkins. The boys gathered around Leslie full of questions and excitement.

Mr Atkins sent the boys off to attend their books and homework for school in the morning. 'Come with me Leslie,' he said, leading the boy into the private room. 'You may sit there' he said, pointing to a hard wooden chair. 'The gardener, a Mr Lane I believe and the one who took you to the hospital, did he have anything to do with your injury?'

'No master. One minute we were talking and the next I woke up in the hospital.'

'Tell me what you know of this man.'

Leslie thought about the two occasions he and Rob had met. 'I know he is an under gardener. He says that he did not grow up here in the village. He lives up near the stores with Mr and Mrs Breen and two other gardeners. He was planting some bushes and bulbs when I first met him, and I helped him with some of the bulbs along the avenue, I found him to be kind and friendly, jovial too. After my visit to Dr Hendricks, I thought

Rob would be planting some more bulbs along the avenue, but he was not. When I was down by the river, I heard him telling some town boys they should not be in the village. They were on the far bank. I was going to ask him about planting some more bulbs.'

The master thought about what Leslie had recounted. 'You said the two of you were talking. You have not said what it was you were discussing.'

'I do not recall that we said much, except about my sister telling me off' he lied, hiding his fear of psychiatrists and such folk.

'Yes. Paul was the last person to see you here. He told me about Mary.'

Leslie giggled, recalling Paul's description of her. 'Sorry master, a firebrand in pigtails.'

The master gave a little smile. 'She heard about you and came over to see me. She was most concerned and accused us of neglecting you. I think Paul gave a good description.' They both laughed, and Leslie felt more relaxed.

'What do you think made you faint?' the master asked in a friendly tone.

'Well I do not know really, master. I recall feeling a bit weary late that afternoon' he rubbed the bandage to scratch an itch. 'The doctor and I had done a lot of talking and playing games at the lodge as I recall, and, oh sir, he has a most beautiful garden with a fish pond.' Seeing that the master was not interested in the doctor's garden he continued, 'We had some lunch, chicken pie; I think his housekeeper made it. Anyway, later on I walked down the lane and cut through the woods to the river. When I got there, I remember feeling tired and sat on the fallen tree we always sit on. I was feeling quite hot, so I rested for a while. That is when I saw the town boys on the far bank with their fishing poles and heard Rob telling them off. It lifted my spirits to see Rob again and I ran just a short way to meet with him and we spoke for only a moment I believe. I cannot remember any more master.'

'Well, thank you, Leslie. I am relieved that no serious harm befell you. But in future, you may want to take things a little easier; no running about in the sun, as it can be exhausting with the heat.'

Leslie regarded their talk as a step toward a friendlier relationship. Mr Atkins applauded the candid manner of the boy, but the lad was keeping something from him; he was certain of it.

Leslie could not reveal his secrets to this man, the boy lacked confidence in Mr Atkins and for now, his secrets remained his own.

Chapter 3

The Education Years and a Summer of Discovery

School was an obligation Leslie welcomed with pleasure, unlike many children; he had an insatiable thirst for learning. He had missed much of his schooling in September but soon caught up with his peers. As winter eclipsed autumn, he absorbed more and more, every syllable of every word, devoured the information like a hungry wolf at a carcass in the midwinter snows.

The hours passed – English, French, Latin, Greek, geography, history, mathematics, biology... He looked forward eagerly each evening to the next exciting instalment, and as always, he scanned his dictionary each evening.

***

He had become close to the two Spanish housemaids, mentally noting any deviation into their native tongue. He would enquire constantly, what is the Spanish for this or for that? How would I say this? If one said this, how would someone respond and vice versa? All the time, he was building his knowledge and vocabulary and adding the subtle cadences to his growing mastery of the tongue. The maids were only too happy to oblige; many peoples with a native language other than their own, become impressed by somebody who would take the trouble to learn and attempt to communicate in their mother tongue. Often, Leslie would try to compose simple sentences to be corrected by the native speakers. Most children would see a correction as a failure in communicating; on the contrary,

Leslie would purposely phrase incorrectly and wait for the correction. This was how he affirmed his own level of understanding of the tongue.

He was confident that his mastery of languages was advancing well, and now he had two new strong companions to aid him, Spanish and French dictionaries. The weekly money he received for his chores was aiding and abetting his advancement in both languages.

***

Each Friday, the boys received pocket money in return for the chores they had completed to the master's satisfaction. The more impressed the master was, the more money there was available. The old adage, 'A job worth doing is worth doing well,' seemed to be the rule of the day. Every boy strove to outdo the others – to be the best. Above all, being the best at everything was the ultimate goal. The payment mattered, but it was the kudos and the status that mattered more. One's reputation reigned supreme in this closeted realm.

The world outside had no interest in the life of the village, to them, it was a closed community, cutting itself off from the realities of the post-war years of struggles and hardships and financed by someone with more money than sense; and they dismissed the village as the obsession of a grand eccentric.

***

Three days each week, Leslie had permission to read in the dean's library, and he indulged in the range of books available to him, if the dean was away he could visit by arrangement with the librarian. One might think of Leslie as a boy in a sweetshop, this lad had a sweet tooth for books. Sugary sweets were not his thing; he could happily give away a thousand years' worth of sweets for ten hours in these hallowed rooms. His acquired knowledge surpassed that of boys three times his age.

He was aware that other children had not the appetites or passions for learning that he had; so consumed was he in the wealth of learning that he never let it concern him, and apart from Mr McManus, he was always alone in his studies.

***

The librarian had become a personal favourite of Leslie's; the man's understanding and knowledge of the tomes under his care was incalculable. The boy recognised the brilliance behind the man's great love and respect for each book, but he could never explain such things to his peers. Leslie and Mr McManus became good friends, and he would collect the books for the boy, allowing him to read quietly, alone. Sometimes they would sit and discuss the relative merits of a book, its meanings, implied or otherwise. But the librarian always allowed the boy to broach the subject. McManus once told him that reading without understanding was akin to an artist creating without perspective, and that understanding was the vehicle that supported logic. The boy's knowledge and intellect grew greater by the hour in this man's company.

***

He had not had an experience of floating for a long time – nothing of the kind had occurred since he'd been in the hospital. One night, as Paul turned out the light and the other boys drifted into slumber, Leslie lay awake thinking about the events of the day. There was nothing to speak of really, except for a boy missing from class due to some illness. For some reason unknown, he recalled the events that had occurred that peculiar day in hospital some months back. He wondered if he could achieve that same state of floating; he shut his eyes tightly, and after several minutes, nothing had happened. He resigned himself to the fact that it was the bump on the head or the medication that had afforded him this unusual method of travel.

As he lay with his eyes shut, with his hand feeling the slight bump on his head, he thought about the nurse and Hendricks talking on the telephone. He suddenly found himself floating in the hospital room and saw the nurse spoon-feeding a boy some medicine. She tucked the boy up in bed and turned off the light, and then Leslie opened his eyes, he was still in his bed. He did not know if he had drifted into a dream momentarily. He knew a boy was missing from class today. Maybe his mind had played tricks on him; he had known the boy was unwell. Leslie reasoned with what he saw, *I had been thinking about the hospital and my time there. The missing boy, where would one be when ill? The hospital of course. This is a useless exercise*, he thought, and he slept a deep slumber until morning.

***

The weeks passed and cold winter days surrendered to the welcoming buds of spring. He thought often about the gardener, Rob, as he walked to and from the Lodge or the Library. The daffodils and crocuses were a constant reminder. He had seen no more of the man he had grown fond of; so long had passed without a sight or any word. They had been long winter days for Leslie. He filled his time with chores, reading, study and playing draughts and chess and had finally beaten the champion, Paul. But some disquiet ate away at him inside that he could only discuss with the doctor when he felt the time right to do so.

The monthly visits to the doctor had been a requisite that he loved and somehow feared. The games became more complicated, more involved, and required great thought and abstract thinking. He always completed them with a touch of caution and acting, making sure that he took time to calculate the wins and losses here and there. The older he became, the easier he found the games. He had become the consummate actor as well as convincing liar. He was now at a stage where he felt he could construct his own puzzles, ones that the doctor himself could not solve. He possessed a mind of great age and wisdom, living in the body of a child but he could not reveal it, and such was one of his many inner torments.

***

lying in his bed one night on the cusp of summer, he saw a wooded area on the far side of the stores. A fox or badger trail led to a part of the high wall that had fallen into ruins. The approach was thick with brambles and bracken. There were pools of water detained by the sodden clay soil beneath. Alarm calls from blackbirds nearby heightened his senses. He stepped over the fallen debris of the wall, cautiously placing his feet into the spaces between bricks and brambles as though he were there in physical form. Ahead of him loomed the huge and fearful red-bricked building Rob had spoken of, the asylum.

The place he feared most in his thoughts revealed itself as a crumbling mess of decaying brick and half-hearted attempts to repair the time-ravaged building. It may have been the glory of a genuinely concerned benefactor. Once a refuge for injured servicemen and then for the feeble and sick of mind. It now seemed to Leslie to stand as a monument to the folly of those who possessed high ideals but lacked the will or ability to help. The building had become like those who could not defend themselves intellectually, or those who had little or nothing to contribute to society.

The lack of concern or care from their guardians appalled him. How had the grand Woodford ideals he had read about come to this state?

He felt sick as he raised himself from his bed and stumbled to the bathroom.

***

A voice raised him from his sleep. 'We are going to the river today; with the rain yesterday, the water will be high enough to take the boat out.'

Leslie opened his eyes and saw Paul looking at him in excited anticipation. 'It is Saturday, you said you would like to go on the boat. Well today we can, it is a beautiful morning.'

Leslie thought about the library. He had permission to visit today, and the librarian would be expecting him for his arranged time. 'I am sorry,' he said. 'I have other plans made previously for today.'

The other boys laughed and ran down the stairs to enjoy their breakfast. Paul called after them, 'No running in the house, please.' He returned to Leslie's bedside and said, 'Look, you can study as much as you like; it will not make the slightest difference to what you do in the years after you leave the village.'

Leslie had a sudden, sinking feeling that he was losing another best friend. 'I am sorry,' Leslie said, 'but I have made a previous engagement, and it would be quite bad if I did not keep it, do you not agree? If I let you down with a promise, what would you think of me?'

The two boys looked at each other for a moment.

'Leslie, you are excused from fun for today. You will, however, need to pay a forfeit. Are we agreed?'

Leslie thought for a moment, 'no, we are not agreed. Respecting a promise is a thing of honour, and what you propose is something without bounds. Had I made an appointment with you and not kept it without adequate explanation in advance, how would you trust me to honour further agreements?'

The logic hit home. 'I am sorry, Leslie. I retract what I said. You should be true to your promises. If you made me such a promise and let me down, it would hurt me deeply. I really am sorry, and of course, you must keep your appointment. I was being selfish because I like your company, and I feel responsible for you.'

It was a heartfelt admission of the boy's commitment and it warmed Leslie's heart to hear it. 'I mean to keep you as a friend, the best friend someone could have. Perhaps later we can play on the river if my studies allow me, I can join you maybe at the boathouse?'

'Join us when you can. I am so sorry that I made such a stupid mistake.'

Paul felt something was going to change in his life. This young boy was destined for something great. Instead of leading, would Paul have to follow? Leslie could feel Paul's unease. He was not about to usurp his best friend, the friend who'd taught and cared for him, guiding him through the minefields of etiquettes, procedures, and formalities, he truly was a friend indeed.

Thanks to Paul, Leslie had perfected his skills at placing a tablecloth with one flourish and could set a table for a feast for the highest of nobility or a family meal. He could now instruct and guide the juniors in whatever their chores, and pass on to them the things that Paul had taught him, such as standing aside to let a lady pass, opening doors, walking on the outside when accompanying a lady along the street, and standing when a lady enters the room. These matters of etiquette and manners that elevated one from just a man to a gentleman were very important to Paul, and he had instilled them in his protégé. Now, with his perfectly honed skills, Leslie was able to release his mentor from the drudgery of everyday routines, but Paul did not seem to appreciate the freedom. His crown had been removed, and his position of power, knowledge, and expertise had fallen to a minor. His student had become a teacher.

Leslie had not intended to compete with or outdo his friend and mentor and it is where he first learned the responsibility of knowledge and the use of it.

***

Leslie walked up the avenue toward Howard House. He had been aware that the other children associated this place with punishment or expulsion, but there was no evidence of that. For him, it was a place of exploration, where he could read and absorb the writings and knowledge of peoples far more travelled and knowledgeable than he was. He was the sponge that sucked in the juices of other people's travels and experiences. It was as though he had been to those places himself. He could describe the sights and sounds of Morocco, almost smell the spices in the West Indies, and see the blues and the greens of the waters of faraway islands. He had them mapped and recorded.

He knew the accounts of battles between the English and the various would-be invaders of these isles, the heroic and often wasteful cost of lives in battles against the French and the Spanish, and the wars with Germany. He felt the costs to the families that had had to bear the burdens of the decisions of politicians and generals to defend their lands. Looking at battle plans and counter plans, he could see clearly that, on very many occasions, he would have made very different choices given the information available at that time. His ability to see things from different perspectives was indeed a gift. It was also, in a way, a curse; he could do nothing to change the past. The frustrations he felt, as he learned of stupid and sometimes reckless decisions in the historical accounts made him wonder how some commanders had ever risen to such positions.

***

Leslie's mind drifted to his father's situation. *Had his predicament been the result of bad judgement by superior officers, lack of judgement on his part, or just darned bad luck? What had happened to him? Was he living in some jungle as a prisoner? Was he badly injured perhaps and hiding out with some sympathisers, or just dead somewhere, not even buried, a victim of fatal injuries?* A sharp pang of loss hit the boy, and he wondered if he would ever see his father again.

Leslie had not really known his father. Having entered the care of a children's home at such a very early age, he had been too young to have developed a real relationship with him. To him, his father had been a hope of better times to come; a character fashioned from the mind of his sister; and later, a heroic figure and someone who would teach him the ways of the world. He was someone who would describe the wonderful array of sights and sounds that abounded in the wondrous lands he had visited. *He could teach me...* The loss of opportunity hit hard. *He could have taught me so much.* As he corrected his thoughts, tears welled up in him but were not permitted to fall. A void filled the place his father should occupy, and to this boy, it was a tragedy of great dimensions.

***

Mr McManus greeted the boy with a cheerful smile. 'I have collected the books you asked about. They are on the study table. I have to catalogue a section in the west library, so if you need anything, you know where to find me.'

Leslie thanked him and settled straight away to his studies. The books on the table were some very old ones. One in particular was interesting to the boy; it was about South and Central America. It offered accounts of the discoveries of ancient buildings and long past civilisations – Aztecs and Mayans – and the influence of Spanish invaders and their role in the promoting of the Catholic religion with devastating costs. The boy was deeply engrossed with these accounts; he laid the tome on the table and reached for another relating to the same subject. He travelled in the accounts as though there in person; such was his imagination.

***

At school, the teacher had asked the boys to write an essay about any famous person. They could choose the subject, and after the class, Leslie had asked if his subject could be Sir Giles Woodford. The teacher said that it was a very good choice and that he may find some helpful information in the dean's library. This had occurred to him. He started his research by asking Mr McManus for all the books dealing with the Woodford family history. There were eight books. Some were accounts by biographers; two were autobiographies; and the others related to household accounts, records of expenses, and building costs. Leslie set to work reading, making notes and setting them out in logical order.

He learned of the empire built by Sir Giles's father – the varied business interests included gold and diamond mines in Africa; coffee, rubber, and tea plantations in Ceylon and South America; and steel and copper production. There were construction companies in Britain, the United States of America, and South America; agriculture in the Canary Islands and on mainland Spain; olive oil production in Italy, Spain, and Greece; and mineral mines in many countries. The range of interests extended across the world.

One book in particular caught Leslie's attention; it was an account with regard to the last will and testament of Sir Giles. In brief, he had left his entire empire to his son Howard. There was an account of how he had managed to reduce the inheritance tax burden and a list of holdings showing all the companies and their directors and major stockholders. Another list showed charitable institutions financed by income from some of these companies. The village was on the list, as was the Woodford Asylum, now owned by Sir Alastair.

The cover of the book had become frayed and scuffed over the years and was beginning to separate. Leslie noticed that someone had repaired the back inside cover at some time. He was about to ask the librarian about it when he saw a corner of paper very slightly protruding. He gently tugged at the corner, not wishing to tear it. A folded yellowing slip of paper came out from the end cover. The boy turned it over in his hands and carefully opened it. Written in black ink were a series of numbers in groups. This looked to him like a coded message similar to ones he had seen in a book. Nothing else was written on the paper. The numbers meant nothing to the boy. He replaced the slip, inserting it carefully into the end board of the book just as he had found it.

The accounts showed that Sir Giles had ordered the selling of the gold and diamond mines in Africa and the selling of shares in many of the other companies. The Woodford family retained controlling interests, instead of owning them outright. In the light of subsequent events regarding gold and diamond mining in Africa, it was a stroke of genius. With the other companies he had managed to share the risks with interested third parties.

***

A codicil added in 1855, one year after the drawing up of the will, stated that an unspecified amount, separate from the family bequest, was available to whomsoever wished to claim it. This was freely given and with no obligations other than that the claimant must state on application the nature of the bequest and provide proof of the route to how and where it was discovered. There were the names of a firm of lawyers situated in London to apply to for a claim. *Wow*, thought Leslie, *a treasure hunt. Although surely after all these years someone would have found whatever the bequest was?* He scanned the books looking for a reference to a claimant to the bequest but found nothing recorded anywhere relating to a discovery.

The boy's thoughts focused on the list of numbers; *could this be something to do with the bequest?* He put all thoughts of the list aside, he would revisit it later. He collected the rest of the information he needed to complete his essay.

***

It was Friday afternoon. School holidays had begun for the summer, and the boys were free of lessons until the first week in September. Paul sorted the excited rabble into an orderly file as they made their way down the avenue. Leslie walked alongside his friend, and they chatted about the teachers and lessons.

'That essay you wrote about Sir Giles – how did you manage to find out so much about him?'

'Simple, all the information is in the dean's library. Why do you not make use of it?'

'I often wonder what use we can make of what we learn here. In a few years, I will have to leave do my military service and then get a job and earn a living.'

Leslie had not thought about that. 'Perhaps the master or the dean could help you with employment? I think you would make a fantastic butler. Your knowledge of procedure and etiquette is second to none, and you have the temperament for it. Maybe during your military service, you may learn some different skills.'

'Perhaps that is so, but I am not sure yet what I want to do. My French is not as good as yours is, and I have heard you talking to the maids in Spanish. You seem to have a natural flair for languages. Maybe you will become a language teacher or an historian.'

Leslie did not want to pursue this topic. 'That is all a few years away yet. We could go down to the river tomorrow, maybe do some fishing, or take out the boat, perhaps both?'

'Yes. We have not had much time, what with studies and chores.'

***

The two friends spent the whole of Saturday down at the river, and Ralph and Peter joined them. Paul had arranged packed lunches and two flasks of lemonade.

The twins laughed and played at the water's edge under the watchful eyes of Paul and Leslie. Paul had chosen a spot not far from the boathouse where the river veered to the right; the reed beds afforded good fishing. The fishing poles were a rudimentary affair but did the job. Paul caught five fish and Leslie just one. It had been a warm day, but now small black storm flies announced that rain could be on the way.

Leslie decided that now might be their last chance for a walk together along the riverbank before it rained, and Paul agreed. Leslie called the twins and packed up the remains of lunch. The cheerful band of boys strolled, chatting about the fishing rods Leslie had seen the town boys using a week or so back, the last time he was at the river, alone on one of his many solitary walks to organise his thoughts.

'The town boys had brand new rods and lines with reels for winding the line in.' Paul wished he could have one, and Leslie told him the boys had been there all day and caught nothing, they laughed raucously with the twins joining in.

'You see boys; you do not need fancy equipment to catch a fish' said Leslie to the twins. 'It is art and knowledge that guides one to success in this life, use this knowledge as a measure in your future lives, one does not require the very latest model of technology to display skill or talent, that skill comes from within you and not the machine or apparatus you employ.'

Paul thought that the water at this point must have overflowed during the last heavy rain a few days ago. An odour lingered in the air, like that of rotting vegetation. The stench became so strong that Paul and Leslie agreed not to continue. They turned and headed back along the riverbank, the smell slowly fading as they got farther away. 'Well, that was not pleasant so soon after lunch,' said Paul. More chuckles ensued.

The boys walked back to the fallen elm and sat for a while. They could hear the voices of the town boys as they picked their way along the far bank. 'Did you catch any, mate?' one of them shouted across the water.

'Only six,' shouted Leslie in reply.

The town boys picked up their speed, heading for the reed beds. The village boys gathered up their catch and headed swiftly back towards Roding house as a fine drizzle began to fall.

***

There were men's voices in the entrance hall downstairs. The doorbell awakened the boys, Mr Atkins appealed for calm as the maids chatted excitedly in Spanish. Paul went to the top of the stairs to see what was happening below. He came back to the dormitory, explaining that there were two police officers in the hall and had just gone into the private room with Mr Atkins. He had no idea what was going on, he went back and opened the door slightly.

With the door open, Leslie and the other boys heard the maids chattering in Spanish near the stairs :

'Los pobrecitos del pueblo se han encontrado un cuerpo dentro del agua.'

'Por el río?'

'Sí, sí, muerto. Dios mío de mi alma—'

The boys all looked towards Leslie. 'Did you manage to catch any of that?' asked Paul.

'I am afraid I did.'

'So what is happening then?' Ralph asked excitedly.

'Well it seems the town boys found a dead body in the river,' Leslie said.

'Hey, do you recall that horrid smell up near the river bend? That must have been it, the body,' chirped Peter, 'what a rotten smell it was,' he added.

They heard voices again in the hall below. 'I am afraid it will have to wait until the morning officers, the boys are in bed and I will not have them disturbed tonight, if you please?' From the landing, Paul saw Mr Atkins guide the officers to the front door. Once the door had closed, the boys chattered in muffled excitement.

'That will do now boys, settle down now and get some sleep.' Mr Atkins's voice calmed the house into silence.

***

Breakfast time seethed with excited expectations. The boys ate and then cleared the tables, they were to await the master. Normally, he did not attend breakfast or lunch – he had those meals provided in his rooms – but today he had something important to disclose. The boys sat and waited, fidgeting and nudging one another; little whispers here and there received a sharp glance from Paul and the maids.

Mr Atkins entered, and the boys stood. 'You may sit, boys,' he said calmly. 'You are aware that the police visited us last night. There has been an incident in which a body was found near the boathouse at the river. Yesterday, some of you were in that area, and the police need to interview you. Paul, Leslie, Ralph, and Peter, you will accompany me to Howard House. The rest of you should remain in the leisure room for now. You four,' he said, looking at the named boys, 'will want to be properly attired, I recommend school uniforms please.'

He turned to the maids and had some words with them as the boys left quietly to change their clothes.

The four boys walked up to the dean's house in single file led by the master. And on entering, Mr Atkins let them into the library. Four chairs stood in front of the desk, where they were to sit quietly, whilst Mr Atkins left the room. As they sat, Leslie looked at the shelves. He spotted that one of the books on a high shelf protruded. That was not at all like Mr McManus. He was always so meticulous. Staring at the tome, he realised that it was the book containing the slip with the numbers on it. When Leslie required a book, he requested it; he always left the books neatly stacked on the study table when he finished with them. Why was this book protruding and in the wrong place?

The door opened, and the dean and Mr Atkins entered, followed by two police officers, one in uniform and the other in plain clothes. The boys stood as the dean introduced the senior officer, Detective Inspector Morgan, and then he suggested that they interview each boy separately in the west library. The officer agreed and asked for Paul first.

Paul and the officer entered the other wing of the library accompanied by the dean. Leslie glanced again at the book; it was a puzzle to him because the librarian was so organised. The organising of the books was a work of love to him; he concluded that someone had replaced the book other than Mr McManus. The door opened. Next in would be Ralph and then Peter. Paul sat silently and impassively, staring at the floor.

Leslie's turn eventually came, and he was told to sit upon a hard wooden chair he was so familiar with; he noticed that this was a much larger room than the other was and that it contained far more books, some of which he had read thanks to Mr McManus.

The dean began, 'You and the other boys were down at the river yesterday. Tell us all that you remember please.'

The boy related all the events of that day. The officer made notes at various points.

'If I may, sir,' the detective said, looking at the dean. The dean let him continue. 'Can you recall what the boys, town boys you call them, what they carried with them?'

'Yes, sir. They each carried a new fishing rod and a net, not like the poles we use. Proper rods with reels for winding in the line.'

'I see. What were they wearing?'

The boy described each one in detail.

The officer turned to the dean. 'Well, sir, thank you for your time. I must apologise for the officers last night. They can be a little overzealous at times. You can be sure I will have words with them though.'

Leslie re-joined his companions whilst the two men remained in the other room. After several minutes Leslie was asked to return to the room.

The detective asked how it was that he had recalled every detail about the town boys.

'Sir, the memory games that I have with the doctor seem to improve my observation. I could not see the boys' socks or the colour of their eyes, so the description could not be complete. I could only say what I saw, sir.'

'I think that is fair,' said the officer. 'It's just that your description is more detailed than that of the others. Surely they have the same memory games?'

The dean abruptly intervened. 'Thank you, Leslie. I think that will do. I am sure you have been most helpful to the officer.'

He led Leslie to the door and closed it behind him.

Leslie sat with the other boys and some while later the dean entered and asked Mr Atkins to join him. Meanwhile, the officer entered from the hall and had a few words with the constable, and they both left. The boys sat wondering; what was the delay in leaving? They had given their accounts, and there was nothing more to add.

***

The excitement subsided after a couple of days, apart from the maids making reference to a killer on the loose and being murdered in their beds. The vicar had led the congregation in prayers for the 'poor unfortunate soul drowned in the river', and now all was quiet.

Leslie went through the details in his secret room. There was a body found by the town boys somewhere in the river near the boathouse. What questions had not been asked and what details were missing? He made a list:

Was the body male or female?
Had foul play been suspected or ruled out?
How long had the body been in the water?
Had the cause of death been established?
Had the victim been killed elsewhere and dumped here?

Had the body entered the water outside of the village and been washed downstream?

Had the body been identified?

Was the body clothed or not?

What was the age of the victim?

Was he or she child or adult?

Had anyone from the village been in that area on previous occasions?

Was anyone reported as missing?

Had there been similar incidents in the area?

Had anyone reported suspicious activity?

Had there been a motor car accident in the area?

Had there been a report of a fight or an altercation?

Leslie concluded that there were many unanswered questions. It could be that the police were covering these points or that they knew some of the answers but had not divulged them. Their investigation was still ongoing, but the officer gave nothing away during the interviews.

***

On the Monday following the incident, Leslie went to see Dr Hendricks. They played a few games of chess, at which Leslie lost.

'Come now. You seem not to concentrate today.' The doctor expected a tougher opponent.

'I am sorry. I keep thinking about the body in the river.'

'Did you see the body?'

'Oh no, we did not see it, but there was a strong smell in the area, we turned back as it was so foul.'

'If you did not see it, how can it cause such concern to you?'

'Well, if we had continued, it may have been us that had found it. That would have been so awful, especially for the twins.'

Ice cubes tinkled in the glass as the doctor poured another glass of lemonade. 'Why would it be so bad for the twins?'

'Well, they saw both their parents killed when a wall collapsed on them as the boys left a sweet shop on the opposite side of the road.'

'Oh yes, of course, I am remembering now and how tragic for them to witness such a horror.'

'May I tell you something, Doctor? It has been on my mind for some time.'

'But of course, we are the good friends, you can tell me.'

'Well, you remember last year I had a fall down by the river that put me in the hospital' he said, testing the doctor as he spoke.

'Yes, I remember it well, we had to give you the stitches in the head.'

'Well, I was told that the gardener Mr Lane carried me to the hospital. If you recall, he was the last one I spoke to before I fell.'

'Yes?'

'It seemed very odd to me that he carried me that long distance but never came to visit or enquire as to my situation.'

The doctor listened with interest.

'I know we only met on two occasions, but we seemed to get on well together, like old friends. I have not seen him since, not even to thank him for what he did for me.'

The doctor sat back into his chair, pointing his pipe as he spoke. 'I do not know this man personally, you understand.'

'But your garden sir. Perhaps you saw him without knowing who he was.'

'No, I am not in the use of a gardener. I keep my garden myself as my exercise and a personal creation. It is possible that I have seen him in the grounds for working, but I am not aware of it.'

Leslie looked glum.

'This is making you worried for some time, no.' The doctor sensed the boy's unease, 'this body in the river has made you think of him, but why in this context?'

Leslie looked up at the doctor. 'You see, sir, I feared that something may have befallen him. Personally, I would have made some contact if it was me in his situation, which is what confounds me.'

The doctor realised that this had been playing on the boy's mind for some time. 'I will make the enquiries for you, and perhaps the next time we meet, I may have the answers, no?'

'Thank you, sir. I realise that it would be imposing on you—'

'You are correct to tell me of this worrying. It cannot be good for one so young to have such burdens, and it is not the imposition for me.'

They played some more chess, and Leslie beat the doctor in one game.

'You see,' the doctor exclaimed, 'you now have the concentration back, and finally you win a game.'

Leslie had seen the trap before the doctor had sprung it and had taken evasive action. The doctor had not expected it and had concentrated so much on building the trap that he had made a fatal error. Leslie had not pounced but had led his opponent around for a while, as though playing with his good luck.

***

Leslie lay quietly on his bed, supposedly having an afternoon nap. The boy entered his dreamlike state: He was in the dean's library in the west wing, a room he had only ever entered for the police interview. The dean was reading some papers he had taken from the desk drawer. The man looked up, as though someone had entered the room; someone had but not physically, perhaps he heard someone approach the door?

The dean returned to the papers, and Leslie could see they were financial reports, with a list of names, alongside the names of companies, dates of payments, and amounts. The contents were a revelation to Leslie; he stored the information and read on. As the dean turned each page, the information became more incredible. This information answered some questions the boy had had for a while.

The telephone interrupted the dean and Leslie heard the conversation, just as he had heard Hendricks talking to the nurse in the hospital. The doctor could have been talking to Leslie on the telephone the voice was so clear.

'Alastair, I tried to get you earlier.'

'Yes, Ernst, I was at a board meeting and have not long returned. What do you have for me?'

Ernst, thought Leslie, the voice was that of the doctor but he recognised his Cristian name as Ernest, he soon figured that Ernst was the German for Ernest.

'The boy Leslie was with me today. He has some worries regarding Robert Lane.'

'What sort of worries?'

'Well he finds it strange that a man who would carry him so far when he was unconscious would not attempt to contact him again. Also he has not since seen him in the grounds.'

'Do you think he knows anything?'

'Oh it is playing on him, but a simple explanation should suffice no? Maybe the man was offered a better job with prospects or put in prison for some illegal action—'

'Ernst, I think the "better job" sounds more believable. I will leave that in your hands. How about the other boy? Have you managed to get any results yet?'

'Alastair my friend, I think we should give up on him now. It has been many years without the good results.'

'You may be right, but I think we should give him a little longer. Your colleague at St Vincent's assured us of his skill. I have the feeling he can find the answer.'

'Very well I will continue for now. What did you learn from McManus?'

'The list of books Leslie last applied for were all to do with the Woodford family for a school project about Sir Giles.'

From beneath the loose papers, he pulled a file with the handwritten words 'Leslie Johns II. It was a very thick file and volume one must be full. The dean continued, 'I have the file here. Yes, he seemed to spend a lot of time on one book in particular. I checked the volume myself. Nothing but the lawyer's accounts for probate on my grandfather's will – the state of the business at the time of his death and so forth. It was a project for school, and I have a copy here of the boy's project. It is well written and well researched. Ernst, we may have made a good decision bringing him to the village. We have to thank your friend at St Vincent's.'

'Yes. He is a good man and can be relied upon. Well, if there is nothing to do more, I will bid you a good afternoon.'

'Good afternoon, Ernst.'

Leslie watched as the dean organised the papers and files, collected them up, and went to the far end of the room, by the window. The wall, like the others, had floor-to-ceiling bookshelves. This wall had a difference. The shelves were doubly thick and spaced to house taller volumes. The dean removed a heavy book from a shelf at waist level next to the window and crossed back to the centre shelf of the wall. He removed the first book on the middle shelf and replaced it with the one he had selected before. There was an audible click, and a section of the shelving swung out slightly into the room. The dean widened the entrance and inside was a long narrow room devoid of windows. He switched on a light; inside was like an office, with a chair, a table with a reading lamp, and filing cabinets. He removed a key from its hiding place behind a cabinet and opened a drawer. He placed the file on Leslie in the drawer, locked it, and did the same with the other files and papers, placing them into other cabinets.

***

When Leslie awoke, he realised that not one person could be trusted. He had information that could rock the village to its foundations if made public. The dean had a file on him of two volumes, the doctor was in cahoots with the dean, and they both had something to do with Rob disappearing; otherwise, they would not need to concoct a story that would be convincing. *They spoke of an accomplice at St Vincent's. Who is that? Who is the other boy they mentioned and what special skills did he possess?*

Leslie had to obtain concrete information but maintain extreme caution; he was being led on a line – given all the help, advice and education needed to serve a purpose. As to what that entailed, he had no idea. These people appeared benevolent, kind, and protective. And yet, for what? From the information he had seen, they had a very big organisation. The names on the lists included some very high profile people. He had to find out what the payments were for. Leslie felt that he had some advantages, the dean and the doctor were not fully aware of his talents or how much he knew. He must continue to be led by them until he could unravel the spider's web of intrigue that he found himself in.

***

The younger boys were mostly reluctant to go down to the river, despite Leslie's logical interpretation of the incident. He told them that the man drowned accidentally, the parents of the town boys had probably restricted them and the police warned them to stay clear of private property. He told them that he often went alone and sometimes with Paul and no harm befell them, there were no monsters or killers lurking in the shadows, but, they did not see the town boys all summer.

***

When Leslie next visited the doctor, Hendricks fed him the story about the gardener having been offered and accepting a place with better employment and prospects. Rob had given little notice to his employers because the post could not be held open. It was a chance in a lifetime opportunity for the young gardener. The story was well constructed and would have been convincing to one who did not know the truth.

Chapter 4

A New Friend and Devious Deeds Revealed

Over the last few months, he had seen very little of Mary. When he did, it was usually a brief reunion. She would make some criticism about his hair or clothes. 'Getting into mischief by the river. I know what you get up to,' she would say. She had lost the pigtails long ago.

Thanks to his ability to eavesdrop unseen, Leslie had found out much more information surrounding the Woodford empire, but there were still a lot of gaps to fill in. He felt frustrated that he was able see and hear but could only do just that. He had no physical presence. He could not obtain folders and files for himself to read. He knew where they were but could only see them if they were open in plain view. He realised also that, if he had enough information to expose this conspiracy, he had no hard evidence. For the police to investigate, he needed provable facts. Could he trust the police? He had his doubts; the list came to mind… The body in the river?

The newspapers reported that an inmate from the asylum had escaped the confines of the grounds. He had ventured onto the road and had fallen into the river. In an unconscious state, he had unfortunately drowned. Leslie knew that a part of the story was true. The man whose body had been found had been an inmate. The rest was a concoction, "The victim remains unnamed to protect the privacy of his family" the newspapers had reported. Leslie had seen the file and he knew the man's name and background, and falsely the man was recorded as having family but he had none.

Leslie spent much time trying to untangle the strings that bound the companies on the list together. He had worked out that many of the companies were subsidiaries of larger companies and corporations. He had found that a company would trade under a registered name for a few years and then go out of business. The contracts would then transfer to other companies. This was a common practice, but it appeared that the insolvent companies had no assets. The registered offices were always on a fixed lease. The factories and workshops were also on fixed leases. The companies would always cease to exist shortly before the lease was due to expire. There seemed to be a pattern. The same addresses would appear for the old and the new companies. The company names would change, but collectively, they would have the same directors. An example would be:

Company A: Mr Blue, Mr Green, and Mr White
Company B: Mr Silver, Mr Black, and Mr Brown
Company C: Mr More, Mr Less, and Mr Gold
Company A1 (a new company): Mr Brown, Mr Green, and Mr Gold
Company B1 (a new company): Mr Less, Mr Silver, and Mr White

There seemed to be a cycle of the same directors in different combinations. Leslie was not a lawyer, but the whole system stank of fraud and conspiracy to him. Still, he had to be sure. There was yet more to untangle.

***

Leslie had an idea that he wanted to try regarding that list of numbers. He had tackled this puzzle off and on ever since discovering it. He could see the numbers and the sequence. He substituted all the numbers for the letters of the alphabet – 1=A, 2=B, and so on. Then he tried to make sense of the jumble of letters. He would have to think again, this had been constructed to make it difficult to decipher, but what would be the point of an easy code?

***

A floating session drew him back to a place he feared, just as many people who fear something find themselves drawn, nonetheless, he was helplessly attracted to it, he felt himself constantly drawn to this place.

Each time he had been at the asylum he had been standing just beyond the wall looking up at the massive building. This time, he found himself inside an unlit passageway. It smelled dank and musty. He squinted into the darkness, edging his way along the passage. He had no idea how he'd gotten in or how he'd get out, unless he woke up. Rats scurried and squeaked in the murky darkness, and he had the sensation that he was underground. He continued along, looking for anything that might give him an indication of where precisely he was. Occasionally, he could see a grille near the roof of the passage that allowed a brief glimpse of the moonlight. He felt he had walked for half an hour, but probably much less time had passed.

He came at last to a heavy wooden door with a large cast iron ring for a handle. He passed through the door and up a flight of solid stone steps and onto a landing or platform; it was difficult to make out. He could hear the sound of water drops hitting the floor below. He followed the landing for about ten paces. There was a wall to the right and in front. He could feel a cold draught coming from the left and turned that way. Ahead of him, he could see a flickering light from a gap beneath a door.

He approached the door cautiously and stood outside, trying to see the interior through the crack. It was a very restricted angle. He could just see a candle burning on a saucer in the middle of what appeared to be a small room, more like a cell. A voice said, 'Well aren't you coming in then?'

He was already cold, but the voice still sent a chill through him. Was the voice talking to him? Or maybe there was another door to the cell. And how could it be him the voice was talking to? No one could see him.

'You'll find the door's not locked, lad.'

The man beyond the door was talking to him. *How was that possible?* He put his hand to his head.

***

A fox, calling in the nearby woods, woke Leslie from his slumber. He recalled his journey and found it incredible that the man in the room had known he was there. He had visited the dean, the master, the nurse, the doctor, the gardeners, and the vicar. None had shown any signs that they knew of his presence. Well, there was that time the dean had looked up briefly, but that had just been a slight deviation from the norm. He knew he had been in an underground tunnel. But where? He felt certain that the tunnel must be under the asylum.

The summer holidays were nearly over, and it would soon be time to return to his studies. Leslie felt a sense of urgency growing inside him. His schoolwork would have to take precedence over his secret activities. He reviewed his position: There was the code, the list of companies, the accomplice at St Vincent's, the man in the cell, the reasons for the cloak-and-dagger, and the dean's plans for him, all of these issues he needed answers to. He felt daunted; the tasks ahead seemed insurmountable. He decided that he would return to the tunnel. There was a reason he had been there, and he needed to find out what it was.

***

Leslie awaited his opportunity to be alone and undisturbed. When he first realised that he could direct his travel, he travelled usually at night when all were safely tucked up in bed and asleep. On occasions he travelled during an afternoon nap, but over time he had learned that he did not need to lay down and close his eyes pretending to sleep, as long as he remained calm and concentrated he could leave his physical body at any time or place. If someone came upon him and spoke or touched him he immediately returned to his body and could dismiss his trance-like state as a daydream. He was now well practiced in the skill that was so strange to him at first, let alone another person if he ever told them of it, which of course he could not.

***

Paul switched of the dormitory lights, and Leslie gave him time to settle into bed before making his next journey to the tunnel.

He arrived outside the door of the cell, and the same dank and musty smell pervaded the surroundings, and the same flickering light. 'Are you coming in this time, my lad?' the voice said. 'I don't bite you know; despite what they may say.'

Now, Leslie could see a man, perhaps in his early fifties, facing the door and looking directly at him. 'Come on, come in.' He beckoned, and Leslie entered.

'That's a neat trick,' he said, 'walking through doors.'

Leslie approached the man with great caution. This was a new twist, being seen.

'Sit down, lad. You won't get charged more.' The man said with a chuckle.

Leslie gave a nervous smile.

'My name's Peregrine Collins. Yes, it sounds a bit posh. My father was a keen falconer in his day. What might your name be then?'

'My name is Leslie Johns, sir.'

'Please, don't call me sir. Just Perry will do. That's what my friends call me, don't you, lads?' he said waving an arm around the room to a non-existent audience. Leslie observed nervously. 'Just pulling your leg, son. I'm supposed to be mad, so I like to make out that I am from time to time.'

'What is this place?' asked Leslie, looking around him.

'This place, my friend, is the asylum.'

'How do you come to be here then, are you ill of mind?' Leslie asked tentatively, hoping he had not caused insult.

'I might ask you the same, young lad,' Perry replied with a grin. 'Allow me to relate my story, if I may.' Leslie immediately saw that this poor man needed companions, people to talk with and it was clear to Leslie that the wretched man revelled in the opportunity to converse with someone.

The man began his story. 'I worked for the Woodford family as an accountant in London for some years and, of course, got to meet the doctor and the "great" Sir Alastair. When World War II broke out, I enlisted. I joined the army and served in Europe and Africa and was wounded twice.' He showed Leslie the scars. 'After the second injury, I ended up in a military hospital back in England and I suppose an early end to the war for me.

During my recovery period, Dr Hendricks came to visit me. Of course, we knew each other from the old days, and he asked me if I could work on some accounts that belonged to Sir Alastair, who was away on a campaign. Well, I felt I had nothing better to do at that time, my wound was healing slowly, and a few extra shillings could help.

'A few days later, the doctor had me transferred to the village under his supervision and medical care. I was accommodated in what was a gardener's cottage, as all the gardeners were conscripted at the time except for Paddy, being an Irishman. I set to work on the accounts, working from daybreak until dusk in the cottage with what the doctor gave me.

'I spent many days trying to make sense of the bad bookkeeping and felt it would be best to find a reference point, somewhere back before the start of the war. It had all gone haywire since my days, and perhaps an amateur accountant had taken over the books. I asked the doctor if there were any records available that I could use to make sense of the records. The doctor gave me unrestricted access to the library, in which there were many accounts.

'It was a thankless task, trawling through the books, journals, and financial records. It was months before anything had any semblance of order. But cutting to the chase, dear boy, I found a book that had the records of the old man's will.'

Yes, thought Leslie, *I know the very book.*

'In it, I found the list of companies owned or partially owned by the Woodford family. Now you need to remember that I had worked at the London office. All the official company records are held on file at the head office. The records at the library bore no resemblance to what I remembered from London. It struck me as strange, so I dug deeper and deeper. What I found was that they were creating companies that, in fact, did not really exist and that through this deception they were involved in some illegal activities. It is in black and white, in their record; you just have to untangle the threads to see it. It is a complicated system of companies that they control, and there is more to it, bring me a glass of that water over there son.'

Leslie tried to pick up the jug of water but could not, he could not perform a physical task in his ethereal state. 'I cannot do what you ask of me, not because I refuse but because my state of being does not allow me to engage in any physical task.'

'You remind me of another boy so long ago, he had the same gift as you—' Perry's mind drifted momentarily to a time long passed, then he returned his thought to the boy.

'There are people here Leslie who like me have no reason to be here. Things we all have in common are that we have no living relatives but we have connections with Woodford.' Perry had the saddest expression. 'Can you help me, help us?'

The boy was not convinced that he could help the inmates. Although he was sympathetic to the story, he could see no way that he could release Perry and his friends.

'But why and how did you end up here?' the boy enquired.

'Ah now that was because I trusted the doctor you see. I related to him my suspicions about the false companies and the false accounting. I mentioned nothing relating to the children in the village. I had no direct proof about Sir Alastair's motives for the children, but I did see some documents. They were all orphans, you see, gathered into the village and then trained and educated with order and discipline. All the while, the dean and the doctor shaped them for their own purposes. I could not tell what their motives were, but I can tell you that the children were being very well trained, prepared for some important tasks later on.

'I later realised that some old records of the village listed the names of children in the various houses, and many of these corresponded with names on the payments lists. All the names who now occupied high positions in society had been here as children. That is what the village is – a training ground for children with some field of expertise. Anyway, I told the doctor my suspicions about the companies. Like a fool, I trusted him, and I thought that there were others who were abusing the Woodford name.

'He told me to leave it in his hands, and he would investigate. In the meantime, I was to finish the work and set the books straight, which was the job he'd hired me to do. And he would instigate proceedings against anyone that would bring the Woodford name into question. Well, I continued with the books and found that the whole company was rotten to the core. I said no more to the doctor about it; I just carried on until I had the books in order, you know, until they would make sense to an accountant and the taxman.

'Well, what happened next was that, one night shortly after finishing the task the doctor set for me, I was drinking in a pub with a couple of blokes I had never met before. They were ex-army lads. They bought me a drink and another, and we had a good laugh and talked about the army days. I woke up in this place. Not here, you understand, upstairs. They had me drugged day and night until I didn't know my own name. Can you believe it, son, forgetting your own name?

'One day, this other inmate stopped me from taking the medication, and gradually my faculties returned. He had found a way to escape, but he needed help to do so. He told me his plan. But at the moment of almost getting away, we were caught, and they put me down here. I have no idea what happened to him.'

Perry was so convincing that Leslie decided he would go along with the story and assured him that he would see what he could do. Then an idea occurred to the boy. 'In what volume of the books did you find the slip of paper?'

'The slip of paper?'

'Yes, the one with the list of numbers. You found it, you must have if you read the books you speak of.'

'You are a canny one. Are you working for them? You want me to tell you. They sent you here didn't, they boy?'

Perry's tone had become menacing and aggressive, but Leslie did not submit to it. 'You have to convince me that you tell the truth,' said the boy. 'I cannot help you unless you tell me the truth.'

The wretched and desperate man sat with his head in his hands, his long hair and beard obscuring his face. 'Honestly, son, how can I convince you? My days have been long and dark here. My only friends are the rats and the man who brings my food and some clean water. Look around you. I have my washing bowl, my toilet, my table and chair, a bed, and a candle to keep me company. Do I look like an enemy to you for crying out loud?'

The serious expression, the exasperation, and the imploring nature of his question were enough to tilt Leslie. This man was telling the truth about himself, but he did know about the numbers; Leslie was certain of it. He would have to concentrate on the doctor, but he would still tread with caution. 'What should I do?' asked Leslie.

'There are some files that will enable you to set us free. I cannot say where they are now, but you should start with the doctor.'

'Very well. I will see if I can find something that can help you.'

'You come back and see me. Don't forget about me. We can help each other, do you hear me son?' the wretched man implored the boy.

Leslie thought about giving him the numbers to work on. 'Do you have something to write on Perry?'

'Look around, son. I have nothing here, not even life.'

The boy felt sorry for doubting him. 'Before I go, tell me how it is that you can see me when others cannot?'

'Well that's the hardest question of all, but the simple answer is I don't know.' The unspoken thoughts from earlier returned as he recalled a boy with special skills.

'When I was in Africa – it was at some godforsaken oasis that we had been ordered to hold; it was no more than a scrape in the sand, a few buildings, and palm trees – Rommel's lot pounded us by day and by night… Well I saw an Arab boy; keeping low, he scrambled over to me and pleaded with me to move to the other dugout. I told the lads, but they just laughed at me. I did follow the boy to the dugout, and the next moment, a shell landed right in the first dugout and blew them to smithereens – a direct hit. Out of sixteen squaddies, only one other and I survived that day. He died from his injuries a few days later. It was terrible watching him die slowly, but he asked me the same question – about the Arab boy who only I saw.'

'One more question. What is the tunnel down the steps? I mean, where does it lead to?'

'That's the storm drain they built to take the rainwater when it floods. I suppose it runs into the river down the hill.'

***

His first year at the village had been a very eventful one for Leslie. The next four years were consumed with routines and mostly uneventful. The studying was always a priority for the boy. He paid his visits to Sir Alastair and the doctor where he gleaned more information a little at a time. His visits to Perry he enjoyed, the man related so many stories about himself and the people in his life. The boy had a growing fondness for the prisoner in the cell.

***

It rained heavily all day. It was one of those late summer storms, with the lightning and the thunder flashing and rumbling all around. Leslie thought of Perry in that dank underground cell.

'Checkmate,' said Paul. 'You were not concentrating; that was too easy.'

His friend's voice returned Leslie to the chessboard. 'No. Sorry. I was miles away. Thinking about my father and if he was still alive somewhere,' he lied.

'Do you want another game before lunch?'

'No, if I may, I would like to catch up on some studying. We will be back at school soon and I would like to brush up on my French and the British monarchs. History is not one of the easier subjects.'

'Very well. Perhaps later then.'

Leslie went to the dormitory and removed two books from his locker, sat on his chair, and opened one of them. He was alone and knew that he would be for some time, if someone found him it would appear as though he had fallen asleep reading.

***

The doctor had an office at the lodge, a room Leslie knew so well now; the room was empty but the door was ajar. The writing bureau was open, and Leslie was about to look at the papers when he heard someone approaching.

The doctor entered the room, followed by a man Leslie recognised. He did not know the man's name, but he was from St Vincent's. The two men sat at the table. 'Did you bring them with you?' the doctor asked.

'Yes. It was difficult, and I will have to return them before they are missed.' The second man removed several files from a shoulder bag. 'These should be all the ones you need, Ernst.' The second man appeared quite nervous, as though he had done something illegal and was about to be found out.

The doctor opened the files one by one, glancing quickly at the pages and making note of the contents. Leslie could see that they were all files containing the details of children at three children's homes. Their ages ranged from four to seven. One thing connected them all; they were all gifted. 'We have some in the village who will be leaving us next week. These will make excellent replacements. You have done well, George, yes, very well, my friend.'

The doctor made some notes and returned the files to 'George'. 'You will stay for the lunch, no?'

'I really must get back and replace these, but thank you for the offer. How soon will you arrange the transfers, Ernst?'

'We have to make some facility here for them and move some of the children here first; we wish to get them in for the start of the school term. You will need to make up the adoption papers for the charities, no?'

'They are done; I have them with me now.'

'Excellent, George. It may be a week to ten days I think. I will call you a few days beforehand, no?'

'I will take my leave now, if that is all?'

'Thank you, George. As always, excellent work. And you will hear from me soon.'

The doctor rang a bell; the housekeeper opened the door, 'Will you please to show Mr Thompson to the door, Martha?'

Leslie watched as the doctor unlocked a door of the bureau, remove a thick folder, and place it on the table. It contained information on four of the six boys in River House. They were aged fifteen to sixteen. He then turned to a file marked Roding House and sifted through the contents, opening the file on Paul Goodwin and then he removed two files from the Bridge House folder and one from Forest House and placed them together with Paul's folder. Then he made some notes regarding the selected boys.

***

Leslie closed the book on his lap. They were moving four boys from River House, but to where and why? Four boys from the other houses would take their places, and one was his friend Paul. Then four new children would join the village. It was like a slow-moving conveyor belt, with some falling off one end and more added at the other end. The next thing to add to his list of unanswered questions was the destinations of the older four.

He called to mind the accounts of payments he had seen, scanned it, and nodded. Yes, George Thompson was on the list as an administrative officer for the charities that were responsible for the children's homes, and he would have access to all their records, personal, education, medical, and psychiatric. He was the link between the village and St Vincent's. No, he was the procurer. It was a weekend; no one would need access to the records before Thompson replaced them, and that was his obvious concern. *Could this be the man Perry spoke of when I first met him?* He thought to himself.

***

Mr Atkins informed Paul of the impending move to River House, and the boy confided in Leslie. 'I do not want to be transferred; I would rather stay here with my friends.'

Leslie said, 'It could be a good thing for you. I have noticed that you seem a bit unsure of your future, you know, when you have said that we may not be able to make use of what we learn here. It may become something more positive for you.'

Paul felt the response as a prod at the negative side of his nature.

Chapter 5

The Long Cold Winter of 1963

Madame Yvette Silvestre was an excellent French teacher. She was very strict, and she conducted the classes in her native tongue. However, she would always explain how one conjugated verbs, making the students practice repeatedly, emphasising the masculine and feminine forms, and exacting from her students the best cadences and accentuations possible.

Leslie knew that Madame Yvette had not been a child at the village, but her father had. His surname had been Forest, and he'd changed his name when he went to teach in France. He was a lecturer at various universities in his adoptive land and now a well-respected authority on French politics and economics.

Madame was very impressed by Leslie, and to her, his hard work and dedication to the language was outstanding and impressive. His understanding of the language, history, and culture of the land, she felt, was the best of all the children she had ever taught. She had spent some years in France, teaching French language and history before coming to England. She recommended to the dean that Leslie's studies in French step up to a more advanced level than his peers and said she was willing to undertake that project personally.

The dean knew of the boy's talent with languages. Mr Atkins had told him of the long conversations that he held with the Spanish maids in their tongue, and he decided that Leslie would sit an exam to establish if he were capable of a university course. He made four telephone calls.

Mr Atkins told the boys that they were to sit exams, and the dean visited each of the houses and made stirring speeches to the young people in his care. He explained that it was a measure required by the education authorities, obligatory, to assess the levels of teaching at the village; it was a legal requirement. The village children did not usually take exams like the town children; they were subject to a different system altogether, continuous assessment, with teaching plans that the teachers could adapt. Exams were for the final year at the village, when decisions had to be made upon the futures of each child.

The dean impressed upon them that it was as much a test of the teaching quality as an assessment of their ability to learn. They should embrace the exam with the knowledge that they had far superior tutors than were available elsewhere. This would be a chance for the boys and girls to exhibit the standards of excellence to which they had been such privileged recipients.

The day of the exams came, and the village was abuzz with excitement. They were actually looking forward to this demonstration of elitism. 'Of course we are better than the townies,' went up the rallying cry. 'We shall show them all what we can do here in our village.'

Leslie was in a state of deep dread because he knew why this was happening, and he had a duty to do his best in the exams. Everyone knew how good he was, and if he gave less than his best, it would arouse the suspicions of the dean and the doctor. He must be careful to avoid any undue interest in him. That was it; his mind made up – he would do his best but carefully…

***

Leslie floated to the library that night. It was the one place he was sure that the dean and Hendricks would discuss the day's events; the place was silent as the grave. He looked at the volumes of books on the shelves. The odd book, the one that had been out of place, was back in its proper slot.

'He has gone to the lodge today Joan, and he said he will not be back for some time, you may polish the furniture in his room.' Susan's voice in the hall made him realise that he had miscalculated. In an instant he was at the lodge listening to the doctor and the dean discussing the results of the exams.

'You realise that the boy exceeded expectations. In fact, they all have. The rallying call you gave them has resulted in a most amazing display of knowledge for ones so young. Alastair, I fear what the education board will do if these results are published, no? They will bring such attentions upon us, we will not be able to stop the intrusion of the newspapers or the education authorities. For the sake of one very gifted boy, we have ourselves shot in the feet, no?'

The dean paced up and down thinking furiously, then he said to the doctor, 'How can we avoid unwanted attentions without arousing curiosity amongst the outsiders my friend?'

It was evident to Leslie that he personally had not put the cat among the pigeons. It was all the children; they had made the most valiant attempt to uphold the reputation of the village and succeeded in spades. When the authorities measured their results against the national and private schools, they would be quite far ahead; it would bring the most unwanted attention to this small village.

The dean and the doctor began formulating a plan.

***

Two weeks had passed since the exams and Leslie paid an unseen visit to the west wing as he had done on so many occasions. This time he discovered Hendricks sitting with the dean.

'Now, Ernst,' the dean was saying, 'I have had all the examination results for the younger children adapted. They will show good promise for the future of the village but will not arouse suspicions. As for the Johns boy, I have left his results untouched. I expect a response any day from the examining body. If he were to be graded A's, he would qualify for a special case treatment. That means that we will receive all the coursework and oversee it ourselves. He would need to have an assessment every three months by the college' the doctor interrupted him in his excitement.'

'But that is fantastic, is it not Alastair?'

'We still have to await their decision. If it is favourable, he will have a lot of work on his hands. Thank goodness Yvette will be up for the challenge. We will need to employ a Spanish tutor for him, Ernst. His Greek and Latin are excellent, as are his other subjects. I am considering placing him in River House, where he can study without distractions.'

The doctor looked very concerned by that remark, 'Alastair, remember that he is still a boy. We have always ensured that we do not push too hard on the ones so young. They must be allowed some childhood, no?'

The dean replaced the papers in their folders. 'Of course you are right, Ernst. To push too hard may be the undoing of him. We must let this take its course. We do not want another mistake do we?'

Leslie did not know what the dean meant by that or to whom he was referring.

***

The results of the examination board arrived, and as the dean had expected, Leslie was to take university courses in French and Spanish. But this would be in addition to his other studies. He felt he the boy might buckle under the strain.

After breakfast, Mr Atkins made an announcement – Leslie was to concentrate on his studies and was relieved of his duties as head boy but not the stature of the post. Michael had done a sterling job as assistant and would now be in control of the other boys, under Leslie's guidance, consulting with Leslie when and if the need arose.

Leslie, not able now to fulfil his tasks as head boy, was concerned that his weekly payments would cease. He approached Mr Atkins afterwards and voiced his concern.

'I did not wish to announce it in front of the other boys. The dean has decided you will receive ten shillings per week for the duration of your studies. We are so proud of you, and academic achievement has its own rewards.'

Leslie was astounded. This was four times what he could normally earn… And the books he could buy…

Mr Atkins arranged a private 'study room' for Leslie; it was the small room Paul had referred to as the broom cupboard. Cleared of all the utensils and equipment, it now had a desk and chair, a cabinet, writing materials, and shelves for his growing collection of books and study materials.

To relax, he still took his walks along the riverbank, indulging in some fishing occasionally, but that made him think of Paul. The gardens and the avenue reminded him of Rob. He still did not know what had become of Rob, and perhaps he would find out one day, Paul loved fishing, but since his move, he had not been to the river at all. It was as if he had never been there. Leslie played draughts and chess with the younger boys when he had the time to spare, but they were no match for Paul or for him.

***

The Spanish tutor was Professor Antonio Arias Lopez. He was a strict and proud but likeable man. He engaged in conversation with Leslie as though one Spaniard to another and then proceeded to dismantle the content with all the corrections. He did not hold with the Andalucían way of speaking. 'You must speak "Castillano", the recognised language of Spain.' Leslie progressed rapidly, correcting the bad habits he had learned from the maids' speech and honing the intonations and the articulations.

***

It was the coldest winter anyone could remember, and the snow driven by swirling winds, fell heavily and created huge drifts. The village roads, several feet thick in snow, were mostly impassable. The door of Epping House was buried in snow, and its occupants could not see out from the downstairs windows. With school cancelled because the heating system failed, the elated boys rejoiced in their extra holidays.

Leslie organised the boys into work parties. Michael was to take the twins, and Leslie took David and Martin, the new boy. They collected shovels from the coal shed and set to work clearing pathways through the deep drifts. By mid-morning, they'd cleared a path at the back of the house and another from the front door to the road.

They crossed the road and began clearing the snow from the entrance to Epping House. Peering out from the upstairs windows, the girls and Miss Weston watched, smiled, and laughed at the boy's antics as they heaved and shovelled, clearing the path and creating great snow banks either side. By lunchtime, they were all famished.

Cook had prepared chicken soup followed by steak and kidney pudding. She was a genius, and they all agreed to that. The trouble was, they all felt too full to clear any more snow. Mr Atkins and the staff applauded the boys highly for their hard work. They spent the afternoon with their studies, the older boys helping the younger ones by explaining and giving examples.

The days and weeks passed, the snow slowed, thawed and then the freeze came. They were the most bitter of winter days. Refilling the coalscuttle was a job everyone hated; negotiating the slippery yard to the shed and especially the return with the full scuttle was a hazardous endeavour. The store of salt ran out; they had used it up in the futile attempts to keep the paths clear. Leslie suggested to Mr Atkins the use of the ashes from the fireplaces to spread on the path to the coal shed. Michael had experienced a hard fall on the ice, and the master agreed with Leslie.

The boys stayed mostly in their beds fully clothed during the worst of the cold. It was a way to preserve the fast dwindling store of coal and logs. Poor Cook – the smell of fresh bread wafted upward to the dormitory, and she struggled with what she had. She was fast running out of flour, eggs, and fresh vegetables, all the essentials. How could she feed the household with nothing?

The entire country had been in the grip of the worst winter for many years – some said since 1947, and others said it was far worse than that. This winter was lasting longer than any that Leslie could remember but it would certainly be something to remember. Leslie felt a desperate urgency to visit Perry. How would the poor wretch fare in this most bitter weather?

***

Leslie sat warm and cosy at his desk, alone in his private study, and with a feeling of immense injustice as he closed his eyes and thought of Perry.

He smiled at the man although he felt like crying for him, he wished he could offer him something more comforting than his own company or information, but that was all he had and it gave him a sense of futility and helplessness that he hid from Perry. Even in his ethereal state he could feel the cold of the cell as he faced his friend

'The lad brought me more blankets. I'm sorry, but I can't move well. The cold has my bones you see. When it started getting so cold, I thought I would die here… I don't mind dying; it would end my suffering.' The man pulled the blankets up tight around his chin and ears.

'Look, Perry' Leslie said in a soft tone, 'I have managed to put some of the pieces together with the information you gave me and some papers I have seen, but we have a great problem. There are some in the police force who have links with this organisation – I mean high up in the force. To get anywhere, we have to get past them. How do we do that my friend?'

'There is only one option son – the people's force, the papers, newspapers, lad. The thing is, it must be convincing and with proof. That is going to be a hard thing to get. Are you up to it, son?'

'You mean that, if I cannot provide proof, all this could be for nothing, Perry?'

'What a waste it would be, and what a cost if it were all for nothing,' said the man. He looked broken and subdued.

Then Leslie said, 'You talk like a father. You call me son, as if I were your own son. Do you have family who wait for you, Perry?'

The man sobbed like a child. Leslie took in the dismal surroundings – the sounds of water seeping and dripping, the ice melted by this wretched man's own meagre heat. 'I wish you could be my father. I so hope that whatever happened to my own, he had someone like you with him.'

'Oh, no, son. I lost all my lads, every last one of them. It will remain with me forever that I lost them all. They were an unruly bunch, but I suppose I loved them all in my own way. Do you understand? No, how could you. I hope you never ever have to go through that.

'You asked if I had family. Yes, I did. The blitz wiped them out, my wife and two children. A doodlebug hit the house two doors down from us. It brought down the whole street on our side. I lost them all, son – everything in my life gone in a flash, and I was not there to help them. I was taking care of a bunch of lads from all over Britain, strangers who became my family, and I lost them too.'

If he could, Leslie would have wrapped his arms around this distraught man. He could not leave the man in this state, and he thought of the numbers as a distraction. 'If you can write on something, I can give you a task to work on.'

The man seemed embarrassed by his emotions. 'What is it, son?' he said as he wiped his eyes beneath the blankets.

'I can give you the numbers from the book, but you will need something to write with.'

Perry thought for a moment, he leapt from his bed with the blankets surrounding him, he crossed to a corner of the room and produced a large bar of carbolic soap, he folded back the old and dirty tablecloth and rubbed the soap onto the wooden table. He then bit off one of his long disgusting fingernails and used it to scratch into the hard soap slick. 'Pen and paper, sir,' he said, standing to attention, but retaining the blankets.

Leslie laughed warmly at the vision standing before him, 'Get back into your bed now and keep warm, I cannot lose you to the winter old soldier, when you are able you may work on this puzzle. Leslie provided him with the first set of numbers from the slip of paper. Perry memorised the numbers and repeated them twice to Leslie 'See if you can do anything with that, Perry. I have many other things to deal with, and it would be a great help to me.'

***

The last of the cold weather finally yielded to spring, and the boys were elated to be able to go down to the river once more. Leslie had maintained his studies and his secret visits. It was during such a visit to the library that something strange happened to him. He was watching Sir Alastair opening the secret room when he felt himself pulled backwards—

'Leslie, why are you always sleeping?' Leslie was startled, and he opened his eyes to find Michael shaking him. 'How can you be so good at things when you sleep so much?'

'It is just that I need to digest what I have learned – French or Spanish, history or geography, or whatever. I dream and put them into context.' The lie was convincing.

'That says it all, the brain that sleeps, rules' said Michael, laughing as he skipped down the stairs.

The master stood at the base of the stairs with a scowl on his face. 'How will the young ones learn if you are raising havoc and distracting them? Hardly an example of propriety.'

Michael bowed his head and apologised for his inappropriate behaviour. It was a feigned admonition by the master. He was very satisfied by the way Leslie and Michael controlled and commanded the younger boys. In fact, his life had rarely been easier, and he was most pleased with 'his achievements' – *Two very fine young boys who would remember his guidance and counsel.*

***

Since Paul's move to River House and Leslie becoming head boy, a replacement – a seven-year-old called Martin Glaser came to Roding House. Martin was a very bright boy with a gift for drawing and painting. He had all the boys in fits of laughter with the caricatures he made of each of them. Leslie watched in fascination as Martin depicted a crowd scene in pencil, there must have been fifty faces, each different and all made from one continuous line. The lad was amazing to watch with such a skill, and he made a huge impression upon Leslie.

When he thought about the boys and their various skills Leslie realised what they had in common. Each of them had skills so very different from each other but each had mastered them and had confidence in their area of expertise. It did not mean that they had mastered the world, but they did master their own small worlds.

In Roding House, life had become an easy and smooth routine, Michael was very useful as a deputy and took to his responsibilities with ease. Having someone reliable to delegate to made Leslie's studying much easier. Both gifted musicians, the twins were usually in the school music room, practising every spare moment they could find. David's talent was his calligraphy. He never used pencils, always preferring his "special" pen, which was the only treasured possession he had from his late father, even in school he used it.

Leslie sorely missed his friend Paul and wondered what they were doing in River House. The thought occurred to him that in just over a years' time, he would be fourteen himself and would transfer to River House like the other gifted boys of that age. But Paul would not be there. Because Paul was a little more than two years older, he would move on to who knew where; here was one more thing for Leslie to figure out.

Chapter 6

The Strain Begins to Show

Leslie visited River House. It looked the same as Roding from the outside, but inside, what was the leisure room at Roding had been turned into six rooms with a central corridor. Each room had a nameplate with a boy's name. He found Paul's room; it was about eight feet by six feet. It had a desk and chair and a filing cabinet. On the desk were a reel-to-reel tape recording machine and a set of headphones. There were shelves containing books and tapes, a cabinet with paper, a stack of blank folders, writing implements, and boxes of labels. Leslie checked out the other rooms, and they were almost identical.

He heard the boys approaching and went into Paul's room. Paul entered and sat at the desk. He put on the headphones, grabbed a pencil and paper, and sat listening to the tape. Every so often, he would write notes that Leslie immediately recognised as chess moves, recorded at a tournament. Paul paused the tape, reached into a drawer, and took out a chessboard and pieces. He replicated the moves as noted. He then worked out the remaining moves possible and scribbled them down on the paper, thereby predicting the outcome. He placed the notes into a folder and marked it as instructed on the tape, 'Petrosian v. Botvinnik'. Leslie decided to visit another of the rooms.

In one of the rooms, a boy was writing furiously. The voice on the tape was in German, but the boy was writing in English shorthand. At the end of the tape, he did the same as Paul had done, he put the papers into a folder and labelled it. Leslie had no idea what was on the tape because he did not speak German or read shorthand, however, he did recognise the name the boy wrote on the folder from the list of Woodford companies. There was something very odd going on.

The boys gave their folders to the master who handed them to Jackson at the front door. Jackson drove off up the avenue toward Howard House.

Leslie was there when the folders arrived, and Susan handed them to the dean in the library. The dean went into the west wing and sat opposite the doctor. 'Now let us see how good they are,' he said, shuffling through the folders. He handed Dr Hendricks the German folder. 'Well, what do you think?' he asked.

After a few minutes, the doctor replied, 'I think his scribble is incomprehensible. Perhaps we should give him the second machine to record vocally.'

The dean snatched the folder and began to read the contents. 'Of course, he has written in shorthand, Doctor.' He then related the contents whilst the doctor read a German transcript.

'The boy has done well, Alastair. Full marks.'

They went through all the folders, leaving Paul's for last. 'This boy I have high hopes for,' said the dean. He removed a radio set from a cupboard in the desk and tuned into a German station broadcasting the world chess championships. They sat and listened, following every move on the paper. Paul had put down various gambits. Once the play had been established, the moves were just as Paul had predicted.

'If we had gambled, we would have won, no?'

The dean replied, 'It is early days yet. We have others who fill that requirement at present. He is, however, a good investment for the future.' The dean switched off the radio.

***

Sitting in his study, Leslie revisited the list he had seen the dean with some years before. There were many companies and institutions partly financed by him. One stood out, now that Leslie had a better understanding. It was an academy. And that would be his next port of call.

***

Michael was not feeling too well, and a few of the other boys were feeling under the weather too. Mr Atkins called for the doctor, and there was a kind of hospital atmosphere about the house. Leslie was fully absorbed with the situation at hand. All the boys had rashes, and the doctor diagnosed chickenpox. The children and staff were to be kept isolated from the rest of the village with strictly no visitors.

Leslie did not visit the academy or Perry or anywhere else, for fear that he may spread the virus, he was not sure that it was possible to do so in his out-of-body state, and he could not ask anyone. He could not take the risk, especially with Perry. They were harrowing days for the boy; he desperately wanted to get to the bottom of the conundrums.

He was now certain of the purpose of the village. As Perry had said, it was a training ground for the gifted. The students' skills we're honed to a fine pitch and encouraged at every turn without being forced. The village was like a factory, churning out people who excelled in all areas of human enterprise, with the end product nurtured and shaped, moulded and polished.

He could see from the list that many former residents became politicians, economists, consultants, or senior officers in many fields. The list was a revelation now that he saw the background filled in. That was what was in store for all the children of the village. But how did Mary fit into this? She had no special skills or abilities, except being bossy; she was a grand master at that, and perhaps there could be a use for it in the wider world outside of the village. Martin also had a sister in Epping House, and Leslie had met her on several occasions. She was a bright girl but not extraordinary in his eyes. She would be quite a stunning woman in appearance when older, but she had no outstanding talent that he could see.

He visited Perry when he could, but nothing had changed. Perry had not found a solution to the cipher, and Leslie had no time to engage with it at present.

He did manage at last to find the time to visit the academy. It was, as one would imagine, a military-style school. It involved elements of education, discipline, and physical training. Morning drill was standard. The students trained in orienteering and survival, all the usual pursuits for budding members of the armed forces. The courses had been adapted for these young cadets, and they completed them in addition to their academic studies. They also participated in practical applications designed to enhance a variety of personal skills—they planned sorties against other groups, gathered intelligence, and engaged in communication exercises. These cadets would be the soldiers and leaders of the future; in fact, Leslie thought the academy looked like great fun.

***

It was Leslie's own amount of studying and hard work that one day led him to a moment of realisation. He had neglected his other interests, and perhaps he was feeling the pressure of his studies and the daily rounds of conjugating verbs and composing essays in all the languages he was studying. He just felt a need, an urge, to do something different, to get out in the sun and enjoy something just for the pleasure of it. He confided to Dr Hendricks that he was feeling closed in, that his studies were making him a prisoner to the pursuit of academic excellence. Of course, he relished the work; the studying and research led him to untold heights of perception and understanding. It was just that this academic study did not fulfil his life to the fullest. He now had an urge to explore outside the village and to see how his expertise and skills could be of use in that world. He had never set foot outside the confines of the village since arriving there, but all the other boys had. He had not felt a need to visit that other world before.

***

Sir Alastair called in at the lodge on his return from the city, as he often did unless the hour was late. It was almost dusk as Leslie closed the book on his desk. He reached across the desk and pulled down the blind at the small window, switched on the reading lamp and shut his eyes. *You should be arriving any minute Sir Alastair, time for a visit methinks.*

'Alastair, we need to speak, you understand?' said the doctor with some concern.

'What is the problem, Ernst?'

'Your star wishes to explore the outside world. He is with the trapped feelings now in this environment; we must give him the time in the outside, no?'

'You may be right; I will need to think upon it...'

'This may become a serious situation, Alastair, and we must to act quickly to avoid arousing his curiosity. A group outing, something that would not pertain to him directly, perhaps a day on the river. And they could take notes on the local peoples, terrain, and the wildlife, no – a project if you like, to see who notices the world around them with the most detail. They can use it for the school, no?'

'Well my dear friend, I believe you may have the answer. I will inform the teachers at the school and the masters at Roding and the other houses; we cannot afford to waste or lose the talents of such a perfect prospect for the Foundation, can we?'

***

Hill House for girls, was similar in purpose to River House for boys, only the brightest and most skilled of girls transferred to that house, and they could remain there up to the maximum age of 21. Some of the young women from that house chose a career above marriage, others married but continued to work and chose their careers above motherhood, a few managed a career and motherhood.

Girls considered as not up to the standard required for Hill House remained in their original house and acted in place of maids until employment was found for them. The regime gave the lesser girls training in all they would need for their future lives and Mary was considered one such girl as she displayed no art or special talent, and that was her intent.

Mary was a girl of immense talent but none knew of it, she made sure of that to be close to her brother, even he did not know her skills and she was comforted by his ignorance of them.

***

With the day out now arranged, the younger children of the village, those not in River House or Hill House, were going to follow the course of the River Roding from Dunmow to the Thames basin, an estuary important since before Roman times. The teachers instructed them to record the flora and fauna, as well as collecting anecdotes from the local peoples to discover how the river had shaped the lives of local people over the centuries, if they wished, the children could incorporate their findings into a story.

It was a day the children looked forward to with much excitement – 'A day in the outside world, wow.' It began with a charabanc trip to Dunmow, home of the famous Flitch. They learned of the local's terms and accents, what a flitch actually was, (they had no idea that it meant a side of bacon) and the way the river sprung up and spouted out towards the sea without knowing where it was. To Leslie, it was poetry in motion. He saw the children's faces as they learnt and it warmed his heart that he secretly was the initiator of their joy, and that the dean made all this possible to appease him. His joy was not for himself and what he had achieved by devious means, it was for his fellow occupants of the village and the joy they showed lifted his spirits to great heights.

The day passed in pleasant companionship with his fellow adventurers as they made notes on the water clarity, the residents of the river, and the terrain that changed from woodland to open heath and scrub. The children wrote about the birds, such as skylarks, pippins, and kestrels and the plants, including orchids, wild herbs, and the scrubs of yellow gorse, noting way the water lay stagnant in some areas and not in others. The children spoke to the local people, gathering anecdotes and tales of wild duck shoots, smuggling, and tall ships, they took in every drop of the educational excursion. When they arrived back at the village, they were all tired out.

When they'd passed the village on the route, some had exclaimed, 'Look, home!' Leslie had never considered the village as home, to him it was a temporary stop on the way to somewhere unknown.

***

Michael set up the tables and made sure the boys were washed and presentable. He knocked lightly at Leslie's study, 'tea is ready if you are hungry Leslie' he said without opening the door.

As the boys filed into the dining room, it was evident that the day had been well enjoyed, however, it was agreed that they needed more days out like this and Leslie smiled.

Mr Atkins phoned the dean. 'It was a great success, sir, and the boys are full of what they have seen and learned. They must have more days like this sir, for they are rejuvenated and inspired.'

***

Leslie visited Perry. The man was a physical wreck, and he was almost there mentally too. He had used all his powers trying to decipher the code but to no avail. When Leslie saw him, he instantly regretted having given him the task. The man was muttering and mumbling to himself. Nothing he said made much sense.

'Perry, whatever has happened to you? You look a complete wreck and you are supposed to help me.'

'Been sorting these numbers and they don't make sense, lad. Tried all the different ways I could think of. Whoever constructed this did not want the solution found.'

'Nonsense,' said the boy. 'A cipher is meant to be decoded. You just have to work out the key. The same way a key opens a lock in a door, the right key will unlock this puzzle. Show me what you have so far.'

The poor man turned back the tablecloth and showed him the scribbles in the soap. Studying the scrawl, it occurred to Leslie that the man *had* found something. 'Perry, do not do any more with this until I return, will you promise me that?'

'I will indeed son, I feel like I could sleep for a month of Sundays.'

Leslie felt the guilt of someone who had condemned a man to hell. He had not realised that Perry had nothing else in his life, other than to try to help the young boy who in turn could help him.

***

It was two weeks later that Leslie visited Perry again. 'Look what I have for you,' he began. He related to the man a sequence of numbers and letters. 'Try this and see what happens. It may come to nothing, but if so, do not despair my friend, there are always more things that we can try, and in the meantime I am working on how to get you out of here.'

It was not true. Leslie could see no way that he, just a boy, could affect the release of this falsely incarcerated man. However, he desperately needed to know the meaning of the numbers; it was something he wanted to cross off his list.

***

The days of verbs and adverbs, nouns, adjectives and pronouns, masculine possessive, feminine interrogative, the tenses and forms were hard work for the boy. The four languages were beginning to take their toll on him.

'Doctor, do you think I may be taking on too much?' the boy asked.

Hendricks thought before he replied. 'Do **you** think it is too much for you to deal with? If you think so, you must tell me. It is not our intention to exact from you more than you are able to cope with. If this course is not for you, you must tell me or the dean your concerns.'

'I just feel that it is all caving in on me, sir. The work is so difficult and involved, and I do not want to let the dean or anyone else down.'

'You do not let anyone down master Leslie, on the contrary, you have by your own example, lifted the whole village to new levels of achievement. You are a good example to the other children regarding concentration and belief in your purpose.'

'But if I fail in people's expectations of me, shall they understand? Can I live with their disappointment in me doctor? People expect so much from me. I cannot see within my own abilities how I can repay that. I feel expected to deliver more than I am capable of. Please tell me what I should do.'

The doctor had to think, he lit his pipe, and the plumes and rings of smoke rising to the ceiling seemed to give him answers. 'My dear boy, you must always confide in your friends, and I trust you by now consider me your great friend, no? We must examine this step by step. So tell me, when did you first experience this sense of responsibility to others for your own achievements?'

Leslie was not comfortable in the way the question was phrased. His achievements were his own work, attributable to no others except the technical guidance of his tutors. This question was searching for another answer. It was asking how he felt about himself and how others may have contributed to those feelings. 'Doctor, look at it from this viewpoint. All I have learnt is from what has been taught in the village and the books I have studied. I know that there is a world out there, outside the village. How can what I know and learn be of benefit to that world that is so alien to me? Surely, there are people out there in that world more capable than I am; I cannot see how my life and education could affect those people in any way. I feel that my life is lacking purpose. What good does this education do me or those outside the village?'

The scheming boy waited for the response and the doctor responded directly to the boy's so-called dilemma. Leslie knew that the doctor needed to converse with the dean.

'Take some rest time Leslie, a few days to distract you shall not affect your studies but it can benefit you greatly. You enjoy the fishing in the river but choose a spot outside the village and perhaps interact with others who like to fish no?'

'I think that is a superb idea doctor and I wonder why I did not think of it myself, perhaps it is because I see the village as home, secure and comforting and outside the gates lies an alien world that I know little of personally. I know that one day I will have to enter and adjust to that alien world, leave behind me this village with its protection and all it has provided for me. It will be such a sad day for me when I have to leave you, the library and all my friends to face what?'

'You speak of the village as protection, what do you feel it protects you from?'

'It protects me from the unknown I suppose, from what I may not know or understand. All of us village children came here in early years and we cling to the security we find here, change is hard to cope with doctor, but it shall come to us, be we prepared or otherwise.

***

Leslie, in his ethereal form in the library, silently and secretively awaited the discussion he had purposefully provoked, whilst his true form sat at his study desk in Roding House.

'Ernst, tell me what it is that troubles you.'

The doctor had visited the dean on a matter of grave importance. Unaware that the ethereal boy was in the library he expressed his concerns to his friend Sir Alastair.

'The boy, Leslie Johns, he is very unhappy. This is a most promising boy, and upon that we agree. We must indulge him Alastair, however much it goes against the normal routines. I fear we may lose him if we do not. We must not push him beyond his capabilities. So much better to let him feel that he controls his learning at his own speed. As for purpose, he questions the ability to use his knowledge when he leaves the village. I do not think that he realises what a gift he has. He sees the village as a place of safety and security from the outside world and that is not good for him or for you'

Sir Alastair stroked his chin pensively. 'Do you feel that he is not capable of completing his course?'

The doctor opened the file he had brought with him. 'Capable? Yes of course he is; he has the skills and knowledge, they are natural to him. I believe that his friend Paul is the problem here. I recall that Paul often made the same negative remarks. Paul is a gifted boy but somewhat lacking in purpose, and I hope this becomes not the malaise to infect the village. The other younger boys look to Leslie; he is their guide and mentor on many levels, is he not?'

The dean considered the doctor's remarks. 'If we can show him somehow the benefits his learning could have to himself and to others, it may alter his perception of himself and the contribution he can make to society. You will work on this for me, Ernst? I must attend some business in the city for some days and shall be away from the village, I do not see that I shall return before Saturday.'

***

Leslie sat in his study room reading a volume of poems by Miguel Hernandez. He loved and adored the works of some of the great Spanish poets. Among his favourites were Antonio Machado, Hernandez, Gustavo Adolfo Bécquer, and Federico Garcia Lorca. Their poems reflected passion and romanticism in a way that attracted Leslie. Many of the poems contained deep sorrow and suffering, something Leslie felt familiar with, though on a much lesser scale than the poets did.

The idea had not occurred to Leslie before that he may be able to float to where his father might be. He pondered the idea for a while and then thought, *but what if my father is dead?* He felt that finding out for certain his father was dead would take away all hope of re-uniting with the man who meant most to him in his life. Something so final and unchangeable he could not deal with now – no, not at this time. He told himself that if his father were alive, surely he would have come for him and his sister. He decided not to pursue the matter; he would revisit the idea later.

His study visits to the library were now much less frequent, his tutors supplied all the reading material he needed. He would sometimes go just to discuss with Mr McManus, a man whose opinions he valued (even though he knew that the man reported everything to the dean). It was always an opportunity to speak with someone who did not judge or direct or control. Free speech and forthright discussion eased his tensions and released the pent-up pressure that he often felt.

***

Perry had made a major breakthrough with the cipher; he had felt that the answer would not be written in English. Why he had concluded this was not clear, but he now had the first line, in French – 'J'ai ériger un monument pour lui.'

Perry's command of French was basic, so this had been a master stroke on his part, and Leslie knew straightaway that it said, 'I raise a monument to him.'

The path to discovering the code lay in changing the letter/number sequence according to the length of the previous word. It was very difficult to establish the length of a word from a language one could not speak well.

***

Though Leslie had already congratulated the man on a job well done when he'd first made the breakthrough, Leslie mentioned it again when he returned to give Perry the next part of the code. He saw that his praise made the man smile.

'If I could hug you, I would,' he added. 'Your important discovery should lead us to the solution of this demonic puzzle. I realise that you have a limited vocabulary in French. We must proceed one word at a time if that is what will reveal the answer. I believe that this line is from a poem, and I will look into it shortly. You must take care of yourself and not worry too much about this cipher. You must eat and drink normally so as not to attract attention, you do understand, Perry?'

The man was elated that this young intellectual had deigned to praise his discovery (although somewhat accidental). After all, he was just a numbers man with only a basic education in French.

Leslie's concerns for Perry's mental state were at a very high level. This man was spending all his waking hours on the task. He had a half-eaten bowl of food on the table. He had not washed (although he could not shave; he was not allowed a razor) or combed his hair in days, maybe weeks. But then, what need had he to make such attempts?

They heard the key turn in the lock of the top door to the steps to the cell. 'My friend with the food,' said Perry.

The man entered and placed a bowl of lukewarm stew on the table.

Perry asked the man if he could get more soap for him.

'What do you need soap for?'

'Just look at the state of me, can't you tell that I need a wash?'

'Look, I will do what I can, but it is not easy to get anything now. They keep records of what is issued, you know. I'll do my best for you. After all, you're no trouble to me or to them.' The man removed the half-eaten remains and left.

'I need the soap to write with, and pens? Well I have nine more.' He wore the same grin that had endeared Leslie to him at their first meeting.

Leslie had spent more time and conversed far more with Perry than he had with his own father. Their relationship had progressed, and they had gone from being strangers to intimate confidants. Leslie had told Perry his innermost feelings, his desires and darkest moments, and his aspirations. Perry had told Leslie of his feelings and his sadness at the trickery that had imprisoned him in this joyless place.

The boy found himself wishing once again he could hug the man he had become so fond of. Softly and with some concern, Leslie asked Perry if he was ready for the next challenge, and with the affirmation he gave the man the next sequence of numbers. 'You have done so well Perry, and if this leads to a fortune we shall share it.'

The bond between the boy and the prisoner was one of trust and now completely free of suspicions on Leslie's part. He had been right to be cautious of the strange man at their first meeting, he did not know him then as he knew him now. Leslie's regret was that he could not hug this man and let him feel the warmth of his regard.

'I must go now Perry, do not worry too much about the numbers, it may not come to anything in the end. The bequest was not specific in detail and it may already have been claimed but not recorded in the library. Nonetheless, it is a puzzle that intrigues and occupies the brain, do you agree?'

'If it had been claimed son, I am sure that it would be recorded somewhere in that library, I feel that we are on the right track and you can rely on me to help you to solve this puzzle.'

'Thank you dear friend, your efforts shall not go unrecognised by me, whether we find treasure or not at the end of this quest.'

Chapter 7

The Demonic Dances

Leslie thought that, if his father was still alive and in England, he had let him down. He felt that he was in a situation he needed rescuing from, and only his father could do that. At times, he missed and wanted his father so much, at others he wondered why the man had abandoned him. This confusion of emotions exacerbated by the heaviness of not knowing what really happened– His mind and heart suffered the wanting, loving, hating, a sense of abandonment, and a desire for rescue. He no longer knew how he felt about the man. His silent inner torment, created by ignorance of his father's situation ate at him from inside, piece by piece.

If his father ever reappeared in his life, how could they repair the damage already done? To build bridges, you first have to find a starting point, some common ground. Maybe it was already too late for all that; that was how Leslie felt as he lay awake in bed, awaiting the new dawn.

In his bed and without cause, except for his thoughts of his lost father perhaps, he began to cry deep sobs into his pillow that convulsed him and obliterated the entire world from him;

In my dreams, the demon trips,
Cloven feet and crimson lips.
Coal black eyes that shift and dart
Pierce my mind and then my heart.
Gleeful in his ugly dance,
Stabbing with his piercing glance,
Spewing forth his vitriol,
Tempting me to his control.

The words began clear to Leslie, a poem he had read. Then the words swam in his head, he tried to recall the original order of the words as they jumped around but he could not, and his body shuddered with convulsions.

Michael saw immediately that something was wrong as he was about to pass Leslie's bed on the way to the bathroom. Michael quickly roused the other boys and called the master as the other boys gathered around Leslie's bed in awe and fear at the spectacle of their mentor and leader.

The doctor and the dean so immediately informed by Mr Atkins, attended Leslie's bedside. 'What is happening, Doctor? Will he be all right?' 'We must get him to the hospital immediately Alastair, we cannot treat him here in Roding House.'

***

The boy writhed and twisted on the hospital bed, uttering phrases in French, Spanish, Greek, and Latin, none of which made sense. His face mirrored all his demons, which were devouring him with voracious appetites.

Leslie was lost and far from this world of man. The limit of his sight caused dark grey halos around all he saw with open eyes. A light, a blurred face – they came and went and returned. Nothing was clear or defined; he saw only blurred images that made him feel he was insane.

He fell still, and barely breathing, he sank into a long deep sleep that many a sentry would covet.

He dreamed of the boat moored at the jetty, the basket of fish freshly caught, the gardens with the arbour, and the newly planted avenue of tall graceful poplars swaying gently in the breeze. Their leaves turned gold and yellow by the autumnal will of natures' plan. The garden soothed and calmed; the lake waters lapped passively with musical, rhythmic sounds that relaxed and rebuilt the dying mind of a young and brave boy, this victim to the designs of others.

***

Many days passed as Leslie relentlessly fought his demons and the horrors they tormented him with. Escaping to his imaginary world when he felt exhausted, he fortified himself and then returned to the fray. He could not let the demons win, nor could he defeat them all and he knew what the ultimate prize was for the demons, the prize was his mind, complete power and control over it—

***

Leslie opened his eyes and with the most horrendous look of fear and horror upon his face. He had faced and defeated the torments of hell itself. He had dragged himself inch by inch, clawing at whatever life was still within his grasp. He had defeated the demons, or so he thought. What price would he now have to pay?

Sir Alastair exclaimed, 'Doctor, I believe he is back with us. Thank God Almighty, thank you Lord.'

The doctor was not so convinced. 'Look at his face, Alastair. He has the mark of one who has seen death and felt the depths of human despair. He may now not be what we had planned for him.'

'How are you now, young man?' the dean said.

The boy stared at the blurred faces in front of him as they passed into view. He lay motionless, silent, as though his brain had completely switched off.

He struggled to create some order inside his head. He focussed on the shade of the lamp hanging above the bed, and thoughts began to swirl – fragments of conversations; lines of poetry; words in French, Spanish, English, Greek, and Latin. The words tripped and tumbled over one another as though scurrying to find their rightful places in a melee created from chaos. He could not hear the voices from beyond his mind, imploring him to respond. He could not find words to speak; he just lay and stared into the chaos in his mind.

***

The dean paced up and down the library, rubbing the back of his neck and then stroking his chin.

'Is this some mental aberration that has damaged him, Ernst?' The concern showed in the dean's strained expression.

'I would say that the boy is in a catatonic state. The human brain is like a machine, Alastair; it can only do so much before it shuts down. It is like a protective mechanism. The brain is trying to safeguard the boy from complete destruction I believe. I feared something like this would happen. We may have pushed him too far with his studies. It has been so much for one so young.'

'You assured me the boy was capable of the studies, Ernst. How is it that we now find he is not mentally stable enough? And what will happen with him now?'

The doctor sat in one of the armchairs. 'Do you mind, Alastair?' he asked, removing his pipe and tobacco pouch from his pocket.

'I would rather you did not, but go ahead if it aids you to think.'

Dr Hendricks cleaned the bowl of the pipe as the dean removed an ashtray from the desk drawer and placed it beside the doctor. The scraping sound was the only thing that broke the silence. He stuffed the bowl with the sweet aromatic tobacco and lit the match. The puffs of smoke slowly ascended, creating a cloud above the doctor's head. 'We now must wait my friend. The brain is a wonderful and sometimes delicate thing that shall in time sort itself out. How long that will take I cannot predict. It may be days, months, or even years; it depends on if any damage is done.

***

Several more days passed, and the lampshade above Leslie moved in and out of focus. The ceiling light above him the only indications of day and night. The dean brought in Mr Wallace, a specialist, to oversee the boy's care.

Dante, Pythagoras, Machado, Perry – names rolled around in his head and then disappeared, and others replaced them. He wanted to scream but could not; he wanted the names on the lists to let him alone. Lists of people's names, lists of numbers, and names of companies – they all came and danced, leaping and spinning amongst glittering shafts of light and fleeting shadows. Grotesque faces with coal black eyes flailed at his flesh with malicious glances. There were loud discordant sounds – music for the dance and the raucous laughter of revelry – and flashing scenes of chaotic pandemonium.

The demons he thought he had defeated continued to storm his brain with crimson-lipped mouths, vomiting streams of words and numbers, which then took on lives of their own. Words climbed into ever-growing heaps, piling one upon another, and then adopted shapes and forms. They swirled and danced, built and collapsed and then extending upward to become mountains of moving living words vying for prominence. The words at the base collapsed under the strain and toppled the writhing mess, and then became moving rivers of jumbled letters and numbers. The rivers wended their ways across the mass of grotesque faces, only for the red-lipped mouths to devour and spew them out again in other forms. All the while, black eyes glowered intensely in the background, directing and conducting with mere glances, the masses of helpless, hapless, jumbled words, numbers, and letters. Such a madness had haunted the boy, and now he saw it in the raw.

***

Perry had not seen his young friend for some time and was becoming concerned for him. Perhaps the dean or the doctor had discovered his mission and done him in. *They would not be beyond that*, he mused. His work on the cipher had come to a stop because of his lack of French. He was feeling frustrated with his own failings and longed for the company of the ethereal boy with such intellect and knowledge. Yes, he missed the boy more than he would perhaps admit to.'

***

The boys at Roding House had not seen Leslie for over three weeks. Mr Atkins told them that he had a virus and must remain in isolation, and for the safety of everyone, no visitors were allowed.

Dr Hendricks sent for Mary in an act of desperation. She was to attend his office at the lodge. 'Your brother is quite ill, my dear. We feared for his life, but he is now stable we believe.'

The girl looked at the doctor with anxiety and distain. 'Why did nobody tell me before?' Her question was brusque and direct.

'We felt that there would be nothing you could do; you see—'

The girl interrupted him and snapped, 'How would you know what I could or could not do? He is my brother, and you people took away my responsibility for him. I want to see him, and I want to know what you have done to him.'

The abrupt, forthright manner in which she addressed him took the doctor by surprise. He was accustomed to more respect, even reverence; this little upstart had thrown him off balance. 'I shall make the arrangements with the dean and Mr Wallace. He has the very best of care you understand; we have brought in a specialist to attend him. We treasure all the children in our care and your brother especially; we pass the many hours as the friends here, and we wish no harm to him or to any of you. We thought that he was just a little overexerted with his studies. He will make the full recovery soon. I am sure of this.'

Mary detected the lie instantly. 'Now look here, Doctor,' she said, staring him directly in the eyes 'I will see my brother now, today. You may be able to wrap him around your little finger, but me you will find a different prospect. Call the dean now, if you please, and make the arrangements.'

The doctor felt like a schoolboy admonished for some misdeed. How had he not noticed her ability to take control before? The force and power of her commands had left him unable to contradict or defend. He reached for the telephone.

***

Mary looked aghast at the sight awaiting her at her brother's bedside. There were tubes and machines, two nurses in constant attendance, and the specialist monitoring every sign of the boy's 'progress'. 'My God! What have they done to you my dear Leslie?' she screamed, and fell across the bed, trying to hug the motionless figure who just stared at the ceiling. 'My God, you will pay for this. Mark my words, you shall pay dearly.' Her words she directed at the dean and Dr Hendricks.

She sobbed and held her brother's hand, squeezing as though that would transfer something from herself into this poor wretch. The fingers of his hand began to turn white, and Mr Wallace rushed to the bedside, wrenching the girl away from her brother. 'Let go of his hand, miss. You're crushing him.'

The boy sat bolt upright with a loud gasp, and the staff stood in amazement; he had come out of the coma. There was a busied excitement; the girl had raised her brother from his catatonic state, from the dead, to their minds.

Mary had a bed next to her brother in the ward; she adamantly refused to separate from him. She gave him his food, washed him, and combed his hair. She took his pulse on the hour and checked his charts every time with a new entry. She sat beside him recollecting the times they had spent together at Felixstowe and retold stories about their father. She fluffed up his pillows and spoon-fed him his meals. He said nothing.

Two weeks more passed and still not a word out of him. Mary feared that these people had destroyed the mind of her brother. 'Tell me what happened, Leslie. Did they do something to harm you?'

Silence –

***

The golden sun spread down its warm and gentle rays like the touch of a host of angels. The gravel path led him from the house to the arbour, and he sat with his books stacked on the seat; he had not opened one for some time he recalled. He entertained the thought of reading some poetry, something from Bécquer perhaps, a romantic poet perfectly suited to an afternoon such as this. Of all the poets he had studied, this surely was his favourite, or perhaps Machado? He laughed at his indecision as to who was his favourite poet. Choosing instead, a volume of poems by anonymous British authors, he began to read:

In the glorious fading light,
Gliding softly into night,
Slipping down, beyond the deep sea,
Tranquil now...

A voice calling his name interrupted his reading. 'Leslie, Leslie are you there?' He did not have visitors; they did not exist in this haven. He ran along the avenue, across the meadow of wild flowers, scattering red admirals, painted ladies, tortoiseshells, peacocks, and swallowtails, and the voice still called to him. He mounted the steps three at a time and ran around the side of the house to the front drive. He could see no one. The voice continued calling, but there was nobody there. He ran into the house and searched every room but he found no-one.

'Leslie where are you? You little devil, just look at the state of you all dishevelled, and those dirty shoes. Who is supposed to be looking after you?'

He blinked and saw his sister leaning over him. She wrapped her arms around him and squeezed as though his life depended on it. 'Oh, my love, what have they done to you? You have been so far away I thought you would never return.'

'Is Daddy here with you?' he said.

The girl sobbed torrents of tears because she had created Leslie's image of their father and she knew how important he was to her brother. They held each other in an embrace that none dared to break. The staff had felt her wrath in the hospital. This girl was a force to respect, and one crossed her at one's peril.

'How did you find me, Mary?' Leslie asked. 'No one knows where I go to. It is my place – somewhere I can be myself and not worry about the rest of the world.'

'Silly boy, I know what you get up to in that little head of yours. I am your sister, and you are my responsibility. Daddy told me to take care of you and they took that away from me' she said, looking at the dean and doctor Hendricks. 'Look what a mess you are in now. From now on, I will take charge of you as Daddy wanted.' Her words were sincere, heartfelt, and warming. He had never remembered her as being so warm and tender, remembering only the times she had criticised him.

***

He continued his recovery slowly, with exercise therapy to restore his mobility. All books and newspapers were removed to allow him the time to return to his former self. Mary assisted with the exercises, playing ball and enticing him to take that one step more. She was making plans of her own, plans to free them from the clutches of these villains who had almost destroyed her brother. She was an unforgiving person, and a wrong done was a wrong remembered; all should beware the consequences!

The days lengthened as spring gave way to summer. Leslie spoke of returning to Roding House, but Mary had forbidden any such move to put him beyond her reach. She was now in control of her little brother once more, and dean, doctor, tutor would have no say unless she agreed, she determined to reinstate her position.

Leslie was not aware of the powers his sister commanded, and she had made sure of that. She would demand something and tell him that others had suggested this or that. 'What do you think we should do Leslie?' She let her brother make decisions for himself and would then relay them as commands, as though they were her decisions. She was so protective that even the dean could not impose his will.

By mid June, Leslie felt he was ready to face the world and continue to his destiny. He felt now that he was invincible. He could take on whatever came at him and defeat it with all the forces he had at his disposal. He had had a lucky escape. His life's saving grace had been the sanctuary of his haven, that realm in which he could be alone and unencumbered by life's trappings and burdens, the place that gave him inner strength. His secret retreat had saved his life, and perhaps Mary had contributed to some extent.

***

'You must listen to me Alastair The boy is now well recovered and ready to resume his studies. His sister has demanded that he be installed in Howard House instead of Roding House, and she is to be near him at all times.'

The dean held the handset away from his ear. The doctor's voice was excited and alarmed. 'She knows that we do not allow mixed houses. Is that why she has demanded Howard House?'

'But of course, dear friend. She is not the stupid girl as we presumed.'

'Doctor, as you presumed, I believe. I will allow them to be here together temporarily in order to protect our investment, and for no other reason, you understand?'

'But of course, dear friend, of course. It is necessary that we give a little and take a little as you say, no?'

The dean replaced the handset onto the receiver. How had this impudent girl dared to demand anything? *We have fed, clothed, educated, and cared for her and her brother at our own expense; she is going too far for my patience.*

Leslie did not return to Roding House. Now, installed in the dean's own residence, he had his own rooms in the upstairs of the mansion. Mary had rooms next to his, and she had insisted on it.

The dean sat silently in thought, staring out of the window. Susan entered and removed the remnants of his light snack without a word. This whole affair had now come to nothing; their most promising asset had succumbed to human frailty. He had piled all his hopes on this one boy after the failings of so many before him. He was certain that Leslie was the one – the person to succeed him after he was gone; now his hopes lay shattered and forlorn.

Sir Alastair could not rely upon his own son. He considered him a leech and a waster. He would not leave his vast empire to him. His disappointment in and hatred of his own son led him to an outrageous idea. He picked up the telephone and dialled the lodge, 'Ernst, I wish to adopt the boy Leslie and his sister Mary as my own.'

The doctor was astounded. 'But, my dear friend, do you realise what you are doing? What you are saying is that you will disinherit your own son – to leave your life's work and that of your forefathers to the children of a soldier who you knew so many years ago. Is this a feeling of guilt my friend? You did what you needed to do. You achieved what you set out to do, and you took that soldier's life from him; you stole his children. You must not now forget the aims of the Foundation. It is to reinforce and build upon the structure that your forefathers set in motion so many years ago. Alastair, we have the wins and the losses. Life is the table of roulette, no? We win, we lose, and we begin again. We continue until we find the winning combination, no?'

In his private rooms in Howard House, the dean thought about his conversation with the doctor and about the lives that he had destroyed in order to achieve his own goals, the countless people who had had their children torn from them, never to see or hear from them again. The lies and intrigues, the concocted stories that were so convincing played on his mind, and he thought too of the expertise of all those contacts he had built up over the years, people who owed him something and some, everything. He had been vital in the placement of some very influential people. Why did he feel a shudder of fear, a dread, a sense of foreboding, a feeling that everything could come crashing down upon him?

***

Dr Hendricks was concerned about the dean's proposal and called a trusted colleague at the Foundation. 'But adoption?' he said, after bringing the colleague up to date. 'That would be a big mistake; he has not thought this through properly. The girl would be an obstacle, most definitely. He has let his feelings about his son to colour his judgement. The boy, Leslie, is a very likeable boy; that is true. His recent state of mental health would be a forceful argument against handing him the Foundation to run. Adoption, what is the man thinking of?' He urgently needed to discuss the situation with others, before the dean made a serious mistake.

***

Susan and Joan provided every comfort for Leslie and Mary at Howard House. The children took their meals with the dean and were not required to perform any of the tasks they had previously been responsible for. When Leslie offered to help with anything, he was told, 'No, Master Leslie. The dean has forbidden it.'

Susan was happy to have the children at the mansion, she had a fondness for them and Leslie in particular. She recalled those early days and the way he clung to her like a lost boy reunited with his mother. She knew nothing about them other than that the children were orphans, if she could step into the motherly role she would do it without a second thought, such were her feelings for the boy.

Chapter 8

Confidence Restored and a New Experience

At the rear of Howard House, a large wing housed an indoor swimming pool and a games room. The dean told the children they were at liberty to make use of them if they wished. The boy looked longingly at the pool; he always had a fascination with water that was born out of fear. He wished he could swim, and if he could, he felt he would overcome that lifelong dread. Mary was not so enthusiastic about her brother being near the water. She knew perfectly well the cause of his fear but never spoke of it.

The games room had a billiard table and a card table covered with blue baize. The smell of stale cigar smoke indicated that the dean and his guests often made use of this room.

Outside in the rear garden, a wall enclosed a colourful arena, with a large lawn area and a summerhouse to one side. Sir Alastair walked alongside Leslie on the neatly mown lawn, explaining the game of croquet. 'It would be nice to try a game when the weather improves,' said Leslie.

'When time allows, I would enjoy teaching you the game,' the dean replied.

'Sir, how can I learn to swim?' The boy asked out of the blue.

The boy's question surprised the dean. 'Do you not swim? I thought you spent a lot of your time at the river and naturally assumed you could.'

'Oh no sir, I go out in the boat sometimes but not into the water itself. But I think I would like to know how to swim.'

The dean patted the boy on the shoulder. 'We shall have to see what we can do.'

During the next few months, Leslie returned to his studies in earnest. The dean had set a limit on the study hours. Professor Arias came to the library Monday to Friday from nine to ten thirty and Madame Silvestre from ten thirty until noon. His other studies took place in the afternoon, and he was forbidden any study time after four o'clock. He could read all he wanted as a leisure pursuit.

***

Mr Laurence Vance was the master of Bridge House, and in his youth, he had been a competitive swimmer, winning medals and trophies for a swimming club. The dean engaged him to teach Leslie how to swim.

Mr Vance arrived on a Sunday afternoon. 'Well, young man, so you wish to swim, I have been told.'

'Yes indeed, sir,' the boy replied excitedly.

'Well, we will take this slow and easy. We must first get you used to the water and build your confidence. You will need to learn to relax in the water and I shall help you to achieve that.'

Mr Vance entered the water first and held out his hand to Leslie. The boy took hold with a tight grip and descended the steps into the tepid pool.

The water was barely waist high to Mr Vance at the shallow end, but he could feel the tension in the boy's grip. 'We will not go deeper than this, and I will not let any harm come to you. Stay at the edge of the pool here and hold onto the rail, but try to relax, swimming is a most wonderful sensation once you master it. There are skills and techniques I can teach you but we shall begin with the basics.' He gave the boy some bobbing movements to copy, just little jumps that brought the water up to his chest and then to his chin. They continued the bobbing until Leslie had gained a little bravery. 'This is fun.' The boy laughed, bobbing harder and sending splashes over his head. He still held his vice-like grip on the rail.

'Now let us try something a little braver. I want you to still hold the rail and duck your head under the water. Let it flow over you and take all your worries with it. You can resurface anytime you wish; you will not drown with me here.'

The man's voice was calm, warm and soft, tempting and inviting. The boy felt an exhilaration he had not expected or experienced before. He ducked his head into the pool and came up quickly, gasping and spluttering.

'Try again with your mouth closed and your eyes open.'

He ducked again and came up holding his nose. 'The water went up by dose,' he squealed. The sensation stirred something in his memory.

'Let us do this together. One…two…three, duck.'

They both submerged into the tepid water and then erupted into the air of the poolroom, the boy gasping and the man calm and controlled.

'That was good. You are a natural, my boy. Congratulations. Now try that a few more times and become comfortable with it. The boy repeated the task and soon became more comfortable and relaxed. He even opened his eyes under the water on the last two attempts.

'Now let us try something more advanced, I am sure that you are more than capable.'

The boy spat the water out and swept the long curly hair from his face.

'Holding onto the rail, walk your feet up the wall of the pool like so,' he demonstrated the movement.

Leslie slowly imitated the demonstration. He squatted slightly pushing his behind out and away from the wall and walked his feet slowly upwards.

'Well done, my boy, well done. Now relax and let your feet sink down.'

As he relaxed, he lost the grip of one hand. He felt the strong hands grab him gently under the arms and steady him. 'There you see, no harm. Now try that again a few times and become comfortable with it. I will still be behind you.'

The boy regained his grip and proceeded with the exercise. He repeated this six or seven times, gaining in confidence each time.

'Now the last thing for today is far more adventurous. Facing the rail, raise your feet behind you with your legs stretched out.' He showed what was intended.

Leslie looked alarmed.

'Do not worry. Relax and you will float like a balloon.'

The boy gritted his teeth and gradually inched his feet away from the edge. He could feel his body weight transferring from his feet to his shoulders. He froze just as he was about to let his feet go. 'I cannot do it sir.'

Mr Vance placed an arm under the boy's chest. 'Relax and lift.' His voice was calm and soothing.

They stood for a moment, allowing Leslie to summon the will. 'Here goes, sir.' He kicked his feet backward. He could feel that Mr Vance had placed his other arm at his knees and felt him lift his legs. They remained with Mr Vance supporting the boy. 'If you want to let go of the rail, I have you safely under control. Just stay relaxed.'

Leslie slowly released one hand and then the other. He dipped a little as the man adjusted his position. They moved slightly away from the rail. It was now just beyond the reach of the boy. 'Relax. The secret is to relax and enjoy the sensation.'

Leslie tried to relax, but something in him just held that touch of tension.

They returned to the rail and Leslie wildly grabbed at it. The man released the boy slowly letting his feet sink gently. 'I think you have done well, young man. Once we can conquer that fear, you will be more relaxed. They spent another hour repeating what the boy had done, his tutor did not wish to end the session on a negative. I will see you again next Sunday if you wish to continue.'

They both towelled themselves. 'Thank you, sir. It was a bit frightening, but I still enjoyed it, please come again next Sunday sir.'

'Well, I doubt you will make an Olympic swimmer by next month, but you have taken a great step. Now promise me that you will not practice alone.'

The boy chuckled. 'I promise, sir. My sister can swim. Can I practise with her?'

'I would say not, unless she is a strong swimmer. A competent adult would be an advisable choice for you at this stage.'

Leslie was pleased with his attempts to defeat his fear of water. He had briefly experienced that special moment – that moment that does not distinguish between fear and excitement, but lays somewhere in between. He could not wait to tell Mary.

'You did what? I told you to stay away from the water; you always seem to put yourself in harm's way you stupid boy.'

The boy's elation expired like a burst balloon. 'You can swim why not me, why can I not learn?'

'I learned to swim when I was small. I never had a fear of water as you have. Now let us play cards.' Mary was not about to reveal the reason for her brother's fear; her job was to protect him. She admired his will to overcome his fear of water but dreaded that he would recall events whilst in the pool, he could have a panic attack and drown. She knew that he could not recall those events so far back in his life and preferred it to remain so, for his own protection.

Lying in bed that night, Leslie still felt proud of his attempts, regardless of his sister's attitude. He realised that for some time he had not visited anyone, especially Perry.

***

'My dear, dear boy, I thought they had done you in.' Perry was overjoyed to see his young friend again. 'Sorry but I came to a full stop with the cipher. French is not my thing as you know.'

Leslie recounted the events since his last visit to bring Perry up to speed.

'I thought it strange that you didn't visit. Why do you think the dean has installed you in Howard House then?'

'Well I am not certain but I believe it was my sister Mary. She was so annoyed at the state she found me in she threatened to go to the authorities, which is what she told me. She refused to be separated from me again.'

Perry laughed. 'Plucky sister you have there son, I bet that scared the living daylights out of the doctor and Sir Alastair.'

The boy looked at the scribbles in the soap. *I raise a monument to him.* Leslie thought of the garden at the rear of Howard House. Perry was about to say something when Leslie raised a hand to silence him. 'I know this line Perry; it comes from a book of verse written by Sir Giles Woodford. There is a plaque in the garden of Howard House to Sir Howard's twin brother; he died at the age of ten when he fell down a well, Caldwell Prescott Woodford. When I mentioned it to the dean, he said that his grandfather never came to terms with his son's death. He became morose and spent years mourning the boy's demise. He wrote several poems about loss and death, about soldiers killed in action and the debts of those who survived. One poem goes like this:

For now not beats your soldier's breast
Throughout the ageing chimes of time.
Now gone those days of youth sublime.
They took you, at your youthful prime.
Now, sleep, you brother, at your rest.
Wrest not his hand from off his chest.
This fondest son, of our fair land,
Disturb him not, I so command.
Our loss? His life, his heart, his hand,

Now laid in his eternal nest.
Long lost his boyish, foolish zest.
I raise a monument to him
And bide we some, to see within
Ourselves new hope, and so begin
A newer life, forever blessed.
No demons can your will arrest.
I bid you, sirs, now comprehend.
Do not my words now you amend.
Be true and see it to the end
So none, your efforts can contest.
All life is played out as a jest.
So find we answers, false and true.
So make we oaths that we may rue.
Our numbered days here are but few,
So strive as he to do our best.

Perry sat silently, absorbing the words the boy had recited. 'I never knew that Sir Howard had a twin brother. Of course, when I joined the company, they outlined the family history. But there was no mention of the brother.'

They sat thinking about the reason for the verse.

Leslie looked at the man and the conditions he suffered that he was helpless to change. You are a clever man Perry; you may not see it but I believe you have solved one part of the puzzle, and as for the remaining numbers, 'Try a line from the poem. It may fit. If not one line, try another.'

The man looked sceptically at the boy. 'My French is not good enough to decipher this, son.'

'Never mind. Do what you can. I will visit again soon, but I must learn to swim.'

Those parting words puzzled Perry. The boy was learning to swim of course, but he had said it as though he meant something else.

***

The sun shone in through the large window, sending brilliant rays of white and gold flickering across the far wall of the bedroom. August announced her arrival. Leslie arose and stood by the window, absorbing the early morning warmth. He could hear the bustle of breakfast being prepared and the chink of the plates and cutlery in the dining room below. He felt glad to be alive on such a glorious morning. After the pressures of the years of study, illness, worry and stress, he felt as though he'd been dismantled, cleaned, polished, and rebuilt. He was a boy renewed. He was full of the vigour of youth, full of the knowledge and wisdom of age – he was invigorated, rejuvenated, and ready to do battle with any foe that dared to show its dark face.

After breakfast, he decided that he would visit his old friends in Roding House. He asked the dean's permission and was told that, if that was what he wished, he should do it. It was a Saturday, and the boys would be free after their chores. He strolled carefree along the avenue, greeting each tree as if it were an old friend. His step was light, and his mood elated. The dappled sunlight heightened his mood, giving warmth like a mother to her child. He felt so high; it was as if he were drugged. The sense of euphoria almost turned his steps into dance.

This was ridiculous; he was like a six-year-old skipping and gliding along the avenue. Were anyone to observe him, they would say he was the victim of the sun or, at worst, mad. He had not a care for what anyone would think; he basked in the joy of the moment.

Arriving at Roding House sent a slight shiver through him. He shrugged it off. Nothing was going to spoil this magnificent day.

Mr Atkins greeted him at the door, and he offered his hand towards the boy. 'I am so glad that you have decided to pay us a visit dear boy.' Leslie sensed a falseness in the greeting, something did not quite fit to his mind. Mr Atkins had never addressed him before as dear boy—

An alarm bell rang at the back of the boy's mind – an alarm he recalled from before his 'illness'. 'I so missed the company of the boys I had to come and visit. My sister is not the best of company, sir.'

The master understood the meaning; he gave a broad grin and welcomed the boy in. Leslie looked around the entrance hall. Everything was just as before – the gong, the portrait, the coat pegs with one unoccupied. It was just as he had remembered it.

The master led him to the leisure room where the boys were engrossed in puzzles and games and did not even look up as they entered. 'Boys?'

The youngsters stood to attention, bowing their heads; they had been remiss in their respects.

'You remember Leslie; he was here for some years. He has always been a great example of dedication, something all of you should strive for.'

Leslie looked around the room. Michael and David were not here, and there were two boys he did not recognise; they were only about six years old. 'These are Walter and John. The rest you know.'

The boys gathered around him, touching his hands and vying for his attention. Ralph and Peter referred to the days when they went to the river – fishing, sailing, the body, the police, Paul, and Michael. They babbled on like old men recalling their younger days.

'The past is what we leave behind, if not? 'Tis now, or yet to come.' The words from an obscure poem rang in his head. The surroundings, the hard brick and stone, were the same. Everything else had changed. Ralph and Peter were now joint head boys. Leslie recalled when he and Paul had needed to change their wet bed sheets nearly every day. Those boys were now in charge of the youngsters. Returning had been a grave mistake; so much had changed in so little time.

His steps back up the avenue were heavier; his memories had been an illusion, something that once was, but now did not exist. The harsh facts were beginning to bite into his attitude about life in general. The present and future are not prisoners to memory; nostalgia is the prisoner of memory. One must tread carefully and with purpose and never look back; it always brings disappointment. The day had started with such promise and had ended in disillusionment. He avowed that he would not let nostalgia, fantasy, or illusions cloud his judgement again. Another step on his ladder of learning.

Chapter 9

A Demon's Demise and New Allies

The swimming lessons continued to boost the boy's confidence. He could now relax and float on the water's diamond-flecked surface. He was as one with the shimmering, wavering sheet of fluid glass. He could explore the depths of the pool with open eyes, a fish discovering his kingdom. He could twist and turn without restraint beneath the shimmering veil. He felt the exuberance of human exercise, the energy of human expertise; he was a boy becoming man and his confidence blossomed.

The pool was such a release, such a refuge, such a pleasure. The sensation of the water over his flesh was sensual and soothing, how he had feared it all his life was an enigma to him now. He revelled in the sensations – the sway and tussle, the feel of the dive. The exhilaration led him to realms previously unknown. He could float now until his dying breath. He relished the races that he and his teacher would have at each training session. Mr Vance was astounded at the progress and displays of this boy who once had a mortal fear of water. He suggested that Leslie take part in some junior swimming trials he had learned of.

The dean was totally against the idea. He feared that his boy, faced with competition, would crumble under the pressure, and he would do anything in his power to prevent that. Leslie entreated the dean to let him participate in the competition, so that he could measure his own level of expertise. What had they to lose? Had Mr Vance's efforts been for nothing? Mr Vance was a very good teacher, and Leslie's fear of water had evaporated.

Leslie maintained his daily ritual of combating the water demons – they who had held him prisoner for so long and who were now reduced to sediment at the bottom of the pool, flushed and purified by the pumps that constantly circulated the water. As the pumps refreshed the pool, so they refreshed the boy.

Eventually the dean reluctantly agreed to let Leslie participate in the local competition. The scene was set. Seven teams of four would compete against each other at the local baths, and the competitors were all between the ages of thirteen and eighteen. Leslie was still only twelve and according to club rules, not eligible. Leslie's participation was as a result of connections and friendships he was not aware of.

The day was set for the final qualifying rounds. Mr Vance was there beside his young protégé. He whispered words of encouragement, urging his boy to perform to his best. He told him that success was a step on a ladder, some take it by force, and others take it with cunning. He would need to pace himself and leave the remaining surge of force to the last.

Mary sat with a bag of potato chips watching her brother compete; she had seen the previous rounds and dismissed her brother's chances as mere folly. He had qualified in the earlier rounds, but she had noticed that all of the competitors in this final had faster times than Leslie.

The bag fell from her lap as she stood and Leslie edged nearer to the leaders in the pool. She rose to her feet, screaming his name. 'Leslie, Leslie, come on. Come on. You can do it.'

A violent shock propelled the boy as he powered his way to the shoulders of the leading swimmer, a boy three years older than him. Again, Mary's voice cut through the clamour of the leader's supporters. An inexplicable power that was incredibly strong forced him like a torpedo through the moiling thrash of the water created by his competitors. He powered himself to reach the final end, and like a dolphin, he bounced and tumbled head over heels in the water at the final end.

The runner-up came and gave him the customary acknowledgement, albeit with reticence and his own disappointment. Leslie had won the final of the national qualifiers. He had not been aware that this was a competition of such magnitude; he'd just thought it was a local competition of little significance, and now the attentions overwhelmed him.

Mr Vance had entered Leslie's name at the last minute and told him, 'You can only do your best.' Well, he had done his best, and he had demolished the club and national records. He had not sought fame; he did not want the publicity that came with such things. He was, in himself, a quiet and modest person and immediately regretted having won. He did not want to demoralise the club champion, a boy who had destroyed every local record and could have a wonderful career representing his country at the Olympics. No, it was not his wish to be acclaimed or exalted. That was not the purpose of his life, and he tasted sourness in his achievement.

The doctor and Mr Vance were overjoyed at Leslies results – another marker for the village. If only it were so for Leslie. He felt disappointed for the boy he beat. He had been a boy with tremendous strength and courage, a boy who had almost torn his heart out to win the race, expending every ounce of effort to win the one thing that meant the world to him.

Leslie had heard the voice of his sister above the hubbub of the arena, and it had spurred him on like rocket fuel. He wished he had never heard her voice. He made himself a promise that he would never compete again.

***

The dean had not foreseen the consequences of the swimming results. No one could have expected Leslie to win, and win in such style. His only competitor before the trials had been his teacher. The local papers displayed broad headlines: 'Mystery Boy Breaks National Record.'

The dean was furious as he slammed the paper on the desk. 'Ernst, this will attract every journalist for miles. It is going to create more attention than we can deal with. Why did I let him take part? Ernst, something in me said do not allow it, but I succumbed to his pleading and that of Vance. My own failings and lack of judgement have now brought me to this point of conflict.'

'My dear friend, you must not to worry yourself so. It will blow over. In a week or so, no-one will remember his name. What you call a one-minute wonder, no?'

The dean was not in the least bit convinced or appeased. 'No, Ernst, this is going to cause us problems. I can feel it.'

***

Tweety sat in the office with his editor. Harry Bird had written the story about the 'Wonder Boy' who destroyed the national junior record. He felt that there was more to the story because there was little or no information about the kid who won. He had spoken to people at the baths. No one had heard of him or knew where he came from. Some promised to phone if anything came up.

'Look, son, go out and get that story. Don't sit around waiting for a phone call that may never come. Go get the story; it could make your career. Don't take no for an answer. If we all did that, there would be no news at all. See if you can track down that dark-haired girl – you know, the one who kept shouting his name at the pool. Check the registration form; trace his records with his club. What was the name of his trainer?'

'Vance, sir. Laurence Vance.'

'Here, wait a moment my lad' he said as he rubbed his chin in recognition of the name, Good God man, I know that name from years back.' He turned to the open door and shouted, 'Mike, bring me the swimming reports from the archives – twenties and thirties.' He smiled at the young reporter. 'Now you see, son, we have a real mystery on our hands now. You are too young to remember, but an old hack like me? I recall a swimmer of Olympic class who won all the qualifiers, back somewhere in the late twenties I think. I was working for the nationals then as a freelance. This chap was selected to represent his country, but he turned it down. He just disappeared, couldn't be traced anywhere and never took part in any more competitions. Now don't you think that's odd? You go to all that trouble to compete, beat the socks off your competitors, and then refuse to go to the Olympics. We have a scoop here, laddie, a veritable scoop. Now don't mess this up. I'm going to give you a free hand in this. Take your time, get the facts, and check them well. And bring me the story – both stories, the Johns boy and Vance.'

'But what about the report on the damage to the gravestones?'

'You can leave that. I'll get someone else to do that one. You just get me those stories, I'm putting a lot of faith in you, Tweety.'

***

A prolonged search of all the clubs in London, Essex, and East Anglia produced no results. There were no records of this boy or his trainer being a member of any club. Tweety contacted the secretary of the swimming club that had staged the finals. 'How could this boy compete without being a club member?'

The club secretary explained, 'It was a favour for an old friend. The boy needed some competition experience and was not officially a competitor.'

'But the lad broke the national record. Where the hell did he come from?'

'I'm sorry, Mr Bird, that information is not available.'

'Come now, this is of national importance. Everyone wants to know about this special boy sir.'

'As I said, that information is not available.'

'Okay then, can you tell me how I can get hold of Mr Laurence Vance? Perhaps he will give me the answers.'

'I'm afraid that is not possible either. Now good day to you, sir' said the club secretary with finality.

***

The dean received a call from an old friend warning him of the press interest. He called Mr Vance to his study at the mansion.

'Why did I not listen to my doubts Vance? This is going to become everything we have tried to avoid. Vance, I do not want anyone talking to the press, is that clear?'

'Yes Sir, perfectly clear, and as you know, I do not wish their attentions either.'

***

Tweety knocked at the editor's door. 'Can I come in, sir? I think I have a lead.'

'Yes, come in, lad. What's this lead then?'

'Well, the news desk received a call from a woman in Salford—'

The editor interrupted, 'Salford? That's bloody miles away.'

'Hold on, sir...she says she has a friend who lives in Ilford and every week her friend sends her the local papers, and of course, she read the report on the Johns boy. Well it turns out that she was married to a Will Johns. They used to live in Sheerness in Kent, and they had two kids called Mary and Leslie. The father was in the armed forces, and he put them in the St Vincent's children's home when he and she got divorced. She wanted to know if it is the same boy, her son!'

'Well I'll be blowed; that's a stroke of luck. Now get onto the records office for the children's home and check it out. Check the records of births on the isle of Sheppey for the late forties and early fifties. Also check the woman's story, even if it means going to Salford, and see if you can trace where the father is. You can start with the army records; check everything twice, three times if you have to. I don't want any slip-ups. Boy this is going to be big; I can feel it.'

The young reporter had made hurried shorthand notes of the salient points. 'I'll get onto the records office right away, sir, before they close.'

***

Perry had deciphered another line of the code. 'You were right, lad. It's been a bit of a slog. Here you better check it.' He showed the soap scribbles to Leslie.

'That looks almost correct. Let us see— The line goes, "No demons can your will arrest." Yes, you almost had it there. Let us check the numbers again.'

They sat and calculated, composed, and translated. The enigma was nearing the end. 'There looks like one line left to do. The thing is, it just seems to lead to another clue, and the answer has to be in the poetry by Sir Giles.'

Leslie talked about the swimming and how the dean was furious with the attention.

Perry said, 'I can see why he wouldn't want the papers poking about. They are like ferrets that lot; if you have something to hide, they'll dig it out. This could be the chance we are looking for.'

Leslie looked a little sullen. 'We have all been made to promise not to talk to the press,' he said, 'and I cannot break a promise.'

'Not even to save a life,' snapped Perry. 'Your life or mine?' He sat with his arms folded across his chest and glowered at the boy.

'I am sorry, Perry. I know the time may come when I may have to make that choice, but for now, I must keep my word.' He did not like upsetting his friend but he had strong feelings about promises. He gave his friend the last of the numbers.

***

Leslie secretly visited the doctor and found that the 'procurer' was with the doctor in his office.

'The reporter said his name was Harry Bird, he wanted to see the records of the Johns children,' Thompson said, as Leslie arrived unseen.

'I have no idea how he found out they were at St Vincent's. It has me worried, Ernst.'

The doctor sucked silently at his pipe and then said, 'Of course you told him nothing-'

'No, nothing at all. I told him that all the children's records were confidential, and I could neither confirm nor deny they were ever at the home.' Thompson answered nervously.

'Do you think that will satisfy the reporter?' The doctor enquired, noticing the distress that the procurer displayed.

'If he keeps coming up with blanks, he will eventually give up, surely' answered Thompson.

'Blanks, you say. He has a source somewhere.' The doctor said.

Leslie could see the concern etched deep in Thompson's face. That would be the next stop – the reporter, Mr Harry Bird. Leslie knew the name from the article in the local paper when the reporter covered the swimming trials.

***

Tweety sat with copies of the army records, flicking through them one by one. He was getting nowhere with this. Will's ex-wife could not remember which regiment he had been in or his postings after the war years. To Tweety, it seemed she either had a very bad memory or had lacked interest at the time. He had managed to get copies of the birth certificates for the children and the parents. He had also spent hours at Somerset House, trawling through the records of births, deaths, and marriages since 1953; he had drawn a blank there too. He decided that he should go and give an update to his boss.

Leslie arrived at the editor's office just in time to hear the update.

'Ed, we have the kid's birth records and the parents. There are no records of the father dying or remarrying. We cannot get access to children's records at the home, and we cannot trace Vance. Sir, it seems that the kid's father has just vanished into thin air. If we knew what regiment he was in, we might find it a bit easier. Ten years of records is a lot of blood and sweat.'

The editor sat back in his chair. 'That's what journalism is Tweety my boy – blood, sweat, and occasional tears; another thing is a hunch. Now something made me think of this.' He sifted through the assortment of papers on his desk. 'Do you remember, back in '58, the case of the man found in the River Roding?'

'No Ed, I was still doing my national service then.'

'Three boys found the body of a man in the river. It was inside the grounds of that private school' – he glanced down the page on his desk – 'apparently, the police interviewed four boys from the village.'

'What happened about the body, sir?'

'Oh it turned out that it was an inmate of the asylum. They didn't name him, just said that he escaped and fell from the bridge in the dark and drowned. The police had ruled out foul play and seemed satisfied that there was nothing to indicate otherwise.'

'You think there is a connection?'

'Not necessarily to the event but the place, Tweety – the village; it is a closed enclave. No one knows anything about what goes on in there, and the kids are rarely seen outside of the place.'

Leslie scanned the report and made a note of the names of the officers involved in the investigation. He wished he could somehow let the journalists know that they were on the right track. A gust of wind from the open window sent papers in all directions.

Tweety jumped up and closed the window. He helped pick up the papers from the floor. As he put the papers back on the desk, he glanced at the police article. 'Sir? Why did they underline "foul play" do you think?'

'What do you mean?' He snatched the papers from Tweety's hand. Sure enough, the words had a red line under them. 'That was not there just now, I swear it.'

'Perhaps some ink on the floor… Strange though.'

Leslie had no idea how the line had appeared. It was not his doing, or was it? He had wished he could tell them, and it had happened, although they could just as easily have missed it.

***

It was a long drive to Felixstowe, and the traffic was horrendous. The editor had found the name and address of a woman known to foster children from children's homes; it was a long shot but worth trying. Tweety would have telephoned to save the journey, but there was no number recorded for her address.

He had already been to Salford that week and spoken to the kid's mother. She had remembered that her husband was in the Royal Artillery in 1953 but said that he never spoke about his army days. She couldn't say where he'd served, although that information may have been in the court records when they divorced; it may be another lead.

He pulled up outside an old semi-detached house that had seen better days but was now showing signs of neglect. He parked and took a stroll to the end of the street. The road became a farm track leading to an assortment of cattle sheds and other outbuildings beyond a field of maize; he went back to the house and rang the bell.

A man of about thirty answered the door. 'I wish to speak to Mrs Morton if that is possible?'

The man looked the reporter up and down. 'Is she expecting you?'

'No, I would have telephoned, but I couldn't find a number.' Replied Tweety

'So who might you be then?' the man asked.

'Sorry, the name's Bird, Harry Bird. I am writing an article about children in care – you know, how they get to be there, what sort of care they get, and how people like Mrs Morton take them in. Giving up their own time to care for the children of others—'

'I see. Will her name be in the article?'

'Not if she wishes to remain anonymous. I have other sources if she is not interested. I wanted to concentrate on the foster parent angle.' The reporter assured him.

'You had better come in then. Mum's not well. It's her legs; she's suffered with them for years.'

He showed the reporter into a dingy front room where a large woman sat in an armchair with one leg resting upon a footstool. Both her legs were heavily bound with thick crepe bandages. 'Mum, this is Mr Bird. He wants to talk to you about fostering. I'll leave the two of you to talk, got to see to my pigeons.'

Tweety removed his notebook and pencil and began to ask innocent questions about fostering in general. Mrs Morton was a real character. She may have been infirm, but she had a great memory and a sense of humour. Tweety scribbled notes and interjected with questions here and there. He let her talk until he felt he could direct the conversation to the information he wanted. He stayed for three hours, letting the woman rattle off her anecdotes and tales of sadness when children became adopted or returned to the home. When he had the information he wanted, he thanked her and headed back to his car.

***

During the journey home, Tweety kept thinking about the line in red ink. *If there had been ink on the desk or the floor, it would have stained other sheets of paper. And how was it that the words 'foul play' had appeared to be underlined? Surely a spill of ink would have made an irregular blotch.* How he hated the rush hour on a Friday evening.

***

Over the weekend, Tweety pored over the reams of army information. It was everything he could get regarding the Essex regiment of the RA. He spent all day Saturday and well into the night. The next morning, he had breakfast and returned to where he had left off the night before. He discovered that they had been in action in Cyprus and the Mau Mau Uprising in Kenya during the mid to late fifties. There were reports from the field but no mention of Will Johns. He was not on any of the records relating to those injured or killed in action. Maybe his wife had it wrong; it must have been another regiment.

An idea struck him; he checked the birth record for Will Johns, and his parents were recorded as living in Hampshire. He must have lived his childhood there. He may have joined the Royal Hampshire Regiment. That would be his next line of enquiry but for now he needed to keep Ed up to speed, the editor hated being uninformed of progress, or the lack of it.

***

'Sit down Tweety, you make the place look untidy' Ed chuckled.

'Sir, I talked to Mrs Morton on Friday. She remembered the Johns children very well. She said they were adopted. She didn't know by whom, but that chap called Thompson from St Vincent's was involved. She said he had made all the arrangements – a chauffeur in a big black Wolseley collected them. Must have been a well-off family she thought, and she said the driver had a coat of arms on his cap. She remembered it quite well, a sword over a cross and the words "Cor aut Mors". It means "Heart or Death"; it's to do with morals, duty, and loyalty verses lack of respect or integrity. It turns out she used to teach Latin. Well I've looked it up and guess what I found—'

'The Woodford family motto' interrupted Ed, 'I have been doing some research of my own. Did you know that the Woodford family own the Village for Children and the asylum? That's on top of god knows how many companies.'

Tweety was peeved that the editor had stolen his thunder. He crossed over to the window and started searching around the floor.

'What the devil's your problem?' demanded the editor.

The reporter continued searching the floor as he spoke. 'On Friday, I just could not get that red ink out of my head. I can't find any stain here, and I'm sure if you had spilled ink, you would have remembered. It seemed so strange that it made a straight line under the two words, 'foul play'. You said that it was not there when you read the sheet the first time.'

The editor looked puzzled. 'I swear it was not there. I only use a red pencil to correct copy, and I don't have red ink in my office.'

The reporter grinned at his editor. 'Odd that it involved the village, and here we are talking about it again.'

The editor huffed. 'Now you're not going to get started on some supernatural mumbo jumbo. Come on; get that info on the Tigers.'

'Tigers, sir?'

'Yes, the Royal Hampshire regiment; it's their nickname. God, you youngsters think you know it all.'

***

Leslie had visited Tweety several times and was aware of the work he had been putting in. He admired the man's tenacity. Faced with the huge tasks ahead of him still, he plodded on like a Suffolk Punch, steady and reliable.

It lifted the boy's spirits to know that Tweety and Ed were doing all in their powers to find his father, he felt sure that they would not abandon their quest, at least he sincerely hoped they would not. It could end in heartbreak for Leslie if the research revealed that his father was dead, but it would finally put to rest the uncertainty that tormented him.

Leslie liked the way Ed's mind worked, his hunches and his inexhaustible snippets of knowledge that appeared to lead him in the right direction. And he was the most endearing of Scotsmen with his humour and concern.

***

It was a week later when Tweety reported back to the editor. 'Sir, I've been up to the village, but the maid told me no one is available to comment. I did some digging around and found that the chap Thompson made a visit to the Village a couple of weeks ago, after I had tried to get the info from him. It may be something or nothing.'

'Okay, what plans do have you for the weekend?'

'Well I thought about going to visit my parents, have Sunday lunch with them and—'

'Put that on hold for now. Those are for you,' the editor said pointing to a stack of boxes in the corner.

Harry opened the top one; it contained files from the Royal Hampshire records. In dismay he said, 'This will take me weeks to wade through.'

'If you start now, you'll get done quicker then, won't you?' Ed said with a wicked grin.

***

Having left the reporter to his research, Leslie paid a brief visit to his friend Perry before returning home.

Perry told Leslie that he'd completed the cipher, '—and now it is up to you lad to unravel the meaning.'

'Well done Perry, a brilliant job indeed, I am most indebted to you for your hard work.' He told his friend about the work the reporter had been doing and how he was closing in on the village. 'He still has a long way to go, and hopefully he and Ed may find my father as well.'

Perry looked a little sceptical. 'You're still convinced he's alive then?'

'I have to believe it, Perry. It gives me hope.'

Perry apologised and turned their attentions back to the cipher. They considered the three lines: I raise a monument to him. No demons can your will arrest. So make we oaths that we may rue.

'The lines are out of context, but they appear to me to have something to do with the death of Sir Howard's brother. I do not know why, but I am convinced of it. It looks as though it refers to some kind of marker or tribute – an intention, possibly involving strong opposition and a promise made and regretted. This will need some research and a great deal of thought.'

Perry looked forlorn. 'What should I do now that the cipher's done?'

'Well, you could play with those lines and see if there are other interpretations you could come up with. A thesaurus would be useful, but I can't bring one with me unfortunately.'

***

'So how was your weekend?' the editor said with an impish grin.

The poor reporter looked haggard. 'You always talk about making contacts in this game. Do you have anyone in Military Intelligence who you trust with your life?'

The smile slid from the editor's face. 'For what reason?'

'There you go.' Harry dropped a bunch of documents onto the desk.

'Are you going to tell me or do I have to wring it out of you?'

'A name came up several times with regard to Military Intelligence and attachments to other units, and it seems that they often recruited from the ranks, sir. They chose soldiers who had distinguished themselves in action, especially if they had the Military Medal or the Distinguished Conduct Medal. Colonel Alastair Woodford, Intelligence Corps, was instrumental in the recruitment and training process. He was also stationed in Kenya and Cyprus, involved in intelligence gathering.'

'So you think he may have something to do with the Johns boy's missing father?'

'It is possible but not certain; I need to establish if they met or that Will was recruited. Another idea struck me, so I traced all the records I could get hold of relating to court martials. There are none that I can link to Will.'

'This is some task, laddie – up against the Military Intelligence lot. I won't ask how you came by the records, but you realise we can't use them – OSA, the Official Secrets Act.'

'Oh, I am aware of that. We just need something to point us in the right direction Ed. I still have a box and a half to get through, so I'll get on with that, after I have checked the electoral register at the town hall. I want to know if Vance is at the village. I also need some information from Companies House on the Woodford empire.'

'I can get that for you. An old friend of mine...' Ed tapped his finger against his nose, a gesture Tweety had seen many times before.

Chapter 10

The Explorations

Leslie stopped at the gate of the vicar's cottage. He had been there a few times, mostly with Paul, but it had been some time since they chatted. As usual, Reverend Donald Moxon was weeding and tidying the borders. 'Hello, Leslie. How are you?'

'Very well, thank you sir. And how are you?'

'I've told you before to call me Don; I do detest being called sir.'

'You have been very busy with the borders. They look delightful Don.'

'I was just going to reward my efforts with a cup of tea. Would you care for one?'

The vicar led the boy into the house and sat in the kitchen.

They discussed the plants in the borders and the weather, the problem slugs and aphids, the swimming, the boy's studies, and the damage done by rabbits in the rear garden. The vicar was most annoyed about the rabbits. 'They destroyed my vegetable plot. Here come see for yourself.' He led the boy through the back door and out into a long garden. There were shrubs and flower borders, but it was mostly set out into vegetable plots. The damage by the pests was all too evident. The gnawed stumps of lettuce and ragged, lacy cabbage leaves all around were a gardener's worst nightmare.

The garden extended toward a wooded area that acted as a natural windbreak to the garden. There was the sound of water trickling over pebbles in a nearby brook and the warbling of robins, blackbirds and thrushes trying to out-sing each other. Leslie asked the vicar if he could wander along the brook.

'Of course lad. Make yourself at home.'

The man sat on a stump and mopped his face and brow. Leslie wandered off along the edge of the wood.

The breeze caught the branches of the birch trees, stirring them gently and creating a wonderful rustling that mingled with the tinkling sound of the water, softly tumbling down a sloping stony bank and creating a brook at the bottom. To Leslie, the sounds were a reflective period in a symphony performed by Mother Nature's orchestra.

The boy dipped his hand in the water and found that it was icy cold. And looking up and down the bank, he noticed several rivulets of water trickling down to the brook. 'This must be a spring,' he said quietly. 'The doctor's house would be on the same east west axis, and he had a stream in his garden.' He had not noticed a stream at Howard House, unless it was beyond the back wall of the garden.

The adventurous boy picked his way between the birches rising up the steep bank. At the ridge, he turned in the direction of the school and proceeded to make his way along it. The trees beyond the ridge gave way to elm, ash, and the occasional oak. He decided to keep to the ridge, as the part of the woodland below had a surfeit of brambles and undergrowth.

He could no longer see the brook below to his left; he could just make out the roof of the school through the thicket. He followed the ridge and then could hear the brook to his right; it ran a short distance underground and came up again. He turned in the direction of the sound of the water and stumbled down the far side of the ridge. Beyond dense clumps of ferns and brambles, he could hear the water spouting from its subterranean retreat.

He followed badger's trails around the obstacles and down another small bank to the edge of the water. The brook had become a stream somewhere underground. Perhaps there were other springs feeding into it. He followed the bank and reached a place where the stream turned sharply to the right. Another brook coming from the left joined the stream at this point. *This must be the one from the lodge,* he thought. He followed the stream, aware that it would bring him back towards the thickets behind the wood at the vicar's house and as he progressed along the bank, the sides became higher.

Looking far downstream, he saw a wooden bridge made from roughly hewn tree trunks. It was crude but effective. When he reached it, he cautiously crossed the bridge and made his way through the tangle of fallen branches and undergrowth, carefully placing his feet to avoid getting caught up. He looked up and stopped dead.

In front of him was a clearing and, within it, the remains of a wooden cabin or shed. It was dilapidated beyond repair. Planks of worm-eaten and rotted wood crumbled to the touch. As Leslie pushed open the door, it fell inward with a clatter and a shower of crumbled splinters.

Leslie looked around him and thought, *what a great place for a child to play. A hidden shack, a dense wood with steep banks and a stream. One could be on a deserted island foraging for food, living off fish from the stream and fruits and berries from the trees. Here you could be whatever you wished – a pirate burying your treasure, a conquistador invading the Americas, a fugitive from the posse. The extent of ones' imagination would be the only limit in this wild land.'*

He realised that he had been gone for some time and started to make his way back. He moved quickly and carefully up the steep bank amongst the thickets and arrived panting at the top of the ridge. He made his way down the other side of the bank to where the spring formed the brook. He could see the vicar, asleep upon the tree stump in the garden. He gently shook the slumbering man and said, 'I think I should go now, Don.'

The vicar snorted and shook himself. 'Sorry. I must have dozed off. What time is it?'

***

Several days later, Leslie returned to the newspaper offices and saw Ed talking on the telephone— 'So what's the procedure then laddie? One of your men gets captured by the enemy, and he's held captive for years. What do you lot do? Give up on him? Send a telegram to his family and wipe your hands of him?'

'It's not that way at all, Eddy. We do everything in our power to rescue and recover our servicemen. The problem is when we don't know they are captive, who has them, or where they may be. Sometimes when a conflict is over, the captives are just left to die. The enemy doesn't always follow the rules, you know.'

Tweety walked in on the editor's conversation with his 'contact'. The editor indicated that he should be silent and sit.

'So how would you record that sort of thing? And would it be subject to the Official Secrets Act?' Ed asked.

'If it involved a current operation, then yes, OSA rules would apply.'

'How long do the rules apply after the event?'

'Well currently it is a hundred years.'

'You mean that if a British soldier could be out there somewhere as a captive, no one can talk about it for a hundred years?'

'You take this all wrong Edward. Within the service, it can be discussed and acted upon. But outside of the service, it's a different matter. You see, you never know who you are talking to—'

'Believe me, Major. There are far more moles and traitors inside the service than out. Look, do me the favour you owe me, and we can call it quits. Find me all you can on these men Will Johns and Colonel Woodford. Believe me, it is very important to us, and to the children of Will Johns.'

Tweety heard the click on the phone as the contact ended the conversation. Ed put the phone down slowly and faced Tweety. 'You know, laddie, I think we are going to have some meat with our gravy.' He smiled with his customary cheeky grin. 'My contact knew Will Johns and the colonel. He is going to get all the info he can on both of them. He did say that they knew each other, he witnessed their meeting in Kowloon. The intrigue excites me and gives me the youth and strength I thought I had left far behind me.'

'It is funny to me that you have so many contacts in the military services, as you refer to them, but you never speak of your own service days.'

'Thankfully those days are well behind me laddie and are best left there, in the past where they belong.'

***

Mr Wallace arrived to check Leslie. He prodded and probed and checked his pulse, eyes, reflexes, and movements. 'I am satisfied that the patient is now fully recovered, Sir Alastair. However, should you need my services again, please do not hesitate to call me.'

The dean shook his hand, and the two men left the room together, chatting like old friends, leaving the boy to get dressed.

***

Mary was in one of her bossy moods. 'Are you going to eat that or just keep playing with it?' she demanded.

Leslie put down his knife and fork. 'I am not really hungry today. I was thinking of walking up to the vicar's house. Do you want to come with me?'

She sneered and looked with distain at her young brother. 'That creep? I would not go near him. He gives me the shivers.'

'He isn't so bad, he is quite a nice man in fact. See you later then.' He went to the hall and put on his boots and jacket.

The dean was away on business and would not be back until late.

The boy arrived at the vicar's house, but instead of going in, he passed by and continued to the stores. He entered through the gateway and headed up the road that circled around to the delivery doors. With everything closed and no one about, he left the road and continued up towards the bank of trees at the far end of the yard. He heard voices coming from behind the wall that ran along the side of the yard. He ducked into the cover of the trees. He did not know why he'd done that. He could roam wherever and whenever he pleased.

It had dawned on him while he was in the garden that there were always people around him, discrete and almost unnoticed – Joan washing windows outside the back of the house or Susan sweeping the path or the summerhouse, when he studied, the tutors. In the library, his friend McManus was with him. In the games room, his sister was there, or one of the maids would be polishing or dusting. He just wanted to enjoy some time alone in the open air – to explore like a boy; he would not be a boy for much longer.

The voices faded, and Leslie inched himself up through the trees screening him from the yard. He could not hear the voices any more so he moved on. Keeping low among the scrubs and ferns, he reached the top of the ridge. He wanted to explore the terrain to the right of the vicar's house. He lowered himself down the far side of the ridge to keep out of sight and negotiated the bramble-strewn bank down to the stream. He crossed over the bridge and turned to his right. He found the going quite strenuous; the fallen trunks and branches hindered his progress. The bank reared up higher and steeper, whilst the stream wound its way downward towards the Roding. He followed it as far as he could go.

He found himself on the far bank of the river, where the bridge crossed, and it was contained by the high walls of the village. He retraced his footsteps to a point where he could veer right and follow the wall. He slogged uphill in the swampy terrain, his boots creating squelching noises as he trod the sodden earth.

He reached a gulley, where a constant trickle of water escaped through a large iron grille set into the base of the wall. At this point, a channel allowed the water to flow down to the stream at the bottom of the hill. He carefully negotiated the space between the banks, and clinging to the grille, he edged his way across. The stench of the fetid water was revolting; he leapt the last two feet to the far bank and followed the wall.

He arrived at a place that he recognised; the crumbling section of wall formed an open V shape. He cautiously stepped over the rubble and brambles and stood looking up at the towering red brick walls of the asylum. It was just as he had seen it in his visits – red and austere, depressing and oppressive. Seeing no-one about, he hurried to the cover of the range of outbuildings and looked in the windows.

They were old workshops, disused for years. He took in the woodturning lathes and band saws in the nearest one and realised this one had been a carpentry shop. He found a pottery room and a sewing room, complete with dust-covered mannequins and decaying remains of hanks of cloth covered in moth cocoons. There were the shattered remains of greenhouses long since abandoned and left to rot. He stepped carefully over the broken glass. If he were to meet with an accident here, he would be in trouble. Nobody knew where he was.

He edged his way around the ruins taking care not to be seen or to endanger himself. When he reached the side of the building, he could see the access road that led to the main entrance. He retreated and went back the way he came.

Once back through the gap in the wall, he continued along the bank. The ground sloped steeply downwards from the base of the wall toward the stream, and it made walking difficult. He held onto branches, scrub and rocks, anything to steady himself. After a while, the terrain levelled out, and the going became less laboured. He traced the line of the wall for a half hour. He calculated that he must be somewhere to the north of the cabin. He turned from the wall and slowly made his way down the bank. He followed animal tracks down the wooded slope toward the distant stream. The slope levelled among the trees, but he had to negotiate briars and thick clumps of dense undergrowth, where he could, he detoured around them.

He found a stout pole, with which he beat the briars flat where there was no way around. The thorns snagged and grabbed at his clothes every now and then, and flailing, spiked tendrils tried to take him prisoner at every chance. He fought his way toward the cabin, aware of the alarm calls of blackbirds and the loud flap and flutter of the pigeons as they scattered from the canopy above him. He was close to the cabin now but confronted by a huge thicket of briars at least eight feet high. There was no way through, so he looked for a way around. He spent some time skirting around the obstacle in his path.

At one point, he looked up at the thorny barricade; he could make out what appeared to be some roof tiles within the mass of briars. There was a small brick building inside – captured and imprisoned by these invading tendrils. It excited his imagination and his curiosity. He gathered up some strong sticks and branches and used them as levers and props to create a gap in the thicket. There was a brick wall with a glassless window. He poked his head through the window and peered inside. It was dark; the briars blocked light from entering the interior. He stood with his hands cupped against the sides of his face and let his eyes adjust to the dark. He could make out a door on one side and another window. There were benches set out in rows like in a chapel and an altar at the far end.

He realised that he had been gone for some time, and it must be nearly lunchtime by now. He retraced his steps away from the wall and removed the props. He would come back and investigate another time when he could be better prepared.

***

'Just look at the state of you Leslie, it looks as though you were attacked by a hoard of wild cats. Wash up. It is lunchtime.'

Mary would not understand if he told her what he had been up to, so he said nothing.

After lunch, Leslie went to the library. Mr McManus was away on holiday, so he had the room to himself. He knew where the books on the Woodford family were and selected a tome about the family history. He had read and recorded every word previously, but he wanted to check some details he may have missed.

A Woodford family home stood in these grounds for centuries. It was originally a huge estate in what is now the county of Essex, with its many villages, farms and cottages. Sir Giles's father had the village built to house the seasonal labour necessary for harvesting. The asylum, a large redbrick building was originally a school, hospital, and training centre. He had encouraged his employees to educate their children, as many had been illiterate. Due to the growing mechanisation of farms, and the government's provision of national schools for child education, Sir Giles sold off much of the estate piece by piece. He allowed his tenant farmers to purchase from him at low prices and to repay him over the term of their tenancy.

Leslie paid particular attention to the original layout of the Village. It had been much larger and had extended far beyond the boundary of the Roding to the south. At the northern end, a large farm had also formed a part of the estate; the farm had been sold to the tenant farmer and his family. The farmer was in his late forties when he decided to purchase. The farmer could not afford to repay the cost within his remaining working life, and so an agreement had been made to pass the remaining debt onto his three sons, who would inherit.

There was mention of a chapel that stood between the farm and the manor house. The farmer had elected to draw his boundary along the line of what was now the wall that Leslie had followed. The book noted that the farmer considered the land to the south of this line unworkable due to the terrain and the rocky hillside and woods. As a result of the farmer's decision, Sir Giles had concluded that the access to the chapel from the south side was impractical. Therefore, he'd had a new chapel built, the one that still stands today.

As the size of the estate had reduced, so did the need for a large school and training centre. The large redbrick building became a private institute for the care of war veterans suffering mental and severe physical injury. That was also when they'd erected the huge walls around it and the site the village now occupied. The estate worker's houses were no longer in use, and that prompted Sir Giles to turn the remaining estate into a refuge for orphaned children. He built the smaller school and hospital and had the six houses enlarged to accommodate eight children and six staff in each. It became a project that he was immensely proud of, and over the years, the village built a reputation for good education and high results and became his crowning glory.

Therefore, the bramble and woodbine imprisoned building Leslie had discovered, was the old chapel the farmworkers had used. Leslie could see the logic of abandoning it. He was thinking about what he might need on a return visit to investigate the ruin. A thought nagged at him; there was something he had missed. He checked the book again – nothing. He took another book down and scanned through it; again nothing. He looked carefully at the plan of the village and the old estate, and there it was on the plan, what he searched for was faintly marked, at the back of Howard House, a mausoleum. What had nagged at him was that he had not seen a graveyard in his explorations of the village. All those generations of the Woodford family who had lived and died had to be buried somewhere on the estate.

He had seen the wall at the farthest part of the garden and where a section to the left, jutted beyond the rest of the garden. He had not been down there, but that was where he was going now. He replaced the tome in its appropriate slot and headed outside to the rear garden.

***

The part of the garden he explored was a long tract of lawn, still contained within walls. It was about two hundred feet long and thirty feet wide. It had borders of shrubs and poplars. Halfway along the right-hand wall Leslie saw a pair of padlocked tall wrought iron gates. Peering through, he could see a rectangular formal garden of neatly clipped box hedging and wide steps leading down to a granite mausoleum in the centre. A single line of tall, dark evergreen cypress trees surrounded it. A flagstone path ran around the outer edge of the enclosure, bordered by poplars close to the walls. Above the entrance to the mausoleum was the family coat of arms. There were no flower borders, just the trees swaying gently in the breeze and the sound of the rustling leaves. It was a peaceful and somewhat comforting setting, with the entire dynasty reunited in one place in peaceful rest for eternity.

***

It rained endlessly for a week, for now putting paid to Leslie's exploration of the old chapel. Negotiating the steep banks would be treacherous with the ground sodden and the loose rocky soil.

A visit to Perry had been unproductive with regard to the lines of verse. They'd sat and talked. Perry had recounted his tales of campaigns and skirmishes, his family, and his childhood. Leslie had talked of the old chapel and the cabin in the woods, of the feeling of being an explorer, discovering artefacts from some long-lost civilisation. Perry had listened intently and noticed the boy's excitement as he spoke, 'Do you think that what you've found has anything to do with the cipher?'

The boy had considered the question. 'Hmm, I cannot say really. I need to see inside the mausoleum and the chapel. However, something is for sure. I am drawn to the chapel, like I was drawn here to you. You see,

Perry, when I do this floating thing, I think about someone or a place, and I find myself there. I did not know about you but ended up here.'

Perry had smiled. 'I guess the Arab boy did the same. It must be something to do with a desire to help somebody in a dire situation.'

Leslie thought about the grille in wall. 'I think I have found where the tunnel leads to, but there is no way I could open the grille or break through it.'

'Escaping this place has always been on my mind. But where would I go son? What would I live on? I have no family or money, nowhere to live. I need to get out of here legally.' Leslie saw that the man spoke with reason. To be outside as a fugitive was not an option. He would not last five days. The dean's people would track him down, or he would starve or freeze. If he were arrested for vagrancy, the police would bring him straight back here. There had to be some way to get Perry out and the man's situation worried Leslie immensely. He had said his goodbyes and reluctantly left his good friend in solitude in his squalid surroundings.

As he sat at his desk, the boy thought about his underground friend as hailstones hammered at the window. He really had no idea of how to set Perry free and felt such guilt for the way the man existed whilst he lived in the lap of luxury by comparison. Life to the boy did not seem fair, he himself had contributed nothing to society and yet he was cosseted and pampered. Perry and others like him, and perhaps he could include his father in this thought, had risked their lives and lost all that they left behind them.

***

To the ethereal boy, Tweety looked tired and drawn as he sat in Ed's office, the dark circles under his eyes were evidence of late nights and lots of reading. He had researched all the documents supplied to him. He related to the editor how he had found Will's enlistment records. However, there were no discharge records at all. By all accounts, he was still in the army. But where? Leslie listened with great interest and attention.

The reporter told of another meeting with the boy's mother in Salford. He had explained that they were trying to trace Will but without luck so far. She said that, if the father were dead, she would apply to have her custody reinstated, as she wanted her children back. She told of how they'd had four children at the time of the divorce and shortly after the divorce she had another. The court had given her custody of all of them because her husband was a serving soldier. He had appealed and won custody of Mary and Leslie. Then what did he do? He put them in a children's home. She was bitter and angry about what he had done. How she hated him. She would have tried to get custody then, to keep the children from the home, but she was a single mother struggling to cope with the three children she had.

Leslie was shocked, the news nearly floored him. He had other siblings, another sister and two brothers! Mary must have known and said nothing all these years. He could have been living with his mother instead of in these institutions. What a different kind of life would he have led?

***

'What is the matter? You look like you found a penny and lost a shilling,' said Mary, over the supper table.

The boy looked up from his plate and said softly but inquisitively, 'Mary, why did Mum and Dad get divorced?'

She had expected this question for years, and she could not understand why he had waited so long to get around to it. 'I do not know for sure. I can recall that they had many arguments whenever dad was home, but he was away an awful lot of the time. Maybe she wanted him to leave the army and stay with us. Remember, I was only five at the time. They would not discuss their marital problems with me.' The explanation was sound and convincing, she hoped

Leslie thought that if she knew something, she was not about to tell him. There was only one thing for it. He had only visited locally. He did not know if he could visit Salford.

Chapter 11

A Disappointment and a Treat

The house was a terraced cottage in a rundown part of the town. A row of dustbins punctuated the pavement on each side of the road; none of the houses had front gardens, so the front doors opened onto the pavement. Each door had a painted doorstep, red or black. Two women rested from sweeping the pavement, leaning on their brooms and chatting. Several children in the street were kicking a ball made of rolled-up newspapers and bound with elastic bands and string. Their clothes were clean but tatty; their shoes were scuffed and had seen better days.

Inside the house, the furniture looked old and worn and the rug threadbare. A woman stood at the kitchen sink with her back to him, washing clothes. Her sleeves were rolled up to the elbows and her forearms covered in soapsuds. The wispy trail of smoke from a cigarette meandered upwards. Her hair was blonde with dark brown roots that showed between the rows of curlers and hairpins. 'Tony,' she shouted, 'did you get those potatoes I asked you for?'

Footsteps sounded as a boy, perhaps a year older than Leslie, descended the stairs. 'Sorry, mam, I forgot them.'

'What? One simple thing I asked you to do. Go and get them now, or there's no spuds for supper you bloody useless urchin.'

The boy ran out into the street. The smell of mutton stew pervaded the kitchen, and the lid bobbed and clattered monotonously on the large, chipped enamelled saucepan.

The window beyond the sink looked out onto a despairing, uncared-for garden with a wooden shed, its door hanging from the rusted and broken hinges. The lawn had bare patches, and a scruffy emaciated mongrel dog fixed to a chain. The dog barked incessantly, trying to reach the food bowl that was just out of reach.

'Shut up, you wretch, or I'll wring your scrawny bloody neck' the woman screamed at the dog. 'Peter, go and sort that dog out before I bloody well I kill it,' she shouted.

'Yeah, in a minute, mam.' The boy's voice came from upstairs.

'No now. He's driving me mad with his noise. You wanted the damn thing. You bloody well sort him out.'

The boy leapt down the stairs three at a time. As he passed through the kitchen, he stopped and lifted the saucepan lid. There was a loud slap as his mother smacked his wrist with her soapy hand. 'The dog, now I said.'

The boy had tears welling up in his eyes. A large red handprint emblazoned his wrist. He went out of the back door and sat huddled up with the dog as it licked him excitedly and wagged its tail like a windscreen wiper in a storm.

'What's for tea, mam?' A girl of about twelve sauntered in from the street. She was about to lift the saucepan lid but stopped.

Her mother glowered at her. 'Go lay the table.'

The girl went into the next room.

The mother lit another cigarette from the stub of the other. She placed the dripping clothes into a large enamelled bowl and carried it out to the garden. Leslie watched as she hung the clothes on the line, the cigarette protruding from the side of her mouth and her squinting as the smoke stung her eyes. She picked up a long pole and propped up the line, wiped her hands on her wet apron, and put the empty bowl in the shed. 'When is your brother going to fix that sodding bloody door?'

The boy cowered, hugged his dog and said nothing.

***

Leslie felt a sense of relief lying in his bed that night. He recalled the day he and Mary had arrived at St Vincent's. It had been dark and cold, and the orange glow from the light outside the door had seemed warm and welcoming. The house had been full of little girls. They'd gathered around him excitedly, making lots of fuss and stroking his golden hair. 'What a beautiful boy,' one had said. 'Such lovely hair,' said another. He never saw his father leave; they never said goodbye.

He felt that, as much as he had wished for a normal family life, he was better off than his siblings in Salford. He felt such pity and guilt for their situation. He had put out of his mind the beatings and humiliations he had suffered in the first children's home. Those thoughts were where they should be – shut away and forgotten. At least here at the village, they treated him well; he was never beaten or threatened. Never had he been punished for a mistake or an oversight. In the village the people he interacted with, encouraged him and built his confidence. He felt he had grown into a person they could be proud of. The visit to Salford had left him with a bitter, sour taste in his mouth, and he hoped his mother never regained custody of him and his sister.

He did not stay to see her current husband, a violent man apparently, who liked to drink a lot. Most of the family's money went to support the local pub and his drinking pals.

***

The dean was in the west wing sorting through an assortment of reports. Susan knocked and waited for the reply.

'Just a moment,' the dean said. He hurriedly placed the papers face down and then went and unlocked the door.

Susan entered carrying a tray with tea and biscuits and placed it on a side table. 'You should eat something, sir.'

After she left, he locked the door and poured a cup of tea. He sat munching on the biscuits and deep in thought regarding a proposal he had discussed with his lawyers.

He had expressed his desire to adopt Leslie, even if it meant adopting the boy's sister as well. All the lawyers had tried to talk him out of it – pointing out that the boy could not inherit the family title; his son James would inherit that. If he wished to leave the Foundation to Leslie, and James were to contest the will, there could be years of court battles. They had reminded Sir Alastair that his estate was worth many millions of pounds. How could he be sure that the boy would be capable of running such a massive enterprise or that he would even want to? Sir Alastair felt that those closest to him were dismissing his wishes. He would not hand his empire over to James, a man who would squander the fortune accrued by him and his ancestors. He had searched for years for the best candidate for the task and had seen the future in this strange but wonderful boy he had set his heart on.

***

Walking down the avenue, Leslie thought of Rob as he glanced at the clumps of daffodils and crocuses on his way. The gardener had been right; the flowers were nearly finished now. But when they were in full bloom, they were a picture of colour. He turned into the wooded area between River House and Epping House. It was a cool sunny day with a slight breeze. The dappled sunlight danced in the canopy above, sending flickers of light skipping across the leaf-carpeted woodland floor. The inhabitants sounded occasional alarm calls as the boy disturbed their hunting grounds. He stood for a few moments watching a green woodpecker foraging in the leaf litter for grubs and insects. He marvelled at the beautiful dark green of its back and wing feathers, contrasting with the yellow-green underside and the bright red cap on its head. The bird stopped, observed a jay approaching, and then flew off. Leslie walked on, taking in all the wonders that nature revealed to him. He often walked in the woods and meadows. It was his way of forgetting his worries and putting aside the pressures of study and research. The wood thickened as he neared the centre, and less light penetrated through the dense ash and elm trees.

***

The dean sent for Mary and Leslie. There was something he wanted to discuss with them. Susan reported to Sir Alastair, 'Master Leslie is not in the house sir. He left after breakfast wearing his boots and jacket.'

'He has probably gone down to the river Susan. No matter. I will speak to them later.'

***

The boy continued, unaware that the dean had asked to see him. He came to a circular clearing amongst the trees where a clump of woodbine formed a tangled mound. He removed some of the tendrils and found the lid of a circular brick well. The lid was made of iron and padlocked to an iron frame fixed around the outside. There was no way that he could open it without the key. He felt a little disappointed but understood that, if this was the well Caldwell had fallen into, it made sense to take precautions to prevent someone else doing the same.

He decided to take a different route back to Howard House. He walked along what once must have been an avenue. He could hear shingle beneath his feet, but mossy grasses covered it. Where the sun penetrated, it cast golden beams of light, highlighting clouds of midges as they danced in sprightly courtship. He reached the end of the avenue and entered an open area that may have been a lawn. It appeared as a lawn, the grass neatly mown by the rabbits that had made it their dining room. He crossed the dining table and entered the wood on the other side. An old path led him to the back of the small hospital. He skirted around the building, along the access drive, and out onto the roadway. It was too late now to explore the old chapel. And besides, he did not have his equipment with him.

***

After lunch, the dean asked Mary and Leslie to join him in the west wing of the library; they looked at each other with serious expressions. 'What have you been up to now?' she whispered to her brother in a demanding tone.

'Nothing,' he said innocently, 'nothing at all.'

'Leslie, it has always been our custom here to allow the boys to have long trousers when they move to River House. I know that for you it is still some months away, but I have noticed that both of you are in need of some new clothes. I have arranged for you both to have a trip to London tomorrow. Leslie will come with me. Mary, you will be accompanied by Madame Silvestre. She is a lady of good taste and very knowledgeable regarding fashion. You may replace your entire wardrobe if you wish, but please be guided by her.'

A day out in London – this was something Leslie and Mary had never experienced before. Although they lived close to the city, they had never been there. And new clothes, long trousers – the excitement bubbled up inside him.

'We shall leave directly after breakfast. I need to attend some business for a short while, and then we will have the rest of the day to ourselves.'

Mary sat impassively; there was no change of expression or the slightest sign of excitement. Her lack of response confused Leslie, but he said nothing.

***

Jackson had the Bentley ready as they descended the entrance steps. Sir Alastair and Leslie stood aside to allow Madame Silvestre and Mary to sit in the back seat. Leslie joined them and Sir Alastair sat at the front.

The car stopped outside a boutique and Jackson held open the doors for the passengers to alight. Sir Alastair had a few words with him to arrange a pickup time; Leslie watched the car disappear into the bustling traffic. Madame took Mary by the hand and led her into the couturiers, and Sir Alastair guided Leslie down the street towards Saville Row. The shops had enticing displays set out in the window fronts; Leslie had never seen such variety of shops and restaurants.

They entered a tailor's shop, and Sir Alastair went directly to the owner. They shook hands. 'It is so good to see you again, Sir Alastair. And how may I be of service?'

Sir Alastair explained to the man what was required and turned to the boy. 'I will have to go now, but I should be back within a couple of hours. Mr Britton will take care of you until I return.' He strode off out into the street.

Mr Britton showed Leslie skeins of cloth – checks and stripes, dogtooth and tweed, greys and blues, and blacks and browns. The choice was astounding, and Leslie was not sure what he should choose. He asked Mr Britton what he would recommend.

'For sir, I think something to contrast with the fine head of hair, a navy blue or dark grey, or perhaps something to reflect your colouring, such as beige or a warm brown sir.'

Leslie stroked his chin whilst in deep thought. 'Do you have something that I could see, already made up?'

The man smiled. 'This is your first time to the tailors, sir?'

Leslie nodded.

'I thought so. We make your clothes to order, sir. This is not one of those stores that have "off-the-peg" suits, sir.'

Leslie considered the materials and textures, colours and patterns, and apologised for his indecision. 'I think I like the wool mix in charcoal, if that is all right.'

The man smiled again. 'But of course sir, and if I may say, a very astute choice.'

Later, with all the measurements taken, the manager offered Leslie a cup of tea or coffee whilst he awaited the dean's return. He had never tried coffee before, and that was why he chose it. This was a day of new experiences; he put two more sugar cubes in the coffee. It seemed to have a slightly bitter, burnt taste to it. He watched an elderly man trying on a half-made jacket. It looked as though it would fall apart at any moment.

The man pointed to the sleeves. 'Could you make them just a little longer for me?'

The assistant gripped the sleeve and ripped it off the jacket. He made a note of the length, and then they discussed the vent at the back, the style of the lapels, and whether there should be a buttonhole. How many buttons would he like on the sleeve, and should the pockets have a flap or not, straight across or angled?

The trip bell on the door signalled the arrival of Sir Alastair. He waved to Leslie as he made his way to the manager's desk. 'So, young man, what did you choose?'

The manager showed him the soft charcoal grey cloth. 'My word, the very cloth I would have chosen for you. Excellent.'

Sir Alastair and the manager chatted for a few moments. As they made their exit, the staff nodded and paid their respects.

'We shall need to return for a fitting next week,' the dean said.

They walked along the row of tailoring shops and stopped at a shirt makers' shop. They entered and perused a large selection of shirts wrapped in clear cellophane. The dean prompted Leslie to make his choice, and they left the shop with six shirts. They visited store after store, purchasing ready-made trousers and jackets, ties and pullovers, shoes, and a pair of boots.

At the last store, Sir Alastair instructed Leslie to select a change of clothes from their purchases and change into them. He emerged from the changing room in a pair of long beige trousers, a brown tweed sports jacket, a white shirt and cream-coloured tie, and a pair of brown brogue shoes. Sir Alastair was most suitably impressed.

Jackson met them at the end of the street and placed all the bags into the boot of the car. He then drove them to where they had left Madame and Mary. Jackson entered the shop and returned with the ladies.

Leslie could not believe the change in his sister. She wore a powder blue dress under a short white jacket with matching shoes and handbag. The dress accentuated her curves. She was no longer the girl who set out from Howard House that morning; she was a fine young lady. Jackson placed more bags in the boot and resumed his place at the wheel of the car; he drove them to Claridge's and dropped them off at the entrance.

The door attendant greeted them. 'Sir Alastair, good to see you again, sir.'

Sir Alastair pressed some money into the man's hand as he opened the doors for them to enter. The maître d'hôtel bowed slightly to Sir

Alastair and showed the party into the dining room. This was Leslie's first practical use of the French that he had learned. He consulted Madame on every menu item, ensuring that he interpreted correctly the fare on offer. Sir Alastair made his choice, as did Madame. Mary pondered the menu items, unable to make up her mind. Leslie announced that he would have the melon with Parma ham for hors d'oeuvre, followed by seared turbot with asparagus spears. Eventually, Mary made her choice. As she closed her menu, the maître d'hôtel appeared with a waiter who took their orders.

The dean ordered wines to complement the different dishes. Mary and Leslie had never tasted wine before, and Madame instructed them how they should drink it. The sommelier opened each bottle and poured a small amount of each for the dean to taste. He rejected one white wine and requested something less dry. They enjoyed their meal in the plush relaxing surroundings. An elderly couple with a young boy of about nine years of age sat at a table nearby. Leslie noticed that the boy wore long trousers and was so glad that the dean had suggested changing; he would have felt awkward and uncomfortable otherwise.

After the meal, the dean took them to Cartier's, saying that it was the modern way for young people to wear a timepiece. After they were shown a selection of wristwatches, the dean allowed Leslie and Mary to choose for themselves. Leslie chose a plain gold watch with a white face and brown leather strap. Mary chose a fine gold watch with a gold bracelet.

Over supper, they all agreed it had been a good day out. Jackson had driven them all across the city, and the dean had pointed out the most important landmarks.

***

Susan and Joan marvelled at the new clothes as they unpacked the many bags and placed the contents in the drawers and wardrobes. Susan wondered to herself why the master would have done such a thing. He had singled out these two from among the thirty-six children in the village, and they were living here, at the mansion. There had to be a very good reason that she was not privy to. Stealthily, a seed of jealousy planted itself in that innocent loving heart.

***

Susan had lived at the village since she was a small child. Her father died in the early years of the Second World War, and her mother had become a victim to tuberculosis a few months later. An aunt had cared for her until she was five years old. The aunt had become ill and could no longer give the care and attention required by a small child. She knew of the dean and had begged him to take the child into his care. He had been reluctant to do so at first because she had no special skills. However, he owed a debt to her father and had promised that, if anything should happen, he would look after the family.

Susan had been a trusted and reliable member of his household since the age of fifteen. She learned quickly and always completed the tasks set for her with flair and commitment. The dean was never aware of her feelings for him; she had worshipped him from a distance. He was the most handsome and intelligent man she had ever met, and his bearing and stature was everything she could desire in a man. His black piercing eyes captured her heart and her imagination. She never gave him any sign of how she felt. That would invite disaster if he did not feel the same about her. She waited patiently for a sign that might one day make her dreams a reality. In the meantime, she was content just to be near him, to hear his voice, to serve him. She had long ago mastered the art of suppressing her emotions and yearnings.

***

The dean called a meeting of housemasters; they assembled in the west wing of the library and sat around the large table at the centre of the room. They all stood as the dean entered. He bade them sit and placed a bundle of papers on the table before him. He welcomed them and outlined his plan for days out to London for the whole village. He had felt for some time that the environs of the village confined the children too much. Mixing with the outside world would be of benefit to them. They lived so near to the capital and yet knew of it only from books and school lessons. The trip he'd made with Leslie and Mary had opened his eyes to one of the failings of the village.

'We are shaping these children but denying them the interaction required to make them whole people.' He passed around some sheets of papers to the group. Each house master or mistress would take their charges to the city accompanied by the maids. There was a list of sights and a street map, much like a tourist guidebook would have. The dean felt that a journey by train and underground would be a good experience for the children. Once in the city, they could use the buses to travel from place to place.

He suggested discussing the list of sights beforehand, and the children could select the places to visit for themselves. A little democracy would be a good way to let them learn about negotiation and responsibility. Each house would arrange the trip on different days. As a part of their schoolwork, the children would write an essay about their experiences of the trip. The assembled group agreed the dean had proposed a most suitable distraction for the children. A break from the daily rounds of study and chores would be most beneficial to the children and adults as well.

Sir Alastair began to bring his plans together. By proposing the days out, he hoped to distract attentions from his focus on Leslie. He was treating the boy as a young man and would soon begin to initiate him into his world; he would take a measured systematic approach.

***

Leslie studied hard and completed his dissertation on 'Influences That Shaped the French Language'. He showed his completed thesis to Madame Silvestre for her opinion. She was amazed at how the boy could have drawn some of the conclusions stated in the work. The study books she had supplied had no such content, so she checked his reference list at the end of the work, where she noted the many books he had added to his reading list. She contacted her father at the Sorbonne, and he replied that this could be a work of some importance to academia and wanted to know all about the author and from where he had obtained his information.

The Spanish paper was in the final stages; there were some translations from Galician still to be completed and a section regarding Catalan.

The dean read the French paper and was suitably impressed. 'Madame, I think it is sterling work. I must thank you for your diligence and guidance. It is excellent work indeed.' He felt as though he was the proud father of a talented son. He had plans to reward all the hard work the young man had put into his studies, and he eagerly awaited the Spanish paper.

For days, Leslie spoke to no-one. His head was full of the content of his Spanish thesis. He wrote and rewrote the work in its entirety, in his mind. He had purchased some books from a specialist bookstore in London during their last visit, and those books had clarified for him the last passages needed to complete his studies. He was pleased with the work and submitted it to Professor Arias for his appraisal.

During his own studies, the professor had done a thesis that was similar to the one the boy had submitted. He felt it was unfortunate that the boy had not come to the same conclusions as himself. He discussed the work with the dean at great length, and they studied and discussed the paper's the relative pros and cons. The dean pointed out facts, and the professor would dismiss them as fiction, unreliable sources, and works of the imagination. He agreed that, as a whole, the work was very well written and researched, but he was sceptical with regard to authenticity. He had read some of the source materials annotated but had reservations as to their validity.

The dean concluded that the professor was exhibiting a somewhat biased attitude. He decided to submit the work to the college, and it would stand or fall on its own merits. If the work was accepted as a genuine study based on fact and reasoned conclusions, then the boy would pass. If dismissed, as the professor propounded, it would bring a sense of reality to the strange boy who lived in a world of literature. He realised that the boy had enjoyed a great deal of success in all his academic ventures. Nevertheless, life was also about balancing success and failure and learning to cope with both. Too much success may lead to overconfidence and an exaggerated sense of self-importance, and too many failures would lead to despair and a lack of self-worth.

***

His academic works submitted, Leslie now felt unencumbered by the constraints of endless study. He had not seen the studies as imprisoning but as time-consuming.

He had not visited anyone in a long while. He thought of his poor friend Perry languishing in that hellhole that he called home. How could he help his friend? He paid a short visit to the prisoner of the Asylum and then headed to Tweety's house to catch up on his progress.

Tweety was hard at work with his head buried in mounds of paperwork. He shoved the papers aside, went out to his kitchen, and put on the kettle; it was obvious to Leslie that the man desperately needed some more coffee to aid his concentration. When Tweety opened the refrigerator to get the milk, Leslie could see that he had beers and mixers chilling and the open cocktail cabinet in the lounge revealed that he had bottles of spirits, but he guessed that the man needed to maintain a clear head to untangle the puzzle that lay before him.

The reporter's notebook showed that Will had served in China, Cyprus, and Africa. Tweety had noted that Sir Alastair had also served in the same conflicts. The editor's informant in Military Intelligence confirmed a meeting between Will and Sir Alastair whilst they were in China. They must have met again on other occasions, perhaps in Cyprus or Africa. Tweety had a nagging feeling that told him he needed more information regarding British involvement in China. He needed to talk to someone who knew Will from the army. He scribbled into his notebook. He delved into the copious papers strewn across the table, and reading the documents again, he sorted them into a different sequence. Leslie felt such pity for the man; he had taken on a work of massive proportions. A lot of the information he had was hearsay and conjecture, he had very little in the way of fact. Leslie pondered how he could assist this man; after all, it would be in his own interest to find out what had become of his father.

***

The next day, Leslie visited Perry and told him of Tweety's work.

'My dear boy, he will never find out from official records. Most of what occurs goes unreported. What regiment was your father in?'

The boy gave Perry all the information that he had in relation to Will.

'Yes,' he exclaimed. 'The tigers were in Hong Kong, and so were the Mintell lot. It's what we called the Military Intelligence Service. I recall that Mintell approached some of our lads – the ones who already had medals, that is. One joined, and others didn't; the one who did join, a chap called Dwyer as I recall, they whisked him away immediately. We had no idea where he went to; it was all hush-hush you know. They offered a higher pay rate, and as you can guess, money was tight in those days. I heard say that the rate was the same as a junior commissioned officer at the time. It was a great inducement for an enlisted private with family back home, and a pension went with it. We had some foolhardy lads in our unit who took stupid risks with their own lives and those of the rest of the unit, just to get a medal and hoping for the same benefits. It was all so stupid – the lives lost to greed and fortune. I wept for many a fellow soldier who had chanced his arm in such a futile attempt. Mintell were probably responsible for more deaths than they realised.'

'Were you ever approached by Mintell?' asked the boy with avid interest.

'On two occasions, lad. I did not want the pension or the danger associated with it. I just wanted the war to end and to get back to my family and normal life, like many of my mates. We were there to do a job and get the hell out of it afterwards, and that's how I saw it.'

***

Leslie revisited Tweety. He sat in an armchair with his head in his hands, a cold cup of coffee on the table next to him; he had a look of desperation on his face. The editor wanted a story that he felt he could not supply; it was a tangled web without sufficient reference points to lead him in the right direction. This was all leading to dead ends. His frustration exploded with him throwing the papers across the living room floor. 'Damn that boy and what he started. Damn the father that does not exist. Damn the village that would not let me in. Damn the mountain of papers that reveal nothing to me. And damn Ed for the pressures.' He was at the end of his tether, with nothing in all this investigation that would lead to a conclusive story.

He sidled up to the cocktail cabinet, took down a bottle of scotch and a tumbler, poured a triple measure of the golden poison, and doused it with a splash of soda. After taking a large gulp he said aloud, 'It's one of my days off; I can do as I please in my own time. In my own home, I am lord and master, and if the fancy takes me, I can do whatever I want.' A belligerent mood overtook him. It was as though he was in conflict with some unseen foe as he swallowed another large gulp of the intoxicating liquid and then another and another. Within a few minutes, he emptied the glass. He poured another and turned on the record player.

He selected a blues album from his collection and sat in the armchair listening and sipping the scotch. Before the record ended, he was pouring another drink. He stripped off his clothes and strode around the room in his underwear with the tumbler in his hand. He kicked at the trousers and the shirt, sending them flying across the room. He scowled and derided the forces that had driven him to this state; he felt sick and rushed to the bathroom. He emerged sullen and red-eyed.

The drink had been a big mistake, and gathering up his clothes, he exited to the bedroom. He flopped onto the bed in a stupor and sank into a deep sleep.

Leslie felt that all of this was his doing, and the responsibility to find a solution was his. He studied the papers strewn across the room. After some time, he noticed a name on one of the sheets. He stared at the name transfixed. This man had won awards for bravery and gallantry, mentioned in despatches, he'd received numerous plaudits for his conduct in the face of the enemy. And then, ultimately, he'd been discharged on medical grounds after his second and most serious battle wound, with honour. There was no further record of this man, and Leslie knew why. It was sergeant Peregrine Collins. He concentrated on the name, hoping he could repeat the occurrence in the editor's office.

Nothing happened – no red line to indicate to Tweety that he should follow up on this name. It had no bearing on the case Tweety was working on, but it was of vital importance to Leslie.

Chapter 12

A day in the City and a Prayer Answered in the Chapel

The dawn sun leisurely spread a golden glow from a cloudless pale blue sky, and the sound of songbirds exalted the ever-rising orb of light. The breeze whispered its many secrets that man could not interpret, into the forest of vibrant green beyond the sandstone walls of the garden unseen from his bedroom window. Leslie stood half-naked, as one with the birth of nature's miracle. Nothing could compare with the feel of a new day, and the energy and power that coursed through him was the gift of Mother Nature herself. Leslie spread his arms and veiled himself in the warming cloak that offered itself to him.

He had an abiding love of nature and all her creations – the creatures of the woods and the wind in the trees; the clouds that lingered and then sometimes sped toward a distant horizon. The simplest things in nature enthralled him; the rustling of leaves and the rippling, gurgling waters forming eddies in the shallows of the streams that meandered on their journeys to the seas. Those streams and rivers had an unshakeable urge to unite with their siblings in the deep ocean depths. He felt as if he were a magnificent part of an unfolding drama. The bell sounded to bring him back to the realities of life; breakfast awaited him.

Mary had her usual serious face, and the dean was absorbed in some papers that he had in front of him. Susan served them with her customary grace and silence. Leslie thought that there was some tension in the room but could not identify it. He was inexperienced in the whims of women in love.

The dean looked up from the papers and said, 'Leslie it would please me if you could accompany me today. I have business in the city, and I would be glad of your company.'

Mary looked at her brother with a frown that demanded he say no to the request. He looked at the dean and saw a hint of concern on his face. Perhaps he could be of some service. He was grateful to the dean for his care and the education he'd received. His personal development instilled a sense of confidence, and this request was sincere and heartfelt. He agreed to accompany the dean. Mary was furious but managed to conceal it. Her brother must make his own mistakes and learn from them, and that was her fear. Would he learn in time to save himself?

Leslie hoped that he might learn something of Sir Alastair's plans for him.

***

Jackson stopped the car at the entrance to the Foundation offices in London. Sir Alastair and his companion ascended the wide stairway to the boardroom, employees acknowledging them as they passed. The dean strode into the boardroom, closely followed by Leslie.

The boy had decided to wear the suit that had been tailored for him. With a crisp white shirt and gold-coloured tie, he looked every bit the entrepreneur, albeit a junior one.

The dean ordered another chair placed next to his and invited the assembled employees to sit. They ranged from managing directors to heads of departments. He conducted his usual business, giving out directions and listening to the replies, receiving reports from each company head, and discussing market trends and share values.

After the standard procedures, he made a proposal that would drastically change the way the parent company performed and threw it open for discussion. He considered the opposing views and noted the personnel who agreed but contributed nothing to the discussion. He showed his notes to Leslie and silently emphasized by pointing to the notes where he would concentrate his focus. He singled out certain persons around the table and asked them why they had this view or that. He interrogated passively why one thought in the negative and why others thought in the positive. He wrote on a paper to Leslie, 'Everyone has an opinion. It may be based on fact or rumour or nothing at all. The art is to distinguish between them.'

Leslie considered all the aspects of the arguments, pondered the possible outcomes, and made his informed decision.

The dean silenced the assembly and deferred to Leslie. 'How do you see the outcome of this proposal Leslie?'

The boy felt a sense of dread because he could not agree with the proposal. The argument against was far too strong to his mind. His mouth felt dry, he took a sip from the glass in front of him before speaking, and it gave him a second or two to think. 'Sir, if you wish me to agree with the proposal, I cannot as it stands. The forces that drive your company survive on a very different structure than that of the proposal. Therefore, I would recommend opposing such changes to the structure that is now in place.'

A solemn silence gripped the occupants of the room. No one dared defy the wishes of Sir Alastair. They may put arguments against a proposal, but an outright rebuttal was unheard of. This boy was either a genius or a total fool.

'You would deny me the authority to which I am privileged? You oppose the argument that I put forth and attempt to turn my positive into a negative. How do you explain yourself?'

'I would oppose the proposal from logic, change just for the sake of it is fruitless. You have not provided this assembly with a convincing reason to persuade them that the changes would greatly benefit the company, an old axiom says, if it is not broken don't mend it, but I do not deny your authority here Sir, you asked for my opinion and that is what I give you.'

The group looked on with trepidation. If this youngster was a hope for future development within the company, he had just shot his foot off. Leslie then explained in detail the reasons for his conclusion. Sir Alastair smiled the broadest grin anyone at the Foundation could remember seeing.

He patted the boy on the shoulder. 'My friends, I would like to introduce Leslie Johns. I agree implicitly with his conclusions, and the motion is defeated. Those of you who agreed with the proposal may need to consider your various positions within this company. I do not need yes-men. I require positive thinkers with the will to drive new ideas and innovation but also with the ability to use logic and reason as this young man has demonstrated. Your positions are noted.'

Leslie had realised quite early that Sir Alastair had no serious intention of introducing changes to the structure of the Foundation, as he saw the proposal it lacked detail, there were no specific plans or graphs to show how to get from A to B or anything to demonstrate the benefits of change. This had been an introduction, a chance for Leslie to dip his toes into the world of commerce and serious business matters. Sir Alastair not only tested the boy's integrity, he tested the assembly and Leslie saw that, even if others at the meeting did not.

***

Sir Alastair and his young protégé lunched at Claridge's and then went to explore the wealth of interests on offer in the city. The museums, libraries, and art galleries and the waxworks at Madame Tussaud's fascinated the boy.

By far, the greatest pleasure for Leslie was the planetarium. He marvelled at the expanse of stars and planets that rivalled nature in its clarity and dimension. He had studied the night skies on numerous occasions but had never seen the expanse of constellations with such a clear and gripping view. He was in a state of ecstasy, identifying the constellations well before the commentary that accompanied the display. The dots of light showed themselves to him as drawings of Perseus and Andromeda, the Great Bear, and the twins Castor and Pollux that lived in the Gemini constellation. The heaven above his head absorbed him. The dean had trouble tearing him away from this marvel of nature's works reproduced by man. To Leslie, it was a revelation of what technology could achieve; to the dean, it was an enterprise designed to generate money. After all, it only showed what one could see if one took the trouble to look upward on a clear night. Leslie saw it as an education for the uninitiated; the city lights at night could never afford city dwellers such a view of the mantle that encompasses the whole of humankind.

With their heads firmly back on earth, Sir Alastair took Leslie to visit the seat of government. Sir Alastair explained the procedures within the houses of parliament, the Lords and the Commons, the peers and the elected. Leslie took everything in; he revelled in the process of debate and reasoned argument. He considered the proposal a politician placed before the House of Commons and drew his own conclusions. The MP making the statement either did not have all the facts or had misinterpreted them, which led Leslie to a different opinion. The debate passed from one side of the house to the other, back and forth.

On the journey back to the village, the dean asked the boy for his view of the debate. Leslie outlined the argument of the proposer and the opposing views. He gave a considered opinion on the content and stated that a logical outcome would be the failure of the proposal. The dean was impressed by the display of reasoning and logic.

'It may still succeed. Not all MPs have your analytical brain, and some will have ulterior motives when they vote on it.'

The boy considered the dean's words. 'Surely the purpose of parliament is to govern in the interest of the country as a whole, not for personal gain or glory.'

The dean let a smile escape the usually impassive facade. 'In an ideal world, that would be so young man. But human failings govern as well as strengths. Greed and corruption are persuasive companions and mighty adversaries.'

***

Leslie sat on the edge of the jetty in his unseen world, his feet stirring soft ripples in the quiet lake, and on the gleaming white hull of the motor launch, dappled spots of reflected light danced and bobbed rhythmically to the tempo of the ripples. He was whittling a piece of wood with a pocketknife and pondering the discussion that he had had with the dean. A gull swooped down to investigate the little woodchips floating on the surface of the water. Steadying itself with powerful wingbeats, it dipped and scooped up a woodchip. Leslie watched as the bird flew away across the water. It dropped the woodchip, having decided that there were tastier and more tender morsels to be had elsewhere. Leslie tossed the unfinished carving into the water and walked along the jetty towards the house, grabbing his towel as he passed.

Inside the house, it was cool and bright, and from the large south-facing windows, the sun's rays illuminated the marble-tiled floor, creating a crisp cleanness that accentuated the sharp angular lines of the rooms. He left the damp towel in the bathroom and went to his secret room. He perused the spines of the books and selected one of his favourites, a book of poems by Miguel Hernández Gilabert, he did not need the book but he liked to see the written words. Leslie connected heart and soul with the suffering of this man from a lowly background, a goatherd of little education who led many of his compatriots during the Spanish Civil War – leading his band of soldiers of the Republican Front, reciting his poetry to inspire the weary throng – and his sad death in the last of his many prisons that had become his home. Hernández was meticulous in the use of the metric and the rhyme. His descriptive narratives brought to life his experiences, sentiments and suffering. The poor man lived a brief but productive and inspiring life in his writings.

Leslie's thoughts turned to another person who had languished in captivity, his friend Perry. But first he must see how Tweety was doing.

***

Leslie was in ethereal form in the reporter's office when Ed entered.

The journalist was at his desk packing the military records into their boxes. The editor went over to him and asked what he'd managed to discover.

'Well I feel exhausted; to tell the truth boss, I found nothing of any significance.'

The editor patted him on the back and said, 'Well, sometimes we can't see the wood for the trees. Did you find any other names that could link us to him, other soldiers in his regiment we could contact?'

Tweety continued to pack away the reports. 'I wrote down a few names that popped up. I will need to do more research to try and find them. They are on my note book there.'

The editor looked at Tweety with some concern; 'Look, laddie, if this is going to make you ill, leave it.'

The thought of the reporter abandoning his quest disturbed Leslie. How else could he find his father if these people could not? Even with all their contacts and resources, they had thus far failed.

***

When Leslie explained the situation and the newsmen's lack of results to Perry, the man considered the consequences. 'I may never get out of here if they give up son, and you may never learn about your father, we are in a state of limbo and nothing we can do will change that.'

Leslie agreed that it looked ominous. 'Can you think of any way they might find more information, Perry?'

The sullen man sat on the edge of his bed. 'What about ex-servicemen's clubs and the Royal British Legion? They may be able to trace him or someone who knows him.'

Leslie felt it was a long shot but worth trying all the same. How he could pass that information to Tweety was another matter.

He told Perry of the visit to London and the Foundation offices. He recounted the incident and the dean's response.

'It sounds to me as though he is preparing you to become part of his company. You need to watch out for him, son, or you could end up in a sticky mess. From what you have told me of your part, you are playing right into his game.'

Leslie assured Perry that he had given a lot of thought to the dean's attentions to him and that it was a way to get to the heart of the organisation. He intended to expose it from the inside.

'They are ruthless people you are dealing with, son. Take great care my lad.'

***

Sir Alastair and Dr Hendricks had gone away together on business and would not be back for two days. Leslie had previously assembled the equipment he needed to explore the old chapel and stashed them in a garden shed.

Prepared with his equipment he made his way through the woods and followed the trail to the stream. When he arrived at the site of the chapel, he set down his bag and removed a 'borrowed' billhook and set to work hacking at the prickly stems and branches. At last, he could see the solid oak door with iron hinges and lock. He cleared away a path to the door and tried the handle. It had rusted over the years and would not turn. He thought about bashing it with the hammer but that could attract attention. He selected an iron bar with a flattened end and used it as a jemmy, levering the door handle against the frame. After a long struggle, the handle freed, and he managed to turn it. Thankfully, the door was unlocked. He pushed against the heavy door, and inch-by-inch, creaking and groaning, it gave way, allowing the boy to enter.

Sunlight streamed in through the open doorway, illuminating the gloom with rays of glimmering, sparkling dust. He looked around the small chapel with its layers of dust and decayed leaves on the floor. Twisted tendrils of woodbine had broken through the windows and climbed up the walls and across the floor. The rows of benches faced an altar on a raised platform at the far end of the single room. A simple, carved wooden crucifix behind the altar, peppered with woodworm holes, hung upon the wall that would have faced the congregation. He looked in the cupboards below the crucifix. They were empty, the trappings of holy worship long since removed.

The altar was covered in what once would have been a pure white cloth but was now grey, stained with watermarks and dust. He lifted the cloth to find the altar made from white marble blocks in the shape of an arc with a flat top. Leslie replaced the cloth and shuffled around the room inspecting the walls. Carvings occupied recesses in the walls, and they appeared to be victorious saints and vanquished demons. Centred on the wall opposite the altar was a large single carving of St George slaying a dragon.

Leslie took a torch from his bag and searched the walls. He felt that he was close to finding an answer to the puzzle. He was looking for a link to Sir Howard's brother, Caldwell, and their father, Sir Giles. He was adamant that the solution lay in that direction. Sir Giles had been so distraught at the death of Caldwell, and perhaps that was the reason for such an odd bequest in his will.

The cipher mentioned a monument, demons, and an oath. There were demons and monuments here in the form of carvings, but an oath he could not find. He scoured the chapel, searching on the roof beams and in the corners. He inspected every bench and again he studied the altar and the crucifix but to no avail.

He was about to leave when he noticed in the torchlight that, where he had disturbed the debris against the walls, the floor slabs had inscriptions on them. They were faint and dusty, so he cleared the debris away and followed the slabs along the course of the wall. The names of all the generations of Woodfords had been chiselled into the floor slabs – one name to each slab, along with the dates of births and deaths. The inscriptions ended with 'Caldwell Prescott Woodford'; no further slabs were inscribed.

Leslie examined the slab closely with its crudely cut words – unlike the others, which appeared to have been done by a stonemason. The inscription below the name was, 'I could not protect you as I promised; please forgive me my dear son." This was it, his father had surely inscribed the words himself as an act of penitence. This had to be the answer to the riddle he and Perry had worked on for so long.

Now, he had to discover the nature of the legacy.

The young boy felt a deep sense of disgrace and disrespect as he used the iron bar to score around the slab. But something drove him to continue as he worked. He selected a lump of rock from outside to use for leverage. He prised the slab from its setting and searched under it. There was nothing to see, so he dug away some of the earth. A few inches below the surface, he discovered a decayed sackcloth bag containing a small glass box. He brushed away the dirt and studied the box. Inside, all he could see was something like cotton wool. He would need to clean up the box and try to open it.

He replaced the soil and the slab, filling in the gaps around the edges. He turned to the altar and made a silent, heartfelt apology for the disturbance. He collected up his equipment and closed the door behind him. He replaced as much of the bramble as he could and went down to the stream to wash the box.

The box was made of thick glass contained within an intricate silver framework. The hinged lid opened stiffly, and inside, nestling in its bed of cotton wool – he found a lump of glass and a small key. Leslie turned the lump of glass repeatedly in his hands; it was a little smaller than a golf ball. A tremor of excitement coursed through him. He could not tell, but he presumed that it was an uncut diamond. He replaced it and the key in the box and headed for Howard House. He would need to find a hiding place for it until he could visit the lawyers in London.

***

Leslie searched his bedroom for a hiding place for the box. It had to be somewhere neither obvious nor discoverable by accident. He considered the floorboards but ruled that out. Lifting them would be noisy and could attract attention. He could not hide it in his desk, the chest of drawers, the wardrobe, or the bathroom. The fireplace was risky and dirty.

He noticed the brass bedstead had large round ball feet. He used a chair to prop up the bed at one corner and unscrewed a foot at the head of the bed. It was tight but eventually came undone. The small box would not fit inside but the stone and key would; he considered that if someone should discover the hiding place, it might be best to separate the stone and the key. He placed the key on a string, and hung it around his neck. He inserted the stone, surrounded by its cotton wool into the ball foot and screwed the foot tightly back onto the bed. Removing the chair, he observed from a distance. It was fine; no one would notice anything even when lifting the bed to clean.

The boy could barely contain his excitement as he related his latest adventure to Perry.

'If they find the stone, you will be finished, Leslie.' Perry gave the boy a very serious look. 'There was a boy they brought here years ago. In the village, they gave him a series of word and number puzzles to work on, and he was very good at it by all accounts. But the last puzzle eluded him. They brought him here, and he worked at it for years but could not find the solution as far as I know.'

Leslie listened attentively.

'Of course I don't know what happened to him after they put me down here.'

'Did you know his name?' asked the boy.

'No. I never met him; it was what I was told by the chap who helped me.'

Leslie recalled the conversation the dean had had with Dr Hendricks regarding 'the other boy'.

Leslie had an idea. 'Do you know the name of the man you tried to escape with?'

'Well only his first name. It was Douglas.'

'Perry, you never told me that before.'

'Why is that important?'

Leslie's face showed some concern. 'The name of the man found dead in the river was Douglas Fairbrother. It was something I found out on one of my early visits to the dean. As I recall, when I arrived the dean and the doctor were in the library having a rather heated discussion. I had arrived part way through the discussion and missed the reason for it but from what I could make out it appears the doctor said that Douglas Fairbrother attacked him when he was doing his rounds; the doctor hit him fatally over the head with a truncheon that he snatched from the guard. During the night, two of the staff dumped his body in the river.'

Perry looked aghast. 'Poor old Douggie. All he wanted was to get out of here.'

'The dean was not too pleased; the doctor had told the staff to dispose of the body discretely; the dean was horrified when the boys discovered it in the river some days later. He did not want the police snooping around,' said the boy.

***

Leslie decided he should visit Tweety at the newspaper office again and see if there was some way to give him the motivation to continue after what he had witnessed. He studied the notebook that lay open on the desk but saw nothing useful. The reporter grabbed his notebook and went to the editor's office.

On the editor's desk was a notepad with Ed's notes regarding a telephone conversation earlier that day with his contact in Military Intelligence.

'Sit down Tweety my friend' he said with an air of someone with superior knowledge, I had a call from my old mate in Military Intelligence this morning. He has found an officer who knew Will Johns and he told my contact that Sgt, Will Johns and Colonel Woodford served together in Cyprus. Sgt Johns had been attached to this officer's unit in a clandestine role, along with three other men. They were involved in gathering information on enemy movements. The four would often go off on their own secret missions. The officer told my contact that Will's team reported directly to Colonel Woodford, and that after Cyprus, Will and his team had shipped off to Hong Kong. The officer had supplied the names of the other members of the team—' Leslie could feel a cold chill run down his spine. One of the names was Douglas Fairbrother; the other two were Roger Garner and Norris Dwyer. Perry knew one of them personally.

Leslie concentrated hard on the list of names and on Fairbrother in particular. Nothing happened, much to his dismay. He had to tell Tweety that Fairbrother had not gone to Hong Kong; he was in the Woodford asylum and had been killed there. His inability to communicate with his greatest ally outside of the village frustrated him; he concentrated again but to no avail.

***

Leslie sat at his bedroom window looking out at the rain soaked scene outside. He was waiting for the mail to arrive. He should get his exam results any day now, and the anticipation caused him restlessness. But he decided not to be idle in the meantime, he was desperate to find out what was happening at the newspaper.

***

The boy waited in the editor's empty office.

Ed returned to his office from the print room and sat at the desk. He read the note again. He was sure that there had been three other names on the note. He called Tweety through the open doorway.

'What's up, sir?'

'How many names were on this note?'

'Besides Will's, there were the names of the three others on his team.'

The editor looked puzzled and scratched at his head. He shoved the note into the reporter's hand. 'And now?'

'Just the one, sir. But I don't understand.' He turned the paper over as if the names were hiding on the reverse.

'You remember the red line, sir? That was odd, and this is even stranger. Why is Fairbrother the only name left on here and what does it mean?'

The editor was at a loss for words. 'A good question, and I don't know the answer, laddie.' He sat thinking. 'Tweety, put the two things together and you have "foul play, Douglas Fairbrother". I have a hunch. Do you recall that story about the body in the river?'

'Yes, sir, a chap from the asylum.'

The editor gave a grin. 'Are you thinking what I'm thinking?'

A warm heat flooded the reporter's face. 'One and the same, sir?' he replied.

The editor picked up the telephone and dialled. A few moments later, a man's voice answered. 'Paul, it's Ed from the local. Could you find the information on that body in the River Roding back in '58? The inmate from the Asylum who drowned – we need a name if you can, mate.'

Paul stated that the closed case and file was archived.

'Well that's why I called you. You can access the archives, whereas I can't.'

He replaced the telephone and smiled at Tweety. 'Just when we thought it was all going to the dogs, we get a bone.'

Tweety still could not see how, even if they established the man's name, that could help their case.

Chapter 13

Oxford and the Press

The mail arrived. Leslie rushed down the stairs to the entrance hall and met Susan, whose hand was full of envelopes. 'Susan is there one for me?'

'Come now, Master Leslie. You know I have to give all the mail to Sir Alastair.'

She placed the mail onto a silver salver and knocked at the library door.

The dean sorted the mail and opened the business letters first. He read them and made some notes. There was one from the local newspaper requesting an interview. He put that to one side and continued with the rest. There was nothing for Leslie.

For a whole week, Leslie was fidgety and restless, and his sister noticed. 'I am sure that the letter will not arrive any faster no matter how much you will it,' Mary said, spreading butter thickly on a slice of hot toast.

'It is the waiting that torments me,' he told her. 'It is as if my life is on pause, and there is nothing I can do about it. I cannot make any plans for furthering my education or getting some employment until I know if I have the qualifications.'

Mary pointed her knife in the direction of Sir Alastair's empty chair as she spoke. 'Oh I am sure that "he" has something in mind for you whatever the outcome.'

His sister's tone was vicious and unsettled the boy even more, and he made no reply to her remark.

***

The next week was even harder for Leslie. Postal workers took industrial action and went on strike – no mail for the whole nation. The dean seemed glued to the telephone permanently, keeping his finger on the pulse of his empire.

Leslie visited River House and was surprised to find that Paul was no longer there. Of course, he would now be at the academy.

In the doctor's office, Leslie watched Thompson hand over the files relating to the next proposed transfers. Two of the children were not orphans, Margaret Forde and Gillian Mathews, each with only a single parent. 'This will have to be dealt with, George,' the Doctor said. 'We cannot have parents looking for the little ones can we.'

Leslie shuddered.

'Here are the details of the parents, Ernst; they live far apart, so if accidents occur, they will not arouse suspicions. This one you may find particularly interesting.' He opened a folder with a girl's name on the front – Gillian Mathews. 'She can do the most complicated of mathematic puzzles. Her mother is suffering from circulatory problems and is in a nursing home; her father died on an archaeological expedition in Peru.'

The doctor read the files and offered his hand to Thompson. 'As always, you have done well, my friend. I will make the transfer arrangements straight away'.

After Thompson left, the doctor called someone on the telephone. 'I have some work for you. It must to be convincing and soon. I will send you the information you will need.'

Leslie felt that he was complicit in some huge conspiracy involving kidnapping and murder. He wondered if this was how his own father had disappeared.

Leslie toyed with the idea of trying to visit his father but had a dread that, if he found his body buried somewhere, he would not be able to escape. He imagined himself trapped in his own father's grave, unable to return to his physical body. It was probably a nonsensical notion but he decided not to risk it. He would wait and see what Ed and Tweety could find out.

***

At last, the letter he had so long waited for arrived. And after breakfast, the dean handed the envelope to the nervous Leslie. He opened the envelope slowly and teased out the contents, and hardly daring to read what it said, he passed the folded paper to the anxious dean. 'Please, tell me what it says, sir.'

The dean took the letter without a smile and read the contents. 'Well, my boy, congratulations' his beamed. 'You have two doctorates with honours. This means that you can use DLitt, Hons after your name if you wish. You have doctorates in two languages, I think we should arrange a celebration for your achievements. You will of course attend the ceremonies in Oxford, it is befitting that you do so. I am so proud of you and what you have achieved.'

Leslie looked at the letter and read it several times. He was unable to believe his results. 'Would you like to announce the news to your tutors or should I?' the dean asked.

'I feel that I should tell them and thank them for their diligence.'

The dean applauded the boy's reply.

Now Leslie had to think seriously about what he should do next. He knew that Sir Alastair wanted to induct him into the company, but he was not sure now that it would be the best way for him to proceed. As an employee of the company, he would be in a position of trust and eventually privy to delicate information. It would be impossible to expose what he wished to reveal without becoming a traitor or accusations of complicity.

He decided that he would discuss his future with the dean. They had never openly discussed Leslie's future with the company; it was only through his sister's snide remarks and secret visits that he had surmised that the dean was formulating plans for him. He would propose his own plan before the dean could offer his. That way, if the dean did not agree, he would be countering the boy's visions of his future and not vice versa.

***

On a visit to the cell, Leslie revealed his thought to his dearest friend.

Perry agreed with Leslie that it would be too difficult and dangerous to expose the company from inside. The boy had, at last, come to his senses, though from the outside there would be information he could not access.

'You could perhaps use your powers to visit the company offices and obtain the information that way,' said Perry, pleased with his idea.

'Yes, but the more people I visit, the more chance of encountering someone like you who can see me.'

'Oh…yes, that would be bad.'

They sat in silence for some time, both deep in thought, until Perry broke the silence. 'So what is your plan to foil the dean?'

Leslie outlined his strategy. 'I will tell the dean that I wish to go into the army, and he will counter with the argument that someone of my ability and education would be wasted in the armed forces. I will reply that I have no experience of commanding others. He will counter that I have commanded and instructed others in Roding House as head boy and that instilling leadership is one of the main purposes of the village. I will counter with the fact that we are children leading children, not men leading men. There is a world of difference; I would not dare command an adult. I will point out that my experiences of life, people, and the world in general relate to the village and education, not a sound footing for the realms of international commerce. If the dean tells me directly that he wishes me to join his company, I will tell him that if I do not join the army, I should like to work for an unrelated company for a few years to gain experience and then consider the Foundation later. Who knows? I may learn beneficial ideas and methods from other enterprises.'

Perry considered the boy's statement. 'You have thought this out well, but if the dean insists that your best route is through the Foundation, it all falls flat, doesn't it?'

'I will have to make my case and my argument as strong as possible. If I can make him see logic behind my thinking, half the battle is won.'

***

The information from the police archives arrived, and Tweety and Ed went through the investigation with a fine-tooth comb. Leslie arrives in time to hear part of their conversation.

'Just look at that, Tweety,' the editor said, shoving a report under the man's nose.

He read the name – Douglas Fairbrother. 'It is incredible how this name came to us.'

The editor searched his desk and recovered the note. 'You'll find this even more incredible.'

The reporter took the note. 'But all the names are back on the list. Talk about odd. Who would believe us if we told anyone?'

'And look at this one.' The editor passed Tweety the interview notes. 'So Sir Alastair was at the interview with the four boys, and one was our chum Leslie Johns. He was only seven at the time.'

The editor smiled his wicked grin. 'I have something else for you, laddie. A day out with expenses, and you my friend are going back to school.'

Tweety looked quizzically at the editor.

'It pays to read the nationals laddie. Some ran articles about graduates receiving their degrees at Oxford next week. And guess what my boy? Leslie Johns has a doctorate at the age of fourteen. We need to get the story, and I am coming with you. The hounds will be out in force, and you will need all the help you can get. I've asked Billy to step up for a few days. Sharpen your pencils, laddie.'

The editor set himself the task of listing the questions he wanted answered and phrasing them to avoid single word replies.

Billy came into the office with a story about a gas leak that had killed a man in his flat. The man had done some renovations to his kitchen and had disconnected the gas cooker. He'd installed some new kitchen cabinets, and when he'd replaced the cooker, he hadn't reconnected it properly. A neighbour had smelled gas and reported it to the gas board; they'd had to get the police and a locksmith to gain entry. 'They say it was a miracle the whole block never went up in an explosion,' Billy concluded.

The editor thought about the story. 'What do we know about the dead man? What family does he have? What did he do for a living? How long had he lived there? What friends did he have? Was he a local man? Was he skilled at anything? Find out everything about him that you can. Don't just accept the story that's given to you.'

'They are all things on my list sir. I Just wanted to know if you had an interest in the story.'

The editor huffed. 'Of course, but collect all the facts first laddie.'

***

The day before the graduation, the dean announced that they would spend the night in Oxford. After lunch, they changed into suitable clothing and assembled at the car. Jackson held open the door of the Bentley for Sir Alastair, Leslie, and Madame Silvestre. Mary declined the invitation and preferred to remain at Howard House, as each graduate could bring only two guests. The previous day, Professor Arias had stated that he must attend a family problem urgently back in Spain; he left immediately for the night train.

As the car that conveyed the Oxford bound quartet passed the doctor's residence, Leslie noticed a black car discretely parked in the driveway of the lodge. It seemed ominous to him as the car followed them out of the village.

The occupants of the gleaming silver grey Bentley arrived in Oxford. Jackson halted the car outside a plush hotel. When his passengers had disembarked Jackson drove off, Sir Alastair and his companions freshened up in their plush hotel rooms. Later, Sir Alastair suggested a short tour of the city. He would guide them, as he knew the city well having studied there as a student.

When they emerged from the lobby into the street, Leslie was sure he spotted the same black car he'd seen outside the lodge parked down the street.

Sir Alastair recommended a visit to the Ashmolean, and after the briefest of visits, they continued towards Broad Street to see the Bodleian Library and then the Sheldonian Theatre where the ceremony would take place. On the tour, Sir Alastair pointed out the various colleges – St Johns, Trinity, and Balliol. Inside the Bodleian, Leslie was in raptures at the array of research material available to students. He could spend the rest of his life here surrounded by his friends. They walked under the 'Bridge of Sighs' and along Queen's Lane down to the high street. They passed St Edmund Hall and Ruskin School of Drawing and Fine Art and arrived at Magdalen College.

Leslie's ears pricked up at the sound of a choir at practice and the strains of cello and violins. His heart jumped at the sight of the deer in the park, and the peaceful surroundings made him feel relaxed and at peace with the world. *I should have done my studies here, as did Oscar Wilde.* On the way back to the hotel, they took a different route so that they could see Merton College and other libraries that Sir Alastair pointed out.

Leslie could not shake off the feeling that they were being followed. There were plenty of people going about their own business, and many times they had to step aside for cyclists, but every time he looked around, he could see no one in obvious pursuit of them.

They had dinner in the hotel and then sat in the lounge going over the procedure for the next day. Leslie memorised every detail.

He mentioned to Sir Alastair his suspicion that they had been followed.

'Nothing to worry about Leslie; just precautionary measures. Your achievements were noted in the press, and I expect there will be some attentions focused on you tomorrow.'

Leslie sighed in relief.

***

Later that evening, alone in his hotel room, Leslie visited Tweety and his editor who he knew would attend the ceremony in Oxford. They were in an old green Morris Oxford and parked at the side of the road with the bonnet up. It seemed they had broken down on the A40 London Road near Wheatley and were waiting for the RAC to come out to them. Arriving back at the car from a nearby public telephone box, Ed told Tweety he'd telephoned the RAC and then the guest house to notify them of their situation. Leslie looked at the engine and underneath the engine block. He could see that the fuel line had loosened and the clip holding it had rusted away. It was not a major disaster, and a mechanic could fix it in no time at all.

***

Leslie thought about the places he had seen on this visit to Oxford and the impressive architecture of the city. *No wonder they call it the city of dreaming spires* he thought. Leslie's play on those words referred to the aspirations of those who aspire to achieve their dreams in this city.

***

Scrambled eggs, toast with just a touch of marmalade, and a cup of black tea was Leslie's favourite breakfast. Madame was nervous and excited, the opposite of her usual demeanour. The dean was calm and cool, in full control of the situation at hand. Leslie had a sack full of kittens scratching at the lining of his stomach and a slight weakness at the knees. Sir Alastair laid his hand on the boy's shoulder. 'There is nothing to worry about. You worked extremely hard to achieve in less than two years what students normally take four years to attain. You should be as proud as we are of you. Think of the way you conducted yourself at the board meeting. In a room full of strangers, and very important people in their various fields at that, you were calm and collected, reasoned and logical. Just treat this the same way.'

The kittens retracted their claws and began to purr softly and soothingly, curling into fluffy balls that exuded a warm cosy feeling.

Outside the entrance to the hotel, Leslie saw Tweety and Ed. Tweety held a camera and Ed, his list of questions.

'Sir Alastair, a comment please on the letter published this morning in *The Times*?'

Sir Alastair looked puzzled and sent Leslie back into the hotel to get a copy of the paper. 'I have no comment to make at this time. If you will excuse us, we have an appointment to attend.'

Leslie returned with the newspaper and handed it to Sir Alastair, and they headed off on foot towards the Sheldonian Theatre. The journalists jostled and harried for an answer, but the dean ignored them and quickened his stride.

Leslie tugged his arm. 'Sir, Madame is in difficulty.'

The man halted and looked back. The reporters surrounded Madame Silvestre; questions were being hurled at her from all directions. She had tried to keep up, but running and stiletto heels are not good companions. The mob had pounced on her like savage dogs with the smell of blood in their nostrils. Sir Alastair waved his hand in the air, and from nowhere, four burly men appeared and extricated the poor victim from the melee. Two men aided her to the side of Sir Alastair, and the other two kept the savage hounds at bay.

They still had ample time to make it to the ceremony; they entered a coffee shop and sat at a table, and Leslie could see two of Madame's rescuers outside the window.

Sir Alastair ordered two black coffees and one black tea. He opened the newspaper and searched through the letters to the editor section. He slammed the paper down just as the waitress arrived with the order. 'Damned Judas!' he exclaimed in a loud voice.

The waitress observed him with a timid expression bordering on fear. 'I am so sorry, my dear,' he said, putting the paper into his briefcase. 'It was something I read. I do apologise.'

The waitress placed the cups on the table and made a swift exit. The outburst had alarmed Madame and Leslie also. Customers at other tables glanced in their direction, tutting and whispering with scornful glances.

The three ignored the looks of admonition and sipped their drinks in silence. After his coffee, Sir Alastair asked the waitress for the use of a telephone. She showed him to an alcove under the stairs. Leslie looked at Madame. Her face was pale, and she had her gaze fixed on the sugar bowl. Leslie felt that silence was the best policy at that moment but he put his hand upon hers to console her. The two guards were still in place outside. He thought it had been wise of Sir Alastair to anticipate the press, but something about the letter in the paper had shaken him badly. It probably would not be prudent to discuss it at this time, he surmised.

***

The ceremony went exactly according to plan except for the graduation gown. They had found it difficult to find one in Leslie's size; even the female-sized gowns appeared to consume him.

Outside the Sheldonian, the few reporters became a throng, each demanding an interview and hurling questions at the graduate and his mentors. Ed and Tweety inched their way up to the front. 'Sir Alastair, what do the boy's parents think of their son's achievements?'

'No comment.'

'What plans do you have for him now?'

'That is for him to decide.'

'What made him give up on the swimming after beating the national junior's champion?'

The gathered journalists were busily scribbling shorthand and taking down the questions and answers. This old hack knew something they didn't.

'Can you explain why one of his tutors has dismissed his studies as "based on mere hearsay"?'

Sir Alastair's face began to redden. He could not use his henchmen in so public a place, and there was no way through the crowd.

'Did you adopt the boy and his sister, sir?'

That was it – the last straw; Sir Alastair pushed his way into the crowd, demanding they let him through. He shoved at Ed, and the man fell backwards into the crowd. Flashbulbs flickered and popped as Tweety helped his editor to his feet.

'Don't worry about me," Ed admonished. "We've got him against the wall.'

Tweety followed the crowd for a few yards and then went back to Ed. 'We can get him at the hotel. I know a shortcut.'

They turned off the main road and crossed the campus of Balliol College, arriving at the hotel moments before the crowd. They rushed into the foyer of the hotel, but the concierge told them. 'Sorry, sirs, no press in the hotel. We have to respect the privacy of our clients.' He ushered them back to the entrance just as the graduation party arrived.

'Sir Alastair, grant us an interview, and we will be glad to tell your story. Here's my card' said Ed as he handed a card to Sir Alastair.

In disgust, the dean flicked it into the street. 'I told you, no comment.'

One of the other journalists waiting nearby picked up the card and put it in his pocket.

Several police officers arrived at the hotel, and one had words with the concierge. He went back to the gathered reporters and told them to disband immediately, as they had become an unruly rabble and were in danger of disturbing the peace.

***

Lunch was a silent affair; apart from placing their orders, not a word passed between the three. What had started as an exciting day had turned into a scary situation. Secretly, Leslie hoped that all the reporters would follow up on the story, he needed all the help he could get.

Sir Alastair's mood was morose. He thought about the questions raised by the journalist with the Scottish accent. This man had obviously done some research. How much did he know? And could he be a threat?

The concierge quietly approached Sir Alastair. 'There is a telephone call for you Sir Alastair, and I can bring the telephone here if you wish.'

'It is no problem, I will take it over there. Thank you.'

The dean walked over to the foyer desk and took the call. When he returned, Sir Alastair looked even more concerned. 'The press are camped outside the village, and Doctor Hendricks has had to call the police to have them restrained. They were in the village trying to interview all and sundry, but the gates are now locked and the police are keeping the press under control.'

Leslie and Madame looked at each other and then at Sir Alastair. Although Leslie wanted the story out in the open, he could not help but feel a pang of guilt at the torment this man was experiencing. However, he had brought it upon himself.

'I think we should allow you some time for a special holiday Leslie. And if Madame agrees to accompany you, you may like to explore the charms that her country has to offer.'

Madame Silvestre's face lit up. 'If you wish me to chaperone, I would be pleased to accompany Leslie.'

'It would please me immensely, Madame. I feel that you also would benefit from a holiday, and you may go for as long as you wish. I can arrange for another tutor for the children unless you have someone in mind, Madame. I will make my private plane available whenever you are ready to leave.

I have a gift for you Leslie that I was going to give you for your birthday. As it is only a few weeks away, and under the circumstances, I think now is the right time—'

He reached into his briefcase and removed a buff -coloured envelope, which he handed to Leslie with a smile.

The boy opened it with hesitation and slowly withdrew the contents – a passport, a birth certificate, and a chequebook. 'But I do not have—'

'Yes you do. I have opened an account for you and deposited one thousand pounds for you to use as you wish. Spend it prudently. I have something else.' He removed another envelope and took from it some official forms. 'I took the liberty of applying for legal guardianship of both you and Mary and it has been granted, You are both now my wards, I am a father to you Leslie.'

Leslie felt as though he'd been hit on the crown of his head with something hard. He had not seen this coming. 'I…I do not know what to say, sir.' The boy's mind was in confusion. Should he be happy or angry? Was this man trying to buy him or outmanoeuvre him? Was he edging him into a corner with cunning skill that would later make him appear to be a spoiled child if he rebelled? The gesture overwhelmed him.

'I understand you may think I have been forward in taking measures without discussing them with you and Mary first. I assure you, it is only to secure your futures and repay you both for the trust you have put in me.'

Leslie could feel the heat of the furnace as demons cast the fetters for his ankles, the clanging of the hammer against iron, ringing out his doom, a life of servitude and gratitude for something he had no power to repay. The debt forced upon him would imprison him; he needed time to think about his next move. Virtually lost for words and in shock, the boy of many words just said, 'Thank you Sir.'

***

Over the years, Leslie had managed to spend very little of his pocket money, only purchasing his books second-hand and never buying sweets as the other boys did at the local newsagent's shop. This had allowed him to put a little of his money aside each week. He knew the cash he had saved amounted to just short of 120 pounds. He wondered if he could manage to have the holiday in France at his own expense. He was reluctant to use any of the 'bribe' money, but the idea of a journey abroad was attractive to him.

***

Alone in his hotel room, Leslie needed the advice of good counsel.

'Oh my word, son.' said Perry, 'you are in a fix. You said before that you would discuss your future with the dean, didn't you? Now he has trumped your ace. Have that talk with him and forego the holiday. He cannot control you in the army unless he sends you to the academy. No… that's what he would do. What about the navy or the air force? Have you considered them?'

Leslie contemplated the dank walls that imprisoned his dearest friend and imagined them as his future. 'I never expected anything like this. He is a clever man. He has moulded me into what he wants. And now I can see it I cannot escape it. Perhaps the navy would be a good move.'

Perry smiled at the thought of the press hounding Sir Alastair and the village besieged by them as well. 'I bet the papers will publish the photos of him pushing the reporter to the ground. They revel in that sort of thing.'

Leslie allowed a smirk to change his expression. 'I just hope that every paper prints the story. It may give some new leads. I think that is why Ed asked those questions in public. I could see that the other reporters let him lead the onslaught, and they took notes. They soon realised that he was onto a scoop and would snatch it from him given the chance.'

The sound of the man with the food signalled to Leslie that he should make his departure. 'See you soon my friend,' he whispered as he left the man to eat in peace, then disappeared in a flash.

***

Jackson had the car ready at the door of the hotel as they made their exit. Reporters jostled each other trying to get photos and answers to their questions. All Sir Alastair would say was, 'No comment.' They pressed against the car as the passengers climbed in. Jackson eased the car slowly along the street and gradually left the crowd behind. Leslie noticed the black car following and the green Morris Oxford ahead of them.

When they arrived at the village, Leslie found the scene unbelievable. The street was full of cars and people. Jackson slowed at the approach to the gates; the Morris Oxford continued towards town. There were a dozen police officers and two more bodyguards. The gates opened, and the car glided up the avenue toward the tranquillity and the secluded safety of Howard House. The gates closed securely behind them.

Over dinner that evening, Mary showed her annoyance. 'A crowd of reporters mobbed me as I came back from the shops,' she said. 'They wanted to know about Leslie and his studies and the swimming; they asked who I was and how many children are in the village. The questions were endless. I had to run to the lodge and beg doctor Hendricks to do something. Thank god, he called the police. They were like ants crawling all over the village.'

The dean looked as apologetic as he could. 'I really am sorry for the upset. Perhaps going to the ceremony was a bad idea after all; we had to face the same thing in Oxford.'

Mary looked at her brother as if to ask something but thought better of it.

'I have offered your brother the opportunity to have a holiday abroad. If you wish you may accompany him and Madame Silvestre.'

'I do not wish it, thank you. I do not speak French as fluently as Leslie, and the thought does not appeal to me. Besides, sailing on a boat is more his cup of tea than mine,' she said, pointing her knife at Leslie.

'What about flying?' asked the dean.

'I could not say, never having had the experience, but that does not attract me either.'

Leslie could see that she was going to be defiant to the end; he admired her strength of character and wished that he had the same temperament.

'I told Leslie today that I have been granted guardianship of you both in the absence of any parents.'

'And what gives you the right?' stormed Mary, standing and facing the dean. 'I suppose you think that we are your property to do with as you wish. There has been no discussion with me on this matter, and I totally object. Our mother and father are still alive until I see proof otherwise.'

The dean's face turned to a scowl. 'I have endured your sullen attitude and your tantrums for the sake of your brother, young lady. I will not tolerate it a moment longer. In my house, you will respect me or suffer the consequences. Do I make myself clear, madam?'

Leslie listened in horror. He began to tremble, fearing the outcome.

Mary glanced at her brother and immediately noticed the pallor quickening across his face. She was about to give hell to the dean but instead rushed around the table to Leslie. She caught him just as he was about to hit the floor. 'How you could send such a fragile boy away to foreign lands?'

The dean realised that there was no way he could separate these two. If he wanted to keep the boy, the girl was the price he would have to pay.

Chapter 14

A Serious Diagnosis

There were no demons to harangue or torment him, just the soft whispering of the breeze playing with the golden leaves of autumn.

Leslie continued his careful brushstrokes along the slats of the garden table, following the grain of the wood. He had painstakingly sanded the table, removing the tired and flaking varnish. He brushed the slats to remove the dust and washed them with white spirit. The table was now ready for the teak oil. He poured a little onto a piece of rag and began to caress the slats with the rejuvenating elixir. The sound of music from a quartet playing a Vivaldi sonata wafted on the breeze and mixed with the scent of the oil; it was a heady concoction. Leslie's imagination conjured up a vision of Il 'Prete Rosso', the red-haired priest, conducting the sonata and a choir of girls from an orphanage awaiting their turn to perform.

As the music gradually faded into the distance, he became aware of the hum of an air conditioning unit high up on the wall of the white room. 'Hello, Mary. What is the matter?'

The girl held his hand tightly. 'Thank God,' she said looking to the ceiling. 'You are in hospital, Leslie, in London. This is the third time you have passed out for no apparent reason. The doctors have done some tests on you, but they will need to do more…'

Leslie's expression showed alarm.

Mary squeezed his hand a little tighter, and she stroked his head with the other hand. 'Now stay calm, quiet and calm. The consultant wanted to speak to you when you were awake. How do you feel?'

Leslie looked puzzled. 'I feel fine apart from a slight headache. How long have I been here and why all the fuss?'

'Hush now, you have been here for two days. You collapsed when you returned from Oxford.' She did not go into the details for fear of causing a relapse. 'Listen, I wanted to talk to you myself instead of some strange doctor.'

Leslie tried to sit up in the bed, but Mary gently held him down. He realised that she had something important to relate to him and so relaxed against the pillows.

He became aware that other people were in the room as Mary gently combed his hair with her fingers and said, 'Leslie, from the tests already done, they have diagnosed you as having a brain tumour.' She could feel the shock jolt through him as he became rigid for a moment. She caressed his hand softly, calming him. 'The tests are not complete yet, as you need to be awake when they do them. It does not mean that you are going to die or be very ill for the rest of your life. For one of the tests, they may need to do a biopsy to establish if the tumour is malignant or benign, but that is not for you to worry about now. Let them do the tests and give them your full cooperation. Promise me that you will deal with this like the grown up young man that you are.'

Leslie suddenly put his hand to his neck feeling for the cord.

'I took the key and have it safe' she whispered, placing a finger upon his lips. She said nothing more as a nurse came over to take his pulse. *We will speak again later.* He heard in his head. It was Mary's voice, but her lips never moved.

He could hear muffled voices in the corridor outside the room, and after a few moments, Sir Alastair entered, followed by two men wearing white coats. 'Leslie, I am so relieved to see that you are awake. This is Mr Sangstrom, who is a neurosurgeon, and this is Dr Marston, a specialist in the field of oncology. They wish to undertake some tests to establish the cause of your collapses.'

Leslie sat upright in the bed and replied, 'Mary has explained to me that I may have a brain tumour.'

Mr Sangstrom approached the bed. 'At the moment, we have tests to do that will either confirm or deny our diagnosis. It may involve a biopsy later if our suspicions are correct. At present, it is important that you remain calm and relaxed. I advise no excitement or mental stimulation.' He turned to the nurse and checked her charts and then gestured towards the door. 'Now, Sir Alastair, if you do not mind, we would like to begin the tests immediately.'

The dean turned to the surgeon apologetically. 'But of course. You will keep me informed.'

'Yes we will, sir,' replied the doctor.

The doctors examined his eyes and tested his sight; they pricked his fingers and toes with something sharp. They asked him to articulate his arms and legs this way and that. He turned his wrists and ankles in different directions. They listened to his chest and took more blood samples. They gave him a passage to read from a sheet of paper and asked him to explain the content. All the time, they made notes and discussed the outcome of each test.

They gave him some small weights to lift – first with one hand and then the other. 'Are you right- or left-handed?' asked the doctor.

'Right-handed,' replied the boy.

'Umm…it seems that you have more strength in your left than your right. We will need to await the latest blood results, but I feel that our diagnosis was correct. Nurse, can you prepare him for an X-ray, please. We will have that done right away. I do not wish to delay a moment longer than necessary.'

Sir Alastair spent much of the next day at Leslie's bedside, only leaving to make telephone calls. Mary was constant in her diligent vigil; Leslie wanted to talk to her privately without the attentions of the dean. He tried to talk to her, but she placed her finger on his lips. 'Not now, Leslie. He will have some business to attend to shortly. We can talk then.'

Leslie gave her a quizzical look. The dean returned from one of his calls and explained that something urgent required his attention, but he would be back as soon as he could. Leslie stared at his sister as the man left the room.

Although they were now alone in the room, she gently covered his mouth. 'Say nothing.' she whispered.

Then Leslie could hear her voice in his head. *Say what you want me to hear, in your mind. Close your eyes and think about what it is you wish me to know.*

Leslie pressed back on the pillows and shut his eyes. *The key is important to me; you must take great care that nobody knows of it. If I have to go to surgery, there are risks involved. They say that, if I survive, I may lose some of my faculties, and I have many things I must see concluded. If I lose my memories, I will not be able to complete what I have started. There are many things I need to tell you, but I will do that at the last minute before surgery.*

Mary pressed his hand. *Tell me when you are ready. Everything you say will remain secret. And if there is anything you wish me to do, I will make sure it is done.*

Leslie relaxed. Comforted by his sister's words, he drifted off to sleep.

***

Leslie wanted to scratch his head, but he felt Mary's hand prevent him. 'They drilled a hole and did a biopsy,' she explained. 'We are waiting for the results.'

He still felt a dull headache and desperately wanted to touch his head. Mary kept a firm hand on his arm.

Sir Alastair hovered near the doorway like an expectant father. 'What is taking them so long?'

The nurse explained that the tests took some time to do, even though they have given it priority. An orderly entered and asked if anyone would care for refreshments. Leslie said he could murder a cup of tea.

'Sorry,' said the nurse, 'that is not allowed.'

The others refused the offer in deference to the patient.

Mr Sangstrom entered the room, full of apologies. 'I am sorry it is taking so long, but these things cannot be hurried. I would speed things up if I could, but that would not be in the interest of the patient.'

Leslie looked at the surgeon, 'Sir, will you still need to operate if the biopsy proves benign?'

The surgeon stood at the bedside and spoke softly. 'Young man, the tumour is quite large, and if it continues to grow, it will cause severe problems to you. It can affect your eyesight, your balance and mobility, and your cognitive processes and affect a whole list of other problems. You see, the brain lives within a shell of limited size, the skull. As the tumour grows, the space inside the skull becomes increasingly smaller, thereby putting pressure on the brain itself. The pressure causes the symptoms; we need to know if the tumour is benign or malignant in order to operate successfully. If you have any questions, I would be glad to provide answers for you.'

'I have just one question, sir. What are my chances in each scenario?'

'That is difficult to answer…' He paused, trying to construct an answer that would explain without alarming the boy. 'Of course, as with all surgery, even minor ones, there are always risks. However, the risks attached to doing nothing are far greater. It is possible that, if the tumour is benign, it will stop growing and cause few or no problems; I feel that course is most unlikely. If the tumour is malignant, then there are two choices. Operate and face the possible risks or leave it alone and face certain deterioration over a short or long term. One cannot predict the term left in such cases but a short road to death is a certainty.'

The boy considered the facts. 'Sorry, sir, one more thing – after surgery, what are my chances of retaining all my faculties?'

'Leslie, we will do all in our power to avoid damage to the brain itself. We cannot tell at present how deeply rooted the tumour is. Think of the tumour as being like a tree; the roots can go deep. We can cut the tumour, but we have to get the roots to prevent regrowth. At some point, we will need to detach it from the brain matter; that is where the major risk lies with regard to retention of your faculties. The brain does have the ability to repair itself over the long term, but there is the risk that full retention may not be possible. In some cases, but not all, the patient recovers completely within a short time, sometimes weeks. In others, patents recover some of their abilities. And then there are those who do not make any significant recovery. I trust you understand this explanation?'

'Thank you, sir, for your clarity.'

The surgeon shook the boy's hand. 'It is my pleasure to deal with such a brave and sensible young man.'

Leslie had to swallow hard, his mouth felt dry and he was gasping for a drink. The doctor allowed him to have a sip of water. He decided that he wanted to be alone and sleep. Sir Alastair and Mary went to get something from the canteen whilst the surgeon and the doctor had a discussion outside in the corridor.

This may be Leslie's last chance to talk to Perry; he had to tell him urgently about his condition and his plans.

***

The news greatly distressed Perry. 'If things go wrong, it is the end for both of us. You say you will tell your sister everything. But can you trust her? Both our lives will be in her hands.'

'I will tell her about you and what we have discovered," he said. 'She will do everything she can. I do trust her, Perry. And although she can be a pain, she would never harm me.'

'Come back to me, Leslie. I cannot lose another friend. Please promise me.'

'That is a promise I cannot make my dear friend., much as I wish I could, I have no power to affect the outcome, and I am in the hands of fate. Mary will not give up on you or me, she will continue my quests because she will promise to, and you have no idea what a promise means to her.'

***

Mary grinned as she observed her brother.

'What is the matter?' said Leslie.

'You look like an egg,' she replied. 'I never realised that you had such a small head under all that hair.'

Leslie smiled and stroked his head. 'It feels so strange being bald. Now can we talk?'

Mary glanced around the room to ensure they were alone. *As before, think of what you want me to know.* Her lips never moved.

Leslie still had not come to terms with his sister's gift and was amazed at how she could communicate by thought alone. He told her of the stone in his bedroom, the name of the lawyers in London, and of how he had found out about them. He gave her the information required to claim the inheritance. He told her about the acquisitions of gifted children at the village and the principle parties involved. He related the tales of Perry, the body in the river, and the secret room in the library. He explained to her the work Tweety and his editor were engaged in and how they were attempting to track down their father.

He did not tell her how he had obtained the information or how he could 'visit' people or make strange things happen. He outlined his wishes and hoped that it would be enough for Mary to work with.

Mary squeezed her brother's hand, and he could hear her voice in his mind. *When you recover, you will be able to resume this quest that you have been on. In the meantime, I will do all that I can to help. I will do nothing about the stone and the lawyers; you can do that for yourself later.*

Mary, if the worst happens – if I die or irrevocably lose my faculties, please—

I solemnly promise to do all that I can for you, just as I promised to Daddy. But you shall overcome this Leslie. A mind such as yours cannot end in a flash when your purpose has barely begun. Sleep, and I will see you soon sweet angel.

Leslie thought that, if he had been closer to, and had confided more in his sister, they may have solved problems more efficiently by working together. He had always sensed a barrier between them that had prevented them doing so. Only on the occasions whenever Leslie was ill did the barrier come down, and Mary showed a caring, loving side of her that she usually hid well. He gave her hand a squeeze, signalling that he had told her as much as he could or would.

***

At the hospital reception desk, Mary noticed a man with a camera, and a pencil behind his ear. Sir Alastair ignored the man and brushed past him. 'Please, Sir Alastair, I just want the story on the boy. How is he, sir?'

The dean turned swiftly to face the man and snarled, 'You leave the boy alone. Do you hear me?' There was menace in his tone that even alarmed Mary, and she did not frighten easily.

'Please, just grant me an interview, sir.'

The dean swivelled around and strode out of the main entrance.

***

Tweety approached the private room where Leslie was. A burly man was seated in the corridor guarding the door. He rose to his feet as Tweety drew near. 'What is your business here?' he enquired in a gruff voice.

'I wanted to know how the young man is doing today,' he said.

The man made no comment and pointed back down the corridor.

'Just a few words with Leslie is all I need. People are interested in him and want to know how he is.'

The guard stepped towards Tweety menacingly; it was obvious that no story could be had here today.

Tweety retreated towards the lift, a nurse stepped out, and Tweety asked her how the boy was, saying that he was a friend and was very concerned. The nurse looked him up and down. Noticing the camera, she told him that the boy could not have visitors and that she could not comment. And besides, Leslie was not one of her patients.

***

Leslie felt a mixture of relief and trepidation that he had told Mary his secrets. He had entrusted her with an untold fortune and the life of his friend. He had persuaded Perry that she could be trusted, but he had his own doubts. She had never confided in him before or told him of her abilities. On the other hand, he had never divulged his to her. He wondered if she had any other abilities that she had kept secret from him. He was stroking his shaven head when the doctor entered.

'We are going to give you something to make you sleep now.' They gave him an injection and asked him to slowly count to ten.

'...5...6 ...'

Chapter 15

The Hounds Get an Ally and a Bone

Dr Hendricks read the newspaper article with interest; it had a large cover picture of Sir Alastair pushing a reporter backwards into a crowd. The expression on his face was one of frustration and anger. The face of the reporter was of undignified embarrassment. The article covered the graduation of the 'Wonder Boy' and reminded readers of the swimming trials. It went on to say that little or no information had been forthcoming from those around the boy and that he was under guard at an unnamed hospital in London. It told also of the debacle at the village and accused the police of heavy handedness with the press, by interfering with their right to gather information. The editor printed an open invitation to Sir Alastair to tell his side of the story and set the record straight; after all, their purpose was to report the news, not create it.

***

Returning from a visit to her brother, Mary went to her room as she usually did when Leslie was not around. She heard the front doorbell and a few moments later recognised the voice of doctor Hendricks. Susan showed the doctor into the library as usual.

'A journalist has been snooping at the asylum my friend. He tries to get the interviews with the staff regarding the body in the river seven years ago. He would not be redoing a story from so far back unless he had something to go on.'

Sir Alastair was also concerned. The media frenzy had lessened, but those dogged reporters from the local rag were very persistent. Sir Alastair felt threatened by their attentions. 'They must be stopped, Ernst,' the dean stormed.

'Why not just give them the interview they ask for? In this way, we can control the information and to tell the story in the way we want. It may put an end to their meddlesome snooping, no? Ask them to submit their questions in writing before to have an interview.'

The dean considered the doctor's remarks. He had to concede that the doctor had a point. If they could control the interview, they may get the hounds off their backs. There was far too much focus on the village and Leslie. The dean sat at his desk and began to draft a letter to the editor.

***

Mary spent her seventeenth birthday in her room. She only appeared at mealtimes and stayed silent throughout. Sir Alastair tried to engage in conversation, but she stubbornly remained detached. She left the wrapped birthday gift unopened on the dining table. He found the girl difficult to handle; the abrasive attitude she often displayed had softened to an icy cold silence, and he was not comfortable with the change.

He had noticed how she was in the company of her brother whenever he was ill. She became a caring and loving person whose only concern was his welfare. When apart from him, she was as frosty and remote as the peaks of the Himalayas.

He searched his mind for the reasons she may have to abhor him so and could find nothing. He had treated her well, always with respect and courtesy – apart from on occasions he felt she had overstepped the mark. When he had rebuked or admonished her, she'd deserved it. He considered himself a tolerant man, but he had his limits. Then he remembered her words when Leslie was ill before. They rang out loudly in his head. *You will pay.*

He reasoned in his mind that she could not blame him for her brother's condition. It was a medical problem, not something of his creating. For all they knew, he could have been born with the tumour, especially in view of his age when the boy first collapsed. Perhaps it had begun to develop before he had come to the village. With all the medical evidence, surely she would see that he was not in any way to blame. He assured himself that she would eventually come to the same conclusion.

It dawned upon him that he and Hendricks might have been wrong about Robert Lane. The man had probably told them the truth about the boy collapsing. What he and the doctor had done, could not ever be undone.

***

Ed received a call from a journalist who'd picked up his card in Oxford. He wanted to meet with him, as he could not discuss what he had to say on the telephone or write it down. Intrigued, Ed agreed to a meeting. The man had not given his name but had said he would explain everything at the meeting. They would have to meet somewhere well away from the village. Ed felt an excitement growing inside him; this cloak-and-dagger stuff reminded him of his days as a freelancer. They arranged to meet at eleven thirty on Saturday morning at the George Hotel in Colchester, a well-known and respected establishment in the area.

That evening, Ed went to visit Tweety at his home. He enquired how things were going in the Johns case, and Tweety gave him an update. Ed related the events of that day, and Tweety expressed his concern.

'I am surprised that you would even entertain such an idea – I mean, without knowing the man's name. That's most unlike you, sir, and if I may say, a little risky in my opinion. What if it turns out to be a ploy by one of his lordship's heavies? You saw them in Oxford. Great brutes that would crush a man in a trice.'

The editor chuckled. 'Look worry guts; it's in a public place. No harm will come to me there. And besides, I have checked the press pictures, and I have a photograph of the reporter picking up my card. Look that man there.' He showed Tweety the photograph. 'There is a copy of this back at the office. If anything untoward does happen, you will know who I met and where and when.'

Tweety could see that Ed's mind was made up, and nothing he could say would make the slightest difference. Looking sternly at Ed and in a serious voice he said, 'Okay, but promise me one thing.'

'What's that then?' asked Ed.

'I can have your chair if you cop it.'

The editor slapped Tweety gently on the shoulder. 'That chair is too big for you, laddie, but your concern is really sweet.'

They laughed and conversed long into the night.

***

The doctors and nurses gathered around Leslie's bed. No longer in the private room but in intensive care, they removed the bandages to observe the level of healing. A dark red line encircled his head. The edges of the thin flesh puckered where the stitches pulled them together. The doctors had induced a coma to aid the healing and monitored his condition day and night.

***

Ed sat at the table in the hotel drinking a cup of black coffee. He glanced at his watch again for the fourth time. It was already 11:40, and he was beginning to think that the man would not turn up. He had arrived early because he did not know his way around Colchester very well. He had had the car serviced and checked on Friday, not wanting a repeat of the breakdown in Oxford. Finding the hotel had not been difficult, and it had its own parking. He bought a local paper and read it before his contact arrived. He chose a table near the back of the lounge and sat facing the door and window, looking up every time someone entered or left.

At 11:48, he observed a man cross the street and enter the hotel. The man removed his hat, revealing very short fair hair. He was tall, broad-shouldered, and about forty years of age. The man looked around the restaurant and spotted Ed at the table. He went straight over and offered his hand. 'My name is Roger Garner. How do you do?'

Ed asked him to sit. 'Would you like something to eat or drink, Roger?' He recalled the man's name from the list his contact had supplied him.

'Yes, it has been a long drive. How about some lunch? It's on me.'

They each ordered from the menu and then began to talk. 'So, what is all this cloak-and-dagger for?' asked Ed.

'I observed you in Oxford, and a question you asked reminded me of my days in the army. You were in Oxford to cover the story of the young lad graduating I assumed, but you asked questions as though you knew something the other reporters didn't. In particular, was the question about Sir Alastair adopting the boy and his sister Mary.'

Ed stared at Roger. 'I never mentioned the girl's name. How—'

Roger pressed down on his hand and looked over Ed's shoulder; he frowned and sat back in his chair. The waiter placed the plates in front of them and left. 'Let's eat first. I will explain later,' he said in a low voice.

***

Mary stood looking at her brother through the window of the corridor. With no visitors allowed inside the intensive care ward, she attempted to communicate with her mind. Leslie was still unaware of anything around him, and bandages swathed his head. She hoped and prayed that he would return to his old silly self, with all his little intrigues and secrets that often annoyed her. She thought of Sir Alastair, and a growing desire for revenge loomed in her heart. But she had to bide her time, and she was good at that.

***

Sir Alastair discussed the boy's slow progress with the doctors. They managed to convince him that all was going according to plan and that everything was as they expected. He re-joined Mary and escorted her to the exit. The journey home was another silent affair, and she noticed that Jackson eyed her from time to time in the rear view mirror.

Jackson was always impassive, detached from events that enveloped the people around him. Sir Alastair trusted him implicitly; he knew that he could rely on this man's silence and strength.

***

The meal consumed, Ed and Roger ordered more coffee and returned to their discussion. 'You were going to tell me how you know the girl's name…'

Roger anxiously looked around the restaurant. The man's manner slightly unnerved Ed. Roger leaned forward, resting his arms on the table and talking almost in whispers. 'I had not seen Sir Alastair since my army days. We first met on Stonecutters Island in Hong Kong; well, it's Kowloon really. My platoon sergeant was Will Johns.'

Ed felt his blood pump faster.

'We were doing routine drills and training the youngsters who had just joined us from Blighty when this truck pulled up. A sergeant major Walsh steps out with Colonel Woodford. Of course you see, none of us knew who the Colonel was at the time – you know, title and all. Anyway, Walsh called us into the colonel's office, Will and me. Well, they offered us the chance to join the colonel and his lads in Military Intelligence. Will jumped at the offer, and seeing his enthusiasm, I decided that, as we had seen a lot of action together, I would join as well. Besides, we would get more pay and a pension. Who wouldn't jump at it?

'We did parachute training in Hampshire and orienteering and survival training in Wales and Scotland. Then we went to Canada in midwinter and had to survive on our wits and training for three months with no food, water, or shelter. All we had was our kit and the training. The first few weeks were the hardest; the cold got through whatever clothes you wore. We killed a couple of bears and four wolves, used the skins to keep warm, and ate the bear meat. All the time we were there, we had to avoid another team sent to capture us. Anyway you don't want my life story—'

Ed interjected, 'No, go on. Did you succeed?'

'No, sir, we all died in the attempt.'

'You fool, Roger. You know what—'

'We sure did. We captured the other team and held them prisoner for the last two weeks until the training was over. The hardest part was finding enough food for us all, and Will kept us all alive with his skills. He is a great leader, quiet and confident, determined in purpose. I doubt I shall ever meet his like again... Anyway, we still kept an eye out, as he told us, in case they'd sent other teams.

'Once the training finished, we did some recon missions in Egypt and Jordan. Then we went to Cyprus and then to Kenya and back to Cyprus again. During this time, we got to know each other pretty well, and I owe my life to him many times over. Will told me about his kids, his divorce, and how it cut him up putting Mary and Leslie in the home. But what can a serving soldier do in such circumstances? The reason he joined MI was to earn some good money and then buy his own place and take the kids out of there; the pension would come in handy as well.

'Anyway, we were in Cyprus I think – yeah, it would have been about '57 – when he got a telegram saying that his kids had been killed in a car accident on the way back from...I think...it may have been Yarmouth or somewhere close.'

'Felixstowe?' said Ed.

'Yes, I think you're right... Yes, it was Felixstowe. You know this part of the story?'

Ed shook his head. 'No, I'm sorry. Go on.'

'Well, the man just went to pieces. He went on about how hard it was getting custody and how it would have been better to have let her keep them. He was distraught; I tell you, we worried how he would survive it. Well, he spoke to the colonel, and he told Will that he would take care of everything. Evidently, there were few remains to bury, as the car had burst into flames. Will vowed that he would never set foot in England again by choice; it held too many bad memories for him.

'He volunteered for everything, even the most suicidal of missions. I reckon he wanted to die but couldn't top himself. I could tell he wasn't being rational so I always went with him to try and keep him out of trouble. Thing was, he always came out without a scrape, except that time he got stabbed in the arm, oh and when the yanks had to operate on him; they gave him a metal kneecap.'

'Where is he now?' asked Ed.

The man thought for a moment. 'Well, I remember he was sweet on a girl on Stonecutters Island. She worked in the offices there, an Irish girl, not a native you understand. He also had a German shepherd called Oscar. You should have seen the two of them together. My god that dog could do some tricks. Anyways, I know he left the dog with the Irish girl...Marie or Martha, can't remember her name now. Well I'm sure he would have gone back there for them.'

Ed searched the man's face and asked again, 'Why the hush-hush approach with me?'

The man looked furtively around again. 'There's more yet. We always went in groups of four. Will would plan and lead. There would be a communications man, the lingo man, and the backup man; that was me. My job was to be able to do all those things if needed. Whenever we lost someone, he would always be replaced to keep the number at four. Well, we lost a couple over the years. But for the most part, we were the same four for a long time. There was Will and me, Douggie Fairbrother – he was the communications man and a right hard nut, believe me – and then Norris Dwyer. He could speak seven languages fluently. He was a short fellow but fast on his feet; Swifty we called him. He was a great bloke, reliable and clever. We put our lives in his hands a few times, and I would again if I had to.'

Ed recognised all the names from the list, and this convinced him that the man was genuine.

'When we finished up in Cyprus, the CO we were attached to was told that we were off back to Hong Kong. That was not true. We did a couple more missions but without Douggie. The colonel took him off for another group.

'Well, when all the missions ended, I wanted to get back to Civvy Street and pick up the scraps of my life. It was then that the truth hit me.

We had been operating directly under Colonel Woodford. When we got our missions, we also got cash in the local currencies to cover expenses. When we signed up, our pay got put directly into bank accounts set up for each of us. As we were out of the country most of the time, we didn't need it, so it was building up nicely, or so we thought. I remember Douggie going on about his pay not being in his account once. He had a right go in the paymaster's office. They said they would look into it, and it was shortly after that when he went off on that other mission.

'When I left the army, I had no family to speak of, and so I spent some time moving around and odd jobbing just to pay my way. I didn't want to use the money in the bank for a while. I was hoping to buy a cottage later and settle down, maybe a bit of land with it and some hens. Eventually, I went to the bank, and there was less than half the money that there should have been. I got in touch with the paymaster's office, and they told me the same thing they had told Douggie, just that they would look into it.

'A few days later, I had a feeling someone was following me. Well, I was staying in digs at the time and working on a farm up in Norfolk. One day as I was on my way home, a black Austin Westminster stayed behind me. It could have passed many times. I watched it in my mirror. And where the road was narrowest, it forced me off the road and knocked me off my motorbike. I ended up in hospital with a broken leg and arm and the bike all smashed up. I reckon I was lucky to escape with my life. I reported it to the police, but they never found the culprit. When I went back to work, the farmer said he had no more need of me.

'I got a job doing gardening; an old mate from before the army days had a small gardening business in Shenfield and needed some help. A couple of weeks later, I got the feeling of someone following me as I walked home through the village one evening. I ducked into a shop and pretended I was looking at clothes on a rail. I could see through the shop window, but no one could see me from outside. Two burly blokes slowly went past looking in the window and up and down the street. It was so obvious that they were searching for someone; they were the ones following me. When the coast was clear, I went to a phone box and called my mate. I told him my leg was playing up so bad I couldn't walk, and could he come to pick me up and take me home. When I got home, I called the police. They were not the least bit interested as no crime had been committed, and I may have imagined the whole thing they said.

'When I arrived at my mate's house the next day, there were police all over the place. I pushed my way forward and tried to get to the house. A copper grabbed me by the collar of my jacket and twisted my arm up my back. My instinct was to put him onto his back, but I thought better of it. A police sergeant came over and asked what was going on. The constable told him I was trying to push my way through the cordon. I told the sergeant that I worked for the man in the house, and we were old friends. The constable released my arm, and the sergeant took me into the house.

'The place was a mess, and it looked as though there had been a fight – broken glass, furniture, and splashes of blood splattered all over... The sergeant told me that a neighbour had called them to report a commotion about 11:15 the previous night. When they'd arrived, the front door was wide open and they found the owner in a pool of blood inside the hallway. He was not dead but severely injured; he was in hospital under police guard. The sergeant asked me a whole lot of questions and wrote everything down. There were police taking fingerprints and noting all the damage done. He asked if I knew of any problems with neighbours, employees, customers, things like that. I told them that I was the only employee and that he was a very easy-going sort of chap. He never got into fights or arguments, and everyone that he worked for liked him. That's why he always had plenty of work on the go and, in fact, why he needed me to help him out.

'Then, the detective inspector turned up; he asked all the same questions and more. Where was I at 11:00 the night before and so on. You can imagine the questions. This fellow had me down as the prime suspect before the first question. I could feel him rooting around in my words for a contradiction or a lie. He asked the same questions again in a different way, looking to confuse me into giving a different answer. He was a bastard.'

Ed was eager to hear the rest.

'Let's have another coffee. All this talk has made my throat dry.'

They ordered more coffee, and Roger paid the bill.

He got up, went over to the entrance, and peered through the glass panes and windows into the street. He looked up and then down. Ed assumed that this man's behaviour had become a habit, and was glad he did not live with such a persecution complex. The man resumed his seat and sipped the hot coffee.

'I am sorry, sir, but could we change places? I hate having my back to the door. It makes me nervous.'

Ed swapped places to put the man at ease.

He continued with his story. 'Sometime later, the police stuck me in a car and drove me to my digs. When I reached my door, I could see the door had been forced. It was not obvious you understand, no broken splinters or such, just a slight mark where something thin and flexible had been pushed between the lock and the frame. Inside there were little signs to me that someone had been going through my things; to the detective, I was just untidy.

'He asked me to produce proof of my identity, army discharge papers and the like. When I looked for them, all my papers were gone – everything. Passport, birth certificate, bank book, some cash – the lot had been taken. When I told the detective, he said how convenient it was. He called the copper in the hall and slapped the handcuffs on me. I spent two days in the nick before I saw a solicitor.

'When I got back to my digs, the woman asked me to leave. She did not want someone like me in her house. Well, I was almost penniless, homeless, and jobless and had to be available to the police for their investigation. The money I had in the bank I couldn't get at because the bank book was missing.

'I called the paymasters' office again, and they said that they had no records for payments due to me. You can imagine I was fuming, I told them to check my records and gave them my army discharge date.' He reached into his pocket, asking Ed if he minded if he had a smoke.

'By all means, go ahead.' Ed finished his notes and looked at the man. 'You think that Woodford was responsible for all this, don't you? But do you have proof?'

The man puffed at the cigarette. 'I don't think he was responsible. I know for a fact that he was.

'When I was followed and saw the men through the shop window, I recognised one of the men – Sergeant Major Walsh from Hong Kong, who had brought the colonel in the truck. Thick as thieves those two; he never left the colonel's side the whole time they were there, a sort of bodyguard if you like.'

Ed winced slightly. 'Well it may prove they knew each other, but it's not proof of Woodford's involvement in this event. The connection is very tenuous at best and would be classed as circumstantial. Anyway, carry on with your story. What was the outcome?'

Roger seemed a little peeved by the dismissal of his 'evidence'. 'Well as I said, I had nowhere to go, so I went back to my mate's house; probably very foolish, but I couldn't think straight at the time. The coppers had all gone, and the door was locked. I knew where he kept his spare key, so I let myself in. I hadn't eaten for hours, so I made something to eat and poured myself a brandy. I closed all the curtains and left the lights off. Around midnight, I went to the spare bedroom and slept.

'The next day, I went to the hospital to see how he was, but the police wouldn't let me in. I went to the solicitor's office and told him where I was staying. Of course, he told me that I was a fool. Anyway, the fingerprints turned out to be my mate's and mine. There were no other prints in the place.

'That night at the house, the police arrived and carted me back to the nick – charged me with GBH, robbery, breaking and entering, attempted murder, and attempting to pervert the course of justice. So I spent two months in prison before my mate recovered and made a statement clearing me. He told them a man had called at his door looking for me. When he said that I wasn't there, the man let in his companion. The two started to smash up the place, and then they attacked him. I went to see him as soon as I got out. He told me that they had threatened to break his arms and legs if he did not tell them where I was. Lucky for me, he never told them, but not so good for him. He had a broken leg and collarbone, a fractured cheekbone, a skull fracture, internal bleeding, and three broken fingers from trying to defend himself. He said they were like bulldozers, unstoppable, and they had left him for dead. I stayed with him until I found a job in Kent.'

Ed digested the information and asked, 'Did you find out what happened to Douglas Fairbrother?'

The man lit another cigarette, inhaled deeply, and replied, 'No. Since the army days, not a word from him or about him.'

Ed told him about the body in the river and the connection to Sir Alastair.

'Hell, man, you have the connection yourself. There was nothing wrong with Douglas mentally; he was as sane as you or me. That bloody Woodford has a lot to answer for.'

Ed again had to explain the tenuous nature of the connection. 'Woodford is linked to so many companies and organisations it is nearly impossible to avoid a connection. And what I need is positive proof of his involvement. I think that will be the hardest part. He is a clever man, Roger. He employs people he can trust. And if caught, I do not think they would give him up.

'My investigation of Woodford started with the Johns boy, and it has turned out to be the most complex conspiracy I have ever worked on. Finding someone like you has put a new light on the matter. The next thing is to track down Will Johns. Can you remember the name of the Irish girl or where she came from?'

Roger stubbed out his cigarette and ordered another coffee, 'I can't remember her name exactly, whether it was Maria or Martha and I don't think I ever knew her surname. But I could ask Swifty. We still keep in touch from time to time. He lives in Canada now, married with two kids and doing quite well.'

Ed thanked Roger for the meal and the information and asked, 'Is there a number I can contact you on?'

'No,' he replied. 'I move around a lot so they can't keep tabs on me. Look, you are dealing with very dangerous people here, and if they find out what you're up to, your life won't be worth a brass farthing. I'll give you a call at the paper when I have something.'

Ed gave the man his home number just in case there was a problem, and then Roger said, 'By the way, I'm not a journalist. I saw the boy's name in the paper and wondered if it could be the "dead boy"; it just seemed too much of a coincidence. I went to Oxford just to see for myself if this Johns boy was anything like his father, and the similarity is striking. I got a real shock when I saw the colonel acting like he was the boy's father.'

Ed thanked Roger again for all the information and the two men shook hands and parted.

***

When Ed got back to his office, he found that Billy had compiled the article on the gas leak, neatly typed and awaiting him on his desk. Billy was not in the office and Tweety had gone to the asylum again to try to get information.

Ed sat and read Billy's article. The man was Tim Mathews. He had lived at the flat for six months and had bought the lease on it. Employed in the building trade, he had a reputation as a skilled professional; he could do electrical and plumbing work as well as carpentry, bricklaying, and plastering. Born in Cardiff in 1927, he'd lived most of his younger life in and around South Wales and was a great rugby fan. After his navy service, he joined the building trade, learning, working and perfecting his various skills. Once he obtained his qualifications he joined a company with contracts all over the UK and stayed with them for a number of years. He hated the travelling part of the job, as it took him away from his wife, quite often for long periods.

He discovered that his wife was having an affair with one of his colleagues whilst he was away. They ended up divorcing on the grounds of her adultery, and he got custody of their four-year-old daughter; his ex-wife never contested the decision. Tim found it very difficult to work and look after the girl, so after some months of trying to reconcile the situation, he put her into a children's home near where he was living at the time. He worked like mad at every job he could get and managed to save the money to put the deposit on the lease to the flat. He was in the process of renovating the place so that he could bring his daughter home with him. The last job he had to complete was the kitchen. He had already registered the girl at a local school and surgery. He had planned to finish the work on the flat by the end of the month.

Billy had obtained the details of the story from Tim's work colleagues, family, and friends. Devastated by the news, all said what a reliable worker he was. No one Billy spoke to believed he would make a mistake with the gas pipe. He was always extremely safety conscious and meticulous in his work. He would refuse to make a repair if a replacement was essential or an apparatus compromised. They also said he suffered from a sinus problem and had a poor sense of smell. That was why he always tested gas connections with liquid soap.

Neither the neighbours nor the police were aware that he had a daughter; the information came from a work friend. They had worked for the same company before, and it was this friend's recommendation that got Tim the job with his new firm. He also had an ad hoc job with an electrical firm doing rewiring and installing switches and the like.

He was not a regular drinker at pubs or clubs; his colleagues said that he saved every penny he could for the lease. He'd even sold his car and bought a second-hand bicycle.

When Billy checked with the police to see if they had followed up the lead on the girl, they had said the girl was not at the home. He'd also told them about the sinus problem and asked if they had checked for soap residue around the connector. They'd asked him if he was trying to tell them how to do their job, and besides, a sinus problem would be why he did not smell the gas.

Billy had visited the dead man's flat; he was sure there were signs that the door had been forced with something thin and flat like a spatula. The police dismissed Billy's suspicions of foul play.

It occurred to Ed that the police would come off very badly when this story went to print. It was a catalogue of stupidity, incompetence, and arrogance. The backlash could be huge. He decided that, in light of this, he would go to see Tweety and make a proposal for a new line of attack. He left a note for Billy that he would revise the article.

***

Tweety was eager to hear the story of the mystery reporter. Ed related the whole saga to him in summary form. Tweety listened in amazement at the report of the meeting. Ed then told him of the article Billy had written. Straight away, Tweety was in accord with Ed. He put the two stories together with the one about the body in the river, a few other articles they had covered, and they added up to a story of gross negligence that would rock the foundations of the police force.

Ed put his proposal to Tweety; he wanted him to take an extended leave with pay from the paper, to work on an exposé on the failings of the police force. He would edit Billy's article and omit the passages indicating police incompetence. Tweety would bring all the cases together to present a dossier exposing the facts and their own conclusions. His hands would be somewhat tied, as he could not cite Roger as a source.

Ed supplied Tweety with the names and addresses of people he would need to interview – Roger's employer at the farm in Norfolk, the landlady at the lodgings before she threw him out, and the man in Shenfield. He was to check and recheck every source and confirm every statement.

Ed saw this as an article people would want read and was going to check with the directors of the paper to ensure that there would be no conflict of interest. He envisaged a special edition. But if the director didn't agree, a national or something like *Punch* magazine would take it. Ed still had plenty of contacts from the old days.

***

A letter from Sir Alastair inviting a list of questions prior to an interview intrigued Ed and Tweety, who jumped with surprise at the offer. 'He wants to control the interview and concoct his answers so that we can't take him by surprise,' exclaimed Tweety.

'Of course, laddie. He is not about to 'go gentle into that good night'. To quote Dylan Thomas.'

Tweety looked a little sourly at Ed. 'I suppose you want to do the interview yourself?'

'Yes, but not for the reasons you think laddie. I want you to stay away from the Woodford story for now. I'm not taking it away from you; don't get me wrong. I want the police story and the Woodford one. But in view of what Roger told me, it's best that it looks as though you are not connected. I will do the interview, for what it's worth, and let you write it up later so you share the credit. Will you be happy with that?'

Tweety had no choice other than to agree, but he would dearly have loved to interview the man himself. He thought about what Ed said and agreed that it was the sensible approach. Ed also mentioned that he was certain the Woodford story would link at some point with the police corruption story. That was why he wanted to keep them separate for now. There would be risky days ahead for them both.

Chapter 16

A New Day Dawns and a Chasm Yawns

Leslie sat up in the bed to answer the doctor. 'Well, I feel a slight lightness in my head, probably because you took something out of it.'

The boy and the doctor laughed. 'It is so good to see you display a sense of humour.'

The boy stroked his head and felt the stubble that had begun to reforest his head. The doctors were very pleased with the healing of the wound. They left off the bandages to aid the repair and now, with the risk of infection greatly reduced, agreed that he could have visitors.

***

Mary stood at the reception desk, desperate to get permission to visit her brother, 'Could you please ask Mr Sangstrom?' she asked in a childlike manner. 'I promise I will not tire him or put strain upon him. Please let me see him. I beg you.'

The reception nurse was still trying to get the surgeon to answer the call sent over the PA system. 'He has not answered yet. He is probably with another patient or the relatives.'

Mary went and sat on one of the chairs in the waiting room, opposite the desk.

She noticed a man looking in her direction several times from a seat nearby. After some time, she went across to him and asked abruptly, 'Is there something you want from me?'

The man turned bright red and was completely flustered. 'I…I… Are you…er.' He regained his composure and continued. 'Sorry, Miss. Are you the sister of Leslie?'

'Yes I am,' she replied. 'And what is that to you?'

The man was unsettled by her abruptness. 'I am a reporter from the local paper. We have been trying to get some news about Leslie, but nobody will tell us anything. You see, Miss, many people out there have taken an interest in your brother. We are all concerned about his health, but they won't tell us a thing here—'

She cut him dead. 'You just want to sell papers; my brother's welfare is not your business.'

'On the contrary, Miss. You don't know how important your brother's welfare is to us and to the folks who have written in to the paper asking for information about him. There is much concern about his health and welfare, Miss. Did you know that prayers are said for his recovery at the local churches and that collections are being made to pay for the medical treatment?'

Mary's face showed her complete ignorance of the facts the reporter had revealed. She felt ashamed of her attitude and lowered her voice slightly. 'I did not realise that anyone apart from me cared in the slightest about him. I'm sorry I snapped at you.'

The reporter immediately felt that slight tug of a fish on the hook. He had to take great care; this was an important fish that he could not allow to escape. 'Miss, I am sorry too. I'm not going to pressure you or anyone else. You have your own worries and I truly sympathize with your predicament.' They sat in silence for a few moments.

'My name is Billy, and if there is anything I can do, please let me know, Miss. My mate Tweety has spent hours here. In fact, he followed the ambulance here.'

Mary was contemplating her shoes as a tear dropped onto the laces. She quickly wiped her eyes and looked at the reporter. 'Tweety?'

'Oh, yeah, his name is Bird. Tweety is his nickname. Our editor has put him on another assignment, and so it's just little old me now to do the pleading and waiting.'

Mary asked, 'Can we talk somewhere privately?'

He looked about them and replied, 'Not here.'

Mary had an idea. 'Wait for me here,' she said and went off down the corridor.

Within a few minutes, she returned and sat next to him. She removed a plastic bag from her handbag and passed it to him discretely. 'Go to the men's room and put this on. You are wearing a suit, so do not button it. Just leave it open like a doctor.'

The reporter nodded and crossed the crowded waiting area.

Billy had only been gone for a few seconds when the reception nurse told her she could go to see her brother. She explained that she did not want her brother to see that she had been crying and would wait a little longer and freshen up.

Mary permitted herself an inward chuckle as she watched the reporter stride though the waiting area in the white coat. He stopped halfway and turned some pages back and forth on the clipboard she had also given him, and keeping his face turned away from the desk, he went straight up to Mary. 'Come along, Miss. We need to do more tests to establish his progress...'

They passed into the corridor, and Mary ushered him into the empty consulting room she had borrowed the coat from. 'Have you ever considered acting?' she asked with an impish grin.

'It was clever of you to think of this,' he replied.

Mary pressed his arm anxiously. 'Look, we don't have long; I am allowed to see Leslie now. What do you want to know?'

Billy had resigned himself to the fact that no one would speak to him and was now lost for words. The questions jumbled in his head.

'Come on,' Mary said in agitation.

'What is the relationship between you and Sir Alastair?'

'He is our legal guardian. Next.'

'What happened to your parents?'

'My mother lives in Salford, and my father was reported missing in action, presumed dead in 1957. Next.'

'Why did Leslie give up the swimming?'

'I don't know. Next.'

'What do you know about Douglas Fairbrother?'

'He was found dead in the river Roding in 1958, an inmate of the asylum and killed by Dr Hendricks, the result of a blow to the head with a truncheon. Next.'

'What do you know about sergeant major Walsh?'

'He is one of Sir Alastair's private assassins. Next and last.'

'Who did the sergeant major kill?'

'The list is too long to cover now, but Robert Lane and Tim Mathews you can start with. But now I must go to see Leslie.'

Billy offered his hand and thanked her most sincerely. 'Good luck with your brother, and we all hope he makes a full recovery. By the way, what is wrong with him?'

'A massive brain tumour,' she said, and adding, 'A word of advice Billy – make copies of everything and store them away from the office buildings,' Mary left the room with great speed to see her dear brother.

Taken aback by the last remark, Billy saw it as ominous.

***

A guard positioned outside the room was not one of the usual team. 'What do you want here?' he growled.

'I am here to see my brother.'

He placed himself in front of the door, his arms hanging by his side and fists clenched tightly. 'No visitors,' he said.

Mary looked up at the blank face and said, 'I will see my brother, and you will sit on that chair and not interfere. Is that clear?'

His face unchanged, the man sat on the chair, and Mary entered the room.

Leslie watched as his sister drew up a chair and sat beside his bed. 'How are you doing, Leslie?' she asked in a very calm soft voice.

'Not too bad,' he replied. 'Who are you?'

Mary was shocked that he did not recognise her; she knew that he may not have all his memories, but to forget her was something very unexpected. 'I am your sister, Mary. You remember me?'

'I have a sister?' the boy replied with a puzzled expression.

'Leslie, it is me, Mary. I have been here all the time you have been ill – Mary your sister.' Anxiety began to rise within her at his responses.

The boy still had the same expression as he stared at her. 'I did not know I had a sister. Nobody told me. Why did no one tell me, Mary?'

It was too much and so unexpected; the girl ran from the room with tears streaming down her face and deep sobs that shook her off balance. She stumbled and fell in the corridor; a passing nurse helped her back to her feet and asked what the problem was. As they returned to the reception area, Mary explained as best she could what had happened. But she found it nearly impossible to speak coherently. Tears and saliva drowned her. She could not control the waves of shock that shuddered through her, the sobbing and the tears blurred her vision, and her body convulsed with tremors. As they entered the reception area, the nurse signalled to the desk for a doctor.

***

Mary awoke with a throbbing headache pounding like a jackhammer inside her skull, Sedated and placed in a side room in the hospital, she looked around and tried to get up; rails on the side of the bed prevented her from getting out. A nurse took her pulse and told her why she was there. She slumped back in the bed and asked why her brother did not recognise her. The nurse told her to relax and that she would call for the doctor.

Mr Sangstrom stood by Mary's bed. 'I am sorry I could not get here sooner.' He reached down and held the girl's hand. 'It must have come as an awful shock to you. We wanted to see you and Sir Alastair before you visited your brother, but I had to attend another hospital on an urgent case. It is most unfortunate, truly unfortunate.' He let go of her hand and sat on the chair. 'When we brought him out of the coma, he seemed to be fine. He could read, count, and move his limbs as normal. It was only when we started to ask about you and Sir Alastair, the village and the tutors, his studies and his friends that we realised that he had no memory of them at all. I must warn you, Mary. Sometimes when he speaks, he sounds like a six-year-old. His intellect is fine. It just sounds strange when he speaks. I hope he will pass out of this stage, and his memory will return to normal. It is early days yet, and he may have a long road to full recovery. You are suffering from a mixture of shock, grief, and helplessness, and it is normal for you to feel such emotions. But try to be strong for him.

The rage began to rear its ugly head inside her. *You will pay* she screamed in her mind, convinced that somehow the dean, the doctor or both were responsible for the tumour and therefore his condition now. It was a totally irrational idea and one that Leslie would have dismissed if she had told him her thoughts.

The surgeon said, 'We will monitor his progress constantly; it is a good idea if you can continue to visit him. But try not to let emotions get the better of you. I realise that I am asking you to do something very difficult. If your brother is to recover fully, we want to avoid emotions and confusions. If he sees that you are upset, he may not be able to understand why. And remember, Mary, in his head, he is only six at times. He uses the vocabulary of an adult but escapes into childhood, and that may be a good thing for him now, until he recovers his memories. You do understand what I am telling you?

'Did something happen to him when he was about six years old, a major event or a life-changing occurrence, something that would be fixed in his mind for life?'

'Of course,' said Mary, 'that is when we went to live at the village and when the dean…Sir Alastair, he told us about Dad being missing in action or dead. I remember it so vividly. Leslie wet himself, and he had never done that before. And it is also when he swallowed the three pennies at Felixstowe a while previous. They all happened when he was six.'

The surgeon smiled at Mary. 'An eventful year for a small lad. I did not see any scar from an operation.'

'No, he did not have one.'

'What? They let the coins pass right through him.'

'Well…nobody believed he had swallowed them.'

'You are so very lucky to still have a brother, young lady.'

He allowed Mary to leave the room and visit Leslie, on the solemn promise that she would not become emotional. 'And we want to keep you in overnight to ensure that you have fully recovered. Is that okay with you?'

She gave the surgeon a hug, and the tears started to run again.

'Now, Miss, you did promise.'

She wiped her eyes whilst trying to laugh. 'Yes…yes I did. And I do keep my promises. Thank you, sir. Thank you.'

***

It annoyed Sir Alastair that the hospital staff had allowed Mary to see Leslie without informing her of his condition first, and he was just as annoyed at her display of hysteria. Mr Sangstrom managed to calm the man as they sat in the canteen. He told Sir Alastair everything that he had told Mary and emphasized the importance of remaining calm and unemotional. 'As for the hysteria, she has had a hard time controlling her emotions in front of Leslie. And after all, he is her only kin. She cares for him deeply, sir, and that is evident.'

When he entered Leslie's room, Sir Alastair found Mary with her head resting against the chair back and both of them fast asleep, hand in hand. He decided to leave them resting.

***

Billy was excited as he reported to Ed the events at the hospital. He was not in competition with Tweety, but he'd had a result on his second day, in contrast to Tweety's weeks of blanks.

'The right time in the right place,' Ed reminded Billy. 'Write up your notes and let me have them. Oh, and by the way, intrepid one, you understand that all is hearsay unless Mary actually witnessed anything, which I sincerely doubt. But good work anyway.'

Billy stopped suddenly as he was on his way out of the office. 'Ed, she said something rather odd right before she left. 'Make copies of everything and store them away from the office building.'

'What do you think she meant by that?' Ed looked alarmed. 'Get everyone in here now please, Billy, and I mean everyone.'

Billy shrugged and went to gather the staff.

Twelve people crammed into the editor's small office. The only staff missing were Tweety and a cub reporter out on assignments. Ed stood and addressed the employees. 'It is possible that something untoward may happen in the very near future. I can't go into details as to how I know, but I do not want anyone in these premises after 18:00 until I tell you otherwise. Is that understood?'

The staff muttered and mumbled to each other.

'I said is that understood, dammit.'

As one, the staff replied, 'Yes, sir.'

'Be vigilant at all times. Do not open any unexpected parcels or packages. And watch out for anything unusual. Nobody is to enter this building except staff or invited visitors. Keep the doors locked, and make sure you have your keys with you at all times. Billy and Mike, stay here. The rest of you can return to work. And thank you all. Remember, vigilance at all times.'

Ed withdrew eight folders from a cabinet and handed them to Billy. 'I want you to make two copies of each of these and do it now. Mike, I want you to return all those boxes. You will find the addresses on the senders' labels. Now please. Oh, how are we on this week's issue?'

'Up to speed, sir. Just two articles for you to check.'

Ed nodded. 'Good. Send in the copy boy with the articles, and I'll check them now.'

There was urgency about Ed and the way he had spoken that spurred the staff into hectic activity.

Ed composed his list of questions for Sir Alastair, along with a letter explaining his reasons for requesting the interview. He called Mike. 'How are we doing with the boxes?'

'All downstairs and awaiting the courier, sir.'

'Good. Now I want you to get on your bike and deliver this letter in person.'

Mike stood, reading the address on the envelope.

'Come on, laddie. Chop-chop,' urged Ed.

Billy entered the office pushing a trolley laden with papers. 'We have run out of folders, sir. Do you have any?'

Ed told him to close the door and he retrieved some blank folders. They sorted the papers and placed them into the folders in three identical piles. From his desk, Ed placed two typed sheets of paper on top of each pile and put each pile into box files. He handed one box to Billy. 'I want you to take this box home with you and keep it in a very safe place. Should anything happen to me or to Tweety, you are to open the box and follow the instructions I have put inside. I presume that you read as you did the copying?'

Billy looked sheepishly at Ed.

'No. It's okay, laddie. You should know what we are getting into. We are involved with some dangerous characters, and you have a right to know. Just keep it to yourself, you understand?'

Billy donned the mantle of responsibility and felt immensely proud that the editor trusted and had confided in him. 'Sure thing, sir. How risky is this?'

'There's no telling with this lot, but on a scale of one to ten, twelve is close,' said Ed.

***

Mary continued to visit Leslie every day. She caught the 9:35 underground train and changed at Mile End for South Kensington on the District line. From the station, it was a short walk to the hospital. She much preferred to travel alone by train than to go in the car with Sir Alastair. Besides she could arrive and leave as she pleased. She did not wish to conform to her guardian's busy schedule.

Leslie's progress was slow. He never thought about his sublime retreat, Perry, Tweety or Ed, the village, or his vow to amend the situation. All was lost to his mind, forgotten, as were his studies and his achievements. He could still converse in the languages he had studied but was confused by people's lack of response when he spoke so. He had tried to communicate with a nurse in French and then in Spanish, but she did not understand him. His mind struggled to decide which of his languages was appropriate. He had done the same with Mary; she understood the French but urged him to speak in English.

On the occasions that Sir Alastair visited Leslie, he always found the boy sleeping and was reluctant to awaken him, especially with Mary on guard! Sleep for Leslie was his refuge now. He did not dream at all. Mary talked about their father and told stories of their days in Felixstowe, but she avoided any references to what Leslie had told her of his plans. She wanted him to recover under his own volition at a pace that he could cope with; she would not coerce him in any way. She waited patiently for signs of him returning to his former self.

***

Eventually Sir Alastair made an appearance when Leslie was awake. He entered the private room accompanied by Mr Sangstrom. And as usual, Mary was already at her brother's bedside.

Leslie studied the man's sharp features and the dark piercing eyes; he huddled himself tightly and held onto his sister. A terrible fear gripped him, and he began to babble in the childlike voice that he sometimes adopted. The surgeon was so alarmed at the boy's reaction that he swiftly led Sir Alastair back towards the door. In the corridor, he expressed his concern to Sir Alastair. 'It appears he has forgotten you as he did his sister. It is most disconcerting I know, for you and the boy. It may be best, sir, that, for the time being, you do not visit him and allow him to recover. I noticed that he expressed some alarm, and that is not good for him. He may just be confused at present, but I am sure the situation will resolve with time. We shall inform you of his progress, but please do not worry. He is improving slowly.'

Sir Alastair was startled by Leslie's reaction to him and not at all happy to feel excluded from the boy's recovery, but he would comply nonetheless. He felt that he and Leslie had built a strong bond between them. He was immensely fond of the boy and proud of his development into a young man. A thought nagged at him from deep in his mind; Mary had constant access to Leslie and could poison her brother's mind against him.

***

Ed drove to Tweety's flat and parked a few streets away. He walked the rest of the way in the dark, his senses heightened, alert to every sound and movement. He gave Tweety one of the boxes of files and explained the situation. Ed urged Tweety to put the box somewhere safe.

'I'll take it to my parent's house and leave it in my room there,' he said.

Ed made him aware that this could involve them in some risk; it would be more prudent not to involve his parents at all. Tweety agreed.

They sat talking about Tweety's assignment. The reporter had plans to visit Norfolk the next day and would stay at a guest house for a few days or until he got the interviews and information he was after. He gave Ed the details and a contact number.

Tweety left his flat before dawn, hoping to avoid the morning rush hour. He made a stop in Braintree to breakfast and to stretch his legs. He constantly checked that no one followed him, every so often pulling over at the side of the road and letting the traffic pass for five minutes or so. Each time, he would take the opportunity to refer to his road map; this was unknown territory for him.

He headed for Mundford and found the minor road heading for Methwold but continued past it for about a mile. He parked and had a walk around, looking in a shop window and checking the reflections in the glass to make sure no one was watching him. He entered a newsagent's shop and bought a national paper, a local paper, and some barley sugar sweets. Satisfied that he was alone, he continued his journey. He arrived at 'Wood Farm' and turned into the drive after checking what vehicles were close by.

'Good morning, Mr Stratton? I'm Harry Bird. We spoke on the telephone yesterday.'

'Ah, yes. Do come in, Mr Bird. Can I get you a tea or coffee?'

'A cup of tea will be most welcome, sir.'

'Take a seat, please. Make yourself at home.'

The man went out to the kitchen, and Tweety had a look around. There were some photographs of prize bulls and framed certificates and rosettes. 'I see you have done well with your animals over the years, Mr Stratton.'

A voice from the kitchen replied, 'Yes. I been lucky with me stock, but they needs a lot of lookin' after. Trouble is, y'see, prices 'ave gorn up an 'taint cheap breeding nowadays. I only keeps a dairy 'erd now and some arable crops.'

He re-entered the front room carrying a tray with tea and biscuits. 'Now you wanted to talk 'bout that chap who worked for me a ways back.'

'Yes, Mr Stratton. I am following up on a story regarding the accident that he had on his motorbike.'

The man looked surprised. 'Accident, don't know about no accident,' he said. 'He went home one day an' din't come back for a couple o weeks I think it were; might have been longer see. Then this bloke comes asking for im. Says did I have problems with im, and I told im what 'appened like. An he says he knew im, and he weren't to be trusted like – unreliable he says; owed him money like. E says Roger was a gamblin man and owed lots of people money like. Says he robbed some folks he worked for to pay his gamblin debts. Thing is, I did like Roger, an easy-going sort a chap that you could get on with, a bloody good worker too. But after what that fella told me, I had to think about me farm and the little I got put away for emergencies like.'

Tweety took notes and asked, 'What did this fellow say his name was?'

'Oh I don't think e gave me is name, just that he were looking for Roger and did I knows where he was.'

'Did you tell him where Roger lived?'

'Well yes, course I did. See, if Roger owed him money, e ad the right to get it back I reckon.'

'Did you discuss it with Roger when he came back?'

'No, sir. I just wanted him off of me property like.'

'Could you describe the man who came to look for Roger?'

'Well, tall like, ad to be about forty, really well built and big shoulders like. Oh, e had a broken nose like a boxer and a shaved ead and all.'

Tweety put his notebook in his pocket and thanked the farmer for his time. He wanted to tell the man that he had all the facts wrong about Roger. But at this stage, he couldn't honestly say if the story was true or false, so he said nothing more and made his departure.

Tweety drove to a detached house in Stoke Ferry, a short distance from Methwold. A notice in the window announced that there was a room to let. He rang the bell and waited. A short woman of about seventy-five opened the door. 'Have you come about the room?' she asked.

'No, ma'am, we spoke on the telephone yesterday. Mr Bird?' he said in an enquiring tone.

'Mr Bird? Oh dear, do I know you?'

Tweety felt straight away that this was going to be a difficult interview. 'Yes, Mrs Purcell. We spoke on the telephone about an article I am writing.'

'An article? Would that be for the newspapers? I can't imagine what they could want from me.'

They entered the house and went into a lounge. 'We don't get many visitors from the papers you know.'

Tweety removed his notebook from his pocket and began. 'Mrs Purcell, do you recall a Mr Roger Garner who stayed here a while ago?'

She searched her memory such as it was and replied, 'I don't think I remember that name Mr…'

'Bird,' said Tweety. 'My name is Harry Bird.'

'That is such a sweet name; I like to feed the birds in the garden. I always make sure I put some bread out for them. Do you have a bird table, Mr…?'

'People call me Tweety, Mrs Purcell. We were talking about Roger Garner?'

'Yes, Roger, such a nice man, always very polite. The sort of person I like to have staying here.'

Tweety was beginning to feel frustration build inside him. 'Do you remember if anyone came looking for him after he left?'

'Oh dear, did he leave? I do hope I didn't upset him. I have my rules, you see. No lady friends in the room. And the front door is locked at eleven. And no loud music… I do so detest the loud music they play these days, don't you, Mr…'

Tweety closed his notebook and thanked the woman for her time.

His next stop would be the friend in Shenfield. He felt he was closer to home ground with this one. He telephoned Ed to tell him of the change of plan, and then he called the guest house to cancel the booking.

He parked outside the detached bungalow and met David Giles in the front garden. Tweety introduced himself and they went into the house.

'How long did you know Roger Garner?' was Tweety's first question.

'We used to live next door to each other as kids.'

'Did you know him well?'

'Yeah, we must have been neighbours for sixteen years or so before I left to do my military service.'

'So you run your own business now, doing gardening I believe.'

'Well I wouldn't call it a business as such. I get by, just doing people's gardens who can no longer manage them alone. My son used to help me out before he married. Now he has a family of his own I don't see that much of him. He works for the telephone company.'

'You engaged Roger to help you out. Is that right?'

'Yeah, good egg that bloke and a shame what happened to him.'

'Can you tell me the story of what happened? I realise that it may be painful for you to recall it.'

'Not at all, young feller. This bloke calls at my door about twenty past ten at night looking for Roger. I told him that Roger didn't live here. He asked me for Roger's address, and I refused to tell him. You see, Roger had told me what happened in Norfolk, and I suspected that this man calling late at night was a bit fishy. He went to the front door and let this other bloke in.'

'They started to break things, demanding that I tell them what they wanted to know. I tried to stop them, but they attacked me, and one of them smashed my leg with his boot. All the time they were beating me, they kept demanding the same thing. I never told them a thing because I knew that they would kill Roger if they got hold of him. I wanted to phone him after they left, but I passed out.'

'Did you get a name?'

'No. They never said their names. Oh…except when the first guy opened the door for the other one to come in; the second guy called him Greg.'

'Did you tell all of this to the police?'

'I sure did. And just as well. They had Roger in the frame for it. They questioned me in the hospital for hours, suggesting that Roger had concocted the story and was putting pressure on me to tell a pack of lies to them. That detective inspector was an arrogant sod; he treated me like a criminal, not a victim. He threatened to charge me with perverting the course of justice. I told him to get the bastards that did this to me,' he said, pointing at his head and leg.

'Can you describe the two men?'

David shifted his position in the chair. 'This Greg, well he would have been probably late thirties or early forties. About two inches taller than me, say six foot. Strong, broad shoulders like a fighter. He had a shaved head, a broken nose, and huge fists like hams. The other fellow was shorter, about my height, stocky…short mousy hair…a moustache and small beard, a goatee I think they call it. And though it wasn't cold, he had black gloves on. I noticed their car when I first opened the door. It was a black Austin

A90 Westminster. I'd say about ten years old. I remember it because a bloke I used to work for had one the same. Oh, the shorter guy carried a short length of pipe. That's what he hit me over the head and shoulders with. I put up a fight, but they were too good for me.'

Tweety checked his notes. 'Whilst you were in the hospital, Roger came here didn't he?'

'Yeah, he told me about that. I didn't mind. I'd told him before that he could stay here. I have three bedrooms, and he could have saved on rent and such. He said he preferred to live away from the job, but I think he wanted to keep trouble at a distance from me.'

Tweety gave the man his card and said, 'If you think of anything that might help us, could you call me or my editor on this number?'

Tweety looked up and down the road as he left the house and got into his car.

He drove to Hutton Village just on the edge of Shenfield and rang the bell of the Edwardian style house. Whilst he awaited a reply, he observed a woman at the window of a house across the road.

A tall, slim woman looked down at him from the open doorway. 'Yes?'

'My name is Bird.'

'Oh yes. Do come in, Mr Bird.' She showed the reporter into a large comfortable lounge with heavy brocade curtains and highly polished antique furniture. The smell of lavender-scented beeswax pervaded the house. 'Do please sit, Mr Bird. And may I get you some refreshments?'

'No, thank you, ma'am,' he replied.

'Tell me again what it is that you are writing about. The telephone is quite crackly.'

Tweety opened his notebook and licked the end of the pencil. 'I am writing an article on the effects of crime – how people deal with crime and the effects on the victims.'

She gave him a sharp glance. 'It is about time that someone paid attention to that sort of thing. There is far too much violence and robbery these days. I blame the influence of the television and the cinema; there are far too many violent films. How can I help you?'

She spoke with a posh voice in a manner that one could describe as haughty. She had well-defined (although not well-considered) views on the world and its problems, as well as their causes and solutions. She reminded Tweety of a history teacher from his schooldays. 'Do you remember Roger Garner, ma'am?'

'Of course I do. I still have all my faculties, young man.'

'I do beg your pardon, ma'am. I can see that you do. Perhaps I should have asked, what do you remember about Roger Garner?'

'I thought at first that he was a real gentleman. He paid his rent on time. He kept his room clean and tidy, and I felt that he was reliable. That day when the police brought him here in handcuffs, well, I have never had such goings on in my house. This is a respectable establishment.'

Tweety made his notes and asked, 'Did Roger or the police explain to you what was happening?'

'I did ask, but the police detective said it was an official investigation, and they could not divulge information. I read in the local newspaper how he had attacked a friend and nearly killed him and how he was arrested when he went back to rob the house whilst the poor man was in the hospital fighting for his life. Such shocking behaviour. When he came back to the house, I asked him to leave immediately.'

'Did anyone come to the house looking for him in the days before or after the incident?'

She thought for a moment. 'Yes…yes, on that very morning, a man came to the door just as I was leaving to go to the bank. I did not let him in, as I did not want to miss the bus. It must have been about 10:20 because the bank shuts for lunch at 12:30, and the bus to town leaves here at 10:37. He asked if Mr Garner was in and said that he was a friend of his. I told him that he was not in, and would he excuse me as I had a bus to catch. He got back into his car and drove away.'

'What kind of car was it?'

'I am not good with motor cars, Mr Bird. It was black, and there was another man driving.'

'Can you describe the men?'

'Well the one that came to the door was tall… He had no hair – not bald; I would say he shaved his head… He had a flat nose… He was powerfully built, broad shoulders and thick neck. I thought at the time that Mr Garner surely did not associate with persons of that type. He looked like a ruffian to me. The man in the car I could not see very well, except that he had a moustache and a beard. It was odd that he wore gloves on such a warm day – yes, black leather gloves.'

'Is the room let now? I wondered if I may just have a brief look at it.'

The woman stood and said, 'He took all his possessions, and there is nothing of his left upstairs.'

'If you would kindly indulge me, ma'am. I am not interested in his personal belongings. There is something I need to check. I promise I will explain everything to you in a few moments.'

'Very well,' she said, retrieving a pass key from the sideboard drawer.

They ascended the stairs, and she opened the door. Tweety inspected the door frame closely. 'Mrs Munns, did you notice that there is a mark just here?'

She peered at the frame, moving her head up and down. 'I have no idea how that got there. I have not noticed it before.'

Tweety removed a thin rectangle of strong flexible plastic from his pocket. He closed the door and placed the plastic between the door and the frame, in line with the lock. He gave a swift push to the plastic, and the door swung open.

'What on earth?' exclaimed the woman.

'Can we check the front door, ma'am?' said Tweety.

'I hope you have not damaged the door,' she said as they descended the stairs.

'Not at all, ma'am,' he replied.

He opened the front door and immediately noticed the curtains move across the road.

He examined the door lock and the frame. 'Look! You can see here, Mrs Munns; this frame has the same marks.'

She bent low to examine the faint traces on the door frame.

'I suggest that you change your lock and install a deadlock. This door opens as easily as the one upstairs. 'Now if you will kindly indulge me just a few moments longer.'

He crossed the street and knocked at the door of the house opposite. A stout woman answered the door. Tweety gave her an explanation and asked if she could spare a few minutes of her time. He asked if she recalled the day of Roger's arrest.

'Yes I do, sir. Such a scandal. The talk was all up and down the street—'

'Did you see anyone, strangers, at the house that day?'

'I saw two gentlemen in a black Westminster when they were talking to Gloria. Oh that's Mrs Munns. I assumed she had given them a room because they came back about fifteen minutes later. They seemed to have some trouble with the key though. Well they were only in the house for about twenty minutes, and then they were gone again. I presumed they had gone to collect their luggage, as they had none with them at the time.'

'Was it the same man who spoke to Gloria earlier?'

'Oh most definitely.'

'Well thank you for your time, ma'am. You have been most helpful. Oh, just one thing more. Did the police interview you?'

'No. They were in and out of Gloria's house all afternoon, but they never came to any of us neighbours.'

Tweety returned to Mrs Munns and explained the whole story to her, including what the neighbour had told him.

She was shocked and apologetic. 'That poor man. I should have listened to my instincts about him...and I will take your advice about the lock, Mr Bird, thank you so much.'

***

Tweety was very pleased with the information that he had gathered as he sat typing up his notes. He had managed to begin the file on the performance of the police forces involved. However, a problem occurred to him. Once they published all the information and the facts, there would need to be an investigation of the police themselves into the way they perform. The way the system operated was for one police force to investigate another. it was a system riddled with corruption and whitewashes. He felt that an independent body would be far more objective and accountable. The alternative was to hand everything over to the home office and let them deal with it, and that could have its drawbacks as well, at this stage. It was not clear if the case involved mere incompetence or something more sinister. If the latter applied, then how far up the chain did it extend?

Tweety had a lot more work to do yet, and it would be a long road ahead of him. He reviewed the typed sheets and made notes of his thoughts. He wrote down a list of the people he still wanted to interview and the information he hoped to get from each of them. He had decided to leave the interviews of police officers to the last; getting information from them would not be an easy task.

***

Mary knew that her brother was good at playing games, so she took with her a board and a set of draughts. However much she concentrated, she could not defeat him. 'I am getting bored with this game,' she said.

'You need more practice.' He chuckled, 'Paul would thrash you. He is good at draughts and chess.'

The revelation shook her. 'You remember Paul?' she said in amazement.

'I think so,' he replied with some confusion as to where this name had come from. He could not put a face to the name Paul.

Later, as she was leaving, she was on her way to report to Mr Sangstrom the good news. She stopped in her tracks. If the surgeon told Sir Alastair of the improvement, he would probably come to visit her brother. She did not want any setbacks to his progress. She returned to her brother and said, 'Leslie, let us play a different game. Do not say to anyone what you remember – not to the doctors or nurses and especially not to Mr Sangstrom. It will be our own little game, okay?'

The boy looked excited. 'How do we know who wins the game?'

'Simple,' she answered. 'The one who can keep the secret the longest is the winner. When I come tomorrow, I can bring a pack of cards, a chess set, or some books. What do you prefer?'

'Oh, Mary, could you bring me a book of poems by Bécquer from my room at home, please?'

Now she realised how fast he was beginning to remember things. They would not be able to keep this a secret for long.

***

Sir Alastair and Dr Hendricks contemplated the letter and list of questions Ed had sent them. The list looked innocuous enough and the letter contained no hint of malice or animosity, considering that Sir Alastair had shoved the journalist to the ground in Oxford:

1. Can you tell our readers something of the background and history of Leslie Johns? Where he comes from, where he went to school, so that our readers can get a good picture of the boy we get so many enquiries about?
2. Can you tell our readers something about Leslie's parents, his family – where are they now or what happened to them. Does the boy have siblings, where are they? That is the sort of information that grips our readers.

3. Can you provide information for our readers regarding his most amazing performance in the swimming trials, such as his club and trainers?
4. Can you comment on his current illness and his level of recovery? That in itself is a story for our readers.
5. His academic achievements as reported in the national papers fascinate our readers. Can you enlighten them as to his education, what schools he went to, what private tuition, that sort of thing?
6. Why did Professor Arias denigrate the boy's Spanish paper? And how can we get in touch with the professor for his viewpoint so that we can give a balanced view to our readers?
7. The village is a place our readers know little or nothing of. Can you tell them about the village – how it functions and how it benefits the children in your care?
8. We note that you are also responsible for the Woodford Asylum. Could you tell us, without going into personal details of course, something about the establishment, its history, and perhaps its successes in the field of mental illness?
9. In 1958, a police report contained details of an inmate from your asylum found dead in the River Roding. Could you provide some background to the story, It was reported upon in most local papers, but I feel the reports lacked something?
10. Our readers would be very interested in your own story. You're a man of mystery who controls a business empire, spread across several continents I believe. How does one man cope with such an organisation?
11. Which branch of the military services were you involved with? Could you perhaps share some anecdotes of your time in the services?
12. What connections do you have to Military Intelligence, the police force, or security services?

Sir Alastair was not at all happy about questions 9, 11 and 12, but realised that the newspaperman must know about his connection with MI or he would not have asked. He wondered if they knew more about the body in the river than had previously been reported, and why did they persist with the matter? Sir Alastair and the doctor sat discussing the list and began the task of composing plausible answers that would convince the editor and his readers. They could choose to ignore the questions that were sensitive, but that may arouse suspicions. Sir Alastair wanted to provide some answers that would satisfy and, ultimately, silence the press. He reminded Hendricks, 'If one digs long enough, one will eventually reach the core.'

***

The rain hammered at the window of the hospital room. Leslie sat in the chair wearing a dressing gown and reading his book. He looked up as Mary entered the room, and she looked as though she had swum all the way, fully clothed. 'I bet you are glad not to be out in that weather. It is coming down by the bucketful.' She stood her umbrella by the door and went over to him and kissed him and then took the chair next to his bed and sat beside him. 'How are you getting along with the book?' she asked.

'Great,' he replied. 'I have read it several times. Tomorrow, could you bring me some of the other French and Spanish books from my room?'

'Of course I will. Do you want me to take that one back?'

He closed the book, 'I can recite for you any poem that you choose.' He handed her the book. 'It is no good you reciting to me. I do not understand Spanish, you silly boy.'

They laughed and set up the chessboard she had brought with her.

Whilst engaged in the battle of strategy, Leslie told her of a strange dream. 'I found myself in a sort of chamber, underground I think. There was a man with a long beard, and he smelled a lot. He was drawing something on the table, some numbers and words. I could read the words, "I raise a monument to him". What does that mean, Mary? Who is that man? And why does he smell so bad?'

Mary knew of course. Her brother had told her about Perry before the operation. She thought about how to deal with this new memory. 'He must be someone from the past who you had forgotten about, an old friend perhaps. The chamber could relate to a story that he told you. The writing may be a poem that he told you or you told him, and he wrote it down so he would not forget it. The smell could be because he was trapped for a long time in the chamber; maybe he had fallen into it and could not get out.'

Leslie and Mary continued the game of chess to its inevitable conclusion.

'Did you see Mr Sangstrom this morning, Leslie?'

The boy packed away the chess pieces. 'Yes, he came early today; he said he had to go to see another patient and her parents – a sad case, Mary. She has a malignant tumour, and he will operate this morning. I do hope she will be all right.'

Mary observed the sad expression on her brother's face. He was genuinely and deeply concerned for a girl he did not know. Perhaps he empathised with her due to his own situation and was grateful or felt some guilt, as his tumour was benign. 'I am sure she will be okay, Leslie. She has the same expert surgeon who operated on you, and he is a truly gifted man.'

Leslie gave his sister a very strange look.

'What is it, Leslie?' she said with some alarm. 'What is the matter?'

'You said the surgeon is a gifted man? Do you have any gifts? And what about me? Do I have any?'

Mary was stunned by the question and had to think quickly. 'Dear boy, we all have gifts of some sort. Some people, like you, are good at languages, and others may be clever with numbers. Some are good at music – playing an instrument or singing. Others are clever at designing, architecture, engineering, or writing books, poetry for example. The poets you adore have special gifts that enable them to express in words the beauty or the sorrow of their lives. We connect with their writings because we do not have their gift of expression.'

Leslie still looked a little unsure. 'What are your gifts Mary?' he was not about to let this go.

'I am not sure myself. Maybe I have not found my gifts. Or perhaps I take them for granted and do not realise that they are special. Who knows? I do know one thing though. My special gift is my brother. I would be lost without him.' She wiped away a little tear as it welled up in her eye, remembering her promise to the surgeon.

***

Mr Sangstrom was pleased with the way Leslie progressed. As far as he was concerned, after a few more tests to confirm that, clinically, the boy was recovering to his satisfaction, he could transfer Leslie to a centre for rehabilitation. He had a place in mind that would be ideal. The centre had a lot more facilities than the hospital and it would suit the boy's current needs. Leslie had mentioned that he wished he could go swimming and walking in the countryside. He knew that Mary would be with her brother and went to discuss his proposal with her, before talking to Sir Alastair.

Mary listened attentively to the surgeon and Dr Marston, and was overjoyed that they considered her brother well enough to leave the hospital. However, she was concerned about his slow progress at regaining his memory in full. Dr Marston reminded her that it would take time and was not something doctors could improve clinically. They considered their work at the hospital, apart from regular check-ups, done.

The centre the doctor recommended was set in five acres of grounds and had a heated swimming pool. It also had modern facilities for physiotherapy to rebuild Leslie's muscle strength. Dr. Marston and Mr. Sangstrom agreed that giving the boy some structured physical activities would help to heal him in both mind and body, without incurring any undue pressures. Mary asked if she would still be able to maintain contact with him, as the centre was in Sussex, a long way from the village. Travelling back and forth would be an arduous task. Mr Sangstrom told her she would need to discuss that with the director of the centre and Sir Alastair, her guardian.

***

The conversation between Sir Alastair and Mr Sangstrom became a heated affair. The surgeon insisted that the centre he had proposed would be the ideal place for Leslie. Sir Alastair countered with the argument that the facilities at the village would be adequate for his needs. He had the freedom of the swimming pool and the grounds, where he often took his walks. The school gymnasium was fully equipped and functional, and he would engage a personal physiotherapist for as long as was necessary; he, in fact, had just the person in mind for the job. He stood his ground and won the argument. Leslie would remain at the hospital for the rest of the week, returning to the village on Saturday.

***

Sir Alastair attended his offices in London on business, but on occasions he would stay overnight at his apartment in the city. When staying there, he enjoyed the company of a female companion called Rachel Dorland. Rachel was twenty-two years his junior. However, the relationship had lasted for two years. She was tall, graceful, and elegant, with sparkling blue eyes and a slim figure. She had worked at a teaching hospital in Manchester and then moved to London to take over as the head of physiotherapy at a private clinic. She was in great demand for private consultations, at the teaching hospitals and for seminars. Neither Sir Alastair nor anyone else spoke of the relationship; one other person knew of it – Jackson. His role as chauffeur meant that he knew all Sir Alastair's movements – where to drop him off and pick him up. On some occasions, Jackson collected Rachel from her house in Bayswater to convey her to Sir Alastair's London apartment.

***

Sir Alastair explained to Mary that her brother would be coming home to the Village and not to Sussex. Mary would have preferred to keep as much distance between Leslie and the dean as possible, but she had to agree that there were adequate facilities around them. She also thought that being back at the village might help her brother to recover his memories.

***

The next day on her visit to the hospital, Sir Alastair accompanied Mary. Leslie did not react the same way he had before. He greeted them both and told them of the girl that Mr Sangstrom had told him about. 'You were right, Mary,' he said. 'The girl is making a good recovery, and they will remove the bandages this afternoon. Isn't that good news?'

Mary replied that it was indeed good news.

Sir Alastair told the boy of his plans to return him to the village.

There was a light knock at the door, and a tall slim woman entered. 'Alastair, I see I have the right room.'

Sir Alastair turned to Leslie and introduced the woman. 'This is Miss Dorland. She will be undertaking your physiotherapy and will be staying with us at Howard House. I am sure that you will soon regain your strength and mobility with her expert knowledge. Mary sensed immediately that there was something between Sir Alastair and this strikingly beautiful woman.

'Leslie, I am pleased to meet you. Alastair has told me so much about you, and I am sure we will get you back on your feet in no time at all.'

The boy gazed at the beautiful pale blue eyes and held out his hand. 'Yes, Miss Dorland' Leslie replied.

She shook his hand and said. 'Please, call me Rachel. Miss Dorland makes me sound like a schoolteacher.'

Mary could see that her brother was awestruck by this woman's beauty; this situation could work to her advantage!

The dean introduced Mary and left to attend to some business matters. Rachel sat next to Leslie. She explained some of the processes that she employed to aid mobility and strength. 'Alastair informs me that you like to swim. Is that so?'

The boy nodded, still mesmerised by those blue eyes.

'Swimming is a really good way to recover, but it should be done in a relaxed way at first. No racing up and down the pool.'

Leslie pulled his tongue back into his mouth and swallowed. 'Do you swim, Miss Rachel?'

'I do, yes. Perhaps not like you, though. I don't swim well enough to compete. I just swim for pleasure.'

A thought came to Leslie's mind. 'Do you work here at the hospital?'

'No, I work at a private clinic, but I do some consultations here occasionally. What makes you ask?'

The boy did not know why he had asked. The question had just come into his head. 'Well, I have not seen you here before now. Did Mr Sangstrom ask you to come?'

Rachel smiled. 'No. Alastair and I are old friends, and he asked if I would be able to help you. Of course, I know Mr Sangstrom; we have worked together on several cases.' Rachel performed a brief examination of the boy to establish what treatment she would need to begin with.

Mary stood in the corridor, and noticing Billy approaching from the far end, she walked swiftly towards him and signalled with her eyes that it was not the time or place to talk. She went to the canteen and asked for a pot of tea and a cheese sandwich. After a few moments, she saw Billy join the queue behind her. The canteen was very full, so they had to share a table with another couple. Billy discretely passed her a note that she read and passed back to him without comment. She asked the woman next to her to guard her cup of tea, as she needed to use the services. Once inside, she quickly wrote a message and folded it in four.

Returning to the table, she thanked the woman and finished her drink and sandwich. She slipped the folded paper under the saucer, making sure that Billy had seen her do it. She left the canteen, only looking back to see Billy collect her cup and saucer and place it on a tray along with his own.

***

Alone in the room, Leslie contemplated his impending return to the village. He could not recall ever having been there. He was experiencing a mixture of feelings between excitement, confusion, and trepidation. He pictured Howard House but did not relate it to the village – as if the house stood alone as a mysterious place people told him of. Dr Hendricks, Mr and Mrs Atkins, Don the vicar, Joe Breen, Mr Vance, and all the other people he had interacted with over the years had vanished without trace from his mind. The only exceptions were vague memories of Perry and Paul Goodwin and a fleeting vision of a woman dressed in black and white, with a starched apron that crackled whenever she moved.

It was most disconcerting for him, not being able to recall people or events that had featured so much in his life, such as the swimming contest and graduating from Oxford. Frustration built within him; a sense of being stupid and incompetent tussled with his certain knowledge of languages, poetry, history, and many topics that he had no trouble recalling. The confusion he suffered added to his disquiet. He accepted that Sir Alastair was his guardian and that Mary was his sister because she had told him so. If only he could just remember; that would put everything in its proper place in his mind.

Chapter 17

The Return and Strange Awakenings

Mary assisted Leslie to pack his belongings into the suitcase. Sir Alastair stood in the corridor in discussion with Mr Sangstrom and Dr Marston. The surgeon had visited the village by invitation from the dean, to see for himself the facilities available to Leslie. He was impressed and conceded that it was agreeably comparable to the centre he had suggested, along with the best physiotherapist and maids to attend him. Leslie would be in very good hands indeed.

When they arrived, Susan ran from the top of the steps and greeted Leslie with a hug, something she would never normally do. 'We were so, so worried for you, Master Leslie, and it is so good to have you back home again.'

Leslie immediately recalled the crackling sound and a vague idea that Susan was his mother. After placing his belongings in his bedroom, Leslie and Mary went downstairs to the dining room.

Susan assembled the house staff together on instruction from the dean.

'I Thank you all for attending. I realise that it is a busy time, and I shall not keep you long. I am sure you will all like to wish Leslie a huge welcome home.'

There was a round of applause for this popular boy they had all grown fond of.

'Leslie will be undergoing a period of therapy and will also require rest and calm. I have engaged Miss Rachel Dorland to oversee his recovery, and she will arrive tomorrow evening. Miss Dorland will be staying here at Howard House for the duration of the treatment, and Dr Hendricks will be here to check his progress. Cook, that will mean five of us at lunch until further notice. Susan, is the guest suite ready for Miss Dorland?'

'It is, sir.'

'Very good. Jackson, I would appreciate it if you would monitor the water temperature in the pool daily. If any problems arise, you have the engineer's number?'

'Yes, Sir Alastair,' he replied.

'Rachel…Miss Dorland has decided that, in the mornings after breakfast, Leslie will have a short walk and then spend some time with Dr Hendricks before his swim. After lunch, Leslie will be required to rest. In the evenings, he will be exercising in the school gymnasium when classes end. As his condition improves, we may amend his schedule. Thank you again. You are free to go. Susan, I would like a word in the library.'

Susan had not missed the familiarity with which Sir Alastair had addressed Miss Dorland. The green seed began to sprout a tiny shoot. And Mary had listened with great interest and had watched Susan's face intently during the dean's discourse.

***

When Leslie had heard the dean mention the library, a picture had flashed into his head, and after the dean had spoken to Susan, Leslie asked if he could see the library.

'But of course you can. You have the freedom of the house as before,' said the dean.

The room was not as he'd seen it in the image. The Bodleian Library had flashed in his head. He studied the array of bookshelves and thought of a line from a poem – 'There is a place where I conceal' – and then a book cover denoting the volume.

A rush of blood coursed through his body from his feet to his head. It swirled and pounded in his brain; he staggered towards an armchair and fell into it. Tightly gripping the arms of the chair, he began to recall that day so many years ago. For him, it was more than half a lifetime ago that he'd sat in this very room reciting the poem that meant so much to him. He could not recall the significance of the verse, but he knew the poem line by line. And then something else came to him – sparked by the atmosphere of the room. A man was missing, someone he cared about, someone important to him; someone close to him was missing and 'presumed dead'. Who was it? Who was it that had slapped him so hard on his knee that it had raised a red wheal on his skin? Why were his trousers wet? The questions came and went unanswered.

Mary entered the library and pulled up a chair opposite her brother. The look on his face and the rigid posture sent waves of dread through her. 'Oh no not again,' she groaned.

She was about to call Sir Alastair, when Leslie gripped her arm and began to tell her of the strange experience. She listened to all he recounted and said, 'Your memory is trying to communicate to you. The problem is that it is all jumbled, and some of the details are missing. It is good that they are returning, however confusing. Give it some time, and they will organise themselves correctly. I am sure of it.'

Leslie was now more relaxed, but he leaned forward. And speaking in a low tone, almost a whisper, as if someone might be listening nearby, he said, 'I am frightened of something Mary. There are dreadful things lurking, trying to get out of or into my head. I do not know what they are, Mary, but they scare me.'

Mary took hold of his hands and said, 'Hush now. Nothing shall harm you. I promise you. I will protect you.'

Mary felt her concern deeply. She'd thought that her brother had managed to defeat his demons or that they had been cut from him with the tumour. And yet, here they were again, tormenting him without showing themselves or revealing their purpose. Had they only lain dormant, waiting for the opportunity to resurface and strike at him? Perhaps these were new or undiscovered demons, about to wreak their havoc when he was so lost and vulnerable. She could not let him see her disquiet; she masked it with a smile or a calming word. She would prevent anything from interfering with his recovery even to her own cost.

***

Leslie's night was fraught with dreams and fleeting images – books filled with company names and payments; a huge glass rock with a key embedded within it; a boy struggling to maintain his grip on the edge of a well, eventually to lose his fight and plummet to his meet his doom in the coal-black waters far below; a mess of broken glass strewn around a large metal framework that swayed and bowed with the gusting of the wind; snow piled so high he could not see over the top of it; and an army of boys equipped with shovels, planting daffodils in the snow.

Leslie awoke with a start, and the sweat pouring from him soaked his pyjamas and bed sheets. He sat on the edge of the bed with his head in his hands.

There was a light tap at the door, and it opened slightly. 'May I come in, Leslie?'

'Of course, Mary,' he replied.

'I had a feeling you were in difficulties. Are you all right?' She pulled up a chair and handed him a towel. 'Just look at you. You are soaked right through. Whatever is the matter?'

Whilst he told her of the visions and dreams that had disturbed his sleep, she removed a blanket from the bed and wrapped it around him. 'It will be daylight soon, and you will need to have a bath before breakfast. I expect Susan or Joan will report to the dean that your bed is wet. You must tell him that you had a nightmare and woke up soaking. That is the truth, but make something up about the content of the dreams. Be careful what you tell him because he will discuss it with Dr Hendricks.'

***

After breakfast, the dean sat in the library reading the Sunday papers. Leslie knocked nervously on the door. 'It is such a fine morning,' said the dean. 'However, you looked troubled at breakfast. Is something wrong?'

Leslie cautiously approached the dean. 'Sit down, young man. You look as though you have something on your mind.'

Leslie took a tentative step closer but remained standing, like a small boy having to report his misdeeds to the headmaster. He began, 'I am sorry, sir, but…my bed was soaking wet last night… Oh, I did not wet the bed you understand; it is wet with perspiration. I had nightmares all night long. I would wake and then sleep until another dream came.'

The dean indicated towards the chair. 'For goodness sake, boy. I am not going to punish you. Do not worry about the bed. Susan will attend to that.'

Leslie did as the dean instructed and sat down.

'Do you wish to tell me the nature of the dreams?'

'Well sir, in one I flew like a bird looking down on an island. A terrible storm swamps the whole island, and the island disappears from my sight. The next moment, I am falling to the sea, unable to fly. I am struggling in water with a great weight upon me. And then I woke up.

'In another, I am on a horse riding through a desert, and when I turn in the saddle to look behind me, I see a high range of dark red cliffs. I ride for hours and then for days. Each time I look behind me, the cliffs remain the same distance away. Hot and exhausted with the sun beating down on us, the horse becomes thinner and thinner until it's too weak to ride. I had to leave it and walk, but all the time the cliffs remain, no matter how far away I got.

'A third dream was really strange. I was surrounded by pitch darkness – no floor, walls, or roof, just black empty space. I balanced on a rope like a tightrope walker; it was the only thing I could see. As I walked along it, I could not see either end of it. Each end of the rope disappeared into darkness, so I could not tell how far I had come or how far I had to go. The rope began to change thickness at different points of the length that I could see. It was as if the rope were alive, swelling and shrinking, slackening and tightening. Then I reached a point where there were torn strands. They were slowly breaking one by one and making a twanging sound. That is when I awoke and got out of bed.'

The dean sat stroking his chin and thinking about the possible meanings of the dreams and concluded that Dr Hendricks would be the best person to interpret them. 'I will send for Hendricks, and he may shed some light on these dreams.'

Leslie looked out of the window at the sunlit shingle. 'Would it be all right for me to go for a walk, sir?'

The dean consulted his pocket watch. 'Only a short walk, mind you, and take Mary with you. I have some matters to discuss with the doctor, and I would like you to relate your dreams to him before lunch.'

Mary and Leslie walked out onto the road that led towards the main gate, and Mary was anxious to hear what story he had told the dean.

As they neared the lodge, a stout, round man walked towards them. 'It is Mr Pickwick?' said Leslie in surprise.

'No, you silly thing. That is Dr Hendricks, the man you play chess with.'

As he neared the young pair, the doctor greeted them. 'Hello, Mary. Leslie, you are feeling better now for the walk no?'

Leslie let a slight giggle escape at the sound of the distorted English. 'I feel much better. Thank you, sir,' he replied, puzzled at how the man knew him. He did not recall playing chess with him.

Leslie and Mary went out through the village gates and down the wide greensward to a parade of small shops on the far side of the road. They entered a newsagent's shop and Leslie perused the displays of sweets and toys, games, newspapers, and magazines. Leslie had some money in his pocket and decided to purchase a jigsaw puzzle. He did not see his sister hand an envelope to the shop owner. Mary bought a magazine, and they headed back to the village. Leslie had never been out of the village before as far as he could recall.

Mary told Leslie to report to the dean in the library as soon as they returned. 'And watch out for the doctor. He is a tricky one' she told her brother.

The caution was lost on Leslie, but he remembered the game they had started at the hospital. He supposed that was the meaning of the warning.

***

The armchairs formed a triangle near the fireplace in the library. The dean bade the boy to sit and relate his nightmares to Dr Hendricks.

When Leslie finished relating his nightmares, Hendricks gave him a smile. 'It seems to me now that you are anxious about something. I recall that you told me long ago of the floods where you lived as a small boy. Do you recall that conversation?'

Leslie gave him a blank look.

'I see that you do not recall it this moment, but somewhere in your mind is a memory of the time you were on the island of Sheppey, when most of the east coast of England suffered huge waves and a rise in the level of the sea. You may have suppressed this memory, and it is trying to get your attention now.' The doctor looked for a reaction from the boy that was not forthcoming.

'The dream about a horse and the cliffs – is there something you are afraid of, trying to get away from?'

The boy sat on his hands. 'I cannot remember anything that would cause me fear enough to try and escape from it.'

'Very well. Is there someone you can recall that you needed to rely upon – not for food, clothes, or that sort of thing, but advice, moral support, or guidance, perhaps a parent or teacher, someone of that level – who you feel has in some way let you down?'

'I never knew my mother and father, so it could not be them… Perhaps Mrs Morton in Felixstowe when she called me a liar? I can remember how hurt I felt and also the physical pain I suffered.'

'When you say physical pain, did she mistreat you? Did she beat you?'

'Oh no, sir. It was from swallowing the coins. I thought I would die from the pain, but still she would not believe me. She said I put on an act to convince her, but the pain, sir—'

'You never did tell me of this before. You see, this may be the reason for your torment. Let me explain. The cliffs can represent the memory of hurt, pain, and suffering you felt. And the horse represents Mrs Morton. The horse becomes thinner as you lose trust in her. When you have to abandon the horse, it no longer represents the support and guidance that it once did. It had failed you, but the memory of the earlier support still remains in your mind and causes you some conflict in your thoughts.'

Leslie removed his hands from beneath his thighs and sat back in the sumptuous armchair. He was feeling more relaxed, and his confidence in his ability to fool the doctor was growing, but there was still the third dream to come.

'Leslie, were you ever afraid of the dark?'

It seemed an odd question to the boy. 'Not that I can recall, but someone I knew was.'

It was too late. He had blurted out a secret he'd held for years. He steadied his mind. 'I do not remember his name or where I know him from, but he was terrified of the dark. He would see shapes and monsters, lurking in corners and peering at him from behind objects like trees or buildings.'

'I see. He confided in you, no? He told you of his fears?'

Leslie felt that his attempt to cover his mistake had not been successful. 'I believe he must have. How else could I know?' Leslie could not understand how this memory had suddenly exposed itself. He realised straight away that it was a secret he could not talk about... He had promised.

The doctor removed the pipe from his pocket and glanced at the dean. He received a nod in response and went through his routine of scraping, tapping, filling, lighting, and puffing without speaking a word. It was whilst watching the performance that Leslie began to picture a garden with its array of flowers and a pond full of fish. He saw a fountain and cascades of blooms, smelled a powerful scent of geraniums, and heard the crunch of gravel underfoot. He could recall the garden in all its details and the conservatory, with the doctor dressed in a safari suit. It was all beginning to fall into place – the chess games, the memory games with cards and objects under a cloth. The recollections burst in on him one after the other.

'How do you think of your past, Leslie? And how do you see your future?'

The images vanished as suddenly as they had appeared. He concentrated upon the question. 'I have vague memories of the past; nothing seems to be clear or in order. And as for the future, I cannot say. I need to return to my old self to establish what my strengths and weaknesses are. I know that I can understand several languages, but I am not sure why. That seems to be the only thing I am good at…oh, and Mary says that I am quite good at swimming. But again, I have no memory of swimming. I have a strong attraction to the water, and I can see myself swimming. But I cannot remember having done it.'

Small clouds obscured the doctor's face as he puffed at the briar. 'I see the rope as your path in the life and the darkness surrounding you is your uncertainty about everything. You see nothing clearly. You see no past, no future, only the present. The changing in the rope also conveys the anxiety. You will find that you have to repair the torn part of the rope before you can continue, no? I suggest that you try to put these things into the context. Deal with the dreams as revelations and not the things to scare you. I can understand that to lose your memories is a frightening thing. Perhaps it's like being lost in a forest with nothing to guide you to home, only trees each way you are looking.'

'There are sometimes little things to give us signs that we make the progress. But we must know how to recognise and use them.'

'What does that mean, sir? How do I recognise the signs?' asked Leslie.

'Ooh…let me see now. For example, you know the sun rises in the east and, therefore, sets in the west, as it only travels in the one direction. This is a constant but with a variation. You see in the winter it travels at a lower arc than in full summer but still in the same direction. So, in the winter, it rises more to south-east and sets south-west. How could you use this knowledge?'

The boy followed the doctor's line of thinking very well. 'If my journey started at dawn, and I could see where the sun was rising, I would be travelling south if the sun was on my left but would have to allow for the arc between 11.00 and 13.00. After midday, I would have to have the sun on my right to maintain the same direction. In winter, the hours of daylight are shorter, and so the amount of time I have to use the sun as a guide is less.'

'Very good,' said the doctor. 'You see, it is about making the sense of all the information that we have. If we forget to allow for the arc, we go around in circles, no?' They all chuckled at the remark. 'But that is what is happening to you, young man. You are too anxious to make the sense of everything at once. You must to wait for the sun to rise before you can rely on such things as direction.'

The doctor's explanations went some way to giving the dean an idea of the torment his protégé was experiencing. What neither the dean nor the doctor knew was that these dreams were from a time before he came to the village, before his tumour, and before he lost his memories. The interpretations told Leslie something of his early anxieties and experiences. The doctor had not explained everything to Leslie's satisfaction. What had sent him plummeting into the water? And why did he feel a weight holding him down as he was drowning? He asked the doctor these points.

'When you were flying like the bird, did you also have the wings?'

'I do not think I did, sir.'

'Well then, I would say that your flying is a sense of freedom, and the fall from the sky represents a sudden loss of self-assurance. The event that has made you fearful has made you lose faith in yourself, and so you tumble. You fall out of the sky into the sea, the very sea that engulfs the island. With the faith and the confidence, you must have felt free of the insecurities, no? But when you tumble, the insecurities you did not see before hold you down like the weight.'

Sir Alastair asked Leslie about his walk.

'We, Mary and me went down to the shop across the road, and I bought a jigsaw puzzle. It was a nice walk, and I feel fine now. I am looking forward to swimming tomorrow.'

They sat discussing the various methods of using nature itself as a guide to direction. The dean explained about survival training – where he had learned to look for the way the branches grow on a tree to determine the direction of prevailing winds. He explained how moss grows on the north side of trees and that the south side of a tree or rock is warmer than the north side and noted the different cloud formations that can indicate fair or foul weather to come. The discussion went on with Leslie listening, fascinated, until the gong sounded for lunch.

***

After a light meal, Mary escorted Leslie to his room to ensure that he had a proper rest. She suspected that he would read or do his new jigsaw puzzle. The ever-reliable Susan had opened the window to air the room, changed the bed sheets, and dried the damp patch from the mattress, and there were fresh blankets and pillows. Mary quietly closed the window and left her young brother to rest.

Leslie drifted into a light sleep, at first, he was aware of the sounds of the maids as they busied themselves with the chores of the house; the opening and closing of doors and the occasional distant clatter of a pan from the kitchen. Then he drifted into deep sleep.

He found himself looking at a mansion that seemed vaguely familiar; a wildflower meadow swept from a symmetrical formal area down to a lake bordered by an avenue. He espied a motor launch gleaming white in the sun, moored at a jetty. He turned back to the mansion and walked in through the doors, glancing around him at the marble tiled floors and the staircase. He trod cautiously up the steps to the top floor, looking around him as if expecting to be caught trespassing. Confronted by a steel door, he puzzled over how to open it. It had no handle or lock. He pressed his hands against it. Nothing happened. He went along the corridor to see if there was another way in. He found several bedrooms and bathrooms but no way into the room he wanted to see. He retraced his steps and checked the rooms on the other side – just more bedroom suites. A crunching sound alerted him to something outside.

Mary shook her brother. 'Come. It is time to go downstairs Leslie. Miss Dorland has just arrived.'

He jumped from the bed and rushed to the window. Rachel was checking that Jackson had removed all her luggage from the car, as Susan and Jackson carried her belongings into the house. Leslie washed his face and combed his hair. 'Should I change my clothes?' he asked.

'No. You will do just fine,' Mary answered, noting his excitement. 'Come now. Do not crack the mirror. You know it means seven years of bad luck.'

They hurried down to the entrance hall.

Sir Alastair and the maids were already at the entrance as Jackson returned to the car. Sir Alastair greeted Rachel with a kiss on both cheeks. Mary kept her attention on Susan's demeanour; the blood had drained from her face, and Mary was certain that a pale green tinge tainted those smooth porcelain white features.

This svelte beauty with sapphire eyes transfixed Leslie. She approached Mary and shook her hand. 'I hear you are doing a sterling job taking care of Leslie.'

Mary looked her straight in the eyes and replied in a soft voice, 'I made a promise to do so, and a promise is a promise.'

Rachel admired the girl's remark, but the dean felt a cold wave run through him.

Rachel turned to Leslie. 'I understand you had a walk this morning. Did you find it beneficial?'

Leslie shook her hand, suppressing an urge to kiss her as the dean had done. 'It was only a short walk to the shops and back, and we walked fairly slowly. Thank you, Miss Rachel.'

Susan noticed the way that Leslie could not keep his eyes off this intruder and that he was still holding onto her hand. She wondered if this was an infatuation that should run its course or if it could come to a cataclysmic finale. She observed the dean's face; he alone seemed not to have noticed.

Leslie quickly withdrew his hand, aware that he was making a spectacle of himself. His face flushed hot and red as he contemplated his shoes. In order to distract his mind, he turned his thoughts to the dream he'd had that afternoon. Where was this mansion? Could it be on the Isle of Sheppey, the place he was born? Had that been where they had lived before the sea had swallowed it? It was strange to him that the place had seemed to be deserted. And the door – why could it not open? Something powerful and unseen had drawn him to that place. He must find out what lay beyond that door. He felt it was imperative. He berated his memory for failing him and leaving him with these glimpses of the past, confused and disorientated.

Susan and Joan settled Rachel into the guest suite and returned to their usual tasks. Mary and Leslie sat in the library and began to assemble the jigsaw puzzle, whilst Sir Alastair and Dr Hendricks discussed their business privately in the west wing.

Sir Alastair answered the telephone and had a heated discussion with the caller. From the east wing, Mary and Leslie could not hear the conversation.

'The dean is to go abroad for a while,' said Mary, softly.

'How do you know?' asked Leslie.

'There is some trouble in French Guiana. He has to go to Cayenne to sort it out – something to do with them refusing to honour a mining contract that they had previously agreed to.'

The door opened, and a red-faced Sir Alastair stormed out into the hall closing the door behind him.

Dr Hendricks went over to the table where the jigsaw was almost completed. He observed how all of the completed part of the puzzle was in front of Leslie. The boy was reaching across to complete his sister's half. 'I am afraid that Sir Alastair has to go abroad for a while on business,' he said.

Leslie turned to face the doctor. 'Oh is it something serious?' he asked.

'Just a small problem that he should be able to rectify swiftly,' replied the doctor.

They returned to the puzzle, and Dr Hendricks went to join Sir Alastair.

'That's unfortunate,' said Mary, without looking up from the table. Why did Leslie get the feeling that his sister knew more than she should?

***

At breakfast on Monday morning, Sir Alastair was absent. He had left very early and was on his way to the airport, bound for Cayenne via Paris.

Mary and Leslie tucked into the bacon and scrambled eggs, and as Rachel entered the dining room, Leslie raised himself from his chair and removed the chair next to his, to allow the lady a place at the table.

'My goodness,' said Rachel. 'Such a gentleman. I can see I am going to be spoiled here.'

Leslie just caught Mary's expressive glance and said, 'Paul, who used to be with me in Roding House said, "A gentleman is made by deed and manners.'

'And very astute he was,' replied Rachel. 'Thank you, sir!'

Leslie swelled with pride and offered to serve her the hot breakfast or an alternative.

***

On the morning walk accompanied by his sister, Leslie was deep in thought. He wondered if Rachel had a boyfriend or a lover. Maybe she had a friend that she loved, but he was married and could not commit himself to her fully. Maybe she had not found the man she could give herself to, heart and soul. Maybe she had experienced a troubled romantic interlude that had broken her heart. He could not ask such personal questions. It would not be seemly, and he had shown himself to be a gentleman. He felt a deep gratitude to Paul for his guidance and wisdom.

Mary was the first to break the silent stroll. 'What do you think of Miss Dorland?'

Leslie felt embarrassed by the question. 'What do you mean?' he asked. It seemed to Leslie that she had eavesdropped upon his private thoughts. How could she do that?

'Just…well, what do you think of her as a person? Personally, I like her; I think she will be good for you. She seems intelligent and trustworthy… I do not know if she has a private life, but that is not my concern. I just want her to do her best to restore you to a fairly average specimen of the future for mankind.'

Leslie took a mock swipe at his sister. 'Now you are making fun of me. I hate you!'

She wrapped her arm around his shoulder and pulled him closer to her. 'I only jest. I would not make fun at your expense in front of others.'

He reconsidered his remark; it was harsh and uncalled for.

They walked down to the bend at the bottom of the hill, near the bridge where the road crossed the Roding. He turned back slightly to the left. 'You remember I told you about Perry.' He pointed toward the high wall. 'There is a large tunnel that exits at that point. There is no way to get in because there is a solid iron grille that covers the exit. If I could somehow break through the grille, I could get Perry out of there. He would be free, Mary. Do you realise how much that means to him? This man has done nothing to harm anyone, but he languishes in solitude and despair. Mary… he is like a father to me; he has filled the void left when we were told that Daddy might be dead. I love this man; Mary we must help him!

***

She realised that many things had returned to her brother's memory he had not told her of before and felt a little left out. She thought of the things he'd revealed to her before the operation and the snippets he'd remembered and confided to her during his recovery. But this was a new revelation to her. It was almost as if his whole memories were restored, and he had told her nothing of it. His appeals to her regarding Perry, tugged hard on her leather strapped heartstrings. It was an appeal that hit home with impact and sincerity. She admitted this sentiment into her hard impenetrable shell.

Mary was not a person to be crossed or tricked. She had her fixed views on how people should behave, and any deviation incurred her wrath, dismissal, or retribution. Her brother, on the other hand, whatever he did, said, or thought could never qualify for the responses that others would receive. He was her world –her little brother, her responsibility, and her solemn promise; she could never punish or persecute him for whatever reason. She could keep her distance and let him make his mistakes. She had done so on occasions and had chided and belittled him; it was good for his development. She would personally tear each limb from her own body to protect him and feel no pain. He could never know what lengths she would go to; he was, in effect, an extension of her. She alone knew that, if he ceased to exist, so would she. It was a complicated alliance – unspoken, without communication or understanding.

A mysterious depth exists that human intellect may not perceive, where two people could be one by force of will. One without the other was as a leaf torn from a single tree, blowing in the wind, each finding its own individual resting places, lying down among the intruders and fellows who have fallen to degenerate and rot. Together, they were a part of something whole and purposeful – powerful and dreadful, with mercy and merciless, with forgiveness and unforgiving, vengeful, and exacting. They were an enigma to any who would try to define the two as individuals or as a pair; they could not be accurately defined, and woe betides any who may try. There was an inexorable bond that even he was never aware of, and she would not reveal, unless saving his life would require it.

Mary asked, 'Can Perry get to the outlet of the tunnel?'

Leslie immediately connected with her line of thought. 'Why on earth did I not think of that? Perry can get access to the end of the tunnel. I could have given him pen, paper, clothes, food, whatever he needed. Why did I not think of that?'

'We sometimes cannot see the wood for the trees.'

***

The remark hit him like an arrow shot from an unseen assailant. He recalled the words of Ed. *We cannot always see the wood for the trees.*

More of his forgotten memories began to take form, but he needed clarity to shape them. He saw Tweety, Ed, Billy, and Mike; the local paper; and their pursuit of his life and history and that of his father. And then Salford came to his mind, and resurfacing in his consciousness were his mother and the siblings who struggled in a sea of ignorance, hardship, drunkenness, and brutality. All the revelations were out of context; he had to wait for the full picture. He felt that now that it would not be long for the whole panorama to reveal itself to him, and most perplexing of all to him, how did he know these things? He sensed the impending weight of realisation that would press down so heavily upon him, a burden most would avoid in a rational world. He felt a sickness that urged him to vomit. Mary held him as he spewed onto the grass verge.

They walked in silence for a while, until Mary enquired, 'Do you feel better now? Shall we go back? Or is there more you need to get out of your system?'

The boy was in a quandary. He needed to reconcile the revelations to his memories. He could not make the connections in his own mind's quagmire of confusion, where the inability to distinguish between what was real, imagined, or dreamed still reigned. His mind was awash with facts, figures, intrigues, suspicions, images, and fleeting glances. How on earth he could make sense of it all was beyond his current comprehension.

Leslie considered his newly recovered memory of Perry and the tunnel; it would not be impossible for the man to reach the grille. He had told Leslie that the door was unlocked. He had not observed the man walking, except for a few steps in the small cell he occupied; he may have difficulty due to the injury to his leg. If he could provide clothing and books, the man who brought the food would see them, and that would give the game away. If Perry attempted to reach the grille and had a fall in the tunnel, the man with the food would miss him. It would put both Perry and Leslie at risk. He concluded that using the tunnel was not such a practical solution after all. Leslie confided his conclusions to Mary on the way back up the hill. She agreed that any such risk could put them both in peril.

'Come on,' said Mary, checking the time on her watch. 'You have an appointment with the good doctor.'

Leslie noted the sarcasm and chuckled.

***

Dr Hendricks sat at a table in the library with his bag of tricks and a cloth covering some items spread in front of him. They went through the memory games one by one with Leslie scoring 100 per cent. He had no need to disguise his ability with the games as he recalled doing in their previous sessions.

The doctor made his usual notes and then set up the chessboard. After three games, the score was two to Leslie and one to the doctor. 'I see that you have not lost your skill at the games.'

'No, sir,' Leslie replied. 'I played some in the hospital with Mary.'

The doctor put away the games to concentrate on the state of the boy's memory. 'Do you recall our games at the lodge?'

'Yes, sir. They came back to me slowly. I remembered the garden at first and then the pond with the fish. They were jumping to catch small flies and mosquitoes near the lily pads. Then I recalled the conservatory and you wearing the safari suit and then Miss Martha and the chicken pie.'

The doctor made notes of all the boy's comments and flicked back to the first few pages of the file in front of him. 'That sounds like the first day you came to the lodge and we walked in the garden. Do you recall anything else from that day?'

Leslie concentrated hard; he pictured himself in the lodge and recalled the games and lunch. He searched for what he had done next but could not recall. 'I am sorry, sir. I cannot recall anything more from that day.'

'Oh do not worry. It is not important to recall everything in the detail as you have described already, no?'

Leslie did not realise just how much detail he had given and what would have sufficed. He assumed that detail was an indication of his progress.

They discussed Roding House and the boys, Mr Atkins and the maids, and the cook and her unreliable daughter. Leslie talked of the jumbled visions of boys clearing snow and planting bulbs; that vision had still not become clear to him. He related the image of the Bodleian and his surprise when the east wing had not matched the image he saw. He still had not placed the library in Oxford; nor had he recalled their visit or the reason for it. The doctor conceded that the boy still had some way to go before he had total recollection.

***

It was now 10.30. Leslie took his leave of the doctor and rushed up to his room. He quickly changed into his swimming trunks and wrapped himself in the dressing gown, tying the belt tightly; he grabbed a large towel from the bathroom. He went down to the poolroom and sat on a slatted bench beside the pool, awaiting Miss Rachel.

She entered, accompanied by Joan. 'There you are, Miss,' Joan said and made her exit. No one had thought to show Rachel where the pool was, and she'd asked Joan for directions.

'I am sorry to keep you waiting,' she said as she removed the towelling gown. Leslie struggled to keep his eyes firmly in their sockets. She wore a white swimming costume that hugged her figure and accentuated her fine lines. The costume had a short frill extending down from her narrow waist like a skirt.

They placed their gowns and towels on the bench and entered the water. 'Can you float?' she asked.

'I think so,' he replied. He grabbed the handrail and let his feet float up backwards from the side of the pool. 'There,' he said. He placed his feet back on the bottom of the pool and turned to Rachel.

'Let us see how much you can do but gently now – no exertions.'

Leslie began by floating on his back and gently raised his arms in a clockwork motion, propelling himself along the pool with a backstroke to the far end of the pool. He returned using a breaststroke. When he reached Rachel, he performed a gentle forward somersault and stood beside her.

'How do you feel?' she enquired.

'Absolutely wonderful, Miss Rachel. I feel as though I have done this all my life, and it has been denied me for so long.'

'I must say you swim well and with confidence; it is beautiful to watch such grace in your movements. You must have had a gifted teacher.'

'Yes, Miss. I was taught by Mr Vance. He is the Master of Bridge House.'

Leslie realised that his memory was playing tricks on him because he had not thought of or remembered Mr Vance before this moment.

'Would that be Laurence Vance?' she asked with a quizzical glance.

'Why yes, Miss. Do you know him?'

'Well, not in person. You see, my father was a good swimmer, and he used to compete for his club before he moved to Manchester. He used to speak of this amazing swimmer called Laurence Vance; he compared him to Johnny Weissmuller, the man who played Tarzan in the cinema. My father told me that Johnny won five gold medals and a bronze at the Olympics in Paris and in Amsterdam.

'He said that Laurence could have been as good as if not better than Weissmuller, but he refused to represent his country. My father said that he just disappeared from the swimming circuit after winning the national championships. He could never understand what happened.'

'It is the same man,' said Leslie, 'but he never talked about his past to me. I recall how strong his arms were, and yet he has such gentleness about him. He gradually enticed me and encouraged more daring, convincing me of abilities I never knew I had. Yes, I must agree, he is a terrific teacher, to whom I shall be forever grateful.'

The two of them swam several lengths of the pool side by side, matching each other stroke for stroke in perfect unison.

'Can you swim underwater, Miss?'

She gave a little frown. 'The chlorine in the water irritates my eyes if I am submerged for too long.'

Leslie took a deep breath and ducked under the water. Rachel could see his distorted image through the water as he glided like a shark to the far end of the pool, using only occasional strokes to propel himself. He lurched up out of the water and gasped in a lungful of air.

'I think that we have done sufficient for today,' she said. 'You need to reserve some energy for the gym this evening.'

Leslie climbed out of the pool and stood at the steps, offering his hand to help Rachel out of the pool.

Chapter 18

Love Bites

'Shall I shower first?' he asked.

'If you wish,' she replied.

'I will leave the shower running for you,' he added.

In the changing room, he removed his costume and wrapped himself in the large bath towel. He entered the shower room and turned on the taps but forgot the extractor. He soaped himself and washed away the pungent odour of chlorine. He went over the swimming session minute by minute. He'd enjoyed the exercise and the exhilaration and the sensation of floating on the water, relaxed and calmed.

He was deep in thought when Rachel entered the shower room unseen by him. The steam had created a fog that obscured them both from vision. Rachel placed her gown and towel on a rail and walked towards where Leslie was still showering. He turned with a start to see this goddess in all her naked beauty approaching him through the mist. It was like something from an erotic fantasy. She swiftly covered herself modestly, but Leslie's reaction was apparent and instant. Rachel closed her eyes and remained rooted to the spot. He turned to face the wall amidst apologies and huge embarrassment.

'Leslie,' she said, pleadingly, 'I am so sorry. I thought you had finished. Please, it was not intentional. I am sorry; it was my fault. I should have checked first.'

Leslie groped around for his towel and muttered his apologies.

He fled from the shower, slipping and sliding on the wet floor and the suds sliding down his bare back and legs. He retreated to the changing cubicle and towelled himself dry. His embarrassment had not abated as he sat on the bench, naked beneath his robe.

He wondered if he should leave now and go to his room or wait for Rachel and escort her. He decided to wait for her. If he left now, he would never be able to face her again without extreme embarrassment.

He thought of what he should say, but this was a new occurrence for him. He had never seen a woman naked, except in books relating to art and sculptures. He could not remove her image from his mind however hard he tried; a part of his mind did not wish to.

Rachel sat beside him on the bench and gently stroked his hair. 'I really mean it,' she said softly. 'It was my fault; I did not mean to cause you embarrassment.'

Leslie could not look at her face; he fixed his gaze on the wet trunks as he turned them repeatedly in his hands. He crossed his legs, trying to hide his obvious arousal and flushed bright red as his gown fell open. He leapt from the bench and kept his back toward Rachel, straightening his attire and tying the belt as tightly as he could.

'Leslie,' she said in a firm voice, 'come and sit here.'

He was most reluctant to turn around and face her. He felt shameful and ungentlemanly.

Rachel took his arm and pressed him to the bench. 'Sit and listen to me! What happened is nothing to be ashamed or embarrassed about. You are a perfectly healthy young man, and your reaction is natural. You can do nothing about what God and nature have designed.' She put her hand under his chin and firmly but gently turned his face to hers. 'I am twice your age, Leslie, and I have to admit, I am flattered that I can command such attention.' She gave a saucy smile to the boy that sent him into bursts of laughter.

He felt less awkward and reassured by her gentle manner and the sensible approach to sensitive issues not usually discussed. He certainly had never discussed such matters with anyone, not even the doctor.

'Do you feel better now?' she asked, gazing directly into his eyes from mere inches away. She maintained her soft grip on his chin.

Leslie studied those crystal sapphire orbs; he could feel them pulling him into their azure pools. He would be content to drown in them and succumb to her spell. 'Yes, thank you, Rachel, sorry…Miss Rachel.'

'That's okay. I don't mind if you call me Rachel. You can drop the "Miss", and we will both be more comfortable. Are you feeling more composed?' she asked, glancing down at his lap.

A slight involuntary twitch of the gown answered her question.

'Goodness,' she exclaimed. 'Have you been eating oysters?'

Leslie looked puzzled. 'What do you mean oysters?'

'It is said that oysters are aphrodisiacs, very good for your love life.'

'I do not have a love life,' said Leslie.

'What? You don't have a girlfriend, at your age. You would be a real catch for any girl, handsome, intelligent, and sophisticated, obviously extremely well educated, gentle and considerate. I would take my chances if I were closer to your age.'

It was Leslie's turn now to feel flattered by her description of him, if not a little abashed. He felt a surging force pumping uncontrollably where he felt was inappropriate; he was in a state between pain and ecstasy. She was not helping the situation with her forthright speech and candid manner; she appeared to be flirting with him, which excited him even more. They would have to leave the pool, as it was nearing lunchtime. He stood up and held the damp towel modestly in front of him. He waved an arm gesturing the lady to walk ahead of him, the other hiding his painful excitement.

***

At lunch, Leslie behaved as expected; he offered the various choices to Rachel and served her the items she chose. He treated his sister exactly the same but with less enthusiasm. He wished that Rachel had asked for something more than food. He would have succumbed regardless of the consequences. Just the sight of her reinvigorated him and began the excitement once more.

Mary glanced at him from across the dining table; she sensed his heightened state and the bond developing between him and Rachel. She began to fear that he would let his physical, emotional, and sexual drive push him beyond the boundaries of respectability. He was, after all, a young man burdened with youthful vigour, full of fantasies and whims spurred on by testosterone. This goddess was the catalyst who amalgamated all his youthful desires into one whole living being.

She had to admit Rachel was an extremely attractive, shapely, intelligent example of femininity. What male could resist her obvious charms? She was, however, concerned about how her brother would deal with it; his attraction to her was noticeable, as was his struggle to retain his composure and to conceal his rampant appetite for her. Nothing passed by Mary unnoticed; she excused her brother the ravages of sexual desire, the longing and suffering, the fight to maintain self-control. She knew of and felt his efforts, and she transmitted all the support she could to his feeble mind, for that was what it was.

A boy of his age was not always in control of his thoughts and emotions but driven by primal urges of the male kind that Mother Nature had installed and primed to explode without notice, a force of incalculable ferocity and depth, a force that interfered with normal thinking, rationality, and logic. Yes, it was nature at her most virulent and persuasive, and yes, to any young man of Leslie's age, to deny the gratification was painful indeed.

Leslie ate with a voracious appetite, wolfing down his food as though it were his last meal for an eternity, Mary gave a look of consternation that her brother noticed, and he slowed his pace.

Rachel ate her meal at a very slow pace, completely the opposite to the young wolf by her side. She pondered the sight she had seen in the shower room and wrestled with her desires and emotions. She had an immense physical and mental attraction to this young, virile boy. She could not put the sight of him in the shower out of her mind; the vision tempted and excited her. She made herself aware that this boy was only fifteen and legally a minor. She also thought of her position of trust and responsibility, but desire and danger drew her ever closer to him. He had revealed his most intimate reaction that had shocked and surprised her and would not leave her consciousness. Was it his uncontrolled youthful reaction, his depth of character, the way he glided through the water, the feel of his skin when she touched him, or when he had looked so closely into her eyes during that moment when she'd tried to relieve his embarrassment? She could not be sure if it was one thing or all of them compounded. Perhaps it was just her lust for this specimen of young manhood. She was so unsure of her feelings that she endeavoured to conduct future sessions with more control and formality.

***

Leslie went to his room for his afternoon nap but could not sleep. All he could see was his goddess with her sapphire eyes gliding towards him from within a cloudy mist. He fought the temptation that persecuted him. He jumped from the bed and reached for a book from his desk. He skimmed through the pages looking for something to distract himself. All he found were poems of love and desire – romantic tales of love gained and lost. He flicked from one page to another; all were of the same theme.

What once had penetrated and made him feel as one with the author now tormented and teased him into a state of frustration.

***

It was Rachel this time who knocked at his door. 'It is time for your session in the gym,' she said, from beyond the door.

Leslie had slept a profound sleep and was now disorientated when she awoke him. 'I will be with you directly,' he answered, flustered and embarrassed, as if she could tell he was a victim to his lust for the vision of beauty. He could think of nothing else but her. He had dreamt of her caressing and kissing him, fondling and stroking, and in his dream, he had responded to her every whim. It was a dream filled with desire, exhilaration, rampant excitement, and eventual exhaustion.

How could he face her, his sister, the maids, without them giving him knowing nods and winks? *We know what you've been up to, young stallion.* He felt that it was written all over his face in bold capitals. He recalled how Rachel had told him that his reaction was natural and part of nature's plan. He calmed himself and composed an attitude that said, *So what?*

Leslie descended the stairs with a grace and swagger that befitted his position as the man of the house in the absence of his lordship. He was wearing shorts and a vest suitable for the task ahead. Rachel met him at the foot of the stairs, and the two of them walked side by side to the coat stand in the hall. Leslie removed her faintly scented jacket and helped her put it on. He placed his own jacket over his shoulders, and they exited the mansion towards the schoolhouse.

He felt his left hand touch hers as they walked slowly down the road. He gripped her hand softly, expecting her to pull away. She let him hold her hand with his tender youthful touch; a shudder of expectancy rippled through her. She gripped his hand tightly as they entered the schoolhouse.

She had resolved to be firm and perform the tasks that his lordship had requested of her, but her resolve disintegrated by the second. Her mind was no match for her heart.

Inside the gym, she slammed the door shut, locked it, and grabbed at the boy. She swung him around and wrapped both her arms around his neck, pulling him down to her. She kissed him and licked his soft, youthful face repeatedly. She could feel his response as she pulled him close to her. There was no space between them. Leslie pressed against her, letting her know that he had responded as invited. He submitted willingly to her experience and expertise. He snaked his tongue deep into her mouth as she had done to him. It was a sensation that he had never in his wildest dreams imagined. What he experienced in her capable hands sent him to heights undreamt. The heights he reached were something new, but he reached his climax far too soon for Rachel.

The burst of youth untutored was something she had expected. She guided him to knowledge only women know and screamed with pleasure and ecstasy, writhing and twisting, responding to his efforts to bring her to satisfaction. She reached her zenith repeatedly until she cried, 'Enough, enough. Don't kill me please.'

They lay naked sided by side, soaked in perspiration and the juices of total abandon, all inhibitions gone. Leslie would never again be the boy he had been when he'd entered school that day.

How appropriate, a place of learning gave him his most valued lessons in geography, technical design, biology, and human anatomy. He hugged Rachel as though his life depended on it. He would not let her go as they lay naked together on the mat. He thought that, if he let go, she would vaporise, and he would be alone with his dreams and memories of an experience he could never again feel for the rest of his life. She turned and kissed him with passion and sincerity, a long lingering kiss that said more than words could say. It penetrated so deeply into Leslie's mind, body, and soul that time could not delete it; whatever happened after this did not matter one jot.

Leslie dressed his image of perfection item by item, kissing each part of her body as he clothed it, and every article of clothing made the image disappear from his view. She was in a state of euphoria, helpless, and submissive after leading and teaching. There would never be barriers between her and this Adonis that had exalted her to realms previously unknown. Even Alastair could not achieve what this stripling had achieved. Rachel ached as they walked hand in hand towards Howard House, exercises completed for the day!

At dinner, Rachel and Leslie sat side by side, he the perfect gentleman and she the recipient of his attentions. Mary noticed the change in the way her brother looked and behaved. *Oh God*, she thought, *something has happened between them, and I hope it is not what I think. She could lose her job, face prison even. And he could be headed for a mighty fall.*

***

That night, both Leslie and Rachel thought about what had occurred in the gym. Leslie, now initiated into the world of adulthood, revelled in the experience. He was looking forward to the next lesson tomorrow.

Rachel felt guilty for abdicating her responsibility, tinged with a sense of satisfaction she had not experienced before. She dreaded and anticipated the next lesson, and she knew she had done wrong, very wrong indeed. She had let her lust and desire supersede her responsibility for the well-being of this vulnerable boy. Boy? He was no longer a boy! He was the youthful man that had stolen her heart, mind, and imagination; the boy had taken her to new heights and gently laid her back to earth. Boy indeed. He may have been inexperienced and had rushed into the pleasure headlong. But she knew he was entering a new experience and would not be able to observe the finesses required. How could he know how to perform? Such finesse and delicacy comes from a good teacher, and there was so much she could teach him. She recognised, too, that he was a fast learner. But still it was wrong. *It must not happen again*, she told herself.

What if Sir Alastair found out? That would be disastrous, possibly for them both. She knew nothing of the lengths her lover would go to; to her, he was a business executive who, from time to time, travelled the world to attend his managers and employees. She had no inkling of the extent of his dealings and never showed an interest in them. That suited Sir Alastair perfectly and was possibly why they'd stayed together for so long.

***

Leslie still had the vision of heavenly beauty fixed in his mind. He understood now how one person could become obsessed with another. He had committed himself with abandon to pleasure and ecstasy, and he felt no shame. On the contrary, he felt enlightened and liberated. Rachel had led, and he had willingly followed. Yes, he also knew that it should not have happened, but his willpower had crumbled, far too easily. How could he have refused such a delight?

Together, they shared the secret of their forbidden liaison, a secret that joined them with a special bond. And whatever happened to them in the future, that bond was unbreakable.

***

Leslie eventually drifted off to sleep, happy and contented, wiser and older. In his dreams that night, he saw the man with the white beard cowering in the stench-ridden cell he called his home. He was thin and pale, a sickly colour that precedes death. He could remember the name of Perry and where the man was, but he could not recall how he had gotten there. How he knew this man was a puzzle to him. He had never, to his knowledge, been inside the asylum. He sensed that there was a link missing in his memory. How and what he felt for this man was clear; he remembered the stories and the confidences they had shared. But still he could not add that link. The dream faded, and he slept soundly until the morning.

***

The gong sounded, telling Leslie and the other occupants that breakfast was ready. He was already washed and dressed. He had woken with a feeling of anxiety; a sense of impending doom saturated his mind. He had gone to sleep relaxed and content. What had he dreamt that could cause him such a feeling? He did not remember his dream about Perry.

At breakfast, he was polite and attentive but solemn and silent, almost to the point of being morose.

On their morning walk, Mary asked, 'What is the matter with you today? Yesterday you were full of the joys of spring, and today you are down in the dumps. I hope you are not becoming manic depressive.'

Leslie stayed silent. He felt an unseen burden pushing down on his shoulders that he could not shift and could not understand. He wanted to run to Rachel and lay in her arms for consolation and security. He knew he could not. He knew that their relationship must remain confined to the schoolroom, behind the locked door, where no prying eyes or ears could invade their privacy.

The locked door – it came to him in a flash of realisation and revelation – the locked door of the mansion! It can open without a key. Of course it can, and only I can open it. This is my house, my mansion, my estate, and my island; it's my lake and gardens and my boat. He staggered slightly as he missed his step, and Mary grabbed his arm to steady him.

'Be careful, Leslie. You nearly fell then,' she snapped.

He continued to walk in silence.

'Look, Leslie, if our walks are going to be like this, in the future, you may as well go on your own. I come along to keep you company, and it is also an opportunity for us to talk alone. Suit yourself what you do, but do not rely on me in the future.' Her tone was sincere and direct, she had tried to be all that her brother needed for his return to the person he was, but she could see the walls being erected around him and he was the builder. She could do nothing to stop him; pain seared her as he stayed silent. He did not respond to her remarks, and she saw his silence as if he were saying, *Go to hell*.

Mary turned on her heels and began to march at a furious pace back towards the house. She muttered and mumbled as she stomped blindly up the hill.

Leslie ran after her, and as he caught up, he grabbed her sleeve. 'Stop, Mary, please stop, I am so sorry; there is something I must tell you...but... but...I don't know how to.'

She froze in the middle of the road with her brother still clinging to her sleeve. 'Leslie tell me in whatever way you can. Do not worry about anything. Just get it off your mind.'

They moved to the verge and sat on the grass.

Red-faced and shameful, he told her of the liaison with Rachel.

She jumped up. 'I knew it!' she shouted. 'I knew something like that had happened.'

Leslie pulled her back to his side. 'Please, Mary, tell no one what I have told you. I could not help myself; I know it was not right, but don't blame Rachel either. I know she is the adult and has responsibilities, but it was just something that happened, and it was wonderful.'

Mary sat and held her brother closely. She had known that something would happen, but so soon? This Rachel must be something special to be able to cast her spell on Leslie. Or perhaps the hormones had demolished his defences, leaving him susceptible to the slightest temptation. She did not judge his romantic interlude; she was, after all, a virgin herself. She had not had the sensations that her younger brother had delighted in. She tightened her grasp and kissed his head. 'My poor brother. It must have been horrific for you.'

Lurching his head backward, he caught her under the chin, and blood poured from her mouth as she spat on the road. 'Mary? Mary, I'm sorry. I'm so sorry. What should I do?'

He was panic-stricken and full of guilt. He felt he had caused serious injury to his sister. She held her hand to her mouth, unable to speak.

The blood seeped from between her fingers as they mounted the steps to Howard House.

Leslie was in no state to explain how this had happened. 'Please, get a doctor now,' he screamed.

Rachel appeared at the library door and rushed to give her assistance. 'Whatever has happened?'

'It was me,' cried Leslie. 'Do something. Please, help her. Please help,' he pleaded, imploring and sobbing. He sank into a heap on the floor of the hallway, sobbing like a child. 'It was my fault; it is me to blame… I am sorry, Mary. It was not intentional; it was an accident. Oh, Mary, I would not hurt you for the world.'

Tears blinded him as Rachel opened Mary's mouth to examine the extent of the injury. 'She will be all right in a day or two. She may not say much, but there is no serious damage done. It appears that she has bitten her tongue. Leslie, what did you do?'

'We were talking, and I had my head on her chest. When I raised my head I caught her under the chin, and she poured with blood. It is my fault, Rachel. She will be all right, won't she?'

Rachel cradled his head in her arms and consoled him on the floor of the hallway. He had proven himself a man, but the child in him lingered still.

Susan witnessed the whole drama in the hallway and detected the bond between Leslie and Rachel. The green worm surfaced, wriggling and twisting at the scent of ammunition for its power play.

Rachel escorted Mary to her room, and Leslie followed them, upset and penitent. He knelt by her bedside. 'Please forgive me, Mary. I would never do you harm.'

She could not speak but placed her hand on his head and stroked it. It told him that he was forgiven and not to blame himself; it was an accident, and there were no accusers or people ready to denounce him for some misdeed. He sat silently by her side with his head bowed, admonishing himself for the hurt he had caused her. His tears continued to flow despite her absolution of him.

In Mary's bedroom, Rachel observed the harmony of spirit between this boy and his sibling. She deduced that, in some way, they were one and the same in person. She had discovered the bond that connected them, not in a physical sense but in an ethereal way that was difficult to describe, something like the bond between identical twins. These two were like two halves of one whole being. They lead individual lives but are fused like the two halves of a walnut. Mary planted a thought into Rachel's mind— *My God, she knows about Leslie and me, how we feel about each other and what we did in the school. Oh hell's bells, she knows everything. I will suffer eternal damnation with her as my accuser and witness.*

She ran to the bathroom and vomited quantities of bile and stomach acid. Her head swam with visions of hell's eternal fires and the heat consuming her, heart and soul. She vomited until she could no longer bring anything up. She continued to retch and heave violently until blood bloated her face and head. It caused her to suffer a massive headache that blurred her vision and senses.

***

It was Susan who helped Rachel to her rooms, staggering and lost. Rachel had not been in control of the situation as she would be under normal circumstances. She felt dazed and confused, useless and feeble. It was not like her to lose control to this extent. Yes, she had succumbed to her lust. Was this punishment, the price she had to pay? Her head pounded with a vengeance that a betrayed lover would wish upon his usurper. The pain prevented her from opening her eyes. With each movement her brain banged against the shell that contained it, causing immense pain and discomfort.

Mary considered that Rachel had probably suffered enough punishment and let go her grip on Rachel, letting her slide into a state of release and comfort. She had paid a paltry price for her lust and dishonour, but what she had done would also serve Mary's purpose. That was why she had been so lenient with her! Mary was not an ogre who devoured living souls (she could be if she wanted to). She was just protecting her brother, a natural thing for an older sister to do, was it not? There was no one to agree or deny her the measures she had taken. She felt vindicated by the lack of response.

***

Leslie visited his sister every moment that he could. She still could not speak without a lisp. Her tongue was red and swollen. She pushed it out so that Leslie could see. He sank his head into her abdomen and cried. 'Mary, what have I done to you? You are my life, and I am lost without you.'

It was this that she had longed to hear from the brother she would gladly die for. The boy heard her words in his head, *'Oh, Leslie. Give me a hug. I would never give you blame for whatever reason. Kiss me and be assured that I bear you no ill will.'*

He gave her the kiss that convinced her of his commitment to her and sat beside her in her room. Mary connected her mind to her brother again, *Leslie, I promised long ago that I would do all in my power to protect you. You must listen to me now. I know how you feel about Rachel. Do not get me wrong. I am not criticising or judging. I know your feelings are deep, and she feels the same way about you. Leslie, dear boy, this is going to end badly if you continue. I have to tell you, as you evidently have not worked it out for yourself,* she paused for a moment knowing that what she was about to reveal would be a great shock to him, *Rachel is Sir Alastair's girlfriend.*

The revelation knocked him sideways. *You…you mean…that…that Rachel is—*

Exactly, replied Mary. *You do not realise what a dangerous path you tread.*

The news gave him a jolt. He was all too aware of the dean's power and the resources available to him. He did not wish to be another of those faceless victims. *Shit,* he said and then covered his mouth. *Sorry Mary,* he said from behind his hand.

She caressed his head. *Do not worry; it shall never come from me if he finds out. Susan is the one to watch.*

Leslie looked at her in disbelief. *What do you mean by that? Susan would never do anything so dastardly.*

Oh, you silly boy, she said, stroking his head, *you may think you have reached manhood physically, but you are still so naive in the ways of the world. For God's sake, Leslie. Susan is Sir Alastair's worst nightmare; believe me.* Mary looked at his expression. *Do you not see that she is in love with him? It is written on her face and the way she does everything without question. She is his servant and she loves it that way; she likes to be commanded and ordered. It turns her on, Leslie; you know what I mean now that you are a man of the world.*

You mean she gets excited by him telling her what to do? His disbelief was evident as he questioned her.

Leslie, what am I to do with you? You are so clever and yet so ignorant, so innocent about people and relationships. Mary's words penetrated into his brain. *You are going to fall on your backside with a mighty thud one day if you do not get to grips with reality. Life is not always in books telling you of other peoples' experiences.* Mary paused for a moment and then continued. *Dearest brother, I love you and will protect you from all who would wish you harm, but I cannot protect you from yourself. You, alone, are your own worst enemy until you see the world as it is, instead of images from the thoughts and dreams of others. Yes, poetry and accounts of other people's lives can seem relevant and pertinent, you must distinguish between what is real and what are whim, fantasy, poetry, ideology, and pure rubbish. I am sorry to be so harsh with you, but your brains appear to be in your trousers at the moment. Leslie, shake yourself out of this fantasy, for your sake and mine.*

Mary, with her injury could say nothing verbally. It was difficult for her to speak, and yet he heard her voice as clear as day, directing him as to the path he must take, in order to protect Mary, Rachel, and himself.

Yes, he was well educated, intelligent, and now a man, but his sister had dismissed all this and reduced him to the level of an imbecile, unable to recognise fact from fiction, life from fantasy. He had difficulty reconciling her remarks. He trusted her judgement of him, for she would not lie to him; this he knew. However, he could not see how she meant him to rectify his outlook on life and see people from her different aspect. And when did she become so astute, so deep, and so wise? He had never known her to be so clever, observant, calculating, and analytical. Where had all this come from? Was this really his sister or was an impostor posing as her? No... nobody could know him as she did. He had not reached the conclusion that Rachel had! He was totally unaware of the bond that tied him, and Mary was content for it to remain that way.

Chapter 19

Love Restrained and Horrors Regained

He took his morning walk alone, deep in thought and experiencing the whole gamut of emotions – pleasure, guilt, remorse, and excitement. He thought of Rachel and the warm surrounding comfort that he felt in her embrace, with her arms pulling him tightly to her. He knew that it would be folly to continue with this relationship fraught with danger. And did Rachel know of Sir Alastair's capabilities? He doubted it. He continued his walk with a sense of deep loss; he must end this liaison today. He felt it imperative to return both their lives to some semblance of normality. He would be forever grateful to her, and she would always have a favoured spot in his heart. But it must end now, today.

He sat on the verge sobbing with regret and pain, deep pain for what he was about to do. That morning at the pool, he was going to tell her. He knew it would hurt her and he wished for some other way to soften the blow. It would hurt him too, and it would hurt so deeply that he could already feel it tearing his heart to shreds. The tears rolled down his face; as he wiped them with the back of his hand, he could not control the flow.

Dr Hendricks noticed that Leslie was distracted and distant. 'Why do you not seem yourself today, young man? You are far away and sad I think.'

Leslie made excuses regarding his sister and the guilt he felt for her injury, but his mind was on other things.

'You wish to play the chess to distract your thoughts?'

He had no wish for anything except relieving himself of the position he had created. 'Doctor,' he said, 'could you excuse me for today? I really am not good company.'

The doctor sensed that something was seriously disconcerting to the boy. 'Would you like to talk about it with me? It may be of benefit to you Leslie. To talk is good, no?'

Leslie refused his kind offer and made his excuse to leave.

Beside the pool, he sat waiting for his goddess to arrive. She wore a pale pink costume exactly like the one she had worn in white. He could not control his reaction to her.

They rushed into each other's arms and kissed and hugged, their arms wrapped tightly around each other. It was an eternity before they lessened their grips. Rachel grabbed his hand and ventured towards the shower door. Leslie sat on the slatted bench and held fast, jerking her backwards with their hands still clasped, 'Rachel, my angel, this is so hard for me to say, and here it is so dangerous. We must stop now… Say nothing, but please listen… What we have done is beautiful and heavenly, and I want so much for it to continue. But we must not, Rachel my sweet, we must not.'

Floods of tears streamed down his boyish face as Rachel sat beside him and kissed his salty tears. 'My darling, you are right. I know you are right.' She kissed his face and his head whilst stroking his soft hands. 'But how can I give you up when we have only just found each other, my love?'

Never before had Leslie felt such a physical connection to someone, he recalled his sister's comment about his brains in his trousers, and just that thought brought its own reaction. Rachel saw the movement and slid her hand slowly and teasingly up his leg. He halted her progress with a firm hand. 'Rachel, we must not. It is too dangerous.'

She looked at him and smiled. 'I take precautions, Leslie. I will not get pregnant.'

'No,' he said. 'I am not talking about that. It is Sir Alastair. He will have us both killed.'

She laughed solidly for several seconds unable to speak. 'What…what are you talking about? Oh, you are precious, my love. Here, kiss me, sweet boy. I love you to distraction. You excite me, and you make me laugh. I love you to bits. She teased the evident excitement in him and pulled at the top of his trunks.

His hand again stopped her in her tracks. 'Rachel do you not realise what this man is capable of? What he has done to others far less deserving than us?'

She looked at his serious expression and immediately became concerned. 'What are you trying to say, Leslie? He has always been a perfect gentleman to me, and a softer, kinder man I have never known until you.'

'You know nothing of his dealings, Rachel? Well I am surprised, my sweet angel. He is a ruthless person who will stop at nothing to achieve his ends. Putting people in hospital to him represents failure. He wanted them dead!'

Rachel slapped him hard across the face, knocking him against the wall. 'How dare you? How dare you speak so, against the man who has given you everything and given me such happiness? How dare you, you ungrateful wretch. How dare you,' she screamed at him.

He had not envisioned their relationship ending like this. His face stung where she had slapped him, and as she stormed towards the door, he caught her arm. 'Rachel my love, don't let us end like this. It would hurt us both so much.'

She pulled away fiercely. 'Take your hands off me. You are jealous of Alastair and me, aren't you? Just like a spoilt boy. You think that what we did gives you the right to own me. I am my own person, Leslie. I come, I go when and wherever I please. I say thank you to no one and, I am my own master. I don't need another…'

He pulled her close and kissed her passionately. She softened and melted into his arms, defenceless despite her wrath. 'Oh…my darling boy.'

***

It was sometime later when they sat on the bench by the poolside. 'What did you mean about Alastair, Leslie?'

'Look, please do not get upset with me again, Rachel.'

'No, I want to know what you meant about him being ruthless.'

Leslie had said more than he should already. He should have bitten his own tongue. 'You were right, my love. It is just me being jealous.'

She was not at all convinced. 'Leslie, do not fob me off with that. tell me because I have a right to know.'

He held her hand in his, kissed and stroked it. 'I do not know that I should, my sweet. I can tell you things, but I cannot prove them, and that makes them just stories. And the position I find myself in makes those stories seem like jealousy or lies. Honestly, I did not know about you and Sir Alastair before—'

She tightened her hand into a fist. 'Stop waffling, Leslie, and tell me.'

He could feel the tension mounting in her, and he so wished he had never started on this topic. He stroked her hair and kissed her face. 'Whatever I tell you, my love, regardless of whether you believe me or not, is God's own truth. And, Rachel, I will always love you.'

She had a feeling that what he was about to reveal would change her life in an instant. A sense of foreboding enveloped her.

He told her of the case involving the parents of the Welch twins, of the story behind the death of Douglas Fairbrother, and of his friend Perry, detained behind the walls of the asylum.

She listened with disbelief. 'The boy's parents – that was an accident.'

'Yes a well-executed one.'

'And this man, Fairbrother. You said it was the doctor who killed him.'

'It was the doctor, Sir Alastair knew what the doctor had done and covered it up instead of following the proper procedures. He is just as guilty, Rachel.'

She buried her head in her hands. 'I never knew he could be so evil and devious. Wait until he gets back. I—'

Leslie stopped her. 'No, Rachel, you cannot speak of this. As I told you, there is no proof, and he will demand that you tell him where you obtained this information. Rachel, you will get us both killed and probably Perry as well. If he harmed me, Mary would kill him. Do you not see what we are up against?'

'What do I do now?' she asked 'How can I just carry on as if I know nothing? How can I face him now? I wish you had never told me.'

It was just as well that Leslie had not told her everything; she had trouble enough believing what he had revealed.

***

At lunchtime, Mary stayed in her room; her tongue was still too sore and painful when eating. Leslie, Rachel, and Dr Hendricks sat in silence as they ate their meal. Rachel could not bear to look at Hendricks; knowing now what a demon he was repulsed her, and his appearance belied his true nature.

'Leslie, how are you feeling now?' the doctor asked. 'You were not in the mood for the talking this morning.'

Leslie carried on loading his food onto his fork. 'No, sir, I was not. I have been so worried about Mary; she could have lost her tongue. It is still swollen, you know.'

'Yes, my young friend, but it will pass so soon, and she will be doing the telling off no?'

Leslie gave an affected smile.

The doctor was right though; she would soon be nagging at him once she had recovered. He'd noticed that he and his sister had been confiding more in each other since his operation, but on a second thought, he realised that he had done most of the confiding and she had listened. It struck him then that she never talked about what she liked or disliked, what her dreams were, or what she saw as her path in life. She only seemed to worry about him and his welfare. She was a strange girl in many respects; he became aware that he did not really know her at all.

***

The days passed observing the now regular routine. Mary joined him for the morning walk when she was in the mood to. Doctor Hendricks probed the deep recesses of his memory, and he and Rachel enjoyed their swimming and exercises. They held to their resolve and maintained an appropriate relationship, but they still felt exhilarated by each other's company and hugged and cuddled in the privacy of the showers beside the pool.

Sir Alastair called to inform Doctor Hendricks that the negotiations in Guiana had stalled. It was imperative to his business plans that the situation be resolved, and he would remain until a satisfactory conclusion was obtained. His investments in gold mining and sugar were under considerable risk, and they had to be protected and developed with guarantees from the government. He had been so preoccupied that he had forgotten to enquire about Leslie.

The doctor updated him on the situation at home and told him not to worry. When the dean heard about Mary, he laughed and said, 'How befitting. That has made my day, a speechless Mary.'

***

Leslie could not sleep when he went for his nap. He lay with his eyes closed, but something nagged at him deep in his subconscious. Thoughts began to form into familiar memories, and after a while, he found himself at the mansion, standing again at the steel door. He thought of the various ideas that had flitted through his mind about how to open it. And of course, he now knew that it was his house. But why he had made it so impossible to open the door was puzzling to him. He hoped that, if he could get into the room, he would find all the answers that still eluded him.

I must have been a strange boy to have created such an impregnable door, he thought.

A strange boy! The door vanished in an instant; he stared at the open space dumbfounded. That hated title was the key; he entered and looked around. Everything was just as he had left it. He crossed the room to the filing cabinet behind the desk and opened it. He removed all the files and began to read them one by one.

My God, he thought as he opened the third and fourth files. He read furiously and with great speed, and most of what he read was facts and figures. It made sense now of the lists that had tormented him. But by far the most important to him were the accounts of his visits to Perry, Ed and Tweety, and Salford. He studied his records of the dean's activities and those of Dr Hendricks and George Thompson. His notes explained to him how he had uncovered so much information – he could float, leave his body and cover huge distances in a flash just by thinking about where he wanted to be or whom he wished to observe. The notes said that only Perry could see him. He saw that his last visit to his friend was to tell him of the operation, and that had been months ago.

***

He entered the squalid cell that was home to Perry. It was empty. He searched and called but found no trace of him. Maybe they had relented now that the dean was away and moved him to somewhere more civilised. He concentrated his thoughts and pictured the feeble man with the white beard. He saw before him a patch of freshly disturbed earth. It was about six feet by three. He looked around him and saw similar mounds of earth but not as fresh.

He found himself at a part of the asylum grounds he had not explored before. He was behind the left side of the buildings, and the area was overgrown with grasses, weeds, and brambles. Looking around, he saw grass-covered mounds similar to the bare mound before him now. 'Oh dear Perry what happened to you, my dear friend? I have let you down. I have not kept my promise to get you out of here. But you are free of them now, Perry. I swear I will make them pay for this.'

He awoke feeling sick and rushed to the bathroom, and whilst he was in there, he heard a tapping at the bedroom door. As he came out of the bathroom, he could hear that it was Mary.

'Come in, quickly,' he whispered, urgently gesturing for her to move away from the door.

She entered, and he turned the key in the lock. He took her by the arm, to the window (the farthest point from the door).

His face was distressed and pale. 'Perry is dead, Mary, my dearest friend is dead. I found where they buried him at the back of the asylum' he said, wiping his eyes as copious tears fell freely from his eyes.

Mary looked at his sad face and pulled him close, hugging him as a mother would do with an injured child. He began to judder as he tried to stifle the sobs. *Hush now, dear boy,* he could hear her say in his head. *How do you know that it is Perry buried there?*

He had been reluctant to tell her of what he could do, but he felt now that he had no choice. He had to confide his secret to her.

He told her everything, and without the slightest sign of surprise or disbelief, she sat him gently at the desk. 'Why did you not tell me this before?'

'I thought you would not believe me. I know how incredible it sounds, and I refused to believe it myself that first time in the hospital.'

'Why did you go to Salford? That could only have brought you sadness.'

'Well it was Tweety and Ed. They had been in contact with our mother, and I found out through them that we have two brothers and a sister—'

'I know,' she said, cutting him in mid flow. 'I hoped you would never find that out.'

Leslie glared at her. 'Why? Why shouldn't I know about our family?'

She stroked his hair as she often did when he was sad or ill. 'Okay, I suppose you should know now after all this time, but you will not like what I am about to tell you.

'The dreams you told the doctor about – I told you to make something up, but you told him the nightmares you used to have when you were small, didn't you. When you told me how he had explained them to you, you seemed to be satisfied with the interpretations.'

'Yes, I thought they were quite good actually. They made sense at least.'

'Well what I will tell you is another interpretation but one that is based on fact.'

'You do recall the floods of 1953; you have demonstrated that. But your mind has blocked out something else that happened the same year, something that is also related to water. For many years, you had a justifiable fear of it,' she paused whilst she thought about how to phrase what she had hidden from him and what he had hidden from his conscious mind.

'Well, Mother was in a fury because Dad was on leave but had not yet arrived at the barracks. She had arranged to go out with her friends for a drink, and Dad was late. He had no idea she was going out anyway. You were in the kitchen rooting around in the cupboards and pulling things out onto the floor as small children do. The other children, the ones you refer to as brothers were with a neighbor. Well at that time, we were still on rationing, and you split a bag of sugar all over the floor and played with it. You rendered a whole week's supply unusable. When she saw what you had done, she went berserk and started hitting you about the head and face, slapping and kicking you, I heard the commotion and ran to the kitchen. Leslie, blood covered your face and head; there was blood coming from your eye and your nose, and your chin dripped with blood. I put myself in between you and her and pushed her backwards. She fell onto a chair that toppled and sent her backwards against the table. She dragged herself to her feet. You were screaming your head off, and I have never seen such a look of abject terror on a child's face. Your right eye was swollen and the other huge and staring as she grabbed me and threw me into the cupboard under the stairs. She called it the punishment hole. I heard her slide the bolts on the outside of the door—' She wiped the tears from her eyes that welled up at the recollection.

'The next thing, I could hear her running the bath. You were still screaming and calling my name, but I could do nothing to help you. I banged and pounded at the cupboard door, screaming at her to let you alone. Then I noticed that you had stopped screaming. I strained my ears to catch any sound, and all I could hear was the rushing of the water as it filled the bath. Then I could hear your muffled screams as she dragged you past the cupboard door and into the bathroom. I heard the splash and many strange sounds. For several minutes, this went on, until a silence fell over everything. And then I heard Daddy come in the front door.

'There was an almighty racket and crashing and banging. Dad was swearing, and mother was screaming at him. And then I heard you coughing and spluttering. I banged at the door until my hands bled. I heard the front door slam so hard it is a wonder it stayed on its hinges.

When Dad opened the cupboard door he was holding you so tight in his arms. The two of you were soaked to the skin. He sat you on a chair and untied the stockings she had used to tie you up and took off the gag Dad had pulled away from your mouth. Daddy held us both for ages. There we sat, me with my bloody hands and you with your bloody face – part of your ear was torn where she had dragged you by it I guess – and Dad covered in your blood and his own from scratches from her fingernails. We must have looked a sight. At least Daddy arrived in time to save you from drowning. You were in the hospital at the barracks for a few weeks with a skull fracture, broken ribs, and masses of bruises and stitches, and my hands were covered in sticky plasters. She never came back, and that was when Granny came to stay. Does the water dream make sense now to you now Leslie?'

He was visibly shaking so hard his whole body trembled. She grabbed his hands. They were freezing cold.

'Here, quickly, get into your bed.' She helped him across to the bed and covered him with an extra blanket from the dresser.

He closed his eyes, but this did not shut out the vivid pictures that he saw. He continued to shake as the full memories finally regained their place. He saw her bright crimson red lipstick as her mouth spewed insults at him with hatred and venom, the hands swiping and slapping, leaving him no room to avoid the blows. He could barely see out from under the swollen eyelid and the warm blood stinging his eye. His chin hurt from the gash underneath it, but most of all, his ear throbbed; he could feel the pain as she dragged him to the bathroom.

It explained a lot to him – the inch-long scar on his left eyelid, the scar under his chin, and the one around the top of his ear where they had sewn it up. It also fitted with the demons that haunted him and explained his attraction to some of the more macabre poems about dancing demons.

Mary turned towards the door, unlocking it. 'Do you want me to go now?' she asked softly. 'I think you should be excused from the gym for this evening. I can make your excuses to Rachel for you—'

Leslie was sleeping. She saw the beads of cold perspiration appearing on his forehead and cheeks. She kissed his cold clammy face and left the room.

Mary wondered if she should get Rachel to look at him; she would have to explain his condition. She was seriously concerned that she had misjudged his mental state, and she went looking for Rachel.

'I think he may have a fever; he is certainly cold and clammy' Rachel noted. 'I'll fetch a thermometer from my kit. You stay with him, Mary.'

Rachel quickly reappeared with a black case. She placed the thermometer under his armpit and looked at Mary. 'What has brought this on?' she asked, feeling for the pulse in his wrist.

Mary knew that Leslie had revealed a certain amount to Rachel in order to control the situation between them, but she was now feeling unsure of herself for the first time in her life. Mary went to the open door and closed it. She told Rachel of the water dream and what the doctor had said to her brother as an interpretation. She then related what she had just revealed to Leslie.

Rachel checked the temperature and looked seriously at Mary. 'It's 101, but he's still as cold as ice. He's in a state of shock. We must get him to the hospital, now.'

Mary rushed to the telephone in the hall and made the call.

***

'Mr Marston is on his way up from London,' said Dr Hendricks. 'He should be here shortly.'

Mary would not let go of Leslie's hand, and as she sat beside his bed, she got a distinct feeling of déjà vu. Mary's mind turned to the subject of Perry and what her brother had told her. Should she discuss it with Rachel or keep her out of it? She had difficulty deciding, and then she had an idea. She could communicate to Rachel that Perry was dead. Leslie had told her about Perry and how he felt that he was like a father.

She passed the information in the form of a mound of earth and then an old, thin, dirty man with a white beard lying down for his final rest, sinking into the mound and disappearing beneath it.

The response was unexpected. Rachel had such a vivid picture in her head that it startled her. 'I'm s-sorry,' she stuttered as a tray fell from her hands, sending the hypodermic and ampoule across the floor. She gathered up the items and binned them, retreating to the office to get replacements from the nurse. Mary was surprised at how receptive Rachel was; she had never had someone react so sharply before.

***

The two women had dinner quite late that day and neither of them had much of an appetite. Leslie was in very good hands under Mr Marston's care so they had returned to Howard House to have their meal and get some rest. Dr Hendricks had gone home to the lodge, and Mary and Rachel were virtually alone, apart from Susan. Rachel suggested a short walk before retiring. There was nowhere safe to talk alone in the mansion, and Mary sensed that Rachel wanted to talk urgently.

***

They got some distance from the house before Mary said, 'So what is on your mind, Rachel?'

'You know, Mary, the strangest thing happened to me at the hospital.' She related exactly what Mary already knew.

'What did the old man look like?' she asked innocently.

Rachel gave an exact description and added, 'What on earth do you think that was about? It was almost as if I knew the old man. I thought immediately of Leslie's friend Perry. He seemed to fit the description Leslie gave me of him.'

Mary had already concocted her answer, 'Well, as I have never met him, I could not say. But you are right that he seems to fit the description, now that I think about it. Mind you, I used to think that Perry was his imaginary friend, you know the way that lonely children do.'

'Oh no,' retorted Rachel. 'I believe he is as real as you and me. Do you think something has happened to him and Leslie knows about it?'

'I shall not know until I ask him,' said Mary, realising that she had given him a great shock on top of the one regarding Perry.

Rachel viewed Mary as somebody she could trust and confide in, although there was something strange about the girl she could not define. She had seen how much she cared for her brother and how Leslie confided in her. He appeared to trust her implicitly, so that was good enough for her.

***

After breakfast, Rachel and Mary walked down the hill to the hospital. Don was engaged in his gardening and stopped to ask how Leslie was getting on.

'You talk to him,' Mary said to Rachel forcefully, and carried on to see her brother. She had her reasons not to like this man but said nothing.

Rachel introduced herself and gave an update to the vicar.

He wiped his hands on his apron. 'Can I be of any assistance?' he enquired. 'I'm quite accomplished at pastoral care,' he added with a smile.

Rachel declined his kind offer and went to join Mary.

***

Leslie still had a slight temperature but was not shaking now. He mentioned that he felt a pain above his eye, his chin, and his ear. Mary calmed him as she always could. 'There is nothing wrong with your eyes or ears now. That was all a long time ago, far in the past, a distant, vague, faltering memory. You will feel better very soon and return to the brother I love.'

Even Rachel began to feel relaxed as she listened to the girl's soft tone, consoling and reassuring. This odd girl amazed her with the power she had over her brother.

Rachel was in the hospital office waiting for the kettle to boil so she could make some teas and coffees and offered to make one for the nurse.

'Strange girl that one,' the nurse said. 'When she was here before, she had everyone following her orders like an army officer. The boy was in a sort of coma they couldn't bring him out of, and along comes madam, and hey, presto, he's awake – although he didn't speak, just stared at the ceiling night and day for weeks. Then one day, I heard her telling him off, you know, nagging like an old fishwife, and he just says, "Is Daddy with you?"

'A miracle it was. We all thought from the beginning that he was headed for the reaper. You should have seen his face, twisted and contorted, gruesome it was sometimes. But she just sat with him and held his hand. Except for me and Mr Wallace – he was the consultant – she wouldn't let anyone near him. No one dared to defy her; as soon as she raised her voice, they all submitted like children. You know, it's because of her that they live up at the mansion. Demanded it she did, right here in front of me, and they caved in to her demands.'

'Where did they live before? I thought he was their guardian.'

'Oh yes, he is now; he had it all done legal. Aye, the boy was in Roding, and I think she was in Epping. But, dear God, Mary said they had harmed him, and she would not be separated from him again. You should have seen her have a go at Sir Alastair and Dr Hendricks. Well I don't think they have ever had someone talk to them like that, I mean…disrespectful, to say the least. And her threat to them – "You will pay dearly" – she screamed it. I tell you Miss, I thought all the windows would break, and you could see a look of fear on the master's face. Frightened me too it did.'

This gave Rachel an insight into this girl with strange ways. She had seen that this girl was protective, yes, but able to command grown men when she was just a teenager. What powers she may have; when she became an adult, her power would be awesome to behold. The more she learned of this young woman, the more intrigued she became. Mary had earned Rachel's admiration and respect, if not a little fear. This account had come from a witness to all that had occurred. She almost felt a little envious of the girl. She had power of her own, but transient in nature. Her looks and her seductive figure would not last forever. She hoped they might, but she was, at the very least, realistic in her outlook on life.

***

Mary, aware of the conversation between Rachel and the nurse, connected a permanent transmitter into the nurse's brain. She felt she had to guard her other powers from prying eyes, inquisitive minds and gossips.

The girl thought very little of herself as a woman or as an individual. She had just one purpose in life – the well-being of her brother and his unrealised dependence on her. She had no need of personal relationships or questionable liaisons. She lived vicariously through him. The sadness's and pleasures he encountered, so did she – not as a voyeur or an eavesdropper; no that would hurt her, and him, devastatingly if he ever found that out. She gave her brother his own time and space, to love and be loved; if it made him happy, she was happy too. She would not dream of invading his private moments. That would be intrusive to her, and she would never do that. Her only concern, her only reason to exist, was to further his life and his advancement.

She was glad that she'd never revealed to him the full extent of her capabilities. She wanted to know all his secrets, every detail. There were things he could hide from her, protected by a wall, a dark red bluff that he had built and then tried to distance himself from. After the shock he suffered when she explained about their mother, there was no way she could explain about his dream of the journey in the desert. He had told her about the doctor's interpretation of the dream, but the truth was that he had built the red bluff in his mind, a barrier to protect him from such terrible memories and why he could not escape it, why it followed him to the ends of his worlds. He must trust her with his life and tell her his deepest fears and sorrows, his ecstasies and failures. Everything was of vital importance to her; she must know each beat of his heart, his highs and lows, what excited or depressed him. She must demolish the red wall that oppressed him and weighed so heavily upon him. But she could not do it. Leslie had to demolish it himself.

Hour by hour she stayed by his side, willing him to crush the bluff into sand, to reveal to her all his secrets – not for some form of self gratification, but for the salvation of his soul. She could not command him with this wall of red earth standing in her way; she needed him to demolish it. She needed to find the prairie that lay beyond, vast and deserted, wild and unspoilt, free from danger. She needed to find that space that was free from Sir Alastair and the confines of the village, free from the monster who called himself a doctor, free from the memories of the harm that had befallen him and persuaded him to build this barrier, and free from the loss of a father and a pseudo-personality that had taken his place.

Mary was very well aware of what their father meant to Leslie. He had known his father for such a short time, and it hurt her to think upon it. Those extremely painful memories she had kept far beyond her brother's recollections. She had prevented him from descending into madness and oblivion. Once again she connected to his mind and said, *Dear, dear brother, connect your mind to me. Break down the barriers you have built and let me help you. I implore you. It is the only way I can help you.*

Leslie sat up, choking and gasping. The nurse gave him a drink of orange juice. 'Don't worry, young lad. You'll be right in no time. Now keep calm like your sister says, or my life won't be worth living, you hear, young master?' Her laugh covered the flippant remark as she made her retreat.

Mary entered the room and scowled at the nurse for her incompetence and stupidity. She had no time for gossips and deficient people in positions of responsibility, and this 'creature' was responsible for her brother. Did this woman not realise the importance of the responsibility she had? If she failed in her duty, it would be more than one life in her hands; Mary's vengeance would send her to depths undreamt. Hell's eternal fires were no match for what she could do. She could supersede all that was perceived and imagined, all written of and reported. *Keep my brother safe, for the price of my wrath is something you would never wish to know. Do your work and make him whole again.*

***

The nurse felt a sudden urge to attend the boy and check all his vital signs. Noting each and every disparity and variation, she consulted with the specialist and made her notes accordingly. She felt an anxiety that pervaded her very soul; this boy must survive and be healthy. She rushed and took his temperature and his pulse.

'Doctor,' she reported, 'his pulse has reduced; I think he is returning to normal.'

'Whatever is the matter with you, nurse? You are like a cat on hot bricks,' the doctor said, noting her obviously erratic behaviour. 'Pull yourself together, woman. Remember, you are a professional nurse and not a trainee.'

She had no will power to haul herself from the state into which Mary had plunged her. She must stay beside this boy day and night, without sleep or rest, food or drink. Her life depended upon it with such a depth; she was totally committed and was not yet ready to die.

Mary flexed her arms and stood proud in the moonlit summer night. She was confident, so confident that her power exceeded that of any competitor. She had power over the 'great' Sir Alastair, the 'marvellous' Dr Hendricks, and the ever obedient and submissive Susan and Joan, as well as that ever-watchful Jackson and the creep Don. For the vicar, she felt disgust from the very depths of her soul at so much as the thought of him – what he had done to her friends in Epping House as children curdled her blood. He'd had no success with Mary; her mind and will had denied him his pleasure. But most of all, she had defended Leslie from any untoward advances.

Don was another future victim of her wrath and vengeance. But she was patient, so very patient. She was biding her time, waiting for the moment that she could bring his world crashing down around him and plummet him into depths undreamt of and a pain he could not diminish in a multitude of eternities. A man of God, pah. God – if he were what the Bible and the gospels preached – would not recognise this self-indulgent paedophile who preyed on precious and innocent small children. Such young children had no defences, no ploys to distract him, no defences at all. He represented himself as an agent, a servant of the Lord and the servant of the creator of all life on this planet and beyond – the moon and stars and sun, day and night. The rhetoric he used to vindicate his perverted use of his position and respect was astounding to Mary. To use and abuse the most fragile and susceptible victims within his care was utterly reprehensible and Mary wished him dead.

***

Slowly, ingenuously, and seemingly without reason, Leslie became aware of all that had brought him to this sorry state of affairs. The realisation was something he found very difficult to comprehend; his mind was in turmoil. Had these things happened to him? Or were they things of his, or his sister's, imagination or invention? No, the pain of recollection, the pain above his eye, the absolute knowing that he had been hurt and abused penetrated so deeply into him it had replicated the pains he had suffered as an infant and he had blocked from his mind from such an early age.

That moment he began to raise up the wall, at such a tender age, was because he had realised he could rely on no one for support or succour, the motherly comfort all children require to establish their existence did not exist for him. That inescapable thing had followed and persecuted him in his mind and his dreams, becoming the reason to erect such a monstrosity to block his memory from the suffering. His sister had brought it crashing in upon him with such a force of recollection that he felt unable to defend himself from it. It had been his constant and abiding protector and companion. It had served to protect him from truth and reality; he felt sick and confused, confounded and exposed. He could see the wall crumbling, and it was falling in his direction, catching up to him as he ran faster and faster away from it. He was no match for its speed in this state of despondency and frailty. Now it was attacking and persecuting him, his own wall.

He stepped onto the thin living rope that inhaled and exhaled as he walked upon it. It would not be an escape from his pain and suffering; all vision dissolved from his perimeters and his world descended into that dark empty space he felt he knew and feared. He had been haunted and intimidated by it in his younger life, but now he was escaping the bluff, the wall that followed him. He travelled cautiously along the threadbare length of writhing twine; he had trodden it on many occasions as a small boy. He could not see his destination, and he wobbled and nearly fell. The surging sickness of realisation of what lay below him in the darkness made him more resolved to balance and tread with care.

What lay below him would consume and devour him but would not kill him. Far, far worse, it would change him into something that represented all he despised – something perverted, corrupted, evil, and twisted. He could not let himself fall into that heaving, noxious pit. He could not see it, but the stench from it filled his nostrils. It smelled of Sir Alastair and his faint waft of cologne, Dr Hendricks and the aromatic smell of pipe tobacco, Don and the pungent scent of flowers and incense, Mr Atkins and the aroma of medicaments, and George Thompson and the reek of betrayal and treachery. The smells made his head swirl. It begged him to plunge headlong into its soothing mess of trust, transformed from loyalty, respect, and decency into a mirror image that confused and beckoned him into the opposite of his morality.

The voices called softly and comfortingly. 'Leslie, join with us and be free… Leslie we are here waiting for you… Come now, you are ready… Leslie, we need you now. Do not abandon us. You are one with us… Come to us now; there is nowhere else for you to go…'

He had to steady his balance as he neared the fraying threads. If he went back or continued, he had to consider the consequences of the rope breaking. He recalled the doctor's words. *You must repair the rope to continue.* He fumbled in his pockets and found a length of string, leaned forward, and bound the fraying threads tightly so that the ends could not escape. He strode along the remaining length with vigour and confidence and saw a distant light, warm and inviting, leaving behind him the howling hoard baying for his return

Mary kissed him with warmth and passion. 'My dear, dear brother, do not ever leave me again.'

She was at his bedside holding his hand, as she always did. 'Leslie, I can already see that you are back and well.'

His colour and temperature returned to normal, and he had an air about him that exuded confidence and victory – victory over the demons that had vainly attempted to destroy him. He was not only restored but also instilled with vitality and a sense of purpose that superseded all that he had previously been. This was a new Leslie, the likes of which none had encountered, imbued with his own powers, some freshly strengthened and others newly acquired. It was not yet evident what these new powers were, but they would prove to be of invaluable assistance to him in his quest.

***

Mary sat watching the daily news report on the television in the family lounge. A world renowned and respected expert on Spanish and English language had died in mysterious circumstances on the border between France and Spain. His car had crashed the barriers on the treacherous road near Le Perthus and plunged over the edge. 'His wife and family have been informed,' said the report.

Mary knew this was no accident; she knew the death had been carefully planned and well executed by the sergeant major. That brutal bastard, who enjoyed his work, would come to a sorry end, she vowed. She would expose him for the evil unfeeling monster that he was; he was ruthless, without the slightest semblance of remorse or conscience – a soldier of the most abhorrent nature, a zombie who followed his master's wishes in thought and deed, a man who was the very worst kind of man. In contrast, she was so grateful for the soft, kind, and gentle brother that her own life depended so much upon. He would be, in another form, the type of man she could spend the rest of her days with, in harmony of spirit.

She thudded back to earth as Leslie connected to her mind. Who was there who could measure up to him now? She felt his force growing inside him. The power stunned her. *My God, he exceeds all bounds, he exceeds his previous powers and my powers combined. For God's sake, I hope he uses them wisely and with discrimination!* She juddered again at the force he exuded. *I must see him now.* She rushed down to the hospital.

Mary brushed aside the nurse, and Rachel and waved them away with a sweep of her hand. 'Dear brother, talk to me.'

His face was calm and serene. 'What do you wish to talk about?' he asked haughtily, dismissively, as she had done many times in the past.

'God, what has happened to you? You are no longer the boy you were when you came in. You are like Sir Alastair! Please do not become like him. You must listen to me, do not become like him.'

He raised himself from the hospital bed, stripped naked without the slightest hint of modesty or embarrassment, and then dressed. Mary hid her blushed face as he dressed. 'Leslie, some respect please.'

He felt no shame; he was a creature of nature, proud and unabashed. She had no idea what he had become. He transmitted telepathically, *I am like other men, in shape and form. But now I have the power to destroy all demons.* His calm tone and direct words resounded with a confidence that scared Mary.

Leslie, what are you going to do? she implored.

Her anxiety, obvious and penetrating, spurred the boy into speech. *I will do all I can to avenge my friends and rid this earth of the evil that has been heaped upon us, Mary. Help me in this. Or must I do it alone?*

Spellbound by the transition in her brother, Mary answered, *Of course, I will do whatever you wish and with pleasure.*

He pointed his finger at the trolley containing medication and medical instruments. It sped across the floor and crashed against the wall. 'I have no need of this place anymore,' he said, calmly.

Rachel and the nurse had heard the crash and came running in. 'What happened? Are you both all right?' asked Rachel.

Leslie smiled a wry smile and headed for the door.

'Wait, Master Leslie,' shouted the nurse. 'The doctor has not said you are ready to leave yet and—'

Leslie did not wait, nor did he let the nurse finish.

His power was frightening to Mary as she followed him along the road, 'Leslie, tell me what you are going to do.'

He ignored her and walked from the hospital, striding with vigour and purpose toward Howard House, with his sister tugging at his arm, struggling to keep pace with him. He glanced briefly at the row of cottages opposite the school, the chapel, the vicar's house, and the avenue down to Roding House as he passed them.

Chapter 20

New Life, Death and Destruction

In his bedroom, he told Mary what his first step would be.

You are able to do that? she asked in astonishment.

If you can, then so can I, he said silently. *You will see at lunchtime.*

***

Susan placed the tureens on the sideboard and left the dining room. As they ate, Rachel told them of her decision. 'Leslie, it is obvious that my services are no longer needed here. You have made a surprising recovery, and you are fit and well. There is something I have to tell you, but please keep it to yourselves,' she added in a low voice, looking toward the door to the kitchen. 'I have seen a position advertised for a director of physiotherapy in Australia. I am going to apply for it; I cannot stay here when Alastair returns. I will miss you so deeply, both of you.'

Leslie felt the pain that she felt, tearing her apart from him.

'It is the saddest part of my decision, but if I get the post, I will be leaving very quickly,' Rachel concluded.

Mary looked at her brother. *It worked!*

'Rachel, you have been an unbelievable treasure and a friend. It will hurt me so much, but I understand your position. Oh, and you will get the post,' he added.

Rachel gave him a look that revealed her thoughts.

'Someone of your calibre and abilities would be a very valuable asset. You will get it. Believe me.'

She smiled and thanked him for the flattery, resting her hand on his arm. He did not transmit the deep sadness and sense of loss he felt, almost to the point of desperation at her forthcoming departure. He had designed it and controlled it, contrary to his desire and need for her. His lovely angel was about to ascend to her realm in heaven and leave him bereft and sad at what he had done. It was for her safety and protection.

***

That afternoon, Leslie visited the site of the accident in France. The wreckage had not yet been removed from the site. Leslie inspected every inch of it. He could find no obvious signs such as a bullet hole or tampering with the brake lines. He checked the hillside and the barrier and found nothing; he looked at the black skid marks on the approach to the bend; the brakes must have been working to make those sorts of marks. Across the road, he checked all the way up the mountainside to an area of loose gravel, soil, and scrub that formed a wide ledge. There were sweet wrappers and footprints. It seemed to Leslie that someone had been waiting here for some time. He found two prints in the soil at the back of the ledge that looked as though the person had laid stomach down, the toes of his boots leaving the deep prints. Where his knees would have been, he found more indentations, and those near the shrub would have been from his elbows. He calculated the distance between the indentations and surmised the height and weight of the man. He would be about six feet tall and well built. This fitted the description of his chief suspect, but that was not proof. There were no marks associated with a tripod to hold a rifle and no shell casings either. The sun beat down upon him as it arced slowly westward.

Leslie had a thought. The car had been travelling east to west on this stretch of road. The sun would have been behind the driver at the time of the accident and he would not have the sun visor down. If someone had a mirror up on the hillside, they could blind the driver with it from up here, making him lose control of the vehicle. Leslie connected his mind to the chief investigator and gave him the clues to look for. He checked all the local airport passenger lists for Greg or Gregory Walsh. Just as he'd thought, Gregory Walsh was recorded on a flight to Perpignan four days before the accident and booked on a flight to Heathrow the day after tomorrow. Already armed with the details of the professor's journey, he must have made a detailed reconnoitre of the area. He'd then laid in wait to pounce upon his prey, and with just a flash of light, it was done.

Who could prove he had done anything at all? He did not even know the professor personally. A perfect assassination!

There were the boot prints that could be matched to his boots, the flight records, and the car hire with the recorded mileage, along with the sweet wrappers, which were of a type only available in small London shops that still sold the old favourites. There were no records of him checking in at any hotel, guest house, or gîte in the southern region of France or northern Spain. He had a bolthole or he'd slept in the hired car. Either way, in his mind, he had done the job to perfection.

The police took him in for questioning, at the airport.

***

Leslie concentrated his thoughts on Dr Hendricks, now that the assassin had been delayed. He would distract the doctor in order to take the next step in his plan. If Hendricks were able to have him followed, he could not be sure that his plan would succeed.

The fabulous garden at the lodge, with its scented plants and flowers was always a delight to Leslie. He felt he was destroying a work of art so valuable it was beyond price. It was to him perfection itself. The doctor lived for his garden; he loved and cherished it as much as the vicar did his – two birds, one stone, a mighty hefty one at that.

The vicar called Dr Hendricks. 'Is there a problem with your garden? My plants are shrivelling and dying. There are no more flowers, and the leaves are turning brown.' Panic sounded in his voice. 'All my years gardening have never given me such worry, Doctor.'

'My garden too is dying. I have consulted with the best horticulturalists, and they give me no answers, Don, no answers at all. There is not the blight or infection nationally; it is only here in the village, no? I must find an answer to our problems, Don. Give them the feed and the water every day, as I do. There must be a reason they are so ill. Maybe like the people they become ill also, no?'

***

Now it was time to direct the matters in hand towards Mr Atkins. Leslie learned that the pale, sallow creature Atkins called his wife had discovered the truth within the village many years ago. She had threatened to expose the 'whole disgusting band of kidnappers, perverts, and evil creatures.' When the dean learned of this, he had warned Mr Atkins. 'Control her, or we will.' Mr Atkins had no major part in this scheme except his compliance.

Atkins had few talents or abilities. Without this job he would find it hard to exist in the outside world. He was, in effect, a man of weak character, easily led or persuaded. The threat made to him, put his and his wife's life at risk. From fear and ineptitude, he aligned himself to the purpose of the village. He loved his wife dearly and would see no physical harm come to her, but he had to control her. Hendricks had talked him into giving her some tranquilisers; a powder to mix into her food or drinks, it would be undetected.

The years of being drugged had left Mrs Atkins obedient, quiet and, unresponsive to any communication. Leslie had never heard her utter a word in the years he was at Roding House, not a single word! His next step was to remedy that situation if he still could.

***

Susan was talking to Dr Hendricks on the telephone. 'But you need to get to Roding House. The master there is ill, and Miss Lola is lost as to what to do.'

'My dear Susan, I am not now at my best. I feel like the flowers, sick and dying. You must call for Mr Wallace, and also ask him to come, please, to me.'

All the weight and control of the village seemed to have passed to Susan. She telephoned Mr Vance. 'You must do something. I cannot run the village. I am a maid; I work in the mansion, cleaning and tidying. I cannot take on the work my master does. You will have to stand in for him, one of you... You must do as you are expected to do.'

There was no consensus as to who should stand in for the dean; no one wanted the responsibility or the repercussions. The assembled heads of houses argued and accused, and animosities grew ever greater between them. Leslie was not invited to the meeting; nor was Mary. However, Leslie was there, unseen, unheard, directing and controlling, planting doubts and suspicions of ineptness in the minds of the stronger minded. His work for now was done; chaos was taking control.

***

'Leslie, I love you to bits,' said Mary, as she gave him her most sincere hug and kiss. She nearly strangled him with her arms wrapped around his neck.

He gently separated himself from her and said, 'Why? Why do you love me to bits? It is not sensible or rational—'

'You always have to be so literal, you great elf. I love you because you have not turned out to be one of the monsters or demons that have pursued and tormented you; you have not become the thing you despise. Leslie, promise me you never will. Promise me on pain of death unimaginable, pain that will exceed all that your tormentors could induce...'

Leslie established the space between them; calmly, gently he sat her on the chair and said, 'Mary, I love you too. You have been the one constant in my life. I have connected my mind to yours, and I know now that, as a small child, you risked your own life to save mine; it was an incredibly brave thing to do. I have felt your horror and anguish; I also now know where your dedication to me comes from. It was born and fed by a harsh brutality that should have been a soft and loving nest for us to grow in, warm and secure, surrounded by a mother's love and protection. Animals and birds in the wild protect and defend their young. What went wrong with the creature that calls herself our mother? Did she have no happy memories of childhood? Was she also a victim like us? Mary we know nothing about her and what had transformed her into our memories of her.'

Mary was so overjoyed. For the first time in her life, she was happy to see the tears roll down her brother's face. He had retained a deep, a tremendously deep, morality (a quality she'd always admired in him), and he had almost a forgiveness for the instigator of all his ills. Mary herself could not forgive her mother. She could not defeat her own demons – her desires for vengeance, retribution, and punishment. But Leslie was about to deal with all of that for her, on her behalf.

The news came that Dr Hendricks was so ill with some kind of plant poisoning or allergy he'd been taken to the intensive care unit of the general hospital. Don was not found until Sunday. The Village had assembled for services as usual at 10.00. With the chapel door locked, there was no sign of the vicar; Mr Vance elected to go to his cottage to investigate the problem.

Mr Vance found the vicar dead, impaled on the pitchfork he had placed upside down near the wisteria in the back garden. He had evidently fallen from a ladder whilst tying the tendrils to the framework. Laurence did not know that it had taken him three agonising days to die. Every movement had compounded the vicar's pain, until he felt physical pain no more. During those long days and nights of slowly creeping death, he'd recounted in his head the monstrous deeds he had enjoyed and had slavered over, recounting the sensual delights that deviants savour. They'd bitten, torn, and wrenched and had given him such pain that he'd screamed his silent screams, unheard in this physical world, until he could scream no more.

This was no escape however. Death? Death is a human concept.

***

Human understanding is infantile and meaningless to those vast powers beyond our comprehension. Mary and Leslie believe their powers are given by the Gods, for want of another name. To listen to the Gods sends some people into madness; those unable to use or control the infinite powers given by them, float aimlessly. To understand the power, the possibilities and purpose, and to be able to control or be commanded by them is usually beyond human capability. This power has surrounded us for aeons, eternities, created in the dawn of time as a tool for balance between good and evil. We, humankind, have lost the power of recognition, with our vast technologies; we have, with wisdom and advancement in all things technical, created our own laws and punishments. We scorn and deny the unscientifically proven resources that we may inherit.

There are no machines, techniques, or devices to explain or reveal the true power of man. It is complex – delicate and dispassionate, remembered and forgotten. It remains, despite human dismissal and ignorance, ever forceful and powerful to those who can recognise and control it. Leslie was now such a person. The might and power of the past was now his to understand and employ – but with caution. There are rules that govern how to use these powers, unwritten and unspoken; you knew of them only if you broke them. The blight in the gardens, so lovingly tended, was Leslie's doing, but he had no hand in the demise of Don or the illness that had attacked Dr Hendricks.

***

Sir Alastair could not return due to the accusations made against him by the authorities in French Guiana, he was detained on charges of corruption, blackmail, coercion, and bribery.

This part of Leslie's plan had worked to perfection. Sir Alastair was thousands of miles away and out of contact with his faltering empire. The news of the charges against him hit the world's press offices. The stock markets almost went into free fall, and his holdings suffered badly. The losses were reported worldwide, in the daily papers, radio, and television reports. He lost a large part of his multimillion pound fortune in five hours of trading. Anything connected to him was poisoned. The promises of financial investment by the Woodford Foundation were unusable without value or trust. His 'empire' that had taken generations to build would soon face serious trouble if the situation regarding Woodford interests in French Guiana was not resolved.

***

Leslie now concentrated on the hidden files concealed behind the bookshelves. Susan was cleaning the west wing with her long feather duster, observing the tomes with titles that made no sense to her. She was not as well educated as the other residents of her era. She had problems with absorbing the information, interpretation, calculation, and dissemination. She could not absorb the wealth of information and education. Her mind was not capable or receptive enough. Susan was a lovely person – kind, gentle and lovingly soft of heart; and she had been the source of Leslie's first flights of fancy. He would never let anything untoward happen to her. She was as much a victim as the other children of the village. Don had made her a victim and she was always too ashamed to ever speak of that time. She was happy that he was dead and had beseeched God that his death would be slow and painful. Her wish had been granted but not by her God.

***

Leslie checked on Ed and his companions at the local paper. He did not want them to interfere with his plans, but at the same time, he did not want to hinder them in locating his father. He updated himself on the information they had and satisfied himself that things would soon come to a head.

How he was going to use all the information that he had, how he would bring it to his own personal use, defence, and support, he had no inkling. He had to plan seriously and calculate all the possible lines of attack and defence. Once he had calculated, he could plan his exposure of the Woodford Empire. He decided to put all the information in the hands of 'the press' – his allies, Ed, Tweety, and Billy. They had worked so hard and so long to expose this admired and exalted Woodford character. They had earned his respect, and he would give them their reward, willingly, and with appreciation for their fortitude. 'The people's force,' he recalled Perry's words. He could not just hand over the files that could amount to theft. He planned to visit them and tell them the things they needed to know. It would be for them to decide what way to proceed.

***

Mary languished in her room as Leslie tapped into her mind from his own room. *What is he doing now? He tells me nothing of his plans. It will get him killed.*

I will not be killed or harmed and, more important to me, nor will you. Be calm and trust me, I have power beyond your comprehension and I will use it sparingly and usefully. You are in no danger from me or from any foe in human form, believe and trust in me dear sister he replied.

He meant every word he had said. His sister would come to no harm under his protection; he would ensure the opposite in fact. He would defy the rules and defend her, even at risk to his own life. It was a turnaround of the situation, where she had always protected him. His price may be far greater – unimaginable and eternal. Beware of promises made in haste.

He did not make his promise in haste or out of a sense of payment for a debt but from a deep, deep connection, and that connection responded, with permission for him, to continue his use of power.

He could not sleep; the power that invigorated him drove him. He had to access the files, those files hidden and secret from prying eyes. He descended the stairs on tiptoe. Avoiding the steps that creaked, he trod cautiously and with intent to pursue his mission. Having locked the library doors, he retrieved the volume from the shelf near to the window and exchanged it for the resident tome at the edge of the centre shelf. The door slid open with the sound of a *click*. He spent the rest of the night absorbing the heinous revelations contained within those files he had managed to read.

***

At breakfast, he was in no mood to eat.

'Leslie, you have not touched your porridge.' Rachel's seductive tones still excited him and made him regret the actions he had taken.

He held fast. The road ahead would be long and arduous. Nothing could prevent him from his quest, and she would be his biggest distraction. His devotion and love for her meant that she should be far from harm and danger. The thought of any harm befalling Rachel ate away at him, and later that that morning on their walk he confided in Mary.

'Be strong and continue with what you have started. I will ensure she comes to no harm, and perhaps one day—'

He did not let her finish. 'We have much to do, and for the moment, we are free to continue.'

The tears welled in his eyes, and Mary kissed them away. 'My dear, dear brother, why cannot all men be like you?' She alone could feel his pain and sense of loss.

Mary knew she had to keep him focussed on the tasks ahead, and it was hard for her. She knew how Rachel and Leslie felt about each other and the sacrifices they had agreed to. It was for her the same pain and loss, but she could not tell him that. She had to support him as she had promised.

That night, Mary quietly cried herself to sleep. The pain she felt her brother feeling had driven so deeply into her she could not contain the tears any longer.

***

Sir Alastair languished in a South American prison on unrelated charges to what Leslie and his friends were working on. Greg Walsh was temporarily detained in a French prison, and with Dr Hendricks out of the picture, it was time now to proceed to the next step.

The letter came, telling Rachel of her appointment as the new head of physiotherapy. 'There you see. I said that you would get it. And who is there better for the post?'

Rachel jumped and hugged Leslie and Mary with joy. 'Australia! Wow, I cannot believe it.' She was like an excited schoolgirl but had to calm herself when Susan entered to clear the table.

Susan helped Rachel to pack her things and took them down to the hall. A taxi arrived to take her home to Bayswater; she had much to do before leaving and very little time. She hugged Mary and kissed her face with great feeling. 'Take good care of him. He is something special,' she whispered. She shook hands with Susan and Joan. 'Thank you both for your care and assistance. You have done very well.'

She came to Leslie. 'I am at a loss for words. I think I have said them all.'

A voice in her head said, *And I love you too, my darling angel. You must go now and be happy. Put behind you what you have learned; it can only bring you pain.* He kissed her politely on each cheek and helped Susan to carry the bags down to the waiting taxi. He so wanted to kiss her passionately and say, 'Do not go. Stay with me please. But he controlled his desire… and she, hers. Susan could see that she would be unopposed once again.

***

Laurence Vance had reluctantly taken charge of the general running of the Village. He assigned Jackson to clear the vicar's cottage of personal effects, and he himself was running both Bridge and Roding Houses. Mr Atkins was not well enough to perform his duties. Mrs Atkins was beginning to resemble a human being once more. No longer drugged by her husband, she still did not converse with anyone except by way of a greeting. Even that was new to the boys and the maids.

***

Leslie recalled his first visit to doctor Hendricks when Paul showed him the way to the Lodge. Paul was on an errand for Mr Atkins and this was a monthly occurrence he later found out. The errand was to collect the drug from the local pharmacy, Paul had no idea what the drug was for. After Paul moved to River house years later, Leslie took on the role as the errand boy, therefore he knew what the drug was and how to obtain it. Doctor Hendricks provided the pharmacy with the prescription and one of the boys would collect the drug a few days later.

With his newly acquired skill of being able to move objects by will, even in his ethereal form, Leslie had mixed the drug into sugar cubes. Mrs Atkins never liked sugar in tea or coffee, whereas her husband did and Leslie knew this. The other occupants of the house did not use sugar in cube form, that was only for the master. Leslie had modified the strength of the drug so that Mr Atkins would not end up as she had. The drug, combined with his personality, would keep him gently, but forcefully "out of sorts". The first few doses Leslie had left at their normal strength in order to disable the master enough to prevent him drugging his wife. When Mr Atkins became unwell his wife improved and a role reversal occurred, unrealised by either party. It made sense to Leslie to keep Mr Atkins out of the way for a while, the man knew the purpose of the village and Leslie could not risk him interfering with his plans.

***

Leslie continued his regime of walking after breakfast and then a swim. In the evening, he exercised in the gym for an hour and a half. At every distracted moment, he thought of the love of his life, but by now, she was far beyond his physical reach.

Rachel had resigned from the clinic in London, given up her rented house, and had set out upon a new life. She had mixed emotions. Leaving Leslie grieved her so much it was like losing her soul and something intangible, but the new life ahead filled her with excitement and expectancy and maybe a slight touch of anxiety at the prospect of starting anew.

***

A team of lawyers well versed in the laws of French Guiana and recently updated with regard to political and social situations there, went to the aid of their master Sir Alastair. Not permitted to see him, the lawyers beseeched the British Consul to intercede on their behalf. The political conditions were not good; there had been accusations between politicians and then retractions, defenders and accusers wrangling over the case against Sir Alastair.

The consul arranged a meeting with the prefect 'at his convenience'. The prefect was a very busy official, trying to quell the turmoil amongst the landowners, the natives, and migrant workers. If Sir Alastair's money did not fund the projects, where would the finance come from to improve their lives? Thousands of people would be without work, income, food, or shelter. Sir Alastair was a saviour to these people who had barely been able to survive before his proposed investments and promises of a productive future. Their own government had announced the contracts and made huge promises in the press and on posters around the country. Why had they now gone back on their word? It had inflamed the population, even those not directly connected with the businesses concerned. If the workers had more money, they would have to spend it somewhere. It seemed to

Leslie to be a crazy world: *you have more pay so you spend more, property owners cash in by putting up rents, shop owners increase their prices, and they all win, do they not? They may feel they do for a short while.*

***

Decisions were made at the highest level in French Guiana, and the lawyers delivered the news to Sir Alastair. He was not to face charges after all, but he would have to renegotiate the terms of the contracts. The prices trebled for official guarantees and assurances. He would be freed and exonerated with the apologies of the government and would always be 'welcomed and honoured in our fine and proud country'.

It had been a mighty task, and costly, but Sir Alastair had, with the assistance of his trusty band of experts, resolved the situation regarding his business interests in French Guiana. The agreements would have knock-on effects – the rise in costs of providing South American gold and sugar. The costs to the Woodford companies could be recouped in the long term. More serious was the state of the stock markets. He was confident that, with the news of the contract guarantees, the markets would soar. And they did, instantly.

Sir Alastair had missed the comforts of home, his visits to London, and the soft quiet nights in the arms of his beloved. He would be home soon – as soon as the contracts were signed, sealed, and delivered. There was still much to be done to appease the bandwagon of fortune hunters. It was not quite over just yet.

***

Neither hell nor high water would stop Leslie from his quest; he had a few spanners at his disposal. He changed the lead of the clinic in London to a man who had not known Rachel, arranged for a new owner to take over the house she'd rented in Bayswater, and deleted all traces of her moving to Australia. Only he and Mary would know where she had gone. Mary at least deserved a memory of the woman he loved and who had loved them both in such different ways.

***

Greg Walsh had contacted Sir Alastair's lawyers in London to help him. He was told that no one was available due to a high-profile case that had tied up everyone at the firm. No one told him that the case involved Sir Alastair himself as client confidentiality forbade it. Greg felt abandoned and betrayed. He knew he was dispensable; he was a soldier to the heart. He did feel that he had been a close and reliable friend, a resource from which Sir Alastair could expect the perfect results. Greg had always admired and respected the dean; the man's cold calculation of what was required in any given situation matched his own personality and inspired him, spurred him to give his utmost. He was inventive and intelligent, calculating and cold – just like his master. But he did not have the wealth to secure outcomes. The widespread web of informants and traitors belonged to the master. He felt a desire for vengeance build in him. *After all I have done for him… The ungrateful bastard.*

Chapter 21

Plans, Realisations, and Awareness of the Purpose

Leslie recalled a system he read of called 'brainstorming' or 'mind mapping' and used this to plan and organise how he could proceed. He had never used it, and it was difficult for him to decide the central theme from which the branches would radiate. He first put down his own name and then changed it to 'Woodford'. He finally chose to use 'morality' as the basis for his plan; it was morality, or his idea of it, that drove him. He made a list of supporters and another of adversaries, gave each group different colours, and cut out each name, separating them into the two categories. The victims and allies formed two more groups, with which he did the same. He arranged the colours of the assassins, their masters, and victims and then rearranged them to show where the power lay in the grand scheme of things. He removed them all and restarted. Seven and then eight times he rearranged the plan and changed the main headings and subcategories until he had something resembling the thoughts in his head.

Seeing the scheme on paper made its inner workings clear; that he would and could take action was indisputable. Here, laid out before him, was the hierarchy within Sir Alastair's 'organization', and he would convey what he had worked out to the men at the local paper. From this, they would see how each character was connected and who pulled the strings. Of course, it was his viewpoint; he did not expect them to let it go unquestioned. He anticipated the questions and deliberated over his answers. His reasoning had to make sense without giving too much away. He had to think like a journalist, a detective, and a reader.

To the journalists it would be a work of fiction if there was no proof to back it up – the concoction of a fertile imagination or a story of abuse, hypocrisy, lies, and evil they could not print. He would provide the story, and it would be up to Ed to decide on how to present it once he could provide the proof. If Ed published now, he could not name or allude to a single character; it would then kill the value of the story. The press needed concrete, not wet clay. When the towers begin to fall and the mighty and noble descend to the realms of wretched deceivers exposed, he would provide them with all this, on the solemn promise that they would wait for his sign, his nod of assent and the signal to proceed. They must not pre-empt his moves in this most dastardly game of wits. It could cause all of their deaths!

***

When Mary looked at the schematic of Leslie's outline, she jolted. 'We will be in such peril,' she said, searching her brother's face. 'He will have us both killed, along with your friends at the paper. Do you realise what you are doing?'

He took her hand gently. 'Calm now, Mary. I am not a child anymore; I have calculated what the press's reaction will be. More to the point, I have anticipated how others will react. Yes, the threat to us is not small. I will admit that. But there are forces at my disposal I may use to protect you all.'

His speech did not convince Mary; she did not miss the fact that he had not included himself in the protection. Was he about to sacrifice his own life to save those less deserving than he? What had he planned? She was terrified that he was planning something akin to suicide, for the sake of strangers and so-called friends. These people did not even know him. She felt rage build in her and attacked him. 'Do not do this and risk your life and mine. Think of the consequences, a life of endless hell. Please, please, Leslie, listen to me.' She fell at his feet, imploring him. 'I have given so much to protect you. Do not, please, do not put yourself at such risk.'

He was calm and serene, like one who had already made a pact with his redeemer and master. He laid his hand upon her head but did not answer her.

Mary was beside herself with anxiety. *What has he done?* She fell onto the floor, sobbing. Her dearest love was about to commit the most abhorrent crime – suicide! Some would call it heroism, self-sacrifice in the face of one's adversaries. She could not let him take this route. She had vowed to protect him, and she would do her utmost to keep her promise, however it hurt his plans.

To most people in his life, Leslie had appeared as the perfect child – obedient and polite, intelligent and diligent, attentive and delicate. He was all of these things, but that was not a true picture of him. He had spied on his masters and built cases against them. He had lied and performed to convince and deceive. He had judged and condemned, absolved and pardoned – as though he alone had right on his side. He had been arrogant and self-important in his relationship with Mary and had dismissed her as ineffectual and simple, bossy, and uncommunicative. What drove him was a strong moral sense; there was, for him, a defined and clear line between good and evil (he was naive perhaps) and he used it as justification in his own mind for all he had done and yet detested in others. His morality was his master and the source of his power!

He demonstrated his power to his sister; he invited sparrows to accompany them when they walked and fed wrens and blue tits from his hands. A dark sky became azure blue at his command; a winter's gloom became a picturesque scene of beauty and wonder. A simple touch brought buds into full bloom, and the scent of lilacs surrounded them far from the tree.

This impressed Mary, but she feared for his future; she feared his plans and his demise by his own design. She felt her life draining from her. *What are you doing to me, to us? You stupid boy, you would give up all of this, the wonders you have revealed to me. You cannot and will not give them up, for I forbid it.* She transmitted the words to her brother.

Leslie felt her full force! It was at that moment that he realised what power she had – had always had. He was momentarily stunned. She had taken a lifetime to control her powers, and she had perfected them unbeknown to him.

He apologised. *It never occurred to me that you had the same powers.*

Leslie, it was not you who put the red line on the paper. I am sorry. It was me. The names that disappeared from the list – me also. I am so sorry to have deceived you, but at the time, it was to help you communicate what you were not able to.

Leslie sat on the grass verge in stunned silence. What actions were his own or those of his sister? *The red line was her doing?* His mind pored over all that had happened, and he thought of the open window, that gust of wind – *So, she had deleted the names on the list with father's name, leaving only the name I had concentrated on.* He was astounded and in admiration of her help and secrecy. He realised that it meant she could float out of her body just as he could, and she had followed him to help him, to keep him from harm. He had not seen her do these things because she had not let him.

Mary hugged him and held him tightly. 'Do not ever doubt what assistance I can give to you, silly boy. All those times I told you that I know what goes on in that little head of yours – now you know.'

He felt a shudder surge through him that made him aware that he was still human and was faced with a power equal to his. His arrogance and superiority left him in a flash. He was not the lone saviour of humankind – the destroyer of evil and arbiter of good and bad. He was not the person he imagined himself to be. He had been such a fool, self-indulgent and proud, puffed up like a peacock and as just as loud. Full of his own power and self-importance, he had dismissed all other beings as fodder to his every whim. He had been vain in the extreme; his sister had been the one to burst his bubble. She would moderate him; no other could! No one else had the power.

***

He felt extremely humble when he faced her at supper. He felt awkward and embarrassed in her presence, and the meal passed in silence.

They walked together down towards Roding and Epping. Mary broke the ice and asked her brother, 'Why do you not confide in me? I am your sister and guardian. Your silence cuts me from your life.'

He could not think of an excuse to avoid her question. 'I do not know. Perhaps because I did not know of your powers. I did not realise how much you could help… I am sorry, Mary. At times, I just need to be silent and think – you know, put things in order in my head. You kept your secrets from me; it was only in the hospital that you began to reveal how you can talk without speaking. You have kept that a secret all this time and confided nothing to me. Yes, I suppose the powers that are new to me have made me feel invincible. It was foolish of me to think I was the only person in the world with such gifts. I feel stupid, Mary, really stupid.'

She pulled him closer to her and forgave him all his childish ideas. She had been his protector from so young an age, and she was the nearest thing he had to a mother.

Here he was, almost a man, but still the child in him would not grow up; it was a most endearing quality. It gave him vulnerability and a loveable childishness that made anyone adore him. On meeting him, one could be excused for giving him a hug or a kiss. His outward appearance veiled his intelligence and power.

Mary joined her brother and sat with him at his desk in his bedroom with the mind map in front of them.

'What do you intend to do, Leslie?' she asked.

'What do you suggest?' he replied.

He had finally allowed her into his world, and she put her arm around his shoulder. 'How does this work? Explain it to me. If I am to help you, I'll need to understand it.

He went to great lengths to explain and gave examples that made it easier for her to understand. 'Take Walsh for example' he said pointing out the name and the lines radiating from it. This red line goes to Sir Alastair and another to Hendricks. The red lines denote the chain of command. Then you see red lines from Walsh to his associates. The green lines lead to his victims over here. Once she had the idea of how the map worked, she asked, 'How do you decide what goes into the centre?'

He replied, 'It has taken me a long time to decide that. I have written and rewritten so many times, but I think that this is based on morality.'

She chided him. 'Do you think you can change the modern ways and reinstall the old values? You never will succeed. Let us look at other topics – justice, retribution, revenge—'

He stopped her. 'Mary, I have a purpose. And those things are not mine to use. They are not why I have these powers, and besides, that would make me the same as those we attempt to expose. I will not misuse these gifts.'

How such a boy could be a wise and intelligent person one minute and an insufferable burden the next confounded Mary.

***

She thought long and hard about what Leslie had said. She lay on her bed thinking about her own plans – the fiendish punishments she intended to impose upon her enemies that would have them writhing and begging to die, with her as their judge, jury, and executioner, relishing in the screams and horror they would endure for eternities. She put those thoughts far from her mind, resigning herself to the wisdom of her sibling.

She still wished for those things, but his warning tempered her thoughts. Everything he had said was true. She had never questioned her powers or their origin; she had used them only to safeguard her brother and herself.

Leslie had unknowingly relied upon her survival. Without her, he would have fallen prey to the evils and perversions that abound in this world. She could see now that he was right; she had brought him to this point in his life, and she had done well against the odds. He was the culmination of her vigilance and strength. *That is the answer. I am here to make him what he has now become; to get him to this point has been my purpose. I must now let him guide me, and I must assist him where I can.*

Both Leslie and Mary humbled themselves with their realisations that they were tools for unseen masters and for each other. Leslie's work would now start in earnest. He had experienced loss; pain, both physical and mental; devotion; vulnerability; desire, loyalty, and love; trust and betrayal; success and failure; and arrogance and humility. He was now primed and ready to serve his purpose – with his sister as his trusted confidante and assistant.

***

Leslie rang the bell at the door of the newspaper offices. Tweety had seen him cross the street from the window. 'Ed, it's the boy, the Johns boy.'

'For god's sake, let him in laddie.' He said in his broad Scots accent.

The reporter rushed to the top of the stairs. 'Let him in and then lock the door please Mike.'

Leslie ascended the staircase, and looking upward, he saw Tweety at the top, beckoning him and urging him to join them in the editor's office.

Leslie related to them the vast task ahead and his decision to let them decide how to proceed. He warned them of the consequences of rushing ahead and asked, 'Have you found my father?'

Well, they were all astounded. How could he know of their investigations and efforts?

'Ask me nothing, but tell me all you know.' He was serene and detached but purposeful in his enquiry. 'Tell me everything please.'

The editor could not deny him; after all, he had a right to know. 'Through some contacts that I know, we believe your father is alive and living somewhere in China. We have not been able to trace his current position yet, but we're certain that our contacts will come up with something soon.'

Leslie used his powers to impel and conduct them into finding his father and bringing him home. They must bring him to England and provide a place of shelter for him – for him and his sister too – until he could give them the missing links he had retained.

All three – Ed, Tweety, and Billy – could see that they would have to conform to his wishes to have the story in full, and what a story it would be!

'Bring my father back to me, and I shall be forever in your debt. I will give you all you deserve and more.' The publication Ed managed was a small-town paper, but its honesty and sense of morality and decency defined it to Leslie as a herald of fairness. He chose it for the integrity of its editor and reporters. They had many of the qualities he admired and respected, and he felt a kinship with them.

***

The village was running smoothly and progressing according to Leslie's plans. He decided that a visit to doctor Hendricks was overdue, a real visit, not an ethereal one

Dr Hendricks was recovering slowly. He had absorbed a poison from the chemicals he had used in his garden whilst attempting to combat the blight. He was distraught at the news that the vicar had died in a tragic accident. He enquired about Sir Alastair and the progress in Cayenne. Leslie updated him with the news that he should be back soon. He also told him that, when he'd visited the lodge to check that Martha was all right, he'd noticed that the garden was beginning to recover, although it was mostly weeds now.

***

Leslie wanted to look at Dr Hendricks's files. Martha never went out, not even for shopping. Whatever she needed she had delivered from the stores. Leslie deduced that she suffered from agoraphobia, which made getting to the files impossible. The dean's files Leslie had read, and he had not read them all, did not include information relating to inmates of the asylum. And only contained coded notes, regarding acquisitions of gifted children to populate the village.

***

Mrs Atkins was recovering her wits gradually and was now tending her husband. Miss Weston took over the Sunday school, and Mr Vance efficiently maintained his temporary role as head of the village.

Laurence began to enjoy the added responsibilities. He visited the six houses weekly and sorted any problems immediately – ordering provisions and supervising the maintenance of the grounds and buildings. The one main problem he had was paying wages. He had some savings and had been paying the staff from his own account, in the sure knowledge that his lordship would repay him; Sir Alastair was a gentleman after all. He kept detailed records of all the outgoings and kept purchasing to a minimum. He did monthly stock checks of the stores and recorded every item and where and when it had been obtained and to where it had been issued. He discovered that the masters and mistresses of the village had been previously ordering from the stores, far more than was required, and he put a stop to ad hoc acquisitions without his express approval. Any repairs he authorised, he oversaw their completion to his satisfaction.

But soon, he had only enough money for about two months more. He called a meeting of the housemasters to discuss the financial affairs of the village.

The arguments from the west wing echoed all over the house. The other masters would not cooperate in financing the village. Vance showed them his total outlay so far from his personal savings. 'I have been paying for you and the village to ensure it survives in the absence of Sir Alastair. The least you could do is help me. When his lordship returns, you will pay in other ways for your greed, self-interest, incompetence, and reticence. Support me now or be damned.'

This hit home hard. Vance was an astute man; he wasn't business-minded, but he had pulled off the coup of the century. Suddenly, the housemasters stated their personal wealth in investments and incomes, some of whom had wealth far in excess of Vance's own, and offered to contribute. He calmed them and thanked them graciously for their offers of help. He suggested it would be far easier to maintain the village if each housemaster contributed the same amount to a central fund. Detailed records would be kept, and no one would be at a loss financially. Who knew? The master may show gratitude for their commitments. The suggestion was implied, rather than specified.

***

Leslie admired the way Mr Vance conducted the meeting and had him down as a friend. He could not push the boundary by calling him an ally. Vance was ignorant of the purpose of the village. He just did what he was told or what he believed was required – the perfect employee. If Leslie enlightened him, he would be gone in a shot. He would not hold with the manipulation and contortion of the hopes and dreams of the young. He never manipulated, except in a positive way to improve the young people in his care and to advance their understanding and develop their skills. He would not knowingly exploit or turn his charges into puppets for masters. Sir Alastair had fed him well-rehearsed and practised stories.

Mr Vance's competitive side drove him to push others to do their best and succeed to their ultimate limits. He had set very good examples himself in all he attempted. Maybe that was why the other masters pushed him to lead. Plus, he still had morality – and innocence.

Leslie would do all that he could to protect his former swimming instructor. The man was not evil, but he did have weaknesses that he had now overcome. He was now a whole person, something he had never been before – confident, commanding, and obeyed. He tempered all – all within his power – with humanity and understanding, with compassion and reasoning. He would not stand for ineptitude or laziness; he confronted openly those who opposed him and, by way of persuasion and common sense and, at times, threats and finger-pointing, bent them to his intentions. They had elected him and now respected him.

Leslie was content that things were going to plan in the village. He had chosen Vance as the leader, and the other housemasters had followed like lambs.

***

Susan woke Mary in a state of panic. 'Please wake Master Leslie, Miss. Please wake him. Smoke is coming from the direction of the gates. It may be the Lodge on fire. Oh, do please wake Miss. Martha may be trapped inside. Do please hurry, Miss. Her life may depend on it.'

Mary was out of bed like a shot. 'Susan, call the fire brigade and an ambulance. I will get Leslie.'

Apart from Susan, Joan, and the cook, Mary and Leslie thought they were the only people close enough to save the poor housekeeper if the lodge was on fire.

Leslie leapt naked out of bed and dressed. He ran as fast his legs would carry him to the aid of the poor woman who was so dear to him. He had a soft spot for Martha. Her cooking was divine. Her attentive ways were always unobtrusive and discreet; she was always so careful of the young things who came to consult and divulge their secrets to her master. She loved them all, and they loved her. Martha was another victim in the grand scale of things. Leslie would do all he could to protect her too.

Some of the masters and gardeners were at the lodge, hosing and beating the flames and smoke. Miss Weston had dragged Martha from the smoke-ridden building, before the flames started.

Leslie was relieved to see Martha safe and the attempts of the staff to put out the flames. He rushed to the rear of the lodge and entered the office. He found a holdall and forced open the bureau door. He stuffed as many of the files into the bag as he could and retreated to the safety of the garden.

His actions had not been by his conscious thought, but the fire had served his purpose. He had the files. His concern was for Martha. How was she? Would she be all right? Was she burned or injured. He wished someone would say something about her condition.

He got Jackson to take him in the car and they followed the ambulance taking Martha to the hospital. The doctor who examined Martha told Leslie that her condition was stable and she was not seriously hurt, some smoke inhalation and they would keep her under observation for a few days. He thanked God. Martha deserved no punishment, she was a servant, loyal and obedient. She had harmed no one, and Leslie was relieved to hear the news that she would be all right and was not expected to remain in hospital for long.

He would arrange for Martha to reside with Miss Silvestre upon her return; he figured that the French tutor would be the best help and influence for her.

***

Leslie now had the files, and they contained information that he required to proceed with his plans. The boy opened one file and then another.

Mary came to his room and put her hand on his shoulder. She could tell without seeing his face that he was suffering pain and anxiety. 'Oh, Mary, what are these people? Are they monsters, demons? I feel so wretched

I wish I had never rescued these files. You, me, Paul, all of us are here, our past and our circumstances, our parents and their stories, the stories of so, so many others… Father must come soon. Our friends must bring him, and we have to put an end to this, Mary.' He wanted to scream so loud the whole town would hear it.

She pulled him so close her and her embrace muffled his cries. 'Hush now. Calm yourself and be at peace.'

She could not hold him for long; he had anger and desire for vengeance about him. His mind filled with images of righting wrongs and retribution and of punishment – the things she had wished. With just a nudge, she could tip him into her world, and they would be together, terrible, and magnificent.

Something stopped her. This was not what he had told her he had to do; he had said that what the power impelled and commanded was not his to question. She must let his morality guide with reasoning and logic. It was a fight for Mary to be obedient to her little brother's wishes. Nevertheless, he was better educated and informed in the things she had no ideas of. She reminded him of his own words to her regarding the use of their powers.

Leslie's torment was indescribable. He'd read of the terrors this place and its principals had imparted upon persons both known and unknown to him, of incarcerations and drugging and torture. It made Leslie feel sick, so sick he could vomit his heart and soul into the gutters – gutters filled with evil waste and excrement. Mary feared for his sanity. Her brother was sliding into an abyss she could not pull him from. But it was her duty to attempt to do all that she could.

***

Leslie was not at his best the next morning. He shunned all conversation or contact, confused as to who he could trust and who he could not.

He walked alone. Venturing to the space next to Epping House, he entered the familiar woodland. He walked solemnly and in deep thought, unaware of purpose or direction. He recognized the scents of foxes and badgers, and heard the alarm cries of blackbirds and pigeons warning of his passing through their terrain. He cared not and ignored them.

His mind was fixed on retribution, hell, and damnation for the awful deeds these people had done. He fought a battle between his natural sensitiveness, his sister's quest for vengeance that he could understand, and those responsibilities piled upon him by the unseen masters from where his skills originated.

They must pay with a vengeance...

No, we must judge with caution and measurement.

No, they must pay, must pay with eternal damnation and all its punishments for what they have done.

No, we must have mercy until we know how they reached this point; it is the origin we must destroy.

He walked and walked around the village and eventually out of it, blind to where he was going or had been. As he walked onward, a haze clouded his sight and thoughts, his reasoning and emotions, and even his intellect and logic. He fell to his knees at the kerb, unaware of how far he had walked or where he was.

***

'Ed, Ed, the Johns boy is ill. Look. He is there crouching in the street.'

Tweety leapt down the stairs and rushed into the street. He waved his arms at the onlookers and the traffic, closely followed by Ed, Billy, and Mike. They picked up the semi-conscious boy and carried him to their offices.

'Call a doctor, for God's sake,' snapped Ed. 'He looks all in to me, the poor wee laddie.'

'Do you think they did something to him sir, you know...up at the village. Maybe—'

'Oh do shut up, Mike. Give him some air. Open the window. Did you call a doctor?' he shouted. 'Where the hell are they?'

Leslie was disorientated, confused, and unable to speak.

'Ed, Ed, listen... Ed, listen,' said Billy concerned and excited. 'Get Mary. Get his sister, Mary. Something tells me he must have her here now.' The imperative in Billy's voice compelled Ed to telephone the mansion.

***

Leslie, be calm, I am here, here with you. We are together, calm and peaceful, and serene. Look around you. You are with friends who care for you, whom you trust and rely upon. They are good and kind people and wish you no harm. Be calm, be quiet, be calm. Mary's soothing voice in his head relaxed him as she rode in the taxi.

'Where is that bloody doctor I asked for?' Ed was distressed to see the boy in this state. He liked and respected Leslie and wanted to do his best for him. He wanted to tell him they had found his father and that he would be in England very soon, but he thought the news might be too much for him in such a state.

Ed also wanted to tell him that Tweety had found a cottage for rent on the outskirts of the town. In a village that formed a part of the surrounding group of villages that merged with the town. The cottage, which was only a few doors down from his own place, would give Will a safe place to stay when he arrived from Hong Kong.

Leslie, be strong and trust in me. I will not try to persuade you. I will do as you wish and command. The words penetrated and brought him back to reality. He had heard Mary's voice and Ed's thoughts at the same time.

'Mary, you have saved me yet again,' he gasped. Ed, Tweety and Billy looked at each other with puzzlement.

Leslie regained his composure. 'Mary has told me that you have news of my father.'

The group listened to him in disbelief. How could Mary know of the information they wanted to impart to him?

'Tell me. I must know now. You will tell me.'

Ed gushed out the information. It was so unlike him to reveal all his cards in one go; he was compelled by something he could not control.

Ed began the story. Sir Alastair had tricked and deceived Will into accepting the leadership of a special force, on a 'Royal Commission' to penetrate and infiltrate enemies of the Crown and to relay information concerning present and future plans. He had fallen hook, line, and sinker for the ploy. His loyalty and devotion to his country had been manipulated to serve the aims of one man and his empire; Will and others had been puppets in the hands of a master puppeteer.

Leslie remained calm with the aid of Mary; her voice in his head gave him peace and tranquillity. 'Tell me the rest, please.'

Ed continued explaining what he had found out about the boy's father.

'When he arrives he will be safe?' Leslie asked. 'He must not be a target for the attentions of Sir Alastair's men. We must not bring him here to be killed.'

Ed suddenly realised the seriousness of the situation. He did not have that sort of protection available to him. He needed good security, bodyguards. Who could he find that had no links to Sir Alastair? He made a call to his contact in Mintell.

***

It was 8.37 when Leslie awoke; his head felt fuzzy, and he could not think clearly. He had slept for over sixteen hours, without dreaming or waking. He felt exhausted, listless. He went back to that source of his demeanour – the doctor's files. He read them all again to ensure that he had not imagined, invented or decoded wrongly the information in his head. The doctor used a very simple code but Leslie knew that there was much contained in the files he would not understand. Much of what he read as side notes, translated into German. The accounts the doctor had kept recorded all the circumstances and the 'remedies' that had rendered the children of the village orphans. These were more powerful documents than the ones Sir Alastair had kept of his village activities, as far as he could tell.

He had memorised every detail of all the files, but what should he do with the physical documents to keep them safe? They would be his most valuable asset; they were, in fact, priceless. He took them to Ed and thanked him for his aid and assistance yesterday.

Ed immediately got Billy to copy all the documents in triplicate. 'Put these papers with your files at home,' he instructed. 'The originals I will put in the safety deposit box at the bank, with the other files. At this rate, I will have to rent a new box. They won't all fit into one.'

There was a chuckle from his companions.

Ed had wanted to ask why Mary had given the warning to Billy. 'Do you think we are at risk here at the office?' he asked the boy.

Leslie answered in a confident manner. 'This is important work you are doing. There are many risks involved, unspeakable risks. I trust you and rely on you. I will give to you the weapons to destroy this empire, but I leave it to you to make your own decisions as to how to use them. Be wise and cautious and calculate everything, all possibilities. These people have vast resources they can call upon. They are important and influential people, and they have at their disposal an army of specialist lawyers. Be most certain of what you do and think with detail and care. Above all, protect yourselves. If you feel the risk is too great, do not enter the arena. Leave it alone. Discuss and appraise the pros and cons and then decide your actions. Get legal advice, for I am no lawyer. Tell me what you need, and I will try and deliver it to you. If you use a lawyer, check if he has contacts with Sir Alastair and his cronies. You have a massive task ahead of you. I trust you, or I would not have placed all of this in your hands. We are working together to destroy something beyond even your comprehension. Use Mary and Billy to communicate.'

Leslie noticed Billy's surprised expression. *The newsagent—?* Billy questioned in his mind. Then Mary arrived to collect her brother.

'Before I leave you, I give you my thanks for all you have done. I will not see you for a while, but I know what you have done. I am working on another story that will connect with the one you focus upon. I will give you that story also when the time is right. Do not worry about how to finance it. Leave that to me.' He left the office with his sister, reminding them to safeguard the files.

***

Ed, Tweety, and Billy sat and considered Leslie's words.

'Was that right what I heard?' said Tweety.

Finance them? How could the boy even finance a bus trip? asked Billy.

Ed halted their questions. 'Believe in this boy. He is wise beyond his years; I can hear it in the way he speaks. He is going to make us – us, a small-time local paper – into a force to be reckoned with. I know it. I feel it, and so does he. I think that the next time we see him could be in court, when we will have to provide the proof for our stories. Be assured that Sir Alastair will not lie down and die. He will call upon all his allies to support him, as he has in the past I believe.

Or it could be at the airport when we reunite this boy with his father, that will be a day to savour. Have you noticed how important his father is to him? I have read his notes, the ones he gave me. This boy is so desperate for that reunion and we must do all we can to bring his dream to reality. I lost my father at a young age and it hurt me deeply, perhaps that is why Leslie and I have such a connexion. I do not know; he says many things but hides much from me also. I like the lad, he is one of the most likeable people I have ever met, present company excluded. I value you Tweety and Billy, but you have not experienced what Leslie and I have.'

***

Over a game of chess in the library, Mary and Leslie communicated silently. Sir Alastair would be returning soon, and they had to complete the next step of Leslie's plan before his return.

Susan entered the library and informed Leslie that there was a phone call for him from Mr Sangstrom. Leslie took the call and then told Susan that he must go to London for his check-up and for a new test that would be more precise. He would need to stay in hospital overnight.

Chapter 22

The Value of Trust

Mary and Leslie left after breakfast the next morning, taking a small suitcase each and a holdall. They left the underground station and headed for the address that Leslie had written down. They stood outside a grand Georgian fronted building. 'Yardley & Mosse, Lawyers,' the highly polished sign beside the door announced.

They entered and announced their arrival to the secretary. They were shown into a richly furnished office.

'Erin Yardley at your service.' The man offered his hand and showed them to a pair of chesterfield club chairs. 'I was intrigued by your telephone call. It was my grandfather who prepared the original will for Sir Giles Woodford, and his partner did the codicil a year later. I was not familiar with the outstanding bequest. I have checked our archives and found the relevant documents. It seems such a mysterious bequest, and it has the flavour of a treasure hunt about it.'

He smiled at the pair as the secretary entered with a trolley of refreshments. 'May I offer you tea, coffee?' the lawyer said as the secretary left them to their private discussion.

Mr Yardley referred to the archive documents and said, 'You will be familiar with the terms of the bequest I trust. There are certain formalities to be observed. Sir Giles was quite specific in the detail.'

Leslie heard Mary's thoughts. She wondered how her brother could trust telling this man how he'd found out everything. He replied to her as he sipped his tea.

I have checked him out, and other than holding the will, he has no current connections with the Woodford family or any of his companies. Neither Yardley or Mosse appear on any Woodford list I have seen It is a very successful and well-respected law firm.

'If I may ask,' the lawyer continued. 'How did you become aware of the bequest?'

Leslie told him of the book in the Woodford library with the slip of paper and the numbers.

'What are those numbers and the significance?'

Leslie gave him the sequence of numbers from memory and explained how the code worked in order to decipher it. Erin opened a folder and removed an old yellow envelope. Written on it were the words *encryption* and *cipher*. He opened it with a paperknife and removed a sheet of paper.

He compared what Leslie told him with the contents of the envelope. 'What was the meaning of the cipher?'

The boy gave him the three lines written in French and their English translations.

Erin again checked the words with his paper. 'What clue did these lines give you?'

'They are lines from a poem written by Sir Giles Woodford. Essentially, there are three things in those lines – a tribute, fear, and a promise. The tribute is a memorial stone in a chapel on the estate. The fear was represented by a well. Caldwell Woodford had a fear of it but was constantly drawn to it. He believed that demons lived there. It was where he fell in and drowned in 1855. The promise made by his father – to protect his son from the demons – he failed to keep, and he felt guilt over this for the rest of his life.'

The lawyer listened with great interest to the explanation. He consulted the paper again. 'The clues led you to *what* to look for. How did you know where to look?'

'That was made clearer when I came across a book in the library. It contained a lot of names and their origins. Sir Giles must have used it to name his children. Caldwell means a cold or icy freshwater spring. Prescott is a priest's cottage. And even the surname is a clue. In the village at the back of the vicar's cottage is a cold water spring that becomes a stream. I followed it to a wooden bridge that fords the stream, and I found the old chapel.'

'This transcript does not tell me anything other than what you have related to me,' the lawyer said, waving the paper.

He opened the folder and removed a second envelope. This one was marked, 'Open on confirmation.' He opened it and read the content. 'You have brought something with you that will confirm and support your claim?'

Leslie reached into his pocket and removed the glass and silver box. He opened the lid and passed it to the lawyer.

The content astonished the man. 'Goodness.' he exclaimed as he held up the lump of glass to the light. He looked at the small key and back to the paper. An outline of a key had been drawn on the paper, and the key Leslie had brought matched it perfectly.

The lawyer said to the siblings, 'The key will fit a safety deposit box at a bank very close to us here. This is an uncut diamond, and I would calculate that it is of such significant value. We will need to visit the bank. If you are free at the moment, we could do that now, bearing in mind that you told me you had limited time. We shall also need to have the stone valued and I can make the arrangements for that if you wish.'

The children agreed that the time was perfect to visit the bank. The lawyer telephoned the bank and spoke to the manager. He explained that an appointment was not anticipated, and could he oblige them. After concluding the call, he arose from the desk and gestured towards the door.

They were only a short walk from the bank, and upon arrival, they were shown into a vault, the walls lined with numbered boxes. The manager of the bank produced a key similar to the one Leslie had given to Erin. He turned the key in one of the locks on box 133, and Erin did the same with the other key. They removed a black metal box and carried it to a private side room. The manager left the trio in privacy.

Erin opened the box and removed an envelope. He opened it and read the content. His face turned pale and then flushed. He covered his mouth with a hand and sat down.

'What is it, sir?' asked Leslie, most concerned. 'Whatever is the matter sir?'

Erin handed him the letter, unable to speak.

'Well?' demanded Mary, anxiously as her brother read the letter.

Leslie read the letter again in disbelief and handed it to Mary, speechless.

'But it is incredible. This was written over one hundred years ago... I cannot believe my own eyes.' The lawyer recovered something of his composure. 'If I had not seen this with my own eyes, I would say it was lies – a fake, a hoax of some sort. Those envelopes in my office have never left there, so they could not have been tampered with. They have been gathering dust for over a century. Without the information they contain, there is no way to establish the purpose of the key. It is just so incredible to me.'

Mary and Leslie stared at each other. They thought they had powers.

Erin removed a second envelope; it contained information that led to another bank in Edinburgh.

Back at Erin's office, Leslie and Mary gave him their details – bank account numbers, copies of birth certificates, and so on. Before leaving, Leslie swore the lawyer to secrecy; he must not tell even his partner or secretary about any of this. If he needed anything typed up, he must do it himself and show no one. He must keep the Woodford files locked away for safety.

Erin agreed but questioned Leslie's reasons for the instructions.

'I cannot tell you at the moment, but I will have need of your services again in the near future. I will reveal much to you then. I must warn you that you cannot contact me. Your life would be in grave danger if a connection is made between us.'

The lawyer looked a little startled by the remark and said, 'I have the services of a very good security firm; it is not the first time my life has been in danger.'

Leslie continued. 'No funds are to be paid into our bank accounts, as we are wards of Sir Alastair Woodford and legally minors until the age of twenty-one, as you know.'

The lawyer interjected, 'There is a government debate underway to discuss reducing the age to eighteen, but we will not consider that at present.'

Leslie agreed that doing so would be pointless.

'I will call you to hear the valuation of the stone. You will attend to the setting up of a trust fund and the remaining details for us? You will need a letter of authorisation. Oh and do you think 10 per cent will be a suitable fee for you?'

The lawyer produced a standard form of authorisation and filled in the details, and Leslie signed it. 'A most generous fee, Mr Johns. Do please make use of my services at any time. And shall we call the ten percent of this stone payment in full for a retainer? You mentioned you would require my services again?'

They shook hands on the agreement and the lawyer offered Leslie his card. Leslie read the details on the card and handed it back, if this card is found in my sister's possessions or mine, it could end badly for us all. Thank you for attending us at such short notice, good day sir.

The day ended with three incredulous and unbelievably happy and surprised persons.

***

Leslie and Mary stayed overnight at a small but clean and respectable hotel in the city, and the next day Mary accompanied Leslie to the hospital.

Mr Sangstrom greeted them with a smile. 'How are you doing now, Leslie?' he asked, looking through his notes. 'Oh, I see Dr Marston came out to you. Yes, I have his notes here. Sorry, I seem to be rambling a bit.'

They shook hands and went into a private room. Mary related all the facts to the surgeon regarding her brother's recent condition.

'Hmm, those symptoms seem to be stress-related' Mr Sangstrom said, referring to Leslie's recent episode that had resulted in the newspaper men summoning Mary and a doctor. Are you feeling anxious or stressed Leslie?' he enquired whilst checking the boy's eyes.

Of course, Leslie could not relate their recent activities, and so he talked about Sir Alastair being away, the death of the vicar, the blight, and Dr Hendricks's illness, not to mention the fire. He described his daily physical routine – walking, swimming, and the exercises.

The surgeon was impressed that he had kept to the routine. 'Now we will need to do some blood tests, X-rays, and those tests we did before. Are you all right with that?'

Leslie agreed and laid on the bed.

***

The tests showed no signs of the tumour having returned, and the surgeon was happy with Leslie's progress. He was free to go home, with a caution. 'Please try to avoid tension and stressful situations.'

Leslie and Mary returned to the village to plan their next move, despite the warning.

***

Later that night, Leslie thought about a man he had never met but knew a great deal about, James Woodford. In Sir Alastair's files were the accounts of the trouble his son had gotten into in Brazil. He'd dropped out of university and gone with friends to Rio de Janeiro. He'd stayed as a guest at the family home of one of the friends. They had taken him to the beach and the Mardi Gras and had generally had a good time.

Sir Alastair saw many faults in his son, and one of James's problems the dean recognised was that the boy wore the Woodford name like a shining crown. He was proud and boastful regarding his family fortune and reputation. The young man was rarely short of money due to the generous allowance his father had set up for him.

It transpired that James had become friendly with a young Brazilian girl, also from a wealthy family. After some months of the high life and fun and games, the girl told her mother that she was pregnant. Immediately the girl's father and his extended family besieged the house where James was staying, baying for blood. The girl was underage, and James was accused of rape. Regardless of the girl's protestations. The girl's father threatened to lynch James in the street and drag his corpse through the town. Whilst this was going on, James was on a yacht partying and oblivious to the accusation. Carlos, the friend he was staying with heard it all and set out to warn James to flee the country.

Carlos eventually found James on the yacht moored out in the bay. Meanwhile, Carlos's father and uncle managed to quell the excited band at the gates. They invited the girl's father to enter the house and have a sensible discussion. When James heard what had happened, he denied any such accusations. Against his friend's advice, he went ashore to face his accusers, and when he arrived at the girl's home, her brothers grabbed him and held him captive until the father came back.

Carlos telephoned Sir Alastair. It was then that the army of lawyers had become involved. Ultimately, Sir Alastair paid the equivalent of £50,000 for the release of his son, in addition to lawyer's fees and expenses. Sir Alastair would not listen to his son's denials, and they had rarely spoken since.

***

Leslie concentrated on the name and found himself in an apartment; he could see a man in his mid-twenties. As James turned from the television set, Leslie recognised those same features that distinguished the Woodford line. He had the same black eyes as his father and great-grandfather. Leslie had never seen any other family portraits. James appeared to be well organised and tidy. He was clean-shaven and well dressed and obviously took care of his appearance. Leslie looked around the apartment; it was comfortable and tastefully furnished. He noticed a briefcase near the entrance door, and on the coffee table, a neat stack of papers indicated that he was engaged in some financial investments. Judging by the top sheet, the graphs showed a steep upward trend in the values of four companies and a slight downward trend in two others. A handwritten note beside the two company names suggested his plans to sell these shares; whether personal investments or for a client was unclear. Leslie assured himself that James was safe and well and left him.

***

Erin Yardley spent the day at the same bank that held the safety deposit box, drawing up the conditions of the trust fund. He decided to word it 'legal age of majority' instead of stating the current legal age; that way Mary and Leslie would benefit from the proposed change in the law if it were to come about. He used money of his own to open a new account in their names but with him as joint trustee, along with the bank manager and a trust manager.

The lawyer and the banker chosen to set up the trust for Mary and Leslie, discussed the legal wrangles regarding taxation, deposits, and withdrawals. Both men agreed that a spending limit should be set; if the children required anything above it, they would need a countersignature from Erin. He would decide in their best interests. He also recorded their contact details as being at his offices. That way, all communications between the bank and the clients would go through him. Now he had a lot of typing to do, in triplicate. As he typed, he could not help wondering about the nature of Leslie's future business with him; it had such an air of mystery and danger.

***

Next on Leslie's list was to fix George Thompson and put him out of action. He knew that it was near the time for changes again in the houses. He paid the man a visit. Thompson was travelling between the different homes and gathering files. It was not hard to judge where he would be going next. Leslie concentrated on the director of the children's homes George was on his way to visit next. Leslie planted the idea that he should check the files and update them, as they were to receive an audit by the Charity Commission. He did the same with the directors of the remaining two homes and something similar with the ones Thompson had already taken files from. Somewhere along the line, Thompson would be caught red-handed taking files and in possession of missing ones; Leslie would make sure of it.

***

After his nap, Leslie decided he would like a swim. He had not had one that morning. Mary chose to join him, and it was a chance to update Mary on what he had been doing.

Mary was about to tell him what she had been doing when Leslie said, 'It is done; Thompson has been caught with his hand in the cookie jar – with stolen files. He has been arrested.' He swam a full four lengths at top speed and somersaulted.

'Thank goodness for that,' said Mary, 'the creep!'

'You were going to tell me what you have been doing, weren't you?'

'Do not do that, Leslie. If you can read my mind, then you already know.'

'Not when you block me, dear girl.'

He laughed and swam a length underwater, raising himself up like a dolphin at the far end of the pool. 'Yes, very impressive. Now shall I tell you or not?'

'Of course you shall' said the boy with a smile.

'Some town boys, teenagers a little older than you, were larking about near the main gates, so I planted the idea for them to trash what is left of the lodge. For now, it will cover the loss of the files you gave to Ed. Mr Breen saw the lads and chased them off, so there is a witness.'

Leslie swam several more lengths of the pool and then said, 'Shall we visit the house Tweety has rented for us – get the lie of the land so to speak?'

She thought it a great idea.

***

On the journey across town, Leslie confided to his sister that he felt nervous about meeting their father after so many years apart.

She answered, 'How do you think he will feel after he was tricked into believing we were dead and that we'd suffered such a horrible death? He must have been devastated and full of guilt for years, probably blaming himself for what he was told had happened. What about when he finds out it was all a lie? He will feel he abandoned us. He will find out that the man he trusted most was behind the whole thing. Despite everything, Leslie, we have been well cared for.'

'Oh I quite agree. When I see how our brothers and sister live, I realised we are much better off. You do realise, Mary, that things will soon come to a head. Sir Alastair, Greg Walsh, and Hendricks will all be returning and Dad as well.'

She nodded. 'We shall have to be very careful, especially with Walsh; he is a monster.'

They checked the position of the house. It was set on a hill facing the town, a good vantage point and difficult for anyone to watch the house unseen unless he or she were installed in one of the houses opposite. The road at the front was a minor one with very little traffic, and they were both satisfied that Tweety had done well. He had already secured the house with a deposit and six months' rent paid in advance, a loan from Ed.

***

'Mary, you told Billy that Walsh killed Tim Mathews and Rob Lane. How did you know?'

'I saw him kill Rob Lane,' she answered. 'But I could do nothing to stop him. That first time you were in hospital, I saw Rob leave the lodge, he looked slightly drunk to me, then I saw Hendricks speak briefly to Walsh and hand him something. I followed Walsh and saw him hit Rob Lane in the neck from behind, and the poor man just collapsed in a heap. Walsh and one of his cronies carried him to the well and dumped his body in it. Hendricks had given him the key for the padlock.

'They killed Tim Mathews to make his daughter an orphan. Walsh broke into his flat and tampered with the gas pipe. I have monitored him since he killed Rob. I could not follow him to France because I do not have your level of power. For the same reason, I could not find Dad all those years. He was too far away. You could have found him though. Why did you not try?'

'I had an irrational fear that if he was dead I would be trapped with him and unable to return to my body. Once I found out he was alive, I was very tempted but decided there was so much to do. I let Ed and Tweety follow their leads. If it was not for them, we would never know that Dad is alive. It is their story as much as it is ours, and they have worked so hard at it. When we are with Dad again, do you think we should tell him about our powers?' Leslie asked.

'I do not know. Situations may arise when we will have to, but until then, we better not say anything' his sister answered.

'And the bequest Mary, do we tell him about that?'

'You are so full of questions today Leslie, yes of course we will have to tell him, but not straight away. We do not know his plans or his situation, he may have remarried.'

'Oh no! I never considered that Mary. What if he has other children? What if he wants to go back to China? Oh God no!'

'No, we should wait and see before we tell him anything that we may not need to, agreed?'

'Absolutely.' The boy agreed.

***

The next week, as arranged, Leslie called Erin from the call box outside the newsagent's. 'How did things go with the valuation, sir? … Oh I see. How do we go about that and who would know best? … Yes, please, sir. I would be most grateful. … Once you find a reliable person, could you engage them on my behalf? … Yes, I do agree, sir … Very well. And the trust? … Jolly well done, sir. You have moved very swiftly, and thank you for funding it. … Ha, ha, yes. … You will never need to work again if you so wish. … You have been already, and what was there? I cannot believe it! How many? … And the certificates, are they still valid? … Wow! One hundred and fourteen years at 5 per cent compounded… I make that about two hundred and fifty million; that is an obscene amount! … Ha, ha, ha, yes, I stand corrected, sir. … Plus the stones of course. What would they charge? And would there be inheritance tax to pay? What was that, sir? … Well that is right. … I will leave it in your hands, sir. Thank you, I will be in touch soon. There is a serious matter I need to discuss. … Yes, we did. … Goodbye, sir.'

Leslie could not wait to tell Mary the news; she had floated to London to keep track of Greg Walsh. Leslie had told her that the man would be returning that morning.

***

Leslie and Mary met at lunch, and he was so excited. She said telepathically, *Tell me later. Walsh is back. He met with his cronies at Heathrow airport. I could not hear what they were saying, but they are plotting something judging by the looks on their faces and their body language.*

And Leslie, a little girl saw me, it scared me, Mary transmitted with a look of deep concern. *The girl kept talking to me and telling her parents that I was there. She described me perfectly. It was uncanny, and I am worried now about others who may be able to see us.*

That is exactly what I told Perry. I do not know who can see us, unless they give some indication. We must be more careful.

They finished their meal in silence and consternation.

After lunch, the two went for a walk, and Leslie had the chance to tell Mary his news. 'Erin has already set up the trust fund and opened our accounts with his own money; it's only a few pounds, just to keep the accounts open. He went to the other bank, the one in the letter. Well you are not going to believe this. He showed the letter to the director of the bank, who checked the reference in the archives and found the number of another secure box. Inside was a bag of diamonds – two red ones, the rest white. There are title deeds to properties in London, Paris, and New York managed by an investment company and some investment certificates validated in 1852. They were set in stone. They are still valid and accrued interest at 5 per cent compounded. Mary, they were worth a million pounds when Sir Giles made the investment.'

'How much is that worth now then? A hell of a lot I bet.'

'Hold onto your hat, sister dear – about two hundred and fifty million, less ten per cent of course. The diamonds need cutting by an expert, and Erin is researching that now. I have authorised him to proceed. They cannot be accurately valued until cut. The value depends on carat, cut, clarity, symmetry, and brilliance. Mary, there are twenty more diamonds as big as the one I found. He said the most valuable are the two red ones. I have no idea much they are worth, but the figure has to be astronomical. Sir Giles must have selected and kept the very best ones.

'We are going to do some good with these stones. We are going to help the vulnerable and the victims of evil. Oh, Mary, you told me it was not possible to restore the old values, but they live in me and in you, and we live in modern times. We are modern people. Why should there not be others with our values? Just as that little girl could see you, I could see that you were shaken by the experience. Why can there not be more like us? Look at our trusted friends in the press. Mary, look at Miss Weston. She is blind to what happened to her girls because she only sees the good in people. A mistake, yes, but she has no evil in her. Did she ever do you harm? Was she fair in her judgements? Tell me I am wrong, and I will shut up.' He waited for a rebuttal, but she stayed silent.

'Take Mr Vance; he's such a good man. True, he never reached his true potential, but he has helped and encouraged others to theirs. Mary, there is trust and gratitude; there are people who believe in good and evil. It is the ones who let evil control them that do the harm because evil becomes part of them. Mary, we can only do so much with the powers we have. But we now have money, the language of the modern day. We have the powers of three worlds – human, metaphysical, and financial. Help me put right so many wrongs and abuses. I know you will help me; it is not in your nature to refuse.'

'Mary tell me something of your aspirations' he said, gently touching her arm. I know so little about you. You keep your secrets so well. You have powers – you can control and direct – but what of you Mary? I know nothing of you as a person. As a sister, you do all in your power to protect and guide me, and that is what I am talking about; it seems to be all about me! Am I holding you back because you made a promise? I release you from the promise you made as a small child. You alone, by your devotion and vigilance, have brought me to the person I am now. I love you and thank you so deeply.'

She had a sad look about her.

'You must start thinking about yourself and what you wish and desire. You must have desires, dreams of the perfect man for you, fantasies. You are human the same as me, and I want only the best for you and your happiness.'

She hugged him. 'If only I could find someone as good as you. Kind, sensitive, intelligent, soft.' She stopped. 'But hard-headed, stubborn, and silly. I would be a fool just like you, but I have to admit', stopping abruptly, she tried to block her thoughts from Leslie. 'No, I will not tell you.'

'Billy?' he said smiling.

'You bastard!' she screamed. 'You know, you know how I feel about him, you—'

'Mary, he is a good man and would do no wrong to a living soul. I could sense that there was something different about you when you came to see me at the hospital, you know, after the operation. You did not seem to be what I remembered. It must have been the influence of this budding reporter. You have not done anything, have you?'

She stopped just short of slapping him full in the face. 'How dare you judge me by your own wanton behaviour and lack of discipline, you beast. I am not like you, letting things get out of control…you heathen.' There was vitriol in her admonishment for what he had done.

He had meant no insult or accusation; it was just a jocund remark. Human nature is what it is – nature. He put his arm around her shoulder. 'Dear sister, I would begrudge you nothing. Whatever you wish for, I will help to deliver it if you wish me to. Otherwise I shall leave you to your own devices and not for the world interfere or criticise – unless I thought you'd made a truly bad decision. However, even then I would tell you why I thought it a wrong choice and leave it to you to decide, as it would still be your business and yours alone. I can only give an opinion' he said with a gentle smile. 'I think that Billy is such a good, gentle person. I think he would be good for you, and he's someone you can control if you have to… Honestly, Mary, it is your life; you must live it.'

'Loving is about giving Mary. I do not see you as a giver. To me, yes, you give far too much of yourself. Not to others though. I may be wrong. I see you as a controller, and a loving relationship will not work unless you give yourself completely. Mary dear, do not abandon your dreams for your responsibilities to me. I beg you to fulfil your own dreams. Billy is ideal for you. I am so happy you have told me this.'

'I have told you nothing, you arrogant fool. You assume and presume—'

'Do you like him?'

'Shut up. You have no idea—'

'Mary, do you love him?'

'I would die for him, you bastard.'

She started to cry, and Leslie pulled her closer and kissed her head. 'I understand, you silly girl. How much? I do so hope that you will never ever know.'

She had suffered so much for him that she'd never told him of, but he was becoming aware of it. The realisations drew him ever deeper into her debt, but it was a debt that required no repayment. On the contrary, she was doing her duty in fulfilling her promise – a promise made so long ago, a lifetime ago. Such were her parting words to the father she adored and who her brother had never really known.

She had wanted to keep her father's memory alive and not let the mists of time swallow it. She had told Leslie of the memories she had of this heroic character and maybe added a little seasoning or an extra bone to flavour the stock occasionally. She realised now that, as he was alive, a real person, she would be found out and not trusted by the one person she cared for most in the world. It was a conflict that tormented her. The most horrendous idea came to her; she could prevent her father from returning to save her stories, histories, pictures...or let her brother meet the father he had never known and be exposed as a liar, an inventor.

She had created a character of their father with her stories – a hero, a stalwart of decency – and this was the man Leslie had in his mind. *Oh my God*, she thought suddenly, *my God, that is where his ideas come from. Dad, my daddy, and my stories are the source of his blind obsession with right and wrong. I have been the fool. Leslie has always believed every word of the stories... I am so sorry.*

A realisation dawned on her; her brother was, in thought, deed, and morality the son of her father – the father that she created. Morality was the driving force that helped and spurred him. She thought of the way he had given the story to the local press without the slightest hint of his own involvement. He wanted them to gain the glory and not himself. She realised now how much he was like the father she had created for him – passionate and loyal, reliable and patriotic, single-minded but idealistic. Leslie could be duped just as easily as his father could. She had done well to protect him from his own idealistic ideas in the past, but they'd been resurrected now with a vengeance.

She decided to support him in his altruistic endeavours and not condemn his concern for those less fortunate. She would not condone a mad spree of splashing money in the faces of those who had none, nor any endeavour that would invite those who would to try to exploit him. No, she would control his exuberance and any ideas that he could correct all ills by throwing money at them.

In truth, Leslie and his sister were as Rachel had ascertained, or perhaps two sides of the same coin. She could moderate him, and he could do the same for her, from different viewpoints. She saw money as the root of all evil; he saw money as having the potential to defeat it. Fight fire with fire – use money to defeat those who abused its power and influence. His moral compass came not from the stories his sister had told him, from the knight in white shining armour that represented his father from days of old. No, it was something else – something also bequeathed to him from a man he could never have known, a virtuous man who cared for his people. That man had changed with the times but retained his humanity and thought only of others. More than this, he was a man of foresight beyond imagining. He knew what would become of his empire and had selected someone not even born, to carry his banner – Leslie! The letter at the bank had made that crystal clear to the boy.

***

Leslie wrote solidly and effortlessly for two days; he filled paper after papers with accounts and details known only to him and a few others. Only his sister and he knew all the details gleaned from various sources. He put the papers into a folder to take with him to London.

Leslie made an appointment with Erin to discuss with him urgently matters of a personal nature.

Erin received him with the customary courtesy. 'You come alone today; I sense that this is of grave importance, Mr Johns.'

'I respect your courtesy, sir. But please, just call me Leslie. We have a common bond that I consider makes us friends, and what I am about to give you will compound that. Now, sir – may I call you Erin? Sir is so formal, but I respect your years.'

'My dear Leslie, I am honoured, deeply honoured to be regarded so. Please continue.'

'I have here some information for you – dates; times; facts; and an account of lies, betrayal, and treachery. Erin, my father was taken from me when I was a small child. Having suffered physical and mental abuse from my mother almost to the point of death, my father saved me – not just me; he saved my sister as well. I have never known him. He lives somewhere in China, and I have people working on that for me.

'I want my father back in my life, and I want to be his son. He thinks that my sister and I are dead and has thought that for many years. He would not come back to this country for anything other than us. Erin, read these accounts and my notes, my story. I do not wish you to act on them just yet; absorb the content. I am afraid I may have put too personal a viewpoint in places. Forgive me those faults. I wrote from emotions and not as a report.

'You will see that Sir Alastair has obtained legal custody as guardian of my sister and me. He discussed nothing with us; had we known his intentions we would have refused to entertain them. In short Erin, my father now has no right in law to decide in our lives. Until the age of twenty-one, Sir Alastair is our lord and master. Erin, I have people who are, at this very minute, attempting to contact my father and bring him back to us. Sir, I must have my father back. You must read all these papers and work out how to return my father to his rightful position. Sir Alastair's application for guardianship was based on fabrication and lies, betrayal, and greed. I am not his ward in my heart or mind, but I am under law. Help us please. Help my sister and me and deliver us from eternal damnation. Sir Alastair is an evil man! I will prove that to you later.'

Erin was very shocked. He had never imagined that a man of Sir Alastair's calibre could ever be considered dishonest or less than decent. It was just too much to take in. He had an urge to read these files.

'Mr…Leslie, leave everything in my hands. I will read all you have written and research all the points of law. Be assured, my friend, if I may say so, I will find a way to resolve this ultimately to your satisfaction. I must warn you as your legal advisor; it is a long road ahead and fraught with pitfalls. Sir Alastair has a good team of lawyers, the very best in fact. I will read what you have written and advise you to the best of my ability.

'We must establish in law that he has committed a criminal offence first; if that is successful, we can then accuse him of kidnapping. I will read your papers and consider what route we should take. Leave this in my hands. And trust me, we will have an answer; I can feel it. We will restore the balance, be assured of that, one way or another. May I consult on this matter with my colleague, Leslie?'

'Yes but be careful whom you relate it to. You understand my meaning, sir! You may not have personal connections with Sir Alastair, but many others do, directly or indirectly. Check before you reveal my case; it is of the utmost importance. If you do not do so, we are all at severe risk. Do I need to explain?'

'Leslie, I understand perfectly. Let me read the papers, and we will discuss the appropriate line to take. I will do all that I can and use my resources to bring about a favourable conclusion to your dilemma. It distresses me so to see your concern for my own safety and well-being.'

He opened a safe and removed some papers. 'May I take this opportunity to explain how the trust is set up?'

Leslie listened carefully as Erin went over the details.

A short time later, he led the boy to the door. 'Leslie, trust me. I realise that you have been cheated, betrayed, lied to, and deceived. It leaves you uncertain of trust, but I am your servant. I work for you.'

His tone was reassuring and filled Leslie with confidence that his aims would be safe in this man's hands. This man was a friend indeed; he could be trusted and relied upon, as could his predecessors.

***

Leslie decided to check what was happening in the Thompson case. The man, now freed on bail, was discussing his predicament with his lawyers. He told them that he was doing a research paper regarding the physical and psychological effects of being an orphan – how it drove some and hindered others and whether it interfered with a child's mental and emotional development or contributed to it. He had given his predicament a lot of thought. Perhaps over the years he had envisaged this situation and conjured up this worthless garbage. He had no notes, comparison charts, anecdotes, examples – he had come up with a good excuse, but had failed in his preparations.

The lawyer told him that he would need to provide all his documentation in support of his claims. He had no research documents or case studies and now not even the stolen files or those of the good doctor to fall back on. His world was falling around him.

Hendricks had gotten him into this. He had to get him out, or he would spill the beans and sink the entire Woodford navy. The admiral would go down with the captain and the ship.

***

Pleased with the outcome, Leslie checked on Hendricks. He was now making a good recovery and should be home by the end of the month. He was having some physiotherapy, as the illness had left him weak in the legs, and he could not walk without the aid of two sticks. Leslie felt a little sorry for him; he looked so pathetic performing his exercises, wincing and grimacing with every few steps.

***

Now Leslie had to face the one thing he had put off for so long; he dreaded the thought of the asylum. He floated to that dismal place and visited each of the rooms one by one, identifying the occupants from files he remembered. It was like checking off a list at roll call, and he came finally to a door that he could not enter.

The dread, the fear, and the anticipation were too much to bear. He stood alone, unseen in the corridor. Accompanied only by his worst fears, he finally mustered the courage and entered because he had to know.

Oh God! Oh my God! His worst fears were now realised.

Lying on the bed in front of him was a young man of about eighteen but appearing to be years older. Leslie approached cautiously. The man was thin and sinewy, and his eyes were wild and staring. His hair was unkempt and his face unshaven. But Leslie had no doubt, no doubt at all – it was his old friend Thomas.

What have they done to you?! he screamed inwardly, raising both hands to his head. *They will pay for this, believe me, Thomas.*

The man's eyes gradually began to focus on Leslie as he turned over.

All the devils in hell will not protect these beasts from me.

He heard Mary's voice in his head. *Leslie, it is not your way. Mine is the way of vengeance and retribution. Your way is to help and find solutions. Give comfort not curses to this friend.*

'Leslie? Is it you Leslie…how do you come to be here? What has taken you so long to find me? I hoped you would eventually—'

Thomas fell into another stupor. The poor man was falling in and out of consciousness in rapid succession.

I will get you out of here. Trust me, I will do it.

'Leslie what are you—'

He felt distraught at the sight of his first and best friend in the world, who'd helped and protected him from the harsh beatings, taking them himself to save Leslie. They had been so close, feeling each other's pain like identical twins. Leslie thought about pains he'd suffered in subsequent years that he had not been able to account for – physical pains without cause. Now he realised that it was not his pain he'd felt. He had borne it for his friend subconsciously.

He entered Thomas's head, and it was a scrambled mess of facts, figures, and ideas without reason – a mishmash of broken thoughts. They had reduced his brain to worthless pulp. He had been such a bright and clever boy, and now he was a helpless dependant wretch. It churned Leslie inside out to see this friend in such a state. 'I will keep my promise this time,' he said through clenched teeth. 'Forgive me for taking so long, my dear, dear friend.'

***

He called Erin to inform him of his discovery and sought advice. 'How do we get him out of there? It is urgent that we do something, sir... Please, Erin, we must save him and the others in the asylum, I will explain all to you another time.' He did not reveal how he knew about the inmates, and the lawyer did not ask with Leslie's promise of an explanation at another time.

'I have an idea, Leslie. Here's the scenario – we are looking for a relative of a client and believe he is a patient there. You say the doctor is away, as well as Sir Alastair. So, we introduce a reward. A reward, Leslie, is a great motivator. Shall we say £100 for positive information?'

'Make it thousands if you have to, Erin; it matters not. We must get him out before he becomes a vegetable. Invent what you like. Just get him and the others out.'

'Leslie, a disaster of some kind, natural or man-made has instant results.'

There was silence on the line. Was this man suggesting something abhorrent, a collapse of the building, an earthquake, or something like that? Was he suggesting Leslie create the conditions? How could he know of Leslie's powers? He put his trust in Erin nonetheless.

***

It was at night when the fire began in the boiler room. Smoke wafted through the building, alarms sounded, and the staff galvanised into action got everybody out of the building and onto the front lawns. A mass of ambulances, fire engines, and police cars swarmed the property. There were no flames involved, just thick billowing smoke filling the halls and corridors. The situation was soon under control, but the stench of smoke pervaded the building.

Those inmates able to walk, the police put into handcuffs or straitjackets. The police had no idea of whom they were dealing with and treated them all the same. Staff brought out medications and charts relating to who had what and when. The information went unheard, lost in the night wind and vaporised into the night sky.

A meteorite flashed and sparkled before it vanished into oblivion. 'Thank you…thank you, Leslie,' it whispered in a nanosecond as it disappeared, shattering into a million fragments above the horizon. He had at least given release to so many souls, both living and dead.

The task ahead for the doctors was to examine and assess each patient. These were 'mental' patients, unable to reason or discuss in viable terms their reasons for incarceration. There was much still to do. These people had to have time to recover what senses were still left to them. They were accommodated in the local hospital under the care of Dr Winters, a specialist in all things of the mind and not connected with the Woodford empire. He had records for each patient but he decided to stop the drugs and let the patients resume their natural states. He could not accurately assess a person under the influence of drugs.

Dr Winters's considerations were a revelation and fuel for Leslie's assault on the Woodford regime. None of the inmates' remarks conflicted with the accusations Leslie had made about the asylum and those who ran it. Free from the constraints of the drugs, they gradually revealed the abuses and inhumanities they had suffered.

The doctor would do all he could to save their souls and humanity. He felt it incumbent upon him; he would make recompense in some way.

In his opinion, all the patients were making improvements except one. An elderly and quite feeble man suffering from pneumonia who Dr Winters did not expect to last long. He called for the opinions of two colleagues, both renowned experts in their field of psychology. They each examined the former inhabitants of the asylum and made their individual assessments. All three doctors reached the same conclusions and prepared a joint report to present to the authorities. They sent a copy to the chief constable for the Essex Constabulary.

***

Leslie visited Thomas every day and could see improvements in his friend's condition each time. His old friend told him of the months and years he'd spent working on a series of numbers that appeared to be a cipher. He had not made the slightest inroad into solving it, and he was clever with numbers. He did not know of the poem the cipher related to; nor had he been taught French at school. He'd learned German instead.

It had occurred to Thomas that the cipher might be in German. But of course, that route had led to a dead end. Sir Alastair and Dr Hendricks must have thought the same; they had chosen this boy for his command of the language and his skill with numbers.

Thomas's revelation confirmed to Leslie his idea that 'the boy' the dean and the doctor had spoken of years ago, in the library, was indeed Thomas.

Each time Leslie had tried to float to Thomas in the past, he had been unable to; he now assumed that the boy's drugged state had blocked the connection.

***

The asylum remained uninhabitable; it should have been thoroughly cleaned and redecorated. However, the funds for such an expense were not available and besides, patients could not return whilst the police investigated. The police interviewed all the staff and seized patients' records. The police interviewed Dr Hendricks. As the primary consultant and with his signature on all the records, he would have a lot to answer for.

A special team of investigators assembled; each member of the team was scrutinized to ensure none had links with the asylum or the Woodford Foundation. The head of the team was Detective Chief Inspector Royston, a man with a fearsome reputation. He did everything by the book and expected the same from his team. He made that crystal clear at the preliminary briefing. He would brook no underhand methods, fabrications, or insinuations. Facts – he asked for cold hard facts and logical theories. He was a man of few words, but each member of his team treated each word he uttered with respect and obedience.

DCI Royston divided the asylum files and handed them out. 'Where you do not understand medical terms, ask. Get advice on the effects of the medications listed. Do not make assumptions. Here is a list of experts appointed to this case by the home office. Use it. This is a very high-profile case and monitored from the top,' he said, pointing to the ceiling. 'No slip-ups, no mistakes, and no shortcuts. Got it?' His style was authoritarian and direct; it had earned him his reputation for getting concrete results. He had a clear, analytical, logical, and discerning mind. He used informants and hunches but always made sure of the facts.

***

Leslie told Mary of the police team and about its leader.

'Oh thank God for that,' she replied. 'An honest man with integrity.'

Leslie agreed that this man would fight their fight for them. They may be required at some time to make a statement, and they were more than prepared for that eventuality.

The destruction of the evil empire occupied Leslie's mind. There were things in hand that would cause annoyance and distraction for the lord of the manor. Upon his return, Sir Alastair would be besieged by police and reporters; Mary and he could continue unobserved and unopposed. Everything was falling into place, but they still had to appear innocent and uninvolved. It was critical to his plans that he and Mary did not implicate themselves in any way. He remembered the words Perry had spoken. *Do not put yourself in danger, son.* He included his sister and considered the possible outcomes.

***

Mary considered the actions that her brother had outlined to her. He had given valuable ammunition to the press, furnishing Ed and his two most trusted reporters with documents regarding the children in the village. He had created the circumstances that had allowed the police to launch an investigation into the plight of those imprisoned in the asylum. He had put Sir Alastair and Dr Hendricks under the spotlight. But what of Walsh and his band of cronies? How would her brother deal with them?

What she didn't know was that Leslie had other plans for them, plans he had not discussed with her, plans that would end their devious deeds. He had decided not to tell her of these plans until after they had come to fruition!

***

Sir Alastair booked his flight home. The trip included a stopover in Paris. He would be back in two days, and this did not give Leslie enough time to progress his plans to the next stage. He inspired a strike by air traffic controllers. That would give him a few more days.

Leslie kept his eyes on the clock; every second counted from now on. He skipped breakfast and visited the press and the police. He needed to know every detail of each individual's progress. It was a draining task and not something he would involve his sister with.

Unknown to the boy, Mary was aware of his efforts and followed his every move; he could not escape her attention to his activities.

He had some little power to prevent her. She could often read his mind and see his plans but not always. He had a mechanism to block her intrusion, and she could block him if she concentrated hard enough.

Chapter 23

Many Returns, But Not All Happy

Mary had made her usual visit to the newsagent and collected the note left there by Billy.

'Leslie they have found him. They have found Daddy and made contact with him. They are making arrangements for him to fly to London. Oh what good news!' She jumped like a child, clapping her hands. The excitement she felt made her forget the horrid thoughts she had conjured up before. She could never prevent what must be, what was inevitable.

At last the news that Leslie had waited for so long. And it filled him with excitement and anticipation but also trepidation.

There was so little time left now until the fireworks would begin.

The two of them walked to the town and dropped in at the news desk. 'Leslie, Mary, so good to see you,' said Billy. 'Come on up. Ed wants to talk to you.'

Leslie observed the glances his sister gave Billy. The poor man turned red in the face with embarrassment.

Billy was fairly outgoing, but he was shy. He could overcome his affliction when it was work related, but he was awkward in the presence of Mary. He could feel her power over him, and yet he was attracted to her. He had not given any sign consciously of how he felt. Mary gave a sharp glance to her brother and a mind message, *Do not say a word.*

Ed welcomed them in. 'Have a seat, please. You got the message then? Your father will arrive on Tuesday next; the earliest flight we could arrange. We did not tell him the whole story, just that you are alive. We felt that you should choose what to tell him.'

The group sat talking for a while, Ed punctuating the conversation with instructions to his team.

Leslie told Ed of an idea that he and his sister had worked on. It involved a proposal that Ed was not obligated to answer straight away. He could take some time to discuss it with his colleagues and get their reactions. 'How would you like to run a magazine and be an equal partner in it? It would focus on investigative journalism and be a tool to expose evil and criminal activities. We will finance the costs of setting up, including the premises, equipment, and so forth.' Leslie explained that he and Mary could provide them with leads and that they had discussed the proposal with their lawyer; Erin was working on a contract at that very moment.

Ed jumped at the idea. 'I would need to leave the paper,' he said. 'I feel badly about that. They gave me a job when I was at an all-time low. I would need Tweety and Billy too. It would leave the paper in a tight spot.'

Leslie had considered that. 'Take your time to decide. And as I said, discuss it with your colleagues and prepare your bosses well in advance if you decide to accept. It will take time to find the premises and set everything up.'

'May I ask how you intend to finance this? Forgive me, but this is a huge undertaking, and you are both far too young to have access to that kind of money.'

'You can discuss that with Erin Yardley. Here are his contact details. He will tell you all you need to know.' Leslie said as he wrote down the lawyer's telephone number.

***

After Mary and Leslie left, Ed called Tweety and Billy into the office and informed them the of proposal.

'Wow,' said Tweety 'how can they afford that? And you want us to come with you? I'm up for it. We have several stories already. We could publish those. What about you, Billy?'

Billy was more cautious. It was not in his nature to accept things at face value. 'You mentioned a lawyer in London, sir. Have you spoken to him sir?'

'Not yet. I wanted to discuss it with you two first. Maybe I don't say it, but you two are my most trusted and reliable journalists. If I accept this offer, I will need you both with me.

'With the police story and the one on the village, we do have something to start with. But remember, this has to remain between us. Also, we have stories supplied by Leslie but we have to wait for the go ahead from him' said the editor. 'Think about it Billy, this is a great opportunity for us all and I really need reporters like Tweety and you. I value you both perhaps more than you realise, you have integrity and honesty in your work and that is important to me.'

***

DCI Royston was about to go to see his superior officer when a detective sergeant stopped him. 'If you have a moment, sir, I think I have found something here.'

Royston looked at the papers the sergeant was reading.

'This is the list of patients from the hospital, and these are the records from the asylum. There are records for a Peregrine Collins; he is not on the list or at the hospital. His records show nothing regarding his death, discharge, or transfer. He could still be there, sir.'

'Good work, Sergeant. I am on my way upstairs, and I'll get a warrant to search the whole place.'

'What about the warrant we had, sir?'

'That was only to seize the records. Now we have a missing person.'

Royston left hurriedly to keep his appointment.

***

It was sometime later that DCI Royston returned, waving the warrant. 'Detective Waters, take a search team and two cameras up to the asylum. Search every inch of the place. And be thorough. Search the grounds as well if you have to. Find out where this man is. And don't come back empty-handed. Sergeant Muir, you can lead them.'

***

The police arrived at the asylum. 'This place gives me the jitters,' the sergeant said to Waters.

'Aye, and me too sergeant.'

They split into two teams and searched every ward and side room, every office and cupboard. The search would not take long, as there were no occupants and only two staff on duty. The sergeant took his team to search the boiler room. There were lots of nooks and crannies, but they searched them all.

Waters searched the laundry rooms and the kitchens.

'Sir,' shouted one of the uniformed constables, 'sir, there is a door here, but it is locked. We don't seem to have a key for it.'

Waters went over to the door and tried to open it. 'Get that orderly down here with a key.'

When the orderly arrived, Waters asked him why the door was locked.

'I don't know, officer. I work on the upper floor, and I don't have a clue where the key would be.'

'Okay,' said Waters, nudging the man back from the door and looking at the constables. 'Break it down, lads.'

They looked at each other. 'DCI Royston would not—'

'Orders are to search everywhere thoroughly. Now break it down.'

It was a very solid door, and breaking it open took some time. The sounds of hammering echoed along the corridors and attracted the attention of the sergeant. Having completed his area, the sergeant took his team to see what the commotion was. He arrived just as the door finally gave in.

'What's down there?' Muir asked the orderly.

'I don't know,' the orderly answered blankly. 'Never been down there.'

The officers descended the dimly lit narrow flight of steps. They were aware of the pungent odour rising from below as they reached another door at the foot of the stairway, also locked. They sorted through the bunch of keys and again ended up having to break the door open. Inside, there was no light switch because there was no light. They shone their torches around the dank cell, lit the meagre candle and took photographs of what they found. The sergeant made notes by torchlight and led his team to a door on the far side. This door had no lock, and it led down some steps to a tunnel. They searched the whole length of it in both directions but found nothing.

***

The sergeant began a search of the surrounding grounds, starting with the front tree-lined area that screened the perimeter wall from the building. The two teams began at the entrance gate and worked in opposite directions. The search was long and tiring, and eventually both teams reached the old outbuildings at the rear. They searched every building from corner to corner.

They moved on to the overgrown grassy area; tangled in brambles and stung by the nettles, they persevered. The sergeant asked Waters to stand back. 'Look at all the hummocks; you know, it looks odd. All the rest of the grounds on this site are flat, but not here.'

'Probably rabbits or foxes. It's a bit wild here sergeant.'

Sergeant Muir was not convinced. There were no burrow holes to suggest that Waters was right in his assumption.' The sergeant looked all around, and could not see any signs of burrowing. 'Constables, get some shovels over here please.' Muir said.

The constables started to dig at two of the mounds. They had not dug for long when one called. 'There are bones here, sir.'

Waters and the Sergeant went to see for themselves.

'And here, sir,' went up another shout.

'Dig that one. It looks fairly fresh,' said Muir.

Just a few shovels revealed a partially decayed corpse.

'Okay,' shouted the sergeant. 'We will have to get a specialist team up here. Get the pictures, and I'll call the DCI. You two remain here,' he said, pointing to the nearest two constables. 'No one comes near here unless it is one of us. Is that clear?'

'Yes, Sergeant,' they answered in unison.

'I'll send someone to relieve you later,' he added as he walked towards the front drive.

In the squad car, the sergeant asked, 'What do you make of it, Waters?'

'Well, Sergeant, it seems that some of the remains are quite old, but that last one turned my stomach. Recent, I would say – no more than a couple of months, possibly three. What I don't understand is why they would bury them here in unmarked graves, and they're not properly buried. I mean... well...no coffins, and the graves are shallow. They're barely buried at all. I find it all very suspicious.'

'Thank you, Waters. Exactly my thoughts. Suspicious indeed.'

They chatted about Royston's reputation and the way he wanted things done. Waters confessed that he found the man hard to deal with. The sergeant saw Royston as an icon, a beacon he aspired to emulate. He found himself admiring the way his boss conducted business. He noticed that he always had time to listen to his juniors and extracted from them things they did not realise that they knew. He was a clever manager and manipulator; it was how his reputation had been born and maintained.

Recognised for his diligence and attention to detail, Detective Sergeant Reginald Muir had served in three different constabularies on assignment. He was as thorough a police officer as Royston could ever wish to have on his team. Royston noticed the way Muir got stuck into the heart of things, rooting around and checking his hunches and then rechecking them. Efficient police officers were a rarity in Royston's world; he questioned how many of them had ever passed the exams. Some were clever at wordplay but could not convince him by words alone. He wanted clear thinkers, intuitive people who could spot a falsehood at a hundred paces. He wanted people who could spend hours, days, weeks poring over boring reports and records and come up with a lead from a single contradiction; that kind of dedication demanded a great deal of concentration. He was an old-fashioned peeler and proud of it; Royston was the kind of thorough officer Leslie needed for the investigation and Muir was a bonus for the boy and for Royston.

***

Muir looked up and down the site with horror. He couldn't believe how many shallow graves were here; they'd uncovered almost an acre of bones. Many of the skeletons were those of children, ranging from seven to sixteen years of age; there had to be monsters here to destroy so many young lives.

Some of the police officers had to be excused from duty because they could not deal with the revelations. They became emotional and sick, sickened by what they had unearthed.

The constables kept the press well away from the site on the instructions of DCI Royston. He did not want press intrusions to interfere with his case. 'A statement will be made by the chief superintendent' was all he would say.

***

Mary and her brother were strolling in the grounds of the village when they were photographed by a journalist. 'Can you give us any information on what is happening at the asylum?' the journalist asked.

Leslie carried on walking. 'You should not be in here,' he said. 'This is private property. We have no comment on something that is not of our concern.'

'But the village and the asylum are run by the same man. Come on. Give us something. You must know what's going on up there.'

Leslie and his sister ignored the man and continued with the newshound at their heels.

'Come on, love,' the reporter called, switching tactics. 'Give us a story. You must know what's going on love.'

Mary halted him with just a single thought – *Away with you!*

He left with nothing – no story, no hint, and no clue. All would be reserved for an exclusive in their own publication.

***

Sir Alastair prepared to return to the UK. He had missed Rachel and her soothing touch. He had suffered unimaginable insults, endured accusations and betrayals, and had been denied his comforts and subjected to the horrors of prison life. He would never return to this place for whatever reason.

***

DCI Royston had just finished reading the statement made by Dr Hendricks when Sergeant Muir and Waters returned. They related their findings and handed over their reports. A forensics team was already on site, and a full excavation of the area was underway. At present, they had examined eleven of the shallow graves.

'Listen up,' Royston said. 'I want Hendricks in here as soon as he is well enough. I also want Woodford; he is still in Cayenne according to my sources but he will arrive back any day. As soon as he touches down at Heathrow, bring him in for questioning. He is not to be allowed near the Asylum. Waters, you can deal with that. Sergeant Muir, I want you to go over the asylum files and locate all the records of those listed as deceased.'

'That is already done, sir. I have the list here. It was for—'

'Thank you, Sergeant. Good work. I do like an orderly mind' he said, cutting the sergeant mid-sentence.

Muir felt a deep inner pride; praised several times by his mentor, he strove to maintain his position of reliability to this legend of policing. The DCI's secret was clear organised thinking and attention to all the facts. He would be just like this man, diligent and purposeful in every aspect of his work, looking for the little clues but not obscuring the big ones, sorting the mackerels from the red herrings, and looking for the questions that needed to be asked.

***

Mary was moody and grumpy; she often was. Upset by her mood, Leslie could not understand the reason. He searched his memories for anything that he had done to upset her. It confounded him, and he asked her outright, 'What have I done? Did I say something to upset you?'

'Leslie go away and leave me alone.' This was the answer he always got.

This clever, bright, intelligent boy had no idea of what some women go through. But he was, after all, just a male. There was no way for him to know or understand. Mary herself did not understand why she became this person on a regular cycle. She knew when she would – she had made that connection – but not why. It was something she could not control, something she had no power over.

For Leslie's part, he knew all about the human conditions, the reproductive cycles, a woman's monthly cycles and later the menopause – he was not stupid. But he had problems with fitting the pieces together. He was, for all his brief experience, still a child, an innocent. And so was Mary, to a lesser degree.

She hated the way she treated her brother when the moods befell her. She had done her best to let him discover, explore, and uncover; to make his own friends; and to know a lover. He had experienced more of life's joys and pitfalls than she had because she had given him the freedom to do so. She could have used her powers to bend any man to her will; she had put all of that aside to concentrate on him.

***

Tuesday morning was now upon them, and after a quick breakfast, Mary and Leslie kept their appointment with Ed, who drove them to Heathrow in a large rented car. They watched the information panels and listened to every announcement with eager anticipation. Leslie felt slightly sick with the excitement and expectancy.

Then they heard the announcement; the flight from Paris had landed. Will still had to collect his luggage and pass through passport control. Leslie paced up and down, searching the faces of the passengers as they came through the arrivals gate. 'Where is he? I cannot see him.'

Ed put his hand on the boy's shoulder. 'Calm yourself, laddie. He will be here in a short while. I can see that you've never been to an airport before.'

Ed held a card in front of him with 'Will Johns' printed in capitals. They had no idea what he looked like – nor he, they. A tall slim man with a shock of pure white hair approached Ed and offered his hand. 'I am Will Johns. Are...these... Are these my children, sir? I see it in them. My lord, they are grown.' Tears began to fall as he fell to his knees and hugged them each in turn and again together.

Ed stood back and let the reunion take its course. Will was emotional and transmitted his feelings to the two youngsters, the three of them sobbing and hugging. Ed saw it as a beautiful moment and felt proud that he had been instrumental in its creation.

In an instant, police officers were all about them, checking identities and obviously looking for someone in particular. It was then that Mary spotted Jackson at the far side of the arrivals lounge. 'Leslie, look, over there by the doors. Jackson—' Mary said to her brother. 'I know, his lordship's flight from Paris... Daddy, you have just arrived from Paris... Oh my god, thank you Ed for the economy class...Sir Alastair, that is who the police are looking for from the same flight.'

Ed was not party to this interplay between the two youngsters.

Leslie looked seriously at his father and Ed. 'We must leave now before he sees us. Come' he urged.

There was an urgency in his tone that alarmed Will. 'What's up? What's wrong?'

'We must go now, Dad. Come on.'

Then Will spotted Jackson as they sidled through the crowd. 'Here...I know him...and him—'

'Come on, Dad. Dad!' The boy grabbed his father's hand and hauled him away from the building.

In the car on the way to the cottage, Will mentioned the faces he'd recognised at the airport. 'Jackson, yes, I remember him from the army. And that other fellow...Martins I believe it was. Yes that was it, Martins. He was in league with the colonel and his lot, a right hard nut, vicious and ugly in every sense of the word.'

Ed made mental notes of all the comments. His skills as a reporter had never left him.

Ed took a circuitous route and constantly checked the mirror. A car followed, but it caused him no concern. He had spoken to Erin regarding the boy's proposal and the details of the contract; he also discussed the situation with regard to Will. Ed decided that using someone from Mintell for security would be too risky, and he employed the company recommended by Erin; it was two of their men in the car behind.

Arriving at the cottage, Tweety and Billy greeted them all, and Ed made the introductions. They collected Will's luggage and that of his children, for they had come prepared. Over a cup of tea, they listened to Ed's account of how he and his colleagues had eventually traced Will and made contact; the information on the system Will used to communicate had come from Swifty. As Will had not settled at one address, he used a PO box in Hong Kong. Ed had contacted a friend who worked on the *Sing Tao Evening News* to trace him and make contact. Ed's friend had been a valuable ally. Without him, finding Will would have taken much longer and might even have been impossible.

'Now we will let you settle in, Mr Johns. You must be tired after such a long journey. We have a paper to write. Oh, can we print your story?'

Before Will could agree, Leslie shook his head. 'You will need the whole story, and my sister and I must tell it to Dad, rather than him reading it in the press. I promised you the story, and I will keep my word.'

A mere boy addressing a grown man of some years, as though he were an equal, or even an employee took Will aback. He felt it lacked respect and was about to admonish Leslie for it. A voice in his head said, *Leave it. You do not understand at present, but you will soon.*

'There is just one thing before we go. Leslie, we have decided to accept your proposal – all three of us. Perhaps we can find some time to work out the details?'

Leslie offered his hand and shook hands with each of them in turn. 'Thank you, gentlemen. You have just put the icing on a delicious cake.'

These goings-on confounded Will; he knew nothing of his children's dealings. What proposal could his son have made to these people? What the dickens was going on here?

As the three men turned to leave, Ed asked Leslie, 'How did you know the police were at the airport to pick up Sir Alastair?'

Leslie grinned broadly and tapped the side of his nose. 'I have my sources too, you know,' he said and then winked.

Will was even more lost now. He looked at Mary, and she gave him a big smile, one of her knowing smiles. He shook his head. 'I hope someone is going to enlighten me,' he said despairingly.

His children laughed and ran to hug him; Ed closed the front door quietly behind him.

***

Three uniformed police officers and Detective Waters escorted Sir Alastair from the airport terminal, much to the dismay of Jackson and Martins. Jackson of course was there to collect his master, but Martins was there to warn Sir Alastair of Walsh's plot against him. Martins and Walsh had worked together many times but did not really get on well with each other. Martins always took his orders from Walsh, but in most cases, he would have done things differently. Martins had no quarrel with Sir Alastair and felt the need to warn him.

Jackson followed the police cars to the police station in Cannon Row, Westminster. He parked and entered the building. 'I am here to collect Sir Alastair Woodford,' he said in a dry tone.

The duty officer looked him up and down. 'He is assisting us with our enquiries. You will have to wait...over there.' He pointed to a hard wooden bench.

'Pompous ass,' muttered Jackson.

***

'We have a very serious matter here, Sir Alastair. Fourteen shallow graves at present, with the remains of bodies, found on your property. You can explain, to me surely?'

Sir Alastair squirmed on the seat. 'I know nothing of these graves or bodies you speak of. The asylum on the village property is a private retreat for the mentally infirm. I may own it, but I do not run it. I have no training in such things.' He tried to distance himself from the horrors uncovered.

'As the owner sir, in law you are responsible, accountable for the actions of your employees. Just who is in charge of the asylum, sir?'

He did not want to betray his oldest friend. 'I use various consultants and experts to examine and diagnose—'

'So you do get involved in the running of the place! You just said that you did not, sir.'

Sir Alastair could feel the ground sliding from beneath his feet.

'Someone must have day-to-day control of the hospital … sorry sir, retreat, I believe you called it?'

How could he protect his friend and his own interests? He was beginning to feel tired and slightly confused. It had been a long journey from Cayenne with the stopover, and it had been a long time since he had enjoyed a good night's sleep, the comfort of Rachel's expertise, or the warmth and security of Howard House. He had lost touch with the daily routines – Susan fussing and the boy with his questions—

Yes, the boy! He thought, Leslie, could help him get out of this mess if anyone could. *He is as bright as a spark, as deep as a canyon, and far wiser than his tender years. Yes, yes he will help.*

Sir Alastair had been so blind in his own ambitions for the boy that he had never thought to enquire what Leslie wanted from life. This boy was going to run his empire, and no one was more capable. He had cared for and nurtured this boy; the boy at least owed him something surely – loyalty, respect, obedience even. Surely, Leslie would come to his rescue.

He refused to answer any more questions. 'Get my lawyer before I say another word. I believe you have interrogated me unlawfully.'

'Oh no, Sir Alastair, we have not charged you or accused you. You are free to leave whenever you wish. It's just that we feel you may be able to help us, you know, shed some light on what we have found. Your help would be greatly appreciated, sir. You are a man of good breeding and respected worldwide. I understand that and will not make this more uncomfortable for you than need be. We know you have friends in the force, and we are always in need of friends, Sir—'

'Do not treat me like a fool. A fool I am not, and if I am free to leave, I shall do just that.' He raised himself from the hard wooden chair and headed toward the door.

'There is the charge, or charges I should say, against Dr Hendricks to consider. He works for you, am I right? He has been seriously ill recently. However, we have obtained a statement from him. Oh dear, Sir Alastair, you must be exhausted from such a long journey. How remiss of me, I am such a clam, and I believe your driver awaits you— Oh, by the way sir, you cannot attend the village or the retreat whilst our investigations are ongoing. Where will you be staying if we need to ask you more questions?'

***

It was in his London apartment that Sir Alastair laid his head on the pillows; he had not been able to contact Rachel, and he needed her so much. He fell into a deep, dark dream-ridden sleep, where skeletons taunted him and ghosts haunted and threatened, beckoning and teasing.

He awoke with a sudden jolt. He felt sick but could not vomit. He still saw the images of his dreams. All around him they talked and murmured; mocking and teasing, they goaded him. He could not sleep, could not even rest, although his fatigue left him listless. He felt he was falling, slipping into another world – a world beyond his powers or cognisance. He was slipping slowly and powerless.

***

Leslie released Sir Alastair so that he could face the accusations and fight for his survival. Alastair had felt harshly treated in Cayenne, but what he was about to face would be on a different scale. It may be his home ground, but returning was his biggest mistake.

The cunning and scheming Leslie had awaited his Guardian's return.

***

Aroused by the sound of the doorbell at seven thirty in the morning, Sir Alastair, robed only in a dressing gown opened the door and was shocked to see Royston. 'I am sorry to disturb you at so early an hour sir, but more questions arise that we need answers for. Would you please dress and accompany us to the station?'

***

The team at the paper noted all the events of that previous day. Ed still wondered how Leslie knew about Sir Alastair. How could this boy, barely out of nappies, have contacts and informants on such a scale? He had not known himself that the great man was arriving? And who were Jackson and Martins? What part did they play in this intrigue? He surmised that Leslie was right when he said, "You need the whole story." It affirmed his trust and belief in this strange boy.

***

Both Mary and Leslie were reticent about revealing all to Will. They would have to ascertain what he planned to do next. Would he take them with him to China or just be content that they were alive and well and leave them there without him? Would he stay and help them fight their cause? They had no idea what his plans were.

Mary began the subtle interrogation. 'Daddy, where do you live in China? It sounds so far away.'

'Don't worry your head about that now,' he said dismissively. 'Tell me what's going on here.'

Leslie asked, 'What is your life like in China, sir?'

The very word caught Will by the throat; his own son calling him *sir* was too much for him. 'Never ever call me sir. I forbid it. Do you hear me? I understand that you have no experience of family life but never call me sir.'

Leslie felt sorry that he had offended his father.

Immediately Mary sent her brother a message to console him. *He is not angry with you, Leslie; he associates the title with Sir Alastair, the designer of the guilt Daddy feels.*

Will hugged his children. 'I'm sorry I became cross with you. I would not hurt you for the world. Forgive me.'

Leslie melted into the strength, warmth, and security of his father's arm. He absorbed every molecule and wished that it would never end. This support and love was the single most important thing he had longed for all of his life – the thing he remembered from a lifetime ago. In that lifetime, his father's strong arms had supported, soothed, and caressed him, and Will had stroked his head, easing the pain away.

How had he survived all these years without him? His emotions flooded him as he sobbed and hugged his father tightly. Will saw the small child in him, a child desperate for his father's love. How had he let himself be fooled so easily? He almost crushed his children as he hugged them; he felt so guilty. He'd not had the sense to question the story given to him by Colonel Woodford, and stricken with grief back then, he had not been able to face up to the tragedy. He recalled in his mind the stupid risks he took with his life after he received the news of his children. What Sir Alastair had done to him was unforgivable, and he sobbed with his children. Giving each other comfort with their tears, they were as one.

Leslie, we must talk somewhere private and quiet. Mary transmitted to him.

***

Leslie felt his sister's distress and assented to her pleading. They went for a walk, followed by a man they had never met. The two had no need to worry, he was one of the security team engaged by Ed

'Daddy needs to know the whole story Leslie. I can feel his pain. Leslie, we must be so careful not to shut him out but we cannot reveal all to him just yet.'

'Daddy would never harm us; I feel it and know it. And do not be afraid. He can be trusted. I sensed it the moment I saw him at the airport. I knew he was our father, although he is not what I remembered him to be.'

'A mental connection brought him to us, not the card with his name. Mary, he means us no harm. He is Daddy, our father, and all the gifts we have must have come from him. Hey, maybe he has them too…'

'I think not,' Mary countered. 'He would have seen through the story he was given the way I can see through Sir Alastair. No, he would not have been tricked like that.'

***

Susan called Mr Vance. 'The children are missing and have been gone all night. They did not give any explanation or a reason for their absence.' She was so concerned for their welfare; it was so unlike them not to notify her. She was also concerned that Sir Alastair had not yet arrived home. He should have been home yesterday unless he stayed in London

'The police will do nothing until the children have been gone for more than twenty-four hours,' Vance told her. 'They may have gone to meet Sir Alastair and stayed in London overnight perhaps.'

'Oh, here is Jackson now.' She observed that Jackson was alone and relayed this to Vance before hanging up the phone.

Jackson entered the mansion with Sir Alastair's luggage and told Susan of the events since the master's arrival. The police had detained Sir Alastair for questioning. He knew nothing of the whereabouts of Mary and Leslie.

Susan called Vance again and updated him.

***

Later that morning, Leslie telephoned Erin to tell him the good news. Dad was home, and the men at the paper had accepted the offer.

'Leslie, we are so pleased that you are reunited, but this gives us a problem. Sir Alastair is still your legal guardian, whether we like it or not. This needs a lawful resolution in the courts, as your father is at risk of kidnapping charges. Do you understand what I am saying? You must return to your guardian to protect your father.'

Leslie sat pale faced, the telephone dangling from his hand.

'Hello…hello. Leslie, are you still there?'

Erin heard the line go dead.

'What's the matter, son?'

Leslie told his father and sister what Erin had told him. 'We cannot go back there, not now.'

Will's face showed his anger. 'I won't let him have you. I want to see him and get an explanation even if I have to wring it out of him—'

'No, Dad, Erin is right, and you cannot confront Sir Alastair. You only know a very small part of the story, and he is a dangerous man. No, Daddy, he must not know that you are here, for all our sakes.' Mary said anxiously.

There was a sudden urgency in Leslie's voice. 'We must go to London, today.'

He picked up the telephone and called Erin back. 'Erin, yes it is Leslie. You are right. I am sorry I ended the call so abruptly. Do you have everything ready for the custody case? … You have, good. They will release Sir Alastair today. They do not have enough evidence against him. He could be guilty of negligence at the worst. … They will go after Hendricks, and Sir Alastair will go to visit him today in the hospital. We must prevent him coming back to the village. … I understand, sir. What if we charge him with kidnapping? … Yes, he can bring the evidence with him if he has it. One moment. I will ask him.' He looked eagerly at his father. 'Do you have the telegram still, the one Sir Alastair sent you?'

'Yes of course, son.' He went to his bag and retrieved some papers and an old envelope.

'Yes, Erin, he has it with him,' Leslie said and added after listening for a moment, 'Good. Yes, we will see you later. Thank you and goodbye.'

Leslie turned to Will. 'Dad, is it all right if I read it?'

The man handed his son the telegram. He read it and passed it to Mary. 'Dad, do you still have your bank account details that Sir Alastair set up for you?'

Will looked with surprise at his son. 'What do you know of that… How could you know?'

'It's a long story, Dad. And we will tell you the whole story. But for now, you must trust me. I do not want to tell you in bits and pieces. The bank account and telegram are essential evidence.'

'I have the account book here, for what use it is.'

'Good, then we had better go. Oh, do you have any other papers with you? Bring them, Dad. Bring them all.'

***

Leslie called at Tweety's house to let him know their plans.

'I can take you in the car if you wish. I'll need to clear it with Ed first. It will be safer than public transport and easier for the security guys to keep tabs on us.'

Leslie recovered some files from the box Tweety safeguarded.

This cloak-and-dagger stuff was all so mysterious to Will. He wished his children and these newsmen they seemed to be working with would enlighten him. It also brought to mind his work for Mintel – the top-secret missions and the dangers involved. What were his children mixed up in?

The security men were in a different car than the one they'd used the previous day. But it was the same pair inside. They kept a discrete distance from Tweety.

In Erin's office, Leslie made the introductions and was eager to get straight down to business. He handed Erin the files he'd brought with him. 'These are copies of files from Dr Hendricks's office. I rescued the originals when the house was on fire.'

'You mean you stole them,' the lawyer replied. 'This will not do, no not at all.'

'If I had not rescued them, they would have burned with the others, and we would have little or no evidence. They implicate the doctor, Sir Alastair, Greg Walsh, and George Thompson, who has already been charged with the theft of files from four children's homes and is currently on bail. We must be able to use them, sir.'

Erin opened the file and began to read the account of how Mary and Leslie had been selected, how Will had been tricked and taken out of the picture, and the time the young siblings had spent in St Vincent's and with foster care in Felixstowe. Psychological reports on them that went back to 1953, and the reports included accounts of Leslie's abilities with languages, puzzles, and logic. It gave a full and accurate picture of the children and their acquisition. 'This is powerful stuff indeed, Leslie. But I will need to consult with some colleagues on the legality of how you "rescued" it. You say this is a copy?'

'Yes, sir. The originals are in a safe place. There are many more files, although some got a bit scorched in the fire.'

'You do realise that the police will need these files to assist with their investigations – that is, if they are admissible. Let me call my colleague.'

A much older man with a limp and a walking stick entered the room; the visitors arose and shook his hand whilst Erin did the introductions and explanations. Leslie pulled up another chair as Erin related the problem.

'May I see the content of the file?' enquired Mr Mosse. He skimmed through the pages with speed. 'You say this young man rescued them from a fire? I would say that it would be admissible, but we can contact an old friend to be certain.' Mosse telephoned a friend who was a high court judge and gave him a 'theoretical scenario'. He listened, nodded, and interjected with ums and ohs. A few minutes later, he replaced the telephone.

'A difficult one. If it could be proven that the fire was started by the one who rescued the files, that would be two criminal offences, arson and theft, and possibly other charges, endangerment to life and so on. If the rescuer had no part in the event other than to retrieve the files, a case can be made to uphold the value and integrity of those files. I would therefore have to ask how the fire started and did the police produce a report?'

Leslie briefly glanced at his father. 'Sir, my sister and I were awoken by the maid who told us of the fire. I dressed and ran down to the lodge to see that some of the estate staff were engaged in trying to put out the fire. Miss Weston managed to drag the occupant from the house before the smoke and flames engulfed it. It was then that I thought about the files. I went to the rear of the house and the back door was open – well not open but not locked.

'I managed to find a large holdall in the office and stuffed as many of the files in it as I could before the flames got too close. I hid the holdall in the back garden and went back for it the next day. I realised the importance of the files and arranged for their safekeeping. This is a copy.'

They all looked at the boy as he related the tale. 'You say there are other files. How many?'

'Forty-three, sir. I had to leave many others. The fire was getting too close, and I would not have been able to carry them all.'

'The police and the fire service made reports on the event. The housekeeper had put some washing close the fire to dry. She fell asleep and then was awakened by the smell of burning laundry. As she tried to put out the smouldering clothes, she inadvertently spread the fire. She suffers from agoraphobia, and that is why Miss Weston had to drag her out. Miss Weston discovered the fire as she returned from an evening out and saw the smoke as she entered the gates.'

Mosse looked the boy up and down whilst deep in thought. 'You must have known about the files before the fire and then... You see, we have to establish intention here. What was your purpose in attempting such a risky deed? And what did you intend to do with the files?'

'Well I knew of the files of course. Dr Hendricks always had my file out when I visited him. He made notes all the time and put them into the file. At the time of the fire, I do not know why I retrieved them. I just knew they would be important. It was only when I read them that I realised they needed to be kept safe. After reading my own file, it confirmed to me that Mary and I were not truly orphans. I knew then that Sir Alastair had made us his wards by trickery and dishonesty.'

Mary admired the way Leslie handled the situation. He had managed to tell the truth in a roundabout way by adjusting the timescale of events.

Erin asked for the telegram and any other items that may be useful. Will opened his bag and handed over the telegram, an old bank book, his enlistment papers, a signed copy of the Official Secrets Act, and his discharge papers. Erin examined them all in detail and passed the OSA document to Mosse.

'This is not the correct form for official secrets,' he said.

'That is what we signed, sir,' Will replied.

'No, I have seen the real document many times,' Mosse said firmly. 'This is a forgery, and not a very good one at that. You see, someone has made a huge error here.' He pointed to the top of the document, which stated 'His Majesty's Government'. 'The date on this paper is during our current monarch's reign.'

Will glanced at the lawyer. 'When I questioned that, I was told that they had not yet received the new wording and that this was just as valid.'

'Had this been the genuine article, Mr Johns, you would still be bound by it and unable to disclose any activities governed by it, even in court. As it is a forgery, it has no legality, and you are therefore not bound.'

Erin passed Mosse the discharge papers. 'These also are forgeries, sir. I would say that, officially, you are still in the services. And as such, you are absent without leave for the last six years, a mere technicality that can be dealt with quite easily.'

Several hours passed as the group discussed the legal ins and outs of their case, and Leslie realised they had left without breakfast that morning. His stomach rumbled and gurgled loudly across the office. 'Please do excuse me. I think we should feed the stomach hounds with lunch.' He turned to Erin and his partner. 'May we invite you to join us, sirs, and perhaps you could recommend an establishment locally.'

'What a splendid idea. There is a very good restaurant around the corner,' said Mosse.

As they left the office, Leslie realised that Tweety still waited in the reception area. 'My profound apologies, my friend. It took somewhat longer than anticipated. Please join us for some lunch, my treat.'

Leslie signalled to Erin to settle the bill from his account. He still had much to discuss with Erin, privately. He suggested that he meet up with the others later on, in a coffee house across the road.

***

Mary asked her father what he thought of the events at the office.

'That man Sir Alastair and his henchmen have a lot to answer for. I have seen and done things I am not proud of, but this lot take the biscuit. They should pay for what they have done.'

'They will, Dad. That is what Leslie is ensuring now. There are things we cannot tell you or anyone else now. But have trust in Leslie. He's a very clever and resourceful boy; you will see soon what I mean.'

***

'Erin, did you organise the auction of the stones?'

'Oh yes. That is in hand. Do you wish to see them now?'

'Oh indeed, sir,' he replied eagerly.

Erin removed a cloth bag from the safe and emptied the contents onto the desk. The stones glittered and sparkled. They were huge and beautifully cut. 'I had to get various gemstone cutters to do the work, and I only selected the very best,' Erin explained. 'These are the most valuable in the collection.'

Leslie turned the red diamonds in his hand. 'So exquisite, my friend.'

'They were cut by Harry Winston; he used to own the Hope Diamond. Leslie, the bonds are cashed, and the money is in your account. I suggest that, to get the best from the sale of the diamonds, we sell them at intervals. Flooding the market with so many large stones will devalue them. I took the liberty of anticipating your acceptance and have arranged to auction one red and one clear. The auctioneers have valued the two stones at around 150 million pounds each; they could go for more. I have kept your ownership of them secret, and I will deliver the stones to the auctioneers next week so they can do the publicity work. The auction will take place on the last Thursday of next month.

'Now,' he said grabbing a file from his desk, 'these are the portfolios of properties, and these are the companies that manage them. You will find that they are all located in the most exclusive areas of each city, and as such, they command good rental income. The management companies attend to any repairs and maintenance. May I suggest that, as you have a vast cash reserve, you retain the properties as continuing investment?'

'Thank you, Erin,' Leslie said. 'You have done well. I am glad I put my trust in you.'

'I am happy you think that way. Now to this business with Sir Alastair and Dr Hendricks, here's what I propose...'

***

Leslie left the offices and crossed the road to the coffee house, noting the security men's car a little way down the street. 'Thank you all for being so patient,' he said. 'I am sorry it was necessary to exclude you.' He turned to the waiter. 'Yes, could I have a tea please. No milk or sugar, thank you.'

Will took another sip of his strong black coffee. He felt excluded and wanted to know everything but had listened to his daughter. He decided that she knew her brother better than anybody did, and he would trust her and his son. One of the security men sat at a table near the door reading a newspaper and drinking coffee. *So much more discrete than Sir Alastair's hoodlums*, thought Leslie.

On the way back to the cottage, Leslie asked Tweety to put the car radio on. The last few bars of Bob Dylan's 'Just Like a Woman' faded to the news broadcast. 'J. Edgar Hoover announced that all the evidence indicates that Lee Harvey Oswald, the man who shot President John F Kennedy, acted alone.

'In other news, the multimillionaire business tycoon Sir Alastair Woodford was taken in for questioning by police and released without charge late last night, after spending several hours at Cannon Row Police Station. The police would not give a statement but say that the matter is not related to his recent arrest in Cayenne.

'And now the football results...'

'My God, son, what do you put on your cornflakes, magic dust?'

Everyone chuckled, and Tweety said, 'I certainly wish I had his talents.'

'Don't be so modest, Harry. You have talents of your own,' Leslie said. 'Few newshounds can sniff out a bone like you.'

More chuckles ensued.

At the cottage, they sat around the table trying to decide upon the story they would tell Susan. She must have alerted Mr Vance to their absence by now and maybe even reported it to the police. Mary and Leslie had been so occupied with other matters that they had not tuned in to check on her.

***

Leslie tuned into the events at the village.

Susan was at the front doors of Howard House polishing the brass nameplate and doorknobs but keeping an eye on the road to the gates. Vance was in the library talking on the telephone. The police were sifting through the remains of the lodge in relation to the Hendricks affair.

A man telephoned the mansion demanding to speak to Sir Alastair or Dr Hendricks on an urgent matter. He would not give any details except his name. It was a matter of the utmost importance, and he left a telephone number where he could be reached. Mr Vance asked Susan if she knew who George Thompson was.

'No, sir, I don't think I know the gentleman,' she said.

'No...' said Vance slowly, as if in deep thought, 'he sounds a most unpleasant character.'

***

Leslie told what he'd seen at the village to Mary telepathically and then the two discussed openly so as not exclude their father.

'We could say that we went to meet Sir Alastair as a surprise and it was us that got one instead when they carted him off,' Mary suggested.

'We followed by taxi and waited for him until quite late. We checked into a hotel and slept in late this morning. By the time we got back to Cannon Row, he had been released. And we figured he had come back to the village. We missed breakfast, so we went for some lunch. And on the way back, we went to visit Dr Hendricks, but the police would not let us enter.'

'It sounds plausible,' said Leslie. 'Ah, just one problem though. Jackson would have seen us at the police station had we been there. But then, Jackson says very little to anybody. He's not the chatty type. I think if we leave it so, we may get away with it. The time span is about right, give or take a half hour.'

Will looked distressed. 'When am I to see you again?'

'Do not worry, Dad,' said Mary. 'It will all come good soon, but you will need to prepare yourself for a court case. When do you think, Leslie?'

'Next month I would say, but we had better go now.'

They said their very emotional goodbyes, and Tweety drove Leslie and Mary to a spot just outside the village where he dropped them off. They thanked him and prepared to face Susan's wrath.

'We could just erase her memory,' said Leslie with a smile 'Oh and Vance's as well, and Joan's.'

'And the police if they have told them,' added Mary.

They giggled like naughty schoolchildren as they entered the gates.

They stopped near to the police car outside the lodge, observed the officers picking up scraps of papers and file covers from among the debris, and then continued toward the mansion to receive their admonishment for being so inconsiderate.

***

Sir Alastair was tired and refused to answer any more questions. 'No comment,' he replied to each one lobbed at him. His lawyer had advised him to remain silent.

'Sir, these are very serious allegations. If you continue to refuse to answer, we will have no choice but to charge you. If you have nothing to hide, let us clear this up, and we can all get some rest.'

Sir Alastair remained silent.

'Very well. Sergeant, take him away. And get him something to eat, will you?'

***

Will sat alone with his thoughts in the silent cottage. The strange things going on around him were puzzling. He made another mug of tea. Leslie had made some sort of proposal to the press, *perhaps an exclusive. Yes, that had to be it. They would get the story from Leslie and print a scoop. Why had he needed to see the lawyer alone? He had obviously been there several times. He and the lawyer were on first-name terms, and lawyers are expensive. How was Leslie going to pay for his services and the lunch?*

Leslie had invited everyone, including Tweety. Erin had paid the bill, but it was obvious to him who had sanctioned the payment. Then it dawned on him – *being a ward of Sir Alastair, one of the richest, if not the riches man in the country, Leslie probably got an allowance, a generous one, and Mary too.*

His clothes and Mary's were of fine quality and probably made to measure. The watches they both wore were top-notch. Perhaps these too came from their allowances.

Then another thought struck him. *We were together the whole time, so how did Leslie know what Sir Alastair's movements were and that the police would use the doctor to trap him, unless that was what he had discussed with Erin when they were alone.*

Mary had clearly known what they discussed; she told him Leslie was 'making them pay.'

That's it, he concluded. *Leslie and the lawyer had put some plan together to fix Sir Alastair, and Leslie had known exactly when to turn on the radio. It was well planned and executed. Mary's right,* he realised. *He is a bright boy.*

***

As expected, Leslie and Mary received a good telling off from Susan and again from Laurence; even Joan gave them an admonishing look. They apologised humbly for their lack of consideration and selfish behaviour, and it appeared to be convincing.

That night Leslie went over the results so far:

- The remains of Perry had been found officially and would soon be identified.
- The asylum was now closed, probably never to reopen.
- The inmates had been freed from their tormentors and could take their own legal actions against Hendricks and Sir Alastair if they so wished.

- ❖ He had claimed the inheritance, and the fund had been set up.
- ❖ As soon as Hendricks was fit enough, he would be carted off to prison and would then stand trial for a multitude of crimes.
- ❖ Thompson would be incriminated and imprisoned also.
- ❖ His father was home, and this was his greatest joy.
- ❖ He had found Thomas.
- ❖ He had the go-ahead to set up the magazine, with three very good and reliable men he considered close friends.
- ❖ He had someone honest and worthwhile running the village.
- ❖ He had a better relationship with his sister and confided in her about most things.
- ❖ He had reversed the dependency between the Atkins couple, and soon the drugs would run out.

In all, he was pleased with all that had been achieved so far, but there was still a long road ahead. This was no time to sit back and admire the achievements. He had urgent things to attend. He needed to find a site and set up the magazine, monitor the police investigations to ensure they asked the right questions, and find some way to get his dad involved in their enterprise and some employment for him. Then there was the matter of custody and the court cases to attend too.

He still had not launched the nuclear submarine that would sink the Woodford empire without trace. The fallout would be on a massive scale, and he, his friends, and his family would appear to have no part in it whatever, barring the exclusive inside information ready for publishing.

His submarine would be held back a while longer. He still had Walsh and Martins to deal with and their two colleagues. Perhaps they would be dealt with by the submarine. He had not decided their fate yet, but with Sir Alastair and Hendricks out of the picture, the henchmen had no orders. The police had yet to find Rob Lane's body; there was still plenty to do.

***

He slept soundly all night and, in the morning, enjoyed a hearty breakfast. He sent Mary a message. *We must find premises for the magazine. Let us discuss it with Ed this morning.* She nodded.

When Susan came in, Leslie told her that he and Mary would be going to see what they could find out about Dr Hendricks and the dean.

They walked to town in the cold morning air; the brisk walk was good for the circulation he had been told. At the office, they found that Tweety had brought Will with him. 'I couldn't leave him stuck in the house all day twiddling his thumbs.'

'A good idea,' said Mary.

'Now, we need to find premises, Ed. Any ideas on what sort of space you will need? I would like to get this underway before the court cases start piling up.'

Whilst Leslie and Ed discussed the requirements, Mary sat in the corner of the office with her father, listening to her brother motivating this wise old man. Will tried to put the pieces together without the knowledge required to do so. Mary heard his thoughts and said, 'All will become clear to you soon, Dad.'

Leslie jumped up with a start. 'The police have charged both Sir Alastair and Hendricks with kidnapping on a grand scale, and they are under arrest.'

No one had expected the sudden outburst.

'How do you know?' asked Ed.

'Take my word for it; it will be on the eleven o'clock news.' He turned to the others. 'Hey, Ed has seen a site up for sale that would suit perfectly; shall we go and see it now?'

***

Leslie had expected the arrests to come, and it was with Ed's assistance that they had achieved it. After a private meeting, Erin had telephoned Ed on Leslie's behalf and authorised him to hand all the original files from the lodge to DCI Royston. In the meantime, Erin had called Royston and explained about the files that would arrive shortly. It was volatile ammunition.

An arrest warrant had been issued to apprehend Thompson. Leslie knew he had gone on the run, feeling deserted by his co-conspirators. Leslie would let him run for a while. He had spent years hunting children for the village; now he could become the hunted.

Chapter 24

A Time to Sow Seeds and Gather In

Ed, Will, and his children arrived at the site and met with the agent. The site was listed as 'for sale or to let', so Leslie asked Ed if a let was a more viable idea. He explained that a let was better for short term but that purchasing was preferable for the long term. Leslie was happy for Ed's guidance in these matters. He noticed that the site had good access from the road and was close to the centre of town.

Leslie asked his father to check for security weak spots across the site and make recommendations to improve them.

'What kind of attack are you expecting, son?' Will asked.

'Well, not a major assault, Dad, but things like intruder alarms and automatic lights, that sort of thing.'

'I know, son. Just trying to get a rise out of you. You look as though you are planning a campaign.'

'I suppose that in a way we are – a sort of crusade if you like. We will have to take risks at times and could be a target; I want to keep my friends as safe as possible.'

They wandered around the outside of the building, and Will pointed out the weak spots. 'What is that land to the side of the property. It looks like a farm to me.'

'It is a farm, and this land used to belong to the farmer until he sold it.'

Inside the building, Ed indicated where the printing machinery, inks store, paper, forklifts, storage, and so forth could go. After a couple of hours, they decided that this was the site for them.

Back at the office, Leslie called Erin and gave him the number for the agent and the address of the site.

Leslie struck a prominent pose, addressing each person in turn. From Ed, he wanted a list of machinery, equipment, and materials with estimated costs, along with staffing levels, typical salaries, and a first print run estimation. For the first few runs, they would use a courier service to deliver to the outlets. Then they would re-evaluate whether their own vehicles would be more beneficial. A lot depended on uptake and circulation.

Leslie enquired about the progress on the story on the police force's mishandling of investigations. Tweety had almost completed it and would need another week at the most. He charged the newsman with its completion and noted it would need checking by Ed.

Confident that Tweety would produce the goods, he assigned him the task of preparing an advertising campaign for the launch of the magazine. Billy would source the advertising and forthcoming events.

They would have the resources of a lawyer, one who had been highly recommended by Erin. The lawyer's position was to check for legal points in the drafts before final publication. If the magazine became a success, they would take on a lawyer full-time.

Leslie reminded Ed to include telephones, telex and/or fax machines, photocopiers, a large fireproof safe, and clocks, several of them to show the different times around the world's many time zones. He should also figure in the costs of office staff and what they would need. 'Leave nothing out. Look around the premises where you work and source the very latest models. Everything must be modern and up to date.'

By thought transmittance, Mary reminded Ed that he had been gifted a partnership in this enterprise.

'Oh and figure in a refrigerator, a kettle, mugs, and beverages. Let's have the mugs printed with our names, that way we can see who never washes up.'

The last items brought a round of applause. Leslie had noticed how much tea and coffee they all drunk, and they all knew who it was who never washed his mug.

Will watched all of this spellbound. Was this really his sixteen-year-old son – ordering, inspiring, and controlling grown men with years of experience, in a business he had little or no experience in? He couldn't make sense of what he saw and heard. Nevertheless, he was suitably impressed by his son's confidence; Leslie had conducted these affairs with a sense of purpose and order, and it was clear that he had planned well. He must have worked on this for a long time. He was like the conductor of an orchestra, the music clear in his head, controlling and transmitting his interpretation to the players and driving them to deliver.

'The last thing is a name; we need a name for the magazine. Any ideas?'

'What?' exclaimed Will. 'You've thought of everything except a name?'

'Well I have a name in mind, Dad. But I want to hear other suggestions, and when we get a list we can decide by vote. I think that is fair, no?'

They all agreed with the lad and Ed suggested they all take some time to consider a name for the magazine.

Leslie had a sudden thought that had not occurred to him before.

'Dad, do you have a suit?'

'What do I need a suit for? I'm not selling the magazine door to door.'

'No, Dad, for the court. You will need to make a good impression for the custody case.'

'No,' Will answered. 'I didn't need one in Hong Kong.'

'Right then, off we go.' He turned to his sister. 'Do you want to come, Mary?' Looking at her, he saw that she was gazing at Billy, who was taking notes.

'Oh... Yes...of course,' she answered distractedly. 'See you all later.'

***

In Saville Row, Leslie took his father to a different tailor than the one he had used before with Sir Alastair. 'Now, Dad, you will have to look your best and appear to be a man of means. It is most important that you give a good impression; you will be competing with his lordship. And if you wish me to help you choose, just let me know,' he said, leading his father into the shop.

Will had never owned a suit in his life. The nearest thing was his dress uniform for ceremonies and special occasions, but he had long left all that behind.

Observing the different weaves and thicknesses, he felt the different cloths and textures. He could not decide what colour would suit him best, and Mary sent him a message – charcoal grey with the vertical stripes, the wool mix.

After the measuring and decisions had been made, they went to purchase some other clothes for Will, shirts and such. Mary was also in need of a new wardrobe. She was fast outgrowing the clothes she had. Leslie felt he could last with his for now.

'Dad, do you drive?'

'Of course I drive, since before I was your age too.'

'Right we need to buy a car.'

They left their purchases in the care of the tailor. 'Ah, Dad, do you have a current driving licence by any chance?'

'The one I have will cover me until I am sixty-five years old, son. Now, I know my hair is white, and I am a lot older than you—'

'Okay, Dad. Sorry. It is just that you will need it for tax and insurance. That's all I meant. And I thought that perhaps, living in China, you did not have one or need one; I do not know what I thought really—'

'Ok son, I understand. Your head is so full of what is right and wrong, black and white, and red tape and procedure. You like to stick to the rules, and that's good, son. I'm glad you're the person you are; you make me feel proud to be your father and ashamed I had nothing to do with who you've become.'

'Now do not talk that way. Without you, I would not be here. Neither would Mary.'

Will put his arms around these blossoming adults walking either side of him. A single unnoticed tear welled in his eye, and he was the luckiest man on earth.

'What car should we buy then, Dad?' asked Mary.

'Well, as I don't really know what you are both up to, and given the sinister overtones to it all, I would say it should be ordinary – something that will be reliable but won't attract attention. Second-hand would be best I think. New cars always turn heads. Maybe an Austin… But that may be a bit small for me. No, tell you what, let's get our stuff home and then go and look in that second-hand car place in Ilford we passed yesterday.'

They decided after test-driving several cars that a four-year-old Ford Consul MkII would suit their purposes. It was roomy and could carry them and two or three other passengers if need be; the boot was spacious, and it drove like a dream. The one they tested was a bright red colour. Prompted by Leslie, Will asked for it to be repainted in black; as there were so many black cars on the road, it would not stand out. The deal done, they could pick up the car next week.

It bewildered his father how Leslie was going to pay for everything. He had no way of knowing that these expenses would cost Leslie virtually nothing – all he had spent would come from interest he was earning.

***

Leslie arranged with Erin that the trust should comprise of many smaller accounts that fed each other on a monthly basis; one of the recipient accounts would fund the village. Laurence Vance and his colleagues would be recompensed and able to continue running the village, without having to resort to using their own money.

Thomas was now close to being the person that Leslie remembered, but there was a major problem – not just with him but with other inmates as well. These people had passed many years in a drugged state, with no access to radio, television, or newspapers. They could not know of the events that had occurred during their incarcerations, and Leslie asked Mary to help him to put this right. He made a list of the main topics and gave his sister a copy; they sat and discussed it until Mary had a clear idea of its purpose and content.

Then Leslie realised that his idea of 'educating' the inmates would interfere with the police investigations. 'Mary, we shall have to put this on hold until after the convictions. If we inform the inmates of these events, we shall be weakening our case and those of the inmates who wish to sue. No, this will not do, we must do this later, though it hurts me to leave them so confused.'

***

It had been many years since Thomas had been able to exercise his powers, and as Leslie lay in bed, he received a message from his old friend.

Do you remember when we went to the river and you were so terrified you almost wet yourself? And when we scrumped apples from the orchard and nearly got caught? It is all coming back to me, Leslie – those days we had, those golden days. I wish we could return to them and continue the journey together. Thank you for doing as you promised. It was not a promise you should have made, but I am so glad you did…

Thomas's voice faded as Leslie became aware of Mary standing over him. 'Are you okay, Leslie? I could feel an intrusion. What happened?'

Leslie calmed her and explained that Thomas was like them. No, he could not float – visit places out of his body, whatever the name for it – but he could communicate just like them. He was telepathic.

This revelation put some fear into Mary. *Leslie, after all they have done to him, he could be a pawn. They could be using him to relay everything back to them. Tell him nothing, Leslie. Be careful, so careful of what you reveal to him. I demand that you listen to me.*

Her voice boomed in his head with such a power it shocked him. She had used this method with others before, but seldom with Leslie and usually she was subtler.

He agreed that she could be right. Why had they felt it necessary to keep Thomas drugged? He could not work on the cipher that way. Perhaps they had thought that he could still be of some use to them at a later stage. They knew about his skill and prevented him from using it to transmit their plans to others. Yes, they could have brainwashed him, waiting for the moment to release him and put him to good use. If he were of no use to them, surely they would have disposed of him as they had with so many others. If Thomas was under the control of Woodford and Hendricks, that would be the ultimate betrayal for Leslie. He did not want to believe it could be true, but had to concede that there was risk in revealing too much to Thomas.

***

DCI Royston sent a team to Somerset House to try to trace any living relatives of the inmates. They spent weeks sifting through records of births, deaths, and marriages. They quickly found that Thomas had an uncle living in Scotland and made contact with him. He was horrified to hear of the young man's circumstances and had not known that his brother had married because they had lost touch. The team also unearthed relatives of five more patients and contacted them as well. In each case, the stories were similar. Some of the 'patients' were supposed to have died in accidents and others due to serious illnesses. The relatives of some never knew the person existed.

The forensics department established that the partly decomposed body was that of Peregrine Collins. The cause of death was not clear, but there was damage to the skull. It may have been the result of a fall or a blow.

Dr Hendricks had refused to answer a single question regarding the asylum or the village. Royston and his team had showed him the files and the photographs, but he had not reacted in the least. They'd questioned him about the involvement of George Thompson. How long had he and Thompson been acquiring children from other institutions? How was it that these children were all orphans? Who was Gregory Walsh and where was he? The questioning went on and on without results. The police knew many of the answers because they were in the files Leslie had provided. A team had also gone to the academy to interview the boys there. None of the cadets had spoken a word against the Dr or Sir Alastair. They would only say that they had enjoyed a happy childhood and received a good education; they were indebted to the doctor and the dean.

Leslie arrived unseen as Royston began to read the file on the Mathews girl. The officer sent for the police report into the death of the girl's father. It was suspicious that he'd died just before she moved to the village, and Royston wanted to know who the investigating officers were and how they had reached their conclusions.

Dr Hendricks had used a code to hide information in the files of the children at the village. The information related to how, when, and where the child had been orphaned. It had puzzled the police for some time, and then help had arrived. Leslie had solved it straight away because he knew how Hendricks worked with puzzles. He planted an idea in the mind of Sergeant Muir. The sergeant obtained some graph paper and set out the letters of the alphabet across the top, one letter to each square. In the squares below, he entered the numbers 1 to 26 under the letters, but the result did not correspond to the letters he had. He then rewrote the numbers starting with A=26, B=1, C=2, and so on. The sets of numbers resulted in MFTMJF KPIOT, exactly what he saw in the file. By moving the letters back again a step, it produced Leslie Johns. 'Sir, look at this. I think we have the answers now.'

Muir didn't know where the inspiration had come from, but the code was so simple a child could solve it. For each letter, you moved back one letter of the alphabet. When he saw the letters XBMTI, he knew it spelled Walsh. That name became familiar in many of the files. The main text of the coded notes was in German; Sgt Muir could read only names. He spent hours transcribing the notes and periodically took them for translation, and it revealed the horrendous lengths these people had gone to.

Three more names became mainstays in the village files, and warrants were issued for the arrests of John Martins, Michael Sterling, and Peter Gibbons. Royston figured out that the last two names were associates of

Walsh and Martins. Five suspects were now at large, four of whom were extremely dangerous, especially if they were together.

***

Leslie smiled quietly and passed the information he had obtained to Mary.

'So, are all the hooks now in the stream?' she asked.

'The big fish are about to meet the sharks,' he answered.

'Good,' she said. 'I love a fish supper! How did you do it?

He explained the code to her and how it worked.

'Make mine a large fillet and no chips please.' She smacked her lips in anticipation.

***

Laurence Vance could not believe his eyes when he checked his bank statement. He then checked the village funding account and found it well financed; enough was in the account for a year at least. He called the other housemasters and asked if they had checked their personal bank accounts. None had recently but intended to do so straight away.

The housemasters held a meeting in the library. 'So where do you think this money has come from?' one asked. 'Sir Alastair has hardly been allowed to pop out to the bank,' another ventured, 'and I think—'

Vance stopped the idle chatter and conjecture. 'It is not clear where the money has come from, but it is possible that Sir Alastair has calculated the costs and authorised his lawyers to transfer the funds. I told you that he would not let us down. Now we seem to be in a bit of a spot. The dean has returned but only in a manner speaking. We still have to run the village. I am sure the courts will acquit him of any wrongdoing, and we must press on and show that he can rely upon us. The village is in our hands, safe hands. Are we agreed?'

All in attendance answered as one, 'Yes, sir.'

'Good,' he said. 'We have always given our children 100 per cent. We will endeavour to continue doing just that and to maintain the proud reputation and standing that befits the village. Am I right?'

Again, all agreed; they committed that they would continue to give the best of care to all of the children living in the village.

The only master not at the meeting was the only one of them who knew of the village's true purpose. The drugs had run out, and it was only sugar now in Mr Atkins tea. In a few days, he would be back to his normal self, but he would have to keep his mouth shut. And so would his wife – if they wanted to stay in the village. The loyalty of the other masters to Sir Alastair was born of ignorance of his purpose, and the housemasters would doubtless force the couple to leave.

***

Will and his children went to collect their car.

It stood proud and magnificent on the forecourt of the car sales lot. Will examined every inch of it looking for flaws and could find not even a fingerprint. He was now the proud owner of a perfectly new, old car. He lifted the bonnet, and the engine gleamed and sparkled; not a speck of dirt or a trace of oil stains could be spotted. He turned to the manager and asked who had done the work on it.

'The lad yonder, sir. He is the best mechanic I have ever had working for me.'

Leslie hid himself behind his father. 'Shall we go now, Dad?' he said, keeping his father between him and the young mechanic.

'In a minute, son' he said, looking toward the mechanic as he spoke. I shall bring the car here for servicing and any work that it may need doing in the future. A really excellent job, sir. Thank you. I am most impressed.'

Will was about to go over to the young mechanic when Leslie tugged his sleeve. 'We must go now, Dad. Now!'

Will could see no reason to rush. These people had done a good job, and he wanted to show his respect and admiration.

'Now,' said Mary, 'I told you to trust Leslie in all things. We must go now.'

They got into the car and left the dealership. As they drove, Will asked, 'What in God's name was that about, Leslie? I felt embarrassed by—'

'Dad, please' he momentarily met his father's eyes in the rear-view mirror. 'If I say something in future, could you please not question it?' The boy felt uncomfortable speaking in such a manner to his father, and expanded upon the reason for his alarm. 'We may all be in grave danger now. Don't you see, Dad. The garage has the address of the cottage where you are staying. They already know that we were previously at the village—'

'What is it, Leslie?' Mary interjected. 'You recognised the mechanic, didn't you? Is he someone to be feared?'

'No, no, it isn't him. It's his father! Mary, I know that mechanic from River House… Oh God, what have we done? His father is Greg Walsh!'

'Walsh, you know that bastard, that son of Satan's spawn? How do you know of him?' demanded Will.

Mary again had to calm her father. 'Dad, be calm. Please be calm because it is important that Leslie stays calm. If you get alarmed, he gets alarmed, and we do not know what could happen. Listen to me, and listen well. Leslie is not to stress or become overexcited since his operation. Dad, Leslie had a massive brain tumour removed, and we must stay calm to calm him as well. Help me with this, Daddy, and be calm for him.'

Will had to stop the car. He found the news his daughter had just delivered hard to accept. 'He had a brain tumour?

'Dad we agreed not to tell you. It is done, and it was something you did not need to know. We didn't want you to feel sorry for him or in some way blame yourself. It was nobody's fault, Dad, just one of those things that happen to people. Do you understand now what I'm saying about being calm?'

There was a long pause as Will absorbed the information his daughter had unwillingly revealed. *A brain tumour drives people mad, doesn't it? Is my son mad? He certainly fits the bill. Delusions of grandeur, setting up business with strangers, buying stuff that will cost thousands of pounds, ordering people around as if he is the lord of the manor. And all with an air of 'Money doesn't matter' like a grandee of old, like Sir Alastair perhaps. Maybe that is where this affliction comes from…*

Mary broke into his thoughts. 'Dad, let us go now and get Leslie to his bed. He can rest at the cottage for a while, and you cannot be seen at the village.'

***

Whilst Leslie rested, Mary went down to the car parked a little way up the street. 'I wonder if I could ask you something?'

The man in the car said, 'Fire away, Miss.'

When she had finished talking, he said. 'I am sure we can, but I will have to clear it with my boss first – you know, protocol.'

Leslie had dreams that afternoon during his nap; voices appealed to him. 'Help us, help us; we are in such dire need of your help. We need your help, Leslie, dear sweet boy. Such a dear boy… We love you so, Leslie. … We are the friends, are we not? … You like to play the games. … I have a different game for you now. Close those beautiful eyes, Leslie. What do you see? If I uncover the cloth, you have five seconds, Leslie, five seconds only. Leslie, read me this. Leslie how many can you remember? … My dear friend, my dear, dear friend, how long have you felt this way? We must examine the root of this discomfort. Tell me your deepest desires. Tell me what excites you and what makes you afraid. … You owe us, Leslie; we have cared for you and grown you into the man you are today. You owe us much, Leslie, much indeed. Everything has its price, Leslie. … There are many who would die to be in your place.'

Leslie awoke screaming. 'No, no, no, noooo. I will not bend to your will. I will not be as you, perverted and twisted.'

Will rushed to his room with Mary cutting him off at the point of entry. 'No, Dad. Please, you must let him work out his demons. I will protect him. I promise, Dad.'

All that had occurred bewildered Will. He could understand the strong bond existing between his children; they'd only had each other all those years in his absence. He recalled his words from so far back in time, under the porch light on a cold dark night at a house full of girls. *Take good care of my boy now. I love you both, but I must go now. Kiss him for me.* And he remembered her promise to do so. He had not meant it to take over her life as it apparently had. He could see that she alone understood her brother and knew how to handle him. His sorrow was an issue of guilt and gullibility. He had not been there to provide help and support, and he now had to get to know his children anew. Like turning acquaintances into friends, it would take some time and patience.

Leslie went downstairs to the living room where Mary and Will sat by the roaring fire. He looked pale and drawn.

'What did you dream, Leslie?' his sister asked.

He told her of his dream and the torment. 'They want me to help them, but I cannot and will not. They communicate when I am sleeping. I do not know if I am subconsciously connecting to them or they are using a conduit to connect to me.'

'Thomas,' whispered Mary.

'I hope not. I do hope not, Mary.'

The conversation baffled Will, and he went to make a pot of tea. He knew now not to comment or show his ignorance; he had to just trust his children.

***

Leslie decided that it was time to reveal to Will how they had known he was in Hong Kong. He related the stories of the incident in Oxford, the lead given to Ed by Roger Garner, and the contact with Norris Dwyer and his information about the PO box. The rest he knew. Leslie also told his father of the demise of Douglas Fairbrother. And as they sat sipping their mugs of tea, Will's mind flooded with memories of past escapades with his old friends. 'All this was to find me? But surely you must have believed me to be dead?'

'I had considered the idea at times but refused to accept it. Something told me you were out there somewhere. I realise from what I know now; you were unaware that we had not been killed in a car accident. Ed used his network of connections to track you down. Tweety also put in a tremendous amount of work, sifting through the army records of all Essex regiments until he discovered where your parents came from. He had to start all over again with the Tigers. Perhaps now you can see how Mary and I have developed the relationship with those three at the paper that has puzzled you?'

'Roger and Swifty, my word… It takes me back. I can understand your trust in these men at the paper and the friendship between you. You have both done well to choose the right people to help you. Is this why you are setting up a magazine – to repay them?'

'Not exactly, Dad. Let me explain to you our reasons. You must have seen many evil and twisted people in your life during your army days in the war. Many bad things happened in the name of 'right'; the ends may or may not have justified the means, and it is not for me to judge. Anyway, we too have seen evil – the evil of power and its manipulation to the purposes of a few at the cost of many. We want to create a voice to speak out against it. We require people we can trust, and they must have a moral standard that suits our purpose. Ed, Tweety, and Billy fit perfectly into that slot; they are like-minded, although Billy is the most cautious. They have the knowledge and experience to determine what they can or cannot publish. Ed was a freelance journalist in his younger days, but things turned bad for him, and he hit rock bottom. The owner of the local paper had read his articles. He offered him a job as a reporter and then promoted him to editor. Ed has had many offers from national papers, but he's stayed here out of gratitude and loyalty. He is the type of person we need to spearhead our magazine.

'Tweety is dogged and persistent, a real newshound who can spot a story where others cannot. Billy is the youngest and least experienced, but he has an appetite for the job, he is honest in his work, and he gets to the facts and leaves invention to others less diligent or less talented. Both Tweety and Billy show respect and honesty in their work. And above all, they admire and respect Ed for his integrity and wealth of knowledge. There is a reward involved in this enterprise; we have gifted Ed a quarter share of the magazine, along with you, Mary, and me.'

'My boy, how can one so young be so astute? You are an amazing person in how you see people.' He smiled at the boy, 'but why me? I know nothing about journalism or printing. I know about security work, and I am handy at carpentry and such, but a magazine?'

Mary reassured him. 'Dad, you do not have to work at the magazine or for it. We included you because it is the right thing to do. We have no idea of your plans for the future, and you may not even wish to remain here in England. You have a life in Hong Kong. There may be commitments for you there that draw you back.' Mary had cast the hook.

Will thought about what Mary had said. 'Look, I have friends and a job; my employers were kind enough to give me an extended leave. But I have no family or children there. You are my family, the family I believed for so long were lost to me. No, I will not be returning to Hong Kong. My place is here with you, even though you look ready to fly the nest. We have a lot of catching up to do, and I can see that you have more to tell me.'

Mary looked at her watch. 'Dad, we must be going now. We do not want another telling off from Susan.'

They hugged and arranged to meet the next day.

At supper, Mary and Leslie talked their silent talk. *Well, Mary, you did that with some expertise, getting dad to reveal his situation.*

A question of using the right bait on the hook. But who am I to tell you about fishing? Replied Mary.

Well, now we know he intends to stay. Perhaps we should tell him all. He is confused by what we say sometimes, and he feels strongly that we are excluding him. He is desperate to rebuild relationships, and is unsure if it is possible. And yet, Mary, I feel he is keeping something back from us – something he either does not want us to know or is looking for a way to tell us, something he has blocked from me.

I know. I can feel it too. It has something to do with his life in Hong Kong because he thinks of the place often; he blocks it from me too. I am sure he will tell us when he feels that he can. Leslie, we are unsure of what to reveal to him; he is feeling the same. For now, for the short term, we must be careful what we reveal.

Leslie was in accord with his sister; they needed to be sure about their father.

***

Chief Superintendent Alan Doone headed for the conference room with a wad of papers in his hand. The press had gathered by open invitation to hear a statement on the Woodford and Hendricks cases. Doone read out his prepared statement, outlining the charges against each of the accused. He added that five men were being sought the length and breadth of the country in connection with this case. He gave the names and descriptions of each of the suspects, pointing out that four of them were considered dangerous, possibly armed, and that members of the public should not approach them.

The barrage of questions then began, along with the flashing of camera bulbs, almost blinding Doone as he attempted to give the best answers he could, without tipping his hand or that of Royston. DCI Royston stood by Doone's side and answered the questions passed to him. After three quarters of an hour, Doone closed the meeting with his thanks to the press.

Tweety already knew much of the subject matter, thanks to Leslie's constant updates. He had to show his face among the fraternity to justify the story that would appear in the magazine, with his name on it. He could not write about an event he had not attended, but he wondered how Leslie had known about the press release before the paper had received the invitation. He had told Tweety the place, date, and time two days before Doone made his decision public. Leslie's network of contacts must include police officers, and senior ones at that.

***

'Daddy, can you tell us some stories about China, about the people and the food, the sights and such?'

Seated in the living room of the cottage, in front of the warm cosy fire that glowed, faded and glowed again, Leslie watched as the small flames danced and competed here and there. Mary's question was in her 'little girl' voice, giving her father the opportunity to reveal his hidden secrets.

'Well, where do I start? China is a wonderful and beautiful country, I have been to the Great Wall and walked along parts of it. Workers are restoring it where the centuries have wreaked their havoc upon it, and it is a sight to behold when you first see it.

'Hongcun, an ancient village in Anhui is one of the most beautiful places on earth, it has a lake called Moon Lake, and it is fantastic, beautiful, serene, and enchanting. Huangshan Mountain stands in the background and adds such magic to the surroundings. Oh, you should see it. I believe it is my favourite place on this planet. I have seen many countries and admired their beauty, but this place is heaven itself. Melancholic mists shroud the mountain, and you can believe that you see the ghosts from the past. Peaks jut out above the mists and point sharply at the sky, almost accusing in their gestures. Heaven is not there up above; it is here, down here where we are. It truly is a magical place, and maybe someday I will take you both so that you can experience the uplifting spirit of the magic I found there.

'Then there is a beauty of a different kind in Fujian. Mount Wuyi, what a place, a lake with a flat-topped mountain in the background and a waterfall cascading down to a river that feeds the lake. The waters are so clear and tranquil it's like looking into a mirror.

'In Yangzhou, the food is fresh from the river and lake and always cooked to order. A boat trip from there rewarded me with vistas unseen anywhere else, but if you want to see something spectacular and deafening, the Huangguoshu Waterfall at Guizhou is just the job. I was deaf for a whole day afterwards.

'In my many journeys in China, I have found that the people are the friendliest of any other nation I have encountered. Once you get away from the hustle and bustle of the cities, the countryfolk who have so little give the most. They are an amazing race of peoples, and I have many true, loyal friends there. Don't get me wrong. The Chinese are suspicious of foreigners, but once you gain their trust, you can rely on them for anything, for life.

'At first I found it hard to develop the taste for raw seafood near the coastal areas, and rice, which is the main accompaniment to every dish.

Back here. I miss the food; I guess I have become a victim to the Chinese way of life. The smells from the stalls on the streets attract not only tourists but the locals as well. Why cook when you can eat five-star, on the street?'

Will's words and the images they painted held Leslie and Mary spellbound; the pictures his father described fitted so well with the ones Leslie had gleaned from books. He could smell the ginger and five-spice aromas and the pleasant odour of freshly caught fish cooking, could taste the seaweed mingling with oils and spices. Leslie was feeling and living this experience, absorbing the sensations from his father's account.

Will told his stories so well; he bewitched his captive audience.

'Daddy tell us more, please.' Mary was determined to get to his secret, 'you have been there so long, you must have so many friends. Please tell us about them, go on Daddy, tell us.'

Will had his secret, and he did not want to reveal it just yet. But her voice pulled his secret from him, and he could not resist. He fought it as best he could, but he had to concede. His efforts futile, he related what Mary and Leslie wanted to know. 'It was many years ago that I first saw Martha. I had just gone through a divorce from your mother, here in England. The way your mother dealt you such brutal treatment that no child should suffer' He broke into tears, absorbed by the memories of those days so long ago. For him, it was now; the pain hurt him, cutting and searing him as his son's blood seeped between his fingers and his daughter's terrified expression filled his mind; those images had never left him and could never leave him.

'Daddy, don't cry' Mary said softly.

'I met a lovely Irish girl, the sweetest thing that heaven ever created; I fell in love with her the moment our eyes met. She could reach so deep into me; I felt she could tear my heart out with a single pull. I was smitten. We met at every possible occasion and' he looked from one to the other, well, you do not need to know.' Will stiffened up and spread his broad shoulders. 'Where was I? Oh yes, we were talking about China.'

'Daddy you were talking about Martha. Where is she now?' asked Mary.

'Forget about Martha. I do not want to talk about her and how fate separated us.' Will fell back in his chair, filled with his memories of the love of his life, a love so brief and yet so deep... Their father had his own demons to deal with, but this was the catalyst, the revelation that would cement the bond between this father and his offspring.

'Daddy, hug me so tightly.' He pulled his darling girl close. 'I feel your loss and your pain. Tell me what she was like, Martha.'

Will had no words to explain. He was engrossed in his daughter's concern for him. He snapped himself out of the emotional condition he had allowed himself to fall into. 'There are some things you do not need to know. My private life is none of your concern!'

Mary could see the barriers being erected and had seen it before with her brother. 'Daddy, do not shut us out. We want to learn all about you. We have been apart so many years, we are virtually strangers' she said.

Ooh, that did it. It hit the spot. 'I promise I will never be a stranger to you ever again. My poor children, I should never have left you, but I was in the army, and that made things so difficult. Your grandmother could not look after you when she became ill. It broke me into pieces to leave you in that place. St Vincent's had a good reputation and I could not look after you then.

'My plan was to finish my army service and then take you out of there. When you are in the armed forces, you have to obey orders, and it is no life for a single man with two small children. When I received that telegram, my world crashed down upon me. I was so depressed I just wanted to join you, to die, and give you comfort in that other world. I even put myself in harm's way purposely, risking death so that I could be with you. What that man has put me through I hope you will never experience in your lifetimes.'

Leslie sat silently, listening to his father and reliving his visits to Perry. The bond he had had with that man was the one he should have had with this man with the mass of white hair seated opposite him, a man he could and should hug, often. He said nothing; he went to his father and hugged him tightly.

Will could feel the emotion that the boy had not shown before now. It surged through him with the hug, and the tears that dropped onto his shoulder burned as they wet his shirt and touched his skin. He wanted to hold his children for eternity; the hug told him all he needed to know. Forgiven for the past, he had done what any responsible father would have done. He had no need to blame or punish himself anymore. A huge weight lifted from him, the weight he had borne for so long, bearing oppressively down upon his shoulders, was now gone. He felt light and invigorated. 'Thank you, son,' he said as Leslie released his grip.

He turned to Mary. 'You asked me about Martha. I will keep no secrets from you. It must have been in the mid-fifties. I was stationed on Stonecutters Island, Kowloon, an army base. That's where I met her. She was an Irish girl who worked in the pay corps. I had a German shepherd called Oscar, and I was putting him through his paces when I noticed her watching us. I was not aware of her at first. I was concentrating on Oscar.

'He was the most intelligent dog I'd ever had. He obeyed every command instantly. He watched me for the hand signals he knew so well. I could get him to sit at 700 yards without a word. At that distance, I could make him speak, lie down, stand, sit, or roll over with the movements of my hand or arm. Anyway, that particular day, she was there, fascinated by the dog I suppose. Or it could have been my control over him. I never asked. We got to talking, and I realised how beautiful she was, not in a glamorous pin-up sort of way. Hers was a plain and simple beauty. We became very close, and she even talked of us getting married. I had gone through a very bitter experience with your mother. I had loved her from the moment I saw her – your mother that is. But she was unfaithful. Whenever I was away, she would be with this chap or that – some of them pals of mine. It was all too much. The arguments started, and she would take it out on you two when I was not there to protect you.

'Anyway, when I was posted to Cyprus, Martha looked after Oscar for me, and again when I was posted to Kenya or wherever. Oscar adored her and protected her like she was his master, and each time I returned to the island we resumed our friendship.

'We carried on our relationship, and then I was posted again. And whilst away, I was told she had become ill with throat cancer. It was the most awful of times. They told me that the cancer ate her away. She lost two stones in a month, and by the time she died, she was barely seven stones. It broke my heart. And on top of that, Oscar died very shortly after her. Everything I loved in this world…gone.' He sobbed. 'And each time, I was not around to give help or support.'

He dried his eyes. 'I threw myself into my work, not wanting to have the time to think of them. Even my time off I filled with things to do, like mending roofs or making things from wood, decorating, anything to keep me from thinking of them. Eventually it all caught up with me. I had kept my emotions so tightly bottled up inside me for years, and then I had a nervous breakdown. I was in hospital for several months and given this drug and that, until a doctor told me that I should see a Chinese doctor with a reputation for healing the sick of mind.

'Dr Ma was brilliant. He used herbal medicines and acupuncture. Within weeks I was much better. He got me to talk about the things that had driven me to that state of mind. I talked and talked, more than I had ever done with anyone I realise now. I exorcised my fears and expressed my grief freely.

'Later, I got myself a job doing security work for a large company in Hong Kong and spent my time mostly training dogs. Dr Ma deduced that I needed something to focus my feelings on, and he suggested the dog training. It is the best job in the world, and I must admit that I miss it. I suppose that the dogs were a substitute for you two. I mean, watching them grow from puppies and teaching them tricks, observing their reactions to different sounds and smells and chasing their tails, and laughing as they chased a leaf caught by the wind and twisting this way and that was very healing. You should see the expressions on their faces at some new sound, the way they tilt their heads from one side to the other.' In his mind he could picture what he had just told them. 'Yes, I do so miss my dogs.'

Leslie and Mary could feel that their father had released his soul to them. He had opened his heart and told them his fears and sorrows. 'Dad, why not open a training school here? We will finance the setting up. Do you agree, Mary?'

She nodded in agreement.

'You can have your own school and your own dogs. Hey, we can advertise in the magazine and get people to come to you for training—'

'Now hold on, son. Isn't there something you need to tell me first? Like where all this money comes from that you so easily spend? The magazine, the car, the clothes, and now a dog school? Money doesn't grow on trees. I know that. So, come on, tell me.'

Leslie looked at his sister and then said, 'Dad, as wards of Sir Alastair, we each get very generous allowances. We have no need to buy anything much and our savings multiply with compounded interest. We also made some investments and held them for a while. When the values went up, we waited and then sold them. When values went down, we bought more. When I graduated from Oxford, the dean was very generous indeed.' Leslie was not ready to reveal the truth behind the source of the money to his father and Mary agreed.

'You...you graduated from Oxford?'

'Oh yes,' said Mary. 'He graduated with honours in French and Spanish. He is brilliant at Greek and Latin as well, and now he is learning Portuguese. We should be going now,' she added, tapping her watch and looking at Leslie. 'Susan.'

As they left the cottage, Mary let Leslie walk ahead of her. She waved at the parked car. The lights flashed once. A man got out and followed them to the village on the other side of town.

***

As the children neared Howard House, they caught a glimpse of a furtive figure, a shadow in the moonlight, down near the vicar's house.

'Quickly, inside,' urged Leslie. He bolted the door behind them and went to the telephone on the hall dresser. 'Make sure Susan, Joan, and Cook are okay,' he told his sister. 'Hello, yes the police, please. It is urgent. I need to speak to DCI Royston or one of his team.'

In less than ten minutes, they could hear the distant sounds of police cars weaving through the late rush hour traffic; they turned off the bells well before reaching the village. A police Jaguar pulled up outside the mansion, and Leslie opened the door to DCI Royston, accompanied by Muir and Waters.

'Was it you who called us, lad?' said Royston

'Yes, officer. We cannot find Susan or Joan. They are the housemaids—'

'Now calm yourself, lad. Let's have your names first.'

'Leslie and Mary Johns, sir. We are wards of Sir Alastair Woodford, but Susan—'

'Yes, we will get to that. You said wards. Then he is your guardian. You know, of course, that he is in custody?'

'Yes, sir, we heard it on the radio' said Leslie, wanting to get the focus back to Susan and Joan.

Royston could see the anxiety on the boy's face. 'Okay then, this Susan, you say she is missing? When did you last see her?'

'This morning before we went out, sir.'

'Could she be out somewhere? Shopping? Boyfriend?'

'No sir, she would have been here for supper, and she rarely goes out. I am concerned they are holding her as a hostage, sir.'

'When you say *they*, you mean Walsh and his men?'

'Yes, sir. They are hiding in the vicar's cottage, all four of them.'

'Don't worry, lad. We have the place surrounded… Yes, you wanted to add something?' The officer said.

'Sir, there is a way out of there. A track runs from the back garden up through the woods and leads to the asylum wall. Part of the wall has collapsed, and they can get through to the road from there.'

Royston turned to the sergeant. 'Get on the radio and block off the asylum route.'

Waters had been taking notes on the proceedings. 'Sir, there is another gate to the village at the bottom of the hill.'

Leslie told them that the gate was always locked at night. It was only used for deliveries to the stores on Tuesdays and Fridays.

'We have a car down there just in case. Now I want you two to stay here, and I will leave an officer here with you. I will want to talk with you both later. Is that okay?' said Royston

'Yes, sir,' both the children answered.

Royston, Muir and Waters left, and a constable entered, removing his helmet as he did so.

Mary offered him a cup of tea. 'No thanks, Miss. The DCI would have my guts for garters. I'll just sit here if that's all right.'

The cook brought in the supper, muttering about Susan not doing her job.

'Cook, when did you see her last?' asked Mary.

'Couple of hours ago I reckon.'

'And Joan?'

'Ain't seen her all afternoon. What's going on here? And why's the bobby in the hall?'

Mary filled her in on the events of the last half hour or so.

'Oh my lord, the poor girls, and me berating them so. They will be all right, won't they, Miss?'

Mary sat her at the table and calmed her. The telephone rang in the hall.

'Hello. … Yes it is. … No, he is not here I'm afraid. May I ask who is calling, sir?' Leslie signalled to the constable, pointing at the telephone. He covered the mouthpiece and told the policeman that it was George Thompson. 'Yes. … Yes, Mr Thompson, as soon as I see him I will pass on your message. Is there a number he can reach you on, sir? Yes…yes… very well. Yes I have it written down, sir.' He replaced the handset and told the constable that Thompson was desperate to speak to Sir Alastair.

He had given a contact number that would only be of use for the next twenty-four hours.

The policeman went out to the patrol car and radioed central control. He passed on the information the boy had given him and returned to the house. Cook went back to the kitchen, muttering and sobbing.

Mary sent Leslie a message. *Now is the time to use your powers.*

I have already. The back door of the cottage cannot open from the inside, and the power is off. The windows are stuck fast, so there is no way out. Martins is not in the house, but Susan and Joan are. We must be sure that the police get the credit. Walsh has a pistol, but if he pulls the trigger, it will misfire.

What about the other two thugs? Mary asked.

They are watching the road from the upstairs windows. Walsh is downstairs with the women. Martins is in for a big shock. He is making his way up through the woods towards the gap in the wall. It is pitch-dark in there, and he is about to meet my friends.

What friends? Her brother's remark puzzled her.

The brambles. When they meet, they will love him. They are quite friendly, you see. They will hug him and caress and kiss him, holding him tightly until morning comes.

Leslie you can be so wicked, you bad boy.

They laughed out loud, drawing the attention of the constable. 'Is everything all right here?'

They laughed even louder.

The constable shook his head and returned to the chair in the hall. 'Kids, glad they can find something to laugh at,' he muttered.

They could hear Royston on the loudhailer. 'Walsh, you have no escape. The house is surrounded, so come on out. Send the women out first, unharmed.' He ordered the cars turned to face the cottage, and the full beam lights focussed on the windows. 'Come on, Greg. Don't make things difficult. You can't go anywhere. Let the women go because we are going nowhere.'

Leslie realised that Madame Silvestre was watching from her window. He planted a thought that she should keep away from the windows in case someone had a gun. Joe Breen heard the commotion and was walking towards the police carrying a 12-bore shotgun.

'Stop right there. Put the gun down slowly, very slowly, sir. We don't want anyone harmed now do we.'

Two officers swiftly moved in behind Joe and disarmed him. 'Hold him for questioning' said Royston. The constables ushered Joe, protesting, into the back of a police car.

Royston turned his attention back to the cottage. There had been no response to the police demands from the occupants of the cottage. Leslie felt it was time to bring this to an end. Susan and Joan must be terrified.

***

He floated to the cottage and checked where each person was. Eeny, meeny, miny, moe...

He started with Gibbons. The man heard a high-pitched screech growing louder and louder, fit to burst his eardrums. He held both hands to his ears and scrunched up his eyes in pain.

Next it was Sterling's turn. The two men looked like demented souls as they ran around struggling with the noises in their heads.

And now for Walsh. Susan jumped with a start when Walsh screamed with pain, his face contorted in agony.

'Now run,' whispered Leslie.

Susan ran to the door, dragging Joan with her. She flung it open and dashed into the glare of the car lights. Several officers ran to get the women to safety. Royston, Muir, and a handful of officers rushed into the house, and at that moment, the lights went on in every room.

The sight that greeted them was almost comical. Two men rushed down the stairs holding their heads. A third man was doing some kind of dance in the middle of the room. 'It'll never catch on,' said Royston with a smile.

The Detective Chief Inspector and his men rounded up the fugitives and locked them into the back of the Black Maria. Leslie released the prisoners from their torment and thought about Martins. The police could be there all night searching for him.

Soon, Royston and his colleagues could hear howls of pain emanating from the woodland at the rear of the chapel. Royston despatched four officers to investigate.

Sgt Muir called to his boss. 'Sir, just come in on the radio. Thompson called the mansion earlier and left a contact number. They have traced the number to Cove Bay, a holiday cottage near Aberdeen. It is closed this time of year, so he must think it's a safe place to lie low for a while. The chief super has asked for the Scottish Police's cooperation in apprehending him.'

'Well I must say, Sergeant, a good day's work all round. We've apprehended three of the villains with no injuries to anyone, rescued two maidens in distress, had good news from Scotland, been to a dance, and I think the wild howls from up there must be our fourth villain caught in a trap of some kind.'

'Yes, sir, a very good result, indeed' replied Muir

'Okay, the fellow with the shotgun, bring him up to the mansion.'

***

Mary offered refreshments to the officers.

'Thank you, Miss. We still have much to do tonight.'

Muir wore a pained expression at that remark, he and his wife were to attend a birthday party for one of her nieces.

'May I call you Mary and Leslie?'

'Yes, sir, but do not get them mixed up, please,' said Leslie with a smile.

'Oh I do like someone with a sense of humour,' replied Royston. 'Now, the phone call. I understand that you took the call, Leslie.'

'Yes, sir, I did. Would you like me to repeat it to you verbatim?'

'Well, if you could, that would be perfect. Waters, pencil sharp and on duty?'

'Aye, sir' replied the detective.

'Right, lad, fire away.'

Leslie recounted the conversation word for word.

'Hmm, why twenty-four hours?'

'Perhaps he does not want to stay in one place too long, sir,' piped up Waters.

'Possibly…or he's thinking of fleeing the country – a ferry to Lerwick and then on to Norway perhaps. I hope those Scots know what they're doing. I don't want to lose this one. He is key to our investigations. He is the one who can finger both the doctor and the great Lord himself. No, they had better handle this correctly, or they will have me to deal with—'

'Sir, we have Martins. Looks like he was tied up in barbed wire they say,' relayed Waters.

'Yes a good day, indeed. Now this chap with the shotgun. Is there somewhere I can interview him privately?' asked the DCI.

'Yes, sir, in the library across the hall. Your man is Joseph Breen, the husband of the maid Joan. He is the head gardener of the estate.' Leslie informed Royston.

'Thank you, Mary. Leslie, you have been of great help.'

After a half hour, the police let Breen go with a warning not to approach police officers with a loaded gun in future.

This officer Royston, a champion of law and order, impressed Leslie. He liked the way the man spoke his mind without meaning to offend, apologising if he did so. He was a chevalier of old, noble and virtuous, righteous and decent. This man Leslie had chosen from many candidates; he too, was well pleased with the day's work.

***

Leslie slept a deep, deep sleep. No monsters tormented him. No nightmares assailed him. Only a deep oblivion enveloped him. He was now in the hands of his masters, the nameless unseen and ancient gods that he and his sister believed to be the source of their powers. The gods gave him their deepest rest, undisturbed hours of bliss. He floated and soared, dived and swooped; the sensations filled him and completed him. He was now ready for the task ahead. He was now…the personification – 'a strange boy'.

The unseen masters did the same for Mary, giving her a well-earned reward for her diligence over their project.

***

Leslie had his record player on in his room listening to Roberto Carlos singing 'Quero que va tudo pro inferno' (I want it all to go to hell). Roberto Carlos was his favourite Brazilian artist and learning Portuguese was a joy for Leslie. The language opened up for him the sentiments and the meanings of the lyrics he loved to hear. In spite of the events of the past year, he was now quite fluent. He had purchased many records by Portuguese and Brazilian artists, as well as others by his favourite Catalonian artist, Joan Manuel Serrat. To the boy, Serrat was a poet and a visionary singer-songwriter. But most of all, like Leslie, Serrat was a follower of Machado and Hernandez. The specialist record shop imported the records for Leslie as they were not on general release in the United Kingdom.

Mary reminded him they needed to take Will for his fitting this morning.

On my way, Mary. Leslie transmitted to his sister downstairs

Will proudly drove his shining black car towards London. The two men in the following car had no need to keep their distance; it was not a covert surveillance. They parked and fed the meter close to Saville Row and then walked in the cold winter wind to the tailors'. The trousers fitted perfectly, but the jacket was a tad tight across the shoulders.

'We expected that, sir and it can easily be rectified. Would next Wednesday be all right, sir?'

Will agreed it would, and the trio retraced their footsteps to the car.

The next stop was to see their great friend and ally, Erin.

'The hearing is set for Monday the twenty fourth of April, Mr Johns. I trust that you will be prepared?'

'I think that if somebody could fill me in on all the intrigues and goings-on, I might stand a better chance.'

Erin gave an enquiring glance towards Mary and Leslie.

'Dad, there is a reason we have not told you everything. When you are questioned, you will still only know what you know now. You can answer honestly and with sincerity. You will be questioned about why you put us in St Vincent's, why you did not look for us after your army service, and how you came to know that we are still alive. Dad, we do not want to lose this case. All other information is for you to hear later when the case is over. If we told you all that we could, it would colour your vision and distort your view of things. It would also mean giving up information relating to another case. That would tip our hand and could prejudice what was admissible. No, you must remain ignorant of the things we so want to tell you. It is the only way.'

Erin sat back in his sumptuous chair and looked at the boy; the expression on Will's face; and Mary, silent and inexpressive. He interlocked his fingers, deep in thought. There was a long pause before he spoke. 'Leslie, would you consider it forward of me to make a personal suggestion?'

'Not at all, Erin. Go ahead.'

'You have this enterprise pending. I'm referring to the magazine. You have furnished me with the weapons to… Oh dear, I seem to have committed a faux pas. Mr Johns, Leslie has asked me to give you my services as a lawyer, but I have been remiss in not asking for your approval.'

'Why do I need a lawyer? I am going to tell exactly what occurred and rely on the law to put right the wrong that has been done.'

'Hold there, sir. This is not a perfect world, I fear. If I may say, you will find it rough going in this case. The current focus on Sir Alastair may ease it a little in your favour, but he has friends in high places and has wriggled his way out of accusations against him on occasions in the past. There is not a speck of dust upon him sir. Have you seen the *Financial Times*? His companies have not suffered one jot at the news of his arrest. Companies and share values suffered when Sir Alastair was imprisoned in Cayenne. Now the investors are less jumpy, confident that these allegations are fabrications. The viewpoint is that this private but high-profile man is a target for those who would bring him and his companies down. Professional rivalries cover many ills, sir.

'Well, my services are at your disposal, and if the cost concerns you, there is none; my service to you is gratis.'

Will gaped at this news. 'But...but how?'

'Gratis, sir.'

'Well I don't know... I am confused. I ...'

'Sir, I will give you all the expertise of my knowledge of law and also that of my colleague. Do not confuse us with fortune hunters and charlatans, sir. We have a reputation of which we are proud, and we are also human. We understand how you feel. We will do our utmost to secure what you wish to be delivered.'

Will turned to his children with a look that asked, *What should I do?*

'Dad, Erin is inviting you to accept his services and to trust him implicitly, as do we. Dad accept his offer,' begged Mary.

'Very well, Mr Yardley. I will trust the judgement of my children. They seem to know so much more than I do. I place myself in your hands. And thank you, sir.'

Erin was at the peak of appreciation. 'Well done, sir. Wisely decided. Now, I was talking about young Leslie there, sir. Would you consider learning law? My partner and I would give you the opportunities and facilities without hesitation. We would welcome you into our world and give you the benefits of our collective knowledge. You would be so welcomed into our company. I beg you, Leslie, become a lawyer like us; you could do such good in this world. We can train you and give you all the practical assistance you need, but do not be persuaded by my enthusiasm. Take your time and think about it.'

Erin's words were as sincere a statement as any he'd ever heard. An offer to study law with a firm older than his father and his father's father – how could he refuse? But he did just that – though he had been so flattered by the offer that he'd nearly accepted. He still had so much left to do, and it would be foolish of him to dedicate time to more studies at this moment. 'I thank you so much for your offer, Erin, and would sincerely like to accept, but at this time, it is not possible for me to do so. Perhaps when things are more settled and if the offer is still open—'

'But of course, I understand. Take your time. And when you are ready, the offer will still be there.'

The way this young man dealt with his father so impressed Erin. The boy used sound reasoning and logic on which to base his argument. He had convinced this grown man to accept that he knew best. He would be a phenomenal force for good, and as a lawyer or a barrister, he could do untold good for those who needed and deserved justice. He knew that this boy would not charge a single penny to those who could not afford his services. He was already a multimillionaire at the age of sixteen, and money did not drive him. What motivated and drove him was the cause of justice. He was Erin's kind of person, and he hoped the boy would accept eventually.

Will and his children left the lawyer's chambers and went for lunch, where they discussed Erin's proposal and Leslie's surprise at the offer. It occurred to him that, if he became a lawyer, it would restrict what information he could give to Ed and his team. That would be a serious predicament and conflict with the code of conduct he would be required to observe. He would soon have a difficult choice to make; he would have to decide where he could do the most good.

***

Ed had good news for the Johns family. 'The house close to the entrance of where the magazine is, it is up for sale. The farmer has gone into a nursing home, his wife died two years ago and his children have no interest in farming. The plot consists of the farmhouse and seven fields of a hectare each. If you bought it as a lot, you could lease or rent out the land you do not require, perhaps to the neighbouring farmer.'

'Well that is great news Ed, we shall go to the estate agent right away. The house and land are suitably situated. I noticed it when we went to look at the site for the magazine, and it would include the fields Dad saw when he did his security survey for the magazine site?

***

Will and his children, accompanied by the estate agent, inspected the land and the house. 'The amount of land is far more than I need, and the house, why would I need eight bedrooms, I ask you?'

'Dad, it is perfect for us' said Mary, trying to convince her father. 'As Leslie has said, we can lease out the fields we do not need. As for the house, Leslie will need a room to use as a library and study. We can make each bedroom en-suite with our own personal facilities and still have a guest room.' Mary waited for her father's response.

'You have convinced me Mary but I do not have the finances—'

'Daddy, never worry about finance. My brother and I will take care of that.' Will agreed to the purchase of the site and began to list the things he required.

***

After the purchase of the house and land, the day arrived for Will to attend court for his custody hearing. It did not go well for Will. He could not provide evidence of his income, or how he could support his children. The judge dismissed Sir Alastair as their guardian and made them wards of court. Erin asked to speak with the judge in his chambers.

'Mary, Leslie, I must talk to you both urgently. His honour has listened to me, I have had to reveal my own personal finances to him. The result is that you are no longer the wards of Sir Alastair or wards of court as he stated. I am your guardian now. From my position, you are free to live with your father and you have my blessings. It is as it should be. I am sorry you did not get the result you hoped for, what I hoped for. Be happy with your father and try to repair the damage that the years apart have made.'

Leslie hugged his lawyer. The result of the hearing was not what he wanted or what Mary or Will wanted, but it was, from his point of view, the next best thing.

***

Leslie closed his eyes.

As always, aromatic scents of flowers in bloom greeted him as he passed. The golden sun glistened on the surface of the lake as he turned at the entrance and entered the mansion. He climbed the marble stairs and stood in front of the impenetrable door, and spoke the words he hated so much, 'A strange boy.'

About the Book

This story is primarily about Leslie and his exploits whilst Mary remains constantly in the background, using her powers to guide, protect and influence this strange puzzling boy.

She was now readjusting her father to his new life, with all its revelations and intrigues. She, was the supreme controller and manipulator, shaping and moulding both her brother and her father. She let Leslie believe in his powers and the forces available to him, but she alone controlled him in his use of those powers, so she thought.

Follow their story in the sequel, '*The Promise*'. It may answer some, or all of the questions you may have about these children, the people and events in their lives.